THE
DETAINEE

NO ESCAPE FROM THE PUNISHMENT

PETER LINEY

Jo Fletcher
BOOKS

[First published in Great Britain in 2013 by Jo Fletcher Books
This edition published in 2014 by

Jo Fletcher Books
an imprint of Quercus Editions Ltd.
55 Baker Street
7th Floor, South Block
London
W1U 8EW

A CIP catalogue record for this book is available
from the British Library

ISBN 978 1 78206 035 2 (PB)
ISBN 978 1 78206 034 5 (EBOOK)

10 9 8 7 6 5 4 3 2 1

Typeset by Ellipsis Digital Limited, Glasgow

Printed and bound in Great Britain by
Clays Ltd, St Ives plc

Praise for

THE DETAINEE

'An impressively dark, dystopian piece with much to say about capitalism's tendency to treat human beings as commodities, disposable when no longer useful'

FINANCIAL TIMES

'Equal parts exciting, terrifying and thought-provoking . . . I'm genuinely intrigued to see where Liney takes this story next because if this debut is a well planned bonfire then I'm thinking the sequel will be fireworks'

JFORJETPACK.COM

'In 30 or 40 years time, *The Detainee* could become a work of genius . . . this book has everything and more. Totally recommended'

NEWSIGNEDBOOKS.COM

'I am impressed with the high impact story that Peter Liney has managed to create in *The Detainee*, its unique concept and excellent writing will leave this story in the back of my mind for a long time . . . *The Detainee* has captivated me, and will do the same to you'

THE BOOK PLANK

'*The Detainee* had me gripped . . . I loved the way the story held out a chance of redemption for the common man'

80003346647

To all those who helped on this long road.

CHAPTER ONE

There's a scream inside us all we save for death. Once it's out, once it's given to the world, there ain't no going back on it. It's time to let go, to release your fragile grip on life. Otherwise, God's just going to wrench it from you.

If you've never heard that scream, I hope for your sake you never will. I, on the other hand, must've heard it a thousand times. I can hear it now. A woman somewhere over towards the rocks is squealing like an animal that's just realised it exists to be butchered, her cries issuing out of the fog like blood through a bandage. Now some guy, probably her partner, has joined in. Shouting at them, telling them to leave her alone, as if he has some influence on the situation. But you know he hasn't. Fear's slicing so hard at his voice it's cutting right through. Soon she'll die, and so will he. And I can do nothing but lie here in the dark, listening to my frightened heart pounding; just as all around me, hundreds of others must be lying there, listening to their frightened hearts pounding. It makes you feel sick to do it. But we don't seem to have a choice.

If I could have one wish in life, do you know what it would be? Do you? To be young again. To be thirty, no, shit, forget it, twenty-one.

Oh yeah, I know, 'Age brings wisdom; each age has its own compensations.' That ain't nothing but shit. Nothing but whistling into the grave. There ain't no dignity in getting old. Ain't no honour in being forever sick and your body rotting and being reluctant to mend with you. And I'm weak, too. My muscles hang off my bones now like they're melting, like they're wanting to ooze on down to the floor. Once I could've shifted anything. Anything or anyone that stood in my way, no problem.

Not that I was mean. I worked for some mean sonsofbitches but I didn't do that much myself. Just the sight of me was usually enough. This big, wide bastard, with a face off the side of a cliff, erupting with muscle. I was Vesuvius with muscle to burn. You'd see me come in through the door, blocking all the light and you'd say: 'Yes, sir, whatever you say, sir. It's a pleasure doing business, sir. But don't set that big bastard on me.'

Truth was, I was more of an actor than anything. A frightener. But I was strong if I had to be. Twenty, maybe fifteen years ago I could've taken hold of this sack of old bones wherein clanks my weary heart and crushed it like a bag of broken cookies. So don't you believe any of this shit they give you about getting old. 'Cuz the truth is, it makes you want to weep, it makes you want to cry for the health and strength you once had. Nowadays, if I look in a mirror, there's this old guy staring back at me. I don't know him. His skin's a size too big for his bones, his hair's all dry and drained of colour, and there ain't the slightest flicker left in those sad flat blue eyes. In short, he's old. And for old read helpless. Read unable to stop all these terrible things that've been going on round here.

Jesus! What the hell was that? What are they doing to her to make her scream that way? . . . *Leave her alone!* For chrissake. Let her be. Block it out, that's the thing. Seal off all the entrances and don't let anything or anyone through. Just me in here, inside this tortured old head, surrounded by barricades of fading and fragile memories.

Maybe if I was to share them with you? Pass them on before they dry right up and blow away? Maybe it would help you understand how we all ended up living like this.

How far back do you want me to go? The past seems so far away now. I won't bore you with my childhood. I remember only one thing about my old man: on Saturday nights he'd come home stumbling drunk and either start serenading my mother like a fool, or laying into her like a madman. A combination she apparently found irresistible, 'cuz when he died in his sleep one night she refused to admit it to anyone. Just carried on, getting up, going about her usual business, even sleeping with the body. I tell you, if it hadn't been for me going in there one morning, jumping up and down on his blotched and bloated hide, this terrible stench suddenly ripping out of him, he'd probably still be there now.

It's a sad thing to have to tell you, but, for myself, I never actually been married. Never even had a proper relationship. Don't ask me why. I used to have a perfectly respectable career, working for one of the classiest criminals around, but do you know something, the big guy never gets the girl. Have you ever noticed that? It's the same in the movies. Mind you, the movies are pretty unkind to us all round: the big guy's always stupid, the dope who never gets the joke. My theory is that it's little guys who make movies.

She's making a run for it. Shrieking at the top of her voice, tripping over in the dark with them chasing along behind her. Laughing and teasing in that way they do, working themselves up for the kill. The man's voice stopped some time ago. They must've finished him off already. Please. Don't come this way, lady. I hate myself for saying it, but don't come over here to do your dying.

Where was I? . . . Oh yeah. All this talk about the past, about getting old, you won't be surprised to learn I'm an Island Detainee. Got sent out here almost ten years ago after being means-tested and found wanting. I have this little lean-to, in the middle of the Village, out towards the eastern shore. It ain't a lot, just a few planks and some sheets of plastic, but it's as much as any of us can hope for now. Damp, of course, which don't go down well with my chest. And cold in winter, too. There's a special kind of cold seeps off that ocean, like it's being injected into your bloodstream by icicles.

Then there's the rats. Thousands of them. I tell you, some days it looks like the whole island's on the move. Bold as brass, too. They don't take the blindest bit of notice, no matter what you shout or throw at them. All you can do is look on them as your fellow creatures, living, not so much alongside, as *with* you. Sharing your home, your food, sometimes even your bed. If you don't, it'll drive you crazy.

I guess that makes things sound pretty bad. Endless rows of makeshift lean-tos lurching this way and that, acres of sheets of multicoloured plastic flapping like tethered birds, flies constantly trying to suck the juices from your mouth and eyes. But that ain't the worst of it. That ain't the worst by far. The worst bit is the smell.

They say you get used to it in the end, but even now, after all this time, there are days when I feel nauseous right from the moment I get up 'til the moment I go back to bed. Sometimes I even wake in the middle of the night, retching, spilling my dry guts out across the ground.

A lot of it depends on the weather. Top of the summer, when it's stifling and still, it's more than you can bear. There's a constant sweet and sickly fug so thick it's like someone jamming their dirty fingers down your throat. It ain't something I can truly do justice to, but if you've ever smelled a dead animal rotting on a hot summer's day, well, times that by a hundred, by a thousand, and you'll have some idea.

Garbage. Nothing but garbage. Acres and acres, heaped up, stretching and stinking into the distance like a flyblown corpse dried and contorted by death. Most has been combed out, dragged and checked for anything of value, then just left to rot. Year in, year out, 'til it subsides enough to be tipped on again – and again, and again.

Some places, you dig down deep enough you'll come across the twentieth century. Antique garbage and, believe it or not, there are those willing to excavate for it. Course it's dangerous. You gotta wear a mask. But that ain't much in the way of protection from what's down there. Cancer ain't nothing on the Island. Dead cancer, walking cancer, distended bulges and weeping sores. We don't even think of it as a disease anymore. Just a parasite. Like those flies you got to keep an eye on in case they try to lay their eggs in your cuts and grazes.

Thank God, it's over. Death has come to death and left nothing at all. Just the dark emptiness of the fog, holding us in, keeping us prisoner, whilst allowing them to go free.

At least it was quick, that much I'll give them. I've known nights it's gone on 'til almost dawn. Screams running back and forth, stopping, starting up again, like their victims are being tortured to the point of death and then just held there.

Though the worst part is when someone begs you to help. When they stand outside your lean-to squealing for you to come out and save them. Can you imagine how that feels? To someone like me? Once I might've been able to do something. But not now. Not against them. I wouldn't stand a chance.

*

When I was young and used to see homeless old people hanging round, I never dreamed I would end up being one myself one day. Why would I? I was healthy, strong, and once I started working for Mr Meltoni, always had plenty of money. And there ain't nothing like a pocketful of dough and some bounce in your stride to make you think you're gonna live forever. In any case, everyone always assumed it was gonna get better, not worse. But it's those *with* a home who are the exception now. Those across the water, behind their fortified walls, in their private enclaves, who make all the rules and who decided that by sending us out here, by giving us this 'last chance to become self-sufficient', they'd done everything for us they could. Which, in case you don't know, is how we ended up living on this dollop of crap; four miles long, three across and a little over a mile offshore.

Once it used to be a residential island, part of the commuter belt, the Island Loop, but somewhere along the line someone decided it was the ideal place to start offloading the Mainland's waste. Gradually, over the years, with garbage mounting up and threatening to topple back over everyone, it became less of a residence and more of a dump. 'Til finally, almost thirty years ago, the last inhabitants were forced to abandon it to its rotting fate.

I guess it never occurred to anyone then that it would be lived on again. I mean, it ain't fit for purpose. But there are thousands of us out here. Mostly old people, those with no money, who once might've thought they'd be taken care of. However, no one takes care of you anymore. You either survive or die, simple as that. Sure as hell the State don't. They can't afford to look after anyone. And do you know who they say's to blame? Not incompetent and corrupt politicians, not those pigs gorging themselves down at the stock exchange trough, but us. Old people. Old people 'cuz we got *too* old. As if we had a choice.

Most of the country's population's over seventy. The social safety-net gave way long ago – not enough young people putting in, too many old people taking out – so it's our fault 'cuz we didn't look out for ourselves. Well, I'll tell you something, I thought I did. Mr Meltoni always insisted on me putting away a little something every month in a pension fund.

'Look after yourself, Big Guy,' he used to say. ''Cuz no one's going to do it for you anymore.'

And do you know something? He got it right. Unfortunately though, the pension companies got it wrong. After everything that happened, all the problems we had with banks and the financial system at the start of the century, they still put everything on the market. Can you believe that? An entire society's future. All it took was one tiny whisper on the Internet saying they'd got their sums wrong, the advances in medical science meant their clients would be drawing pensions a lot longer than they thought, and the whole thing came tumbling down. Not just the market, not just the pension companies and the banks backing them, but this time everything else, too.

I mean, you couldn't believe it. This structure we knew as society . . . civilisation . . . everyday life . . . that we thought of as permanent and beyond question, just collapsed around us in a matter of weeks.

'Big Guy!'

Jimmy's slightly quavering voice, just outside my lean-to, suddenly woke me, and I realised that, no matter how tortured the night, I must've finally fallen asleep.

'Big Guy, you in there?'

Jimmy's this little gnome-like character, bent and big-nosed, with a few tufts of white hair on the sides of his freckly bald head that he likes to strain back into a ponytail and a limp that has no story to it. He just woke up one morning and there it was. Later he tried to make up some tale about how he got it – that made him look good – but we all know, as does he, that it's just another symptom of getting old.

He did try a faith healer for a while (there ain't no real doctors on the Island, leastways not for us). For ages he went round with this moss poultice strapped to his leg, well after it had dried up and gone all brown. But it didn't do him any good. Now, when it starts to give him problems he has to use a stick.

I've known Jimmy almost all the time I been out here. I like him, he knows when to back off. I don't even have to say nothing. I just give him the look, and he's gone.

'Big Guy!'

'Okay,' I grunted. 'I'm coming.'

I heaved myself out of my pit and into a morning cold, clear and, thankfully, free of fog. Jimmy was standing there with that slightly shifty expression on his face that means he's about to ask me for something and doesn't know how I'll react.

'Did you hear?'

I nodded. He knew I heard. Everyone had.

He paused for a moment. 'Would you er . . . Would you mind . . . giving me a hand?'

I sighed long and hard, which he took to mean I had no strong objections, and turned and limped away, expecting me to follow.

For a few moments I just stayed where I was, feeling a little put upon, that he was being presumptuous as usual, then I reluctantly tagged along behind.

We made our way down the long line of lean-tos, Jimmy stealing a quick look at his place opposite to make sure he hadn't been seen, then taking a turning towards the ocean, along another line and in the direction of last night's screams.

Soon we reached a lean-to where the plastic had been wrenched from its frame and used to cover something on the ground. It didn't take a genius to work out what.

'I came over earlier. Made a real mess of them,' he said grimly.

I lifted the plastic and peered underneath. He was right. A couple I vaguely recognised had been hacked to death, the final cuts to behead them. I turned away and let the plastic fall from my hand. You just can't believe it. It's like a shock that goes on forever. Hard enough to take in what's being done, let alone who's doing it.

'Jesus,' I muttered.

Jimmy nodded. 'I just think, you know . . . you can't just leave them here.'

I sighed. He was right – someone had to do their 'civic duty' – though knowing him, I was pretty sure he had some kind of ulterior motive.

Taking care not to lose anything out of the ends, we rolled the bodies up into the plastic and dragged them off in the direction of the corrosives pool. Where nobody, nor anything else for that matter, lasts for more than a couple of hours.

All along the way, eyes much older and more weary than mine stared out of the darkened insides of their lean-tos. Yet no one spoke, no one asked what happened. It's as if the longer we live like this, with no meaning or structure to our lives, the more we regress to what we've always been: dumb animals. Eating when we can, sleeping when we can, mutely accepting those who occasionally come to cull this sickly old herd.

I tell you, some days it makes me so mad I want to run around and smash every lean-to I can down to the ground. Just to make them react, to make them say something for once, but instead I become more and more insular, more bad-tempered, more a person that, I know, most Villagers go out of their way to avoid.

We reached the corrosives pool accompanied by a mob of flies that knew there was a banquet somewhere, but weren't exactly sure where. The woman's head fell out as we were unwrapping the plastic and Jimmy looked away as I toe-poked it down the slope. Almost the instant it hit the waiting greenish liquid you could see the flesh starting to pucker away from the bone. It was like some creature we fed, devouring everything we gave it yet always hungry for more.

For a few moments we stood and watched as the two headless torsos slipped out of sight and existence, then Jimmy turned and, with a sudden sense of purpose, began to peg it back towards the Village, unconcerned that he was leaving me some yards behind.

Along the way, from the top of one of many mountains of garbage, I could see almost the entire island. The vomited sprawl of the Village, the ruins of the Old City, and in the distance the pier where the garbage boats come in every day (actually, it's not a 'pier', but all that remains of the bridge that used to stretch out here from the Mainland. It was demolished one foggy night by a tanker, and, as a matter of convenience, never rebuilt). Down in the Camp they had their usual fire going, its rising column of black smoke circling round the Island like some huge snake slowly choking the life out of us.

Of all the hells that humankind's ever created, this is surely one of the worst. Nothing but mile after mile of waste, discharge and debris; the ass-end of civilisation. And we're left choking in its shit, just as one day, you suspect, everyone else will have to do the same.

I turned and looked across towards the Mainland. There was still a layer of last night's fog lingering in the bay and the city rose up out of it like an orchestra; its walls rinsed pink by the early-morning sun. That new building certainly does dominate. Jimmy reckons it belongs to one of the utility companies, but I'm not so sure. Whatever, it's the major piece on the chessboard. I mean, it could be Heaven. Or maybe the Promised Land. Not that I'm saying I envy what they got over there – I don't. They can keep their wealth, their warmth, and their privileged lives. I don't even care that they don't have to worry about who comes for us on a dark foggy night. There's only one thing they got I want. Mind you, I want it so badly, sometimes it feels as if, deep inside me, I'm crying out for it every moment of the day and night.

I want to be allowed to go free. To get off this foul and sickening pile of crap, fill my lungs with fresh air, my heart with hope and believe in people again.

But I might as well sit and howl for the moon. No one's ever got off the Island. No one. They seen to that good and proper. Once you're out here, the only way you leave is by dying. By the wings of your spirit lifting you up and flying you out of this godforsaken place.

CHAPTER TWO

For the rest of the day everyone in the Village kept a real close eye on the weather. The sun's always appreciated at this time of year, giving a bit of relief to old and creaking joints – like a squirt of warm oil. But the fact that it means the fog might return later, and that it might bring *them* with it, is another matter.

I remember someone explaining to me once why it is we get so much fog out here. Something to do with currents and land mass – I don't know, I wasn't really listening. All I do know is that, during some periods of the year, you can go for a week without seeing the Mainland. It's strange, almost as if they've managed to cut us loose. The world goes on spinning whilst we're cast adrift in some silent grey pocket of sodden space. Out of sight, out of mind, and by inference, everything that happens to us out here happens with their blessing.

On the way back from dumping the bodies, Jimmy made some excuse and headed off on his own. I wasn't altogether surprised when later he came struggling up the row with an armful of junk he'd obviously taken from the victims' lean-to.

'I should've guessed,' I grunted, immediately realising that this had been his ulterior motive for helping to move the bodies in the first place.

'Got some really cool stuff,' he told me, indicating the large box that, despite his walking stick, he was still managing to carry.

He angled it towards me so I could look inside and I caught a glimpse of a load of odds and ends that it would be optimistic to call junk: part of an old radio, a metal tube, lengths of wire. God knows what he's going to do with it.

I just nodded. It's not exactly an unwritten law, but having cleared up the bodies, I guess he had every right to be the first to sort through their stuff – and he knows I wouldn't be interested.

He tossed the box down into the entrance of his lean-to and turned to head back for some more. He hadn't got more than a dozen paces before Delilah came rushing out.

'Jimmy! What the hell's this?' she shouted, taking a heavy kick at the box.

The little guy hunched up his shoulders, lowered his bald head into them like some shy turtle and limped on as if he couldn't hear a thing. Though, if he couldn't, he was about the only person this side of the Island.

'*Jimmy!*'

Delilah's Jimmy's companion. I would say lover, but I think companion's more accurate on account of the fact that they keep a great deal of company, but don't show a lot of love. She's this great long, twisted stick of a woman, so thin you wouldn't think she had the strength to stand, but actually she's as tough as old nails. If the human race ever reached a point where the genes of every nationality were poured into one person, I reckon they'd be in her. Her complexion's that browny-grey colour you get when you've been mixing too many paints together and you know you gotta start all over again. Her broad nose, angular cheekbones, huge mouth – any of her facial features –

could easily be laid claim to by a number of ethnic groups. Her temper could only be derived from the most fiery.

Jeez, do her and Jimmy fight. I've known him to come rushing out of there at night, not giving a damn about who or what might be outside, only knowing that it was preferable to what was within.

How long they been together, even they couldn't rightly say. It's a matter of whether you want to include the times she's left him or not. Which, I guess, makes them sound pretty fragile, but you know how those things are; sometimes they can go on forever.

It went through my head to go over to the Old City in the afternoon and do some scavenging. But, with every chance of the fog rolling back in, I decided to stay in the Village and do some of the chores I'd been putting off; like sewing up that big tear in my old overcoat. I hunted out a needle and thread and went to sit outside in the pale warmth of the winter afternoon. I was one of many out there trying to uncurl their locked old spines and I felt a touch embarrassed by my display of domesticity; a guy like me doing needlework.

I'd only been out there a short while when I heard Jimmy screaming for me. I looked up to see him hopping and stepping wildly in my direction, pushing people out of his way, stumbling along with some crazy chasing after him.

'*Big Guy! Big Guy!*' he cried.

It was pretty obvious what had happened. Jimmy'd been sorting through the dead couple's lean-to for more stuff and this crazy had decided to join him. The little guy wouldn't have liked that. He probably got all snippy, tried to shoo the intruder away, to tell him everything was his, and a fight had broken out.

'Big Guy, help!'

It was a noticeably uneven race. Jimmy hop-stepping it along, his stick flailing in the air, legs going at all angles, whilst his pursuer, a look of concentrated fury on his face, was rapidly gaining on him.

My first instinct was to laugh. I mean, he really does ask for it sometimes. But something about how single-minded the crazy looked and how frightened Jimmy was, made me realise this was a bit more than the usual squabbles we get round here.

'Big Guy!' Jimmy wailed, rapidly running out of breath.

With that, his bad leg gave way and he fell over, lurching into the side of someone's lean-to, almost collapsing it.

The crazy was on him in a moment, straddling him, and it was only then – as he drew it out, as he raised it up – that I realised why Jimmy was so frightened. The guy had an axe; big and heavy, with a blade polished and shiny from being forever sharpened.

I jumped to my feet and started to make my way over, but I knew I wasn't going to make it. I shouted as the axe momentarily hung there, like a bird of prey about to dive, then the guy brought it down as hard as he could onto Jimmy's naked head.

Only thing was, it never made it. There was a sound something like the snap of short-circuiting electricity, and the next thing I knew the crazy was flat on his face, his body twitching like he was having a fit.

I tell you, I seen it before, but never up that close. It's so sudden. So absolute. One moment the guy had been about to take Jimmy out, the next he'd been taken out himself.

'Jesus!' Jimmy whined, struggling free of the convulsing body. 'What the hell happened?'

'Satellite,' I growled, with a calm I certainly didn't feel.

Jimmy tried to scramble to his feet, his good leg no more steady than his bad. 'Is he alive?'

'Yeah. Must've seen it as Violent Assault. Or Bearing a Weapon.'

For several moments we stood there looking at the crazy twitching on the ground, his eyes gaping like they were ready to burst out of their sockets, a string of drool sliding from his mouth.

A crowd began to gather, moving tentatively in, as if they were ready to turn and flee at any moment. I mean, it's really something – our new God, this judgement from On High – and to see it up close like that left you feeling like you'd just witnessed some terrible miracle.

I don't rightly know how to explain to you about satellite policing. I guess its roots lie in the early part of this century, when so many cities decided to install surveillance cameras. Gradually, as they cut crime in the immediate area, more and more appeared, but criminals just reacted by going further out. Into the leafier suburbs, the country, the very places that up until then had been more or less free of such things – places where the rich tended to have their rural retreats. A lot of pressure was brought to bear and, finally, some smart-ass came up with an idea that everyone thought would put an end to crime forever: surveillance drone-satellites. Hundreds of them. Low-orbit coordinated navigation, stretching from one side of the country to the other.

Suddenly there was nowhere you could go and not be watched. The countryside, the forest, the desert, the wilderness, it didn't matter. They were spying on you everywhere, with cameras so powerful they could count the flakes of dandruff on your shoulders.

A lot of us panicked and started talking about going straight. I mean, we really did think it was all over . . . 'til it dawned on us that *seeing* what was happening wasn't any use if you couldn't get there to stop it. The police were spread too thin. If you chose your spot – well away from any of the chopper stations they set up – you could just about do whatever you wanted. Soon, everyone was talking about it: how the police couldn't possibly cover such a wide area; about 'inadequate response times', or no response at all. Instead of the ultimate crime deterrent, it became a source of cheap jokes.

But in the end they came up with something that stopped the laughter, that changed our society forever. That gave power to certain people, and tipped the balance in favour of something that should never have existed. I mean, of course, punishment satellites.

Whenever one of those things sees a crime, *Zap!*, it takes you out. Not only that, but in the split second before it hits you, it assesses the seriousness of the offence and delivers the appropriate punishment. If it's a minor misdemeanour – Creating an Affray or Criminal Damage – it'll just knock you out for a few hours. If it's something more serious – Armed Robbery or Violent Assault (like the guy who attacked Jimmy) – it'll hit you so hard it'll take months, sometimes even years, for you to regain your full health and mobility. And if it's Murder, or a Crime Against the State, then say goodbye, 'cuz there ain't nothing can save you from those things.

So who needs the police? Who needs the entire judicial system, when you can be caught in the act, tried, sentenced and punished, all in the matter of a split second? For sure, it was a helluva saving for the government: instant justice from On High, not from God, but through a security system installed by a democratically elected government with the full mandate of the people.

The only problem is, *I* didn't vote for them, and I didn't vote for the satellites either. Nor did anyone else I know. But the thing is, you're only allowed to vote if you got a permanent home. Bricks and mortar. Which means that just over forty per cent of the population controls the rest. Forty per cent who've got one helluvan interest in maintaining the status quo.

Okay, so some days if you're out on the tips getting hassled, being threatened, you can thank the Lord for satellite policing. Plenty of people I know have been saved from a beating. Or maybe far worse. But it ain't the answer, nor is it 100 per cent reliable. Sometimes, in electrical storms, they'll start firing all over the place. Sixteen people got killed a few years back. And, of course, on nights when it's really foggy, when there's not the slightest source of light and we're locked into total darkness, they stop functioning altogether. Which is why there's all this concern about the weather. This fog paranoia. 'Cuz as soon as those we're protected from know we're not protected anymore, they go crazy. Streaming over here, killing and maiming, bathing their bodies in our blood.

You're probably thinking that's all the more reason to keep it then, if most of the time it does a pretty good job. But it ain't that simple. See, I don't believe those satellites are there to protect us at all. Law and order's just a side issue. The real reason they're there is to protect the status quo. To keep an eye on the unwanted majority – all the places they've hidden us away – and make sure we're not doing anything that might threaten them. Which is why one of those 'Crimes Against the State' is attempting to leave the Island. A satellite'll take you out for that. Just blow you away. So in case you haven't already guessed why we're out here, let me tell you. Sure as hell it ain't to be 'pioneers in self-sufficiency'. What we are, in fact, is prisoners; forced to live on this stinking pile of filth until the day we die.

I escorted Jimmy back over to his lean-to, Delilah took one look at him, at how shaken he was, and instantly flipped to another side of her character. Not exactly sympathetic, but certainly fiercely and unreservedly loyal.

'What happened?' she asked.

'Some nut,' Jimmy told her. 'Damn near killed me. Satellite saved me.'

'What? For chrissake! They shouldn't send those people out here!' she complained. 'Haven't we got enough problems?'

'Maybe he wasn't crazy when he arrived,' I ventured.

'Yeah. That'd be right . . . Ohhh, Jimmy,' she soothed, putting her arms around him, pushing his face into her bony chest and kissing the top of his bald head.

I stood there for a while, feeling like I was intruding, then turned to leave.

'Hey. Where you going?' Delilah asked.

'Yeah, Big Guy. You can't go,' Jimmy agreed, emerging out of Delilah's embrace. He took a step towards me, dropping his voice like he had an announcement to make that he didn't want anyone else to hear. 'They're ready.'

'Really?' I asked, immediately knowing what he meant.

'Sure are.'

Jimmy's been growing these MSI patented vegetables in a kind of false wall at the back of their lean-to. Not the normal sad and straggly crap the rest of us grow and have to soak and season to try to transform into something edible, but big clear white potatoes and rich velvet-leaved cabbages. He fixed this guy up with a water tank and got paid in black-market seeds. It's an offence, of course, and he could get into a lot of trouble 'cuz of it, but Jimmy don't care. Which is one of the reasons I'm so fond of the little guy. Unlike most people out here, he hasn't given up. You can't just sit around and wait for death to come, the only unknown factor being what form it'll take. You gotta find reasons to keep going, to nurture hope, and his is through his invention.

I mean, you can probably appreciate, no one's lean-to's exactly a work of art – what with the materials we got available – but Jimmy's turned theirs into something more akin to a funfair tent than a lean-to. He's got all this weird stuff hanging off it. A clock that's powered by rainwater, windmills that – if he ever scavenges the right parts – he reckons he'll be able to create natural energy from. He's even got this idea about revolving solar panels that'll suck power from both the wind and the sun.

Inside, you can't move for stuff he's retrieved from the tips that he's sure'll come in useful one day. You and me might think of it as junk. Certainly Delilah does. Which is why, every now and then, she'll lose her temper and throw the lot out, but to Jimmy, every last piece is a spare part to a possible future.

Course most of it *is* junk, and he knows it. Jimmy's dearest wish is to be allowed to go through the garbage when it first arrives from the Mainland, before it's sorted, before all the good stuff's taken out. He talks about it all the time. Some days he drives me crazy with it. What he might find, what he could do, how he could change everyone's lives. I don't know if I believe him or not. I guess I've heard him say it so many times, I don't even think about it anymore. One way or another, it don't matter. Jimmy ain't ever likely to be allowed on the new garbage. None of us are.

'Sure, you remember!' the little guy was telling me. 'On Union Street. Down towards the end.'

The meal might've been a bit special, particularly the potatoes we smeared with a little fat and roasted on the fire, but our conversation was pretty much the same as ever. We were talking about the 'old days', life on the Mainland. A time when we pale, exiled old ghosts had been normal healthy humans leading normal healthy lives.

I shook my head.

'You *do*!' Jimmy insisted. 'Look. Keep walking. Past the deli, the Italian guy that used to make shoes . . . the laundry, right? . . . there it is!'

I knew he was one street over from where he thought he was, but only 'cuz it used to be my patch. Not that I could be bothered to correct him. We were starting to forget all the time now, almost as if we'd handled our memories so often that holes were starting to appear.

'Best jazz you ever heard. And the best Chinese food. What was the owner's name? Wing or Wang or something? Face like someone hit him with a shovel. When I was working for the department we used to go there every Christmas. They hated us because the boss insisted we used chopsticks and tied up the table all night.'

'I ain't that fond of Chinese,' I told him. 'Nor jazz,' I added, though, actually, it had been called Blue China and I'd gone there once a month to collect protection money for Mr Meltoni.

Jimmy groaned, frustrated not so much by my errant memory as my lack of participation.

'He's younger than you, don't forget,' Delilah reminded him.

'Couple of years.' Jimmy shrugged dismissively, though, in fact, he told me a while back he's turned seventy, which makes it at least seven.

Reminiscing is a bit like scratching an itch: pleasant at first, but after a while it can start to hurt. But just then we needed some ready camaraderie, some ritualised laughter to raise our spirits, and all of us knew why. They were coming. Darkness and its shadow were on their way. Bridging the rocks, consuming the garbage, slithering up the rows of lean-tos towards us.

Delilah refused to be cowed. And maybe as a measure of defiance, took a deep breath and, without so much as a by your leave, started out singing.

Never in your life have you heard a voice like that woman's. Some people might say the sound comes from deep inside her, but I think it's more like there's a door deep inside her, which she occasionally opens and *that's* where it comes from. Sometimes it's a happy song and her face splits open with a big peachy smile; and sometimes it's a sad one and tears well up from deep within her dryness to course haphazardly down her rough cheeks. She's known a lot that woman, and most of it hurt, and I respect her just about as much as anyone I've ever known.

It was the drums that made her stop. They always begin the same way, with a slow insistent rhythm, gradually building, reverberating up the hill like ripples through the fog.

'Aw, shit,' she groaned.

At least we knew. There was that much to it. They don't always come. Some nights you can wait and wait and they never arrive. As if they're just increasing the tension for the next time. But not tonight. They were down there, whooping and dancing round, getting out of their heads, summoning a dark beast for them all to ride upon.

I haven't ever seen it up close myself, I been far too worried about keeping out of the way, but I know they dress up. Weird stuff they've found in the garbage. Women's things, wigs, hats, any crazy costume they can get their hands on. Make-up, too; slashes of bright crimson lipstick gouged across their cheeks, mascaraed holes they drop their wild eyes into. Sometimes they even shave their bodies and paint themselves to look like wild animals; filing their teeth into points, letting their nails grow long like claws. They're insane by any definition I've ever known.

Sure enough, the tempo of the drums began to increase and I felt my heartbeat go with it. There was a distant high-pitched shriek. Then another. They were almost there; the gateway to insanity creaking open bit by bit. Another scream followed, wilder, slightly nearer, and we knew they were on their way.

'I'd better go,' I said.

'Stay if you like,' Delilah offered.

'Yes! Stay, Big Guy,' Jimmy instantly chimed in.

'Gotta look out for my stuff,' I told them.

'Clancy!' Delilah persisted. 'We'll throw his junk out. Make you comfortable.'

She calls me Clancy 'cuz that's my real name, though she's the only one who ever took the trouble to find out.

I stared momentarily at their pale and haunted faces, in danger of breaking the unspoken agreement that none of us ever acknowledged the fear we were feeling.

'It'll be all right. I'm only a few yards away. We can still look out for each other.' And feeling kind of lost, like I wanted to reassure them but didn't want to make a big thing of it, I awkwardly patted them both on the shoulder and left.

When I got outside the fog was so thick I couldn't see more than four or five lean-tos away. Not a soul was around. If you hadn't known better, you might've imagined the whole place was deserted.

From a couple of rows away came a long and tormented scream, and I realised they were a lot closer than I'd thought. I hastily squeezed into my lean-to, lowered the plastic and dragged some bricks across the doorway to weight it down. There ain't much else you can do. Just sit there and wait. Or maybe pray to your God that it won't be you they drag out this time.

It wasn't me they came for that night. Nor was it Jimmy or Delilah. But they came for others. Screaming up and down the rows, pushing lean-tos over, hauling people out, torturing and killing them.

A lot of really weird stuff went on. Ritualistic slaughter, figures dancing around their victims whilst singing songs then hacking them down as if it was part of some macabre theatrical performance. A whole row of lean-tos got torched. In the doorway of one, like some gruesome decoration, they left the impaled heads of the couple who used to live there. I mean, what can you say? Where in God's name does it come from?

Me and Jimmy and, to be fair, a few of the other Villagers, cleaned it all up. Eight mutilated corpses dragged over to the corrosives pool and thrown in. As usual, not one of us said a word. I swear, sometimes it's like we're trying to pretend it ain't happening. That it's just so obscene, the human condition so undermined, no one's prepared to admit to it.

Later, the weather started to change. The wind got up, clouds started blowing in and it began to rain. You could almost hear a collective sigh issuing up over the Village. Each and every one of us had become an expert on the weather and knew that, for the moment at least, there would be no more fogs, and they'd be forced to leave us alone.

CHAPTER THREE

It was late in the afternoon when we finally finished patching the wounds on the Village's scarred old collective body. Afterwards I had an urge to get out on my own, to rid myself of the stain I felt inside, but with winter still leaning so heavy on the day there wasn't enough time. Instead I decided to go to bed early, get up at dawn and spend the day in the Old City.

However, those nights, the tension of not knowing if it's going to be you they next drag out, really take it out of you. When you finally do get a chance to sleep it's like you're tranquillised by security and I didn't stumble out of my lean-to 'til well after nine. Even then I was one of the first up and about.

It was one of those very still metallic mornings, with fingers of smoke from last night's fires trailing straight up into the sky, as if they were wires bearing up the landscape. I cut myself a slice of the salted beef I'd been eking out through the winter and a hunk of that blackened, chalky mix of flour and milk powder that some like to call bread, stuffed them into the pockets of my overcoat, clipped my tool-belt on and set off in the direction of the Old City.

There ain't a great deal to see over there; like a good many cities, most of it was destroyed in the Good Behaviour Riots. Just acres and acres of broken-backed buildings, crumbling walls and scorched rubble. And yet, I still get a sense of anticipation whenever I go over there. Maybe 'cuz of what I found that time.

The thing with scavenging is: you gotta try to think differently, to look for possibilities that others might not see. The Old City must've been searched thousands of times. Every day there are dozens of people over there, scratching and picking away, but that didn't stop me finding what I did. Though I guess the truth was, it was more down to luck than anything.

I was combing through this residential area and noticed a crumbling finger of wall that had recently twisted and keeled over, gouging out an opening at its base. I scrambled up a pile of brownstone, managed to squeeze in through this hole, and found myself in what must've once been someone's kitchen.

One look was enough to see that it had been stripped long ago, and I was just about to squeeze back out, to move on, when I noticed these bricks that looked a bit loose in the cement.

I didn't expect there to be anything. Not after all this time. But I still scratched and prised away 'til I managed to get one out. There was a cavity behind it, with something hidden in the gap. A few bricks later and I could make out this old leather case, covered in dust, with a rope tied around it. Can you imagine? I was that excited I damn near tore the handle off trying to wrench it out.

Turned out to be full of twentieth-century relics: clothes, shoes, a woman's personal items and, most interesting of all, a diary. Scrawled ornately across its faded red cover, as if the writing had been laboured over, were the words 'My Diary – Ethel Weiss – 1987'.

Course I read it. Wouldn't you?

At the time she'd been in her late thirties, married, mistreated by her much older husband, but in love with the guy who used to call round every month to pick up the life assurance instalments. The case was packed and waiting for the right moment for them to go free; her secret in the dark, a tiny glowing candle of comfort, hidden only feet away from what had been a pretty miserable existence.

Lord knows why, but plainly she never made it. Ethel had to be long gone, but the case remained. Whatever happened, it must've been unexpected, 'cuz there were no clues in her diary. It just suddenly stopped:

> *August 14th, 1987*
>
> *Another day gone. It's wrong to wish your life away but how I wish I could forgo this part. Next time I pick up this pen, I'll be a day closer to you. Then another, and another, 'til we can be together forever.*

What happened? I don't know. Maybe her old man found out and went crazy on her? Maybe her lover had been collecting instalments all over? Or maybe the life assurance had been part of a plan and she'd killed her husband, been found out and spent the rest of her life as walled up as her suitcase? Either way, it seems kind of sad that the symbol of her freedom should've ended up that way: lost in the dark and decay of Garbage Island.

In the end, I gave it to one of the guys who sneaks over from the garbage boats. They ain't supposed to, and they're taking their lives in their hands, but they'll trade almost anything with you if they think they can sell it. He gave me some new winter boots (well, new to me), some fishing line and a whole lot of smoked meat, so I guess he thought it was worth something. Still made me feel kind of guilty. It seemed wrong – making gain out of someone else's personal life. But it wasn't any good to her and it wasn't any good to me either. And like I said, when it comes to survival, you gotta do what you can.

Ever since then, whenever I go scavenging in the Old City, I always start at Ethel's place. Just in case she left me another surprise. But if she did, it's an even greater tragedy than the first one – 'cuz it don't look like I'm ever going to find it.

I tapped my hammer round the walls for a while, listening for anything that might sound hollow, and scraped at some bricks, but eventually gave up and wandered on.

One other thing I gotta say about the Old City (and I left it 'til last 'cuz I know you're not going to believe me. In fact, I'm not even sure I believe it myself), some days, when I'm up here on my own, seeking out a little solitude, I don't know what it is but . . . I hear footsteps. Honestly! I swear it! I mean, my old ears might not be what they used to be, but I can hear them all right. Kind of faint and echoey, like they've escaped from somewhere. One day it damn near drove me insane – I started running all over the place, even calling out a couple of times, but I didn't find anyone.

Maybe they're echoes from the past? From the million or so feet that used to walk this place? Or maybe, even after the human race is gone, ghosts will still wander the Earth. Lost and lonely, like elderly parents abandoned by their children.

I slowly worked my way over towards the old jetty where, years ago, fishermen used to unload their catch as part of a thriving industry. One or two other villagers were out doing the same as me: skulking from one pile of rubble to another, picking at this, prodding at that, stopping whatever they were doing whenever someone got too near.

I scraped up some aluminum clips – get enough and you can sell them on to be melted down – and a handful of nails I could trade with someone building back in the Village, but nothing of any real value.

Despite a real chill slicer coming off the ocean, I ambled out onto what remains of the old jetty; its sodden, dank green timbers buckle more with each passing year. Sometimes, in the summer, you can spot stuff that's been missed in the water, but at this time of year, it's too murky.

I turned back towards the shore, about to give up and make my way over towards one of the newer tips we're allowed on, when suddenly something struck me. All the times I've been down there, I can't believe I never thought of before.

It must've been over thirty years since the jetty was last used (when the fishing industry collapsed it had briefly been taken over by pleasure craft – the arrival of the garbage boats soon put an end to that), but surely at some point it would've needed lighting? The nearest remains of a building were eighty-odd yards away. Was it possible they once ran an underground cable out to the jetty, and that maybe, just maybe, no one had ever dug it up? If there *was* a cable, it would probably be made of copper, which would mean it was worth a bit.

It was one helluva long shot, but you get that way after a while. You need a project, something to believe in, no matter how foolish it might be.

I turned and walked to the land end of the jetty, chose a line from there to the remains of the most likely-looking building, unclipped my collapsible shovel and started to dig.

I couldn't believe it. I only went down about eighteen inches or so and damned if I didn't hit right on it: half an inch thick, brown, plastic-coated copper wire. Not exactly buried treasure, but to an Island Detainee, something very close to it.

For several moments I just stood there, my heart going at a canter, looking all around to make sure no one was watching. *Jesus.* I knew I had a problem immediately: how the hell was I going to dig up eighty yards of cable without being seen?

It had to be done in one go. If I did a part, cut it and came back another time, someone was bound to notice the ground had been disturbed, no matter how well I disguised it. I had another good hard look around to make sure I was alone. On the other hand, no way could I leave it, not what it was worth. Then it came to me. Mind you, just the thought made my stomach feel like a frozen pebble had been dropped into it. I could refill the hole, hope no one spotted it during the rest of the day, and come back later. At night. That would give me plenty of time.

Again I glanced all around. Was I serious? Villagers didn't go out at night, not for any reason. And yet, with what was on offer, did I have any other choice?

I carefully refilled the hole, patted down the soil and brushed it over, and got away from there as fast as I could. Not going back through the Old City, but following the rocky shore around to enter the Village from that direction.

No sooner had I got into my lean-to, than Jimmy came over to see if I'd had any luck. I'd already decided I wasn't going to tell him anything. I knew he'd go crazy when he heard what I was planning to do and I didn't want to hear it. Especially as I was aware that everything he'd say would probably make perfect sense.

The little guy let out a long and discontented sigh as I laid out my two paltry finds of the day: the nails and aluminum clips.

'You know what we gotta do, don't you?' he told me.

I nodded, not in agreement, but just to acknowledge that I knew what he was about to say.

'We gotta find a way of getting onto the new garbage.'

'Jimmy.' I sighed wearily. 'You know as well as I do, it ain't possible.'

He went quiet for a moment, then started to play with the nails I'd thrown on the wooden crate before him. 'What do you want?'

'I don't know.' I shrugged. 'Candles?'

'That's cool.'

He went straight over to his lean-to and returned a few minutes later with five candles. It was a good exchange, and if it wasn't him endlessly hammering, it would be someone else.

'Have you any idea,' he said, unable to resist returning to his favourite subject, 'what there is in the new garbage?'

I sighed and shook my head. I really didn't need this. 'No. And I didn't think you did either.'

'I been told!' he snapped, slightly irritated by my attitude.

'Jimmy! Mainlanders don't throw anything worthwhile away. That's how they get to stay Mainlanders.'

'It don't have to be of value to *them*,' he told me. 'But give it to me . . . I could change the world.'

'How?' I demanded, a little harsher than I intended.

Jimmy shrugged, finally giving way to my opposition. 'I don't know, I'd have to see it, wouldn't I?'

I grunted dismissively. I didn't want to be hard on the little guy, but I had other things on my mind.

For a while we both sat in silence, the only sound the occasional creaking of the plastic packing I used as a seat.

'How about a game of chess?' he eventually suggested.

Jimmy and I play chess a lot, though I'm not exactly sure why. Maybe it just gives us an excuse to sit together without having to think up conversation. Sure as hell it ain't for my pleasure. All the times we've played, I've never beaten him once. It just ain't my sort of thing. All that thinking and planning, trying to work out what your opponent's going to do next, and the time after that, and the time after that. He's got a real gift for it though: analysing, breaking things down, working out all the possibilities and then holding it all together in his head.

'Nah,' I said, shaking my head and going into one of my long, stony silences, refusing to respond to anything, occasionally giving him the *look*, so that he would get the message and leave.

I just didn't want him there prattling on when I had so much on my mind. I was worried about digging up that cable. Was it really going to be that easy? How much was it going to weigh, bearing in mind I had to get it back to the Village before sunrise? Even then I had to contact the guy from the garbage boat. What was he going to say? How would he get it down to the pier?

In the end, I guess I decided to do what I always do (the way, Jimmy says, I play chess), which is to just go ahead, do it, and worry about anything else, any repercussions, when, and if, they happen.

I don't know how many times I pulled back the plastic on my doorway to peer out, waiting for night to arrive. So many that it began to feel like the day was simply refusing to move on, that it wasn't going to allow me this act of foolishness. However, eventually darkness did begin to seep across the sky, making it deeper and more bruised, 'til at length it filled every corner. I waited for another half-hour, 'til I was absolutely sure everyone was safely in their lean-tos, then tentatively slipped outside.

The cold, stench-filled night air hit me like the atmosphere of an alien planet. For several minutes I just stood there looking up and down the row, trying to accustom myself to the sensation of being outside at night. All around me hundreds of candles glowed inside different-coloured plastics, shadows of figures moved on multi-hued screens. A couple of rats scurried across my foot as if to emphasise that this was their domain, that I had no right being out at such a time. I took a deep breath, tried to summon up the glory days of an old big guy, and set off in the direction of the Old City.

There was no moon as such, just the ghost of one leaping in and out of clouds, tossing shadows out of garbage piles, giving stuff an eerie glow of momentary life. Everything looked so different. Cold and still, fading from white to black, as if the Island was the body of an old iceberg drifting on the sea.

The noise of my feet crunching across crap sounded like it was echoing right across to the Mainland. As I got nearer to the Camp I glanced down towards it, worried they might spot me. As always they had a huge fire going – it's like their beacon, a warning to everyone. For a moment it went through my head to forget the whole thing, to scuttle back to my lean-to. I mean, if they'd had any idea I was out there, what I was up to, satellite policing or not, they'd come for me. Of that you could be sure.

At that precise instant, almost as if my fears had induced it, one of them started drumming. They do sometimes, even in the daytime. It don't necessarily mean anything, but I gotta tell you, it stopped me dead. I dropped to the ground, the thump of my heart overwhelming the drum. Near the fire I could see some movement, maybe even a little excitement. *Oh shit*, I thought, *don't tell me they know I'm here.*

I turned and looked back towards the Village. I'd gone too far. No way could I get back before they got up that hill and cut me off. If they did know where I was, I didn't stand a chance.

And now, I guess, the time has finally come. No matter how reluctant I am, I can't put it off any longer. I have to tell you who it is down in that Camp. About the devils who terrorise, torture and butcher us. Believe me, no knowledge has ever weighed heavier on my mind, nor caused me greater pain. If I could spare you this, I would.

When I was little, by and large, the state still required children to be educated. But, as the years went by, bearing in mind the cost of education – and the fact that the shift of economic power to Asia had resulted in so little demand for labour – some started to ask why the country should bother. Slowly, what had been a right became a privilege. Schools were 'streamlined', then eventually closed down altogether, and a lot of propaganda about 'new opportunities' and 'a golden age of leisure and independence' was put about. Within five years juvenile crime hit the roof. It was so rife that no one remained untouched. Action was needed and the government came up with this idea of simply paying the kids to behave. I mean, it wasn't a whole lot of money, but with all the other handouts being slowly phased out most of the kids jumped at it.

Course, there were protests. The Church said it was immoral, paying children to be good, but the politicians just argued that it was practical – and what was God if he wasn't the 'big stick' anyway, if he wasn't a means of blackmailing people into behaving? The government were just doing what they could to keep things sweet and the kids knew that, but as long as the money kept on coming what did they care?

That was the trouble. It didn't keep on coming. With the national debt getting ever larger and our creditors squeezing ever tighter, more and more cuts had to be made, and like everything else it was withdrawn. I mean, I think they must've had an idea of what would happen 'cuz it was one of the last things they took away. Long after pensions, unemployment, care for the sick and everything else. But in the end they did it: they stopped paying the Good Behaviour Allowance.

Seems to me the kids started rioting then and never really stopped. And I guess, if you think about it, it wasn't exactly a surprise. No one had ever bothered to teach them right from wrong, just paid them some money. That was the balance, then somebody tipped it.

It was one helluva problem; whole generations with no moral compass. A kid would do anything for money: prostitution, trafficking, even murder. Life had never been so cheap. Want somebody wasted? Give some kid a few notes and send him, or her, off to do it. And if they didn't succeed, well, there were plenty of others ready to try. The authorities didn't know which way to turn. Rioting and looting was everywhere; suburb after suburb, city after city getting burnt down. So many kids were breaking the law there was no way they could incarcerate them all. Of course, just as the authorities must've known it was going to, salvation arrived in the form of the punishment satellites.

Suddenly the government were back in control. Those kids who had parents prepared to pay for their imprisonment were locked up; those who didn't, were, in effect, disowned and sent out here as part of the Island Rehabilitation Program. They became prisoners, just like us, never to leave this place.

With all pretence of a managed environment abandoned long ago, they were left to create their own society. And a pretty sick one it is, too. Over the years the older kids – the first across; hardened criminals, by now in their twenties, or even thirties – have developed into 'Wastelords'; bossing this place, mining the garbage, trading with the Mainland. Whilst the younger and weaker ones, fresh over on the boat or even born out here, work for them. Up and down the tips all day, thigh-deep in the latest garbage delivery, sorting through it twelve or thirteen hours at a stretch. I tell you, it's one helluva pitiful existence.

So guess how thrilled they were to find themselves sharing the Island with us? Old people, the very ones they'd always been taught to blame for their predicament. And it wasn't through idle talk neither, but a government-managed, full-on, save-your-ass propaganda campaign to convince everyone that we were the ones who'd ruined everything, who were responsible for delivering so many citizens of this once great country into poverty and humiliation. And you know something? I actually believe that in doing what they do some of them think they're performing their patriotic duty, that they're exacting a little of society's revenge.

Anyway, now you know. Now you can guess who preys on us on dark foggy nights – those who provoke such fear in us all. Kids, some of them no more than ten or eleven, maybe even younger. The Wastelords fill their bodies with drugs, their heads with nonsense and tell them to get up to the Village and have a good time. Little tots you wouldn't think big enough to talk back to their mothers struggling under the weight of heavy machetes, hacking old people to death without mercy or conscience. And we can't defend ourselves 'cuz, as official garbage sorters, they're the only ones on the Island allowed to carry machetes. Anyone else packing anything that looks like a weapon gets zapped.

And you want to know something? Something you might find impossible to believe? I'm not even sure I blame them. I mean, they're children, for chrissake. Little kids. Do you blame them, or those who paved the way for them? Surely there's some collective social responsibility? And if there is, then I guess I have to take my share. And incidentally, so do you.

For a long while I crouched there in the passing windows of moonlight, cursing myself for being so reckless, convinced a gang was about to come rushing up the hill. When it didn't happen, when the single drummer, as if frustrated no one joined in, ground listlessly to a halt, I got to my feet and moved cautiously on.

The Old City can be a challenge in the day, but at night, I'll tell you, it's another world. Twisted skeletons of buildings writhe against the darkened sky, shadows so black you'd swear if you fell into them you'd never come out again. And everything seems to move slowly, stealthily, only stopping when you finally pin it down with a long hard stare.

At one point I heard this kind of faint swishing overhead and looked up to see two huge eyes and a white face coming for me. Before I could react there was a piercing shriek, it veered away, and I realised I'd been face to face with an owl. I tell you, those things just appear out of nowhere. I saw several of them after that. Just curious, I s'pose. Or maybe hoping I'd scare them up a meal. With all the rats it's a real banquet out here; twenty-four hours a day, all you can eat.

As I walked down the slope to the jetty, the clouds broke and the moon lit a lonely trail out across the ocean and far into the distance; an escape route for fools. I unclipped my shovel and started to dig, soon locating the cable and starting to work my way along it. Not that it would be easy. The soil was soft enough, what with all the winter rain, but I was that apprehensive I couldn't concentrate on what I was doing. Over and over I paused, looking all around me, my ears cocked, expecting to see something or someone come slinking out of the shadows. In the end I had to just force myself to relax. I had eighty-odd yards of trench to dig, and I wasn't going to get it done if I kept stopping all the time.

I got into this routine of working in bursts. Ten minutes or so of giving it everything, resting for a couple of minutes, then starting up again. But it wasn't long before the balance began to change and I needed longer and longer breaks.

You have no idea how frustrating it is – not having the muscles I once had. How much I despise this flabby rusting old iron-lung I'm now locked into. Once I could've dug out the whole trench in a matter of hours. I swear it. As it was, come midnight, I'd only managed thirty or so yards.

A sense of panic began to stir in me. A feeling that maybe I'd bitten off more than I could chew. Perhaps the cable had never been dug up, not because no one had ever found it, but because they all had the good sense to leave it where it was. I took in a whole chestful of air, fit to burst my pained lungs, and began to drive my shovel into the earth as hard as I could.

By two in the morning I was over halfway, by three I'd hit a softer patch and was making really good progress. In fact, I was so intent on what I was doing that I didn't notice the moon dimming slowly.

I think it was the sound of the shovel that eventually alerted me. It didn't echo anymore, just kind of hung there, dull and low. I stopped what I was doing, glanced up and saw something that took my breath away.

There was a mist coming in off the ocean, thin and wispy, slowly wrapping itself around everything in its path. I cursed to myself, leapt out of the trench and was about to head back to the Village when I hesitated.

It wasn't that bad. I could still make out almost the entire jetty. Providing it didn't get any thicker, the satellites would still function okay. I had sixty yards of cable exposed. Was I really going to leave it? In any case, I couldn't help but think that if no one had appeared as yet, surely they weren't going to?

I lowered myself back into the trench and resumed digging, glancing up every few seconds, keeping a real close eye on things, making sure I wasn't presented with any more nasty surprises.

Where he came from I don't know. One moment I looked up and there was nothing, the next he was there. Over towards the ocean, next to some rubble, a slim black figure silhouetted against the pale mist like a shadow on the wall.

He stood there for so long without moving I thought I must be imagining it, that it was just a shape that looked human. Then, as if he'd realised I was staring at him and that he should do something about it, he ducked back down.

I froze where I was, my shovel half raised, wondering what the hell to do. Before I could decide, a brick clattered down a pile of rubble to my right and I realised there were more of them. I stepped out of the trench and started to back away, then noticed several dark shapes creeping up behind me. I raised my shovel, turning circle a couple of times in a gesture of defiance and aggression, but they were all around me.

There must've been at least twenty of them. All ages from maybe ten to late teens; ragged, filthy, mostly boys, but a few girls as well. They came out of nowhere, like they'd been squeezed up out of the ground or something. I don't know what had alerted them to my presence, but the way they were moving in made it pretty obvious what they had in mind. To make matters worse, the mist started noticeably thickening, as if it was their accomplice. I couldn't even guarantee the satellites were still working.

It ain't no use talking to them. No matter what you say, they just laugh at you. As if they no longer speak our language and they're mocking you for not realising.

'Cable,' I muttered, rather stupidly. 'Thought I'd dig it out while no one's around.'

No one answered. They just giggled and jeered, slowly closing in on me, nearer and nearer 'til one suddenly ran at me full pelt, only swerving away at the last moment.

They all cheered him. Then another did the same. Raising his fist and feinting to hit me, checking at the last instant. It took me a while to realise what they were up to. They were playing chicken. Getting closer and closer to me, more and more aggressive, waiting to see if the satellites would take a shot at them or not.

'Out at night,' commented the wiry one I'd first seen, shaking his head as if I'd broken a law and he was the enforcer. 'Out at night.'

Another one came rushing at me, turning away at the very last instant, jumping up and screaming into my face.

They're like animals, ragged and unkempt in their winter coats; all colours, all sizes, each one with the selfsame look in their eyes, kind of glazed, like moonlight has gotten in there and they can't get it out again.

Someone came at me from behind, ran past and pretended to take a swing with a baseball bat. I raised my shovel, ready to hit him, but I was no more sure if those damn things were working than they were.

The thin one, I guessed he was their leader, walked right up to me and spat in my face. I could feel it's moist warmth sliding down my cheek. Then he just stood there, daring me to retaliate. When I did nothing, he started taunting.

'Come on! You wrinkled old pile of dried-up shit!' he hissed. 'Ain't you going to do anything? . . . Hey, dead-dog breath! Come on, give me your best shot!'

I've never seen such an ugly expression on a human face. Like a scar carved by contempt. He started on with all this other sick stuff about old people and what he liked to do to them – what he was about to do to me.

'I'm going to cut out your stringy old guts, wrap them round your neck and leave you out to dry so they slowly strangle you. Got it? . . . Huh? . . . *Do you hear me?*' he shouted, in an exaggerated fashion, as if my hearing was shot. 'Should've been dead long ago,' he muttered.

I couldn't take it anymore. I swore at him and turned to try to walk away. As I did so, something heavy hit me on the side of the head. I don't know what. Maybe a baseball bat. The important thing was that the stand-off had been broken, someone had struck me, and we all waited to see if there'd be any reaction.

I have to confess, in that brief moment I prayed for those damn things to work, for that sudden flash to sear down from the sky. When it didn't, I knew it was all over, that I was about to die. Immediately they gave a kind of loud triumphant cheer and started jostling in me.

Fortunately they didn't have their machetes with them – they hadn't come out with the intention of raiding – but they had other things, like bats and clubs. Somebody hit me a really painful blow from behind. I whirled around and managed to catch him and a couple of others with my shovel, knocking them to the ground. Trouble was, I was surrounded, and it gave another of them the opportunity to crack me so hard on the elbow it jarred the shovel right out of my hand.

Before I could pick it up, it was kicked away and someone else grabbed it. I was now alone, unarmed and surrounded by a gang of over twenty kids, and all I could think to do was run.

I barged a couple of them aside and set off as fast as I could – which, I assure you, ain't that fast – towards the city centre, vaguely hoping that somewhere amongst the fog and ruins I might find a place to slip away. They came after me in a whooping horde, laughing cruelly, knowing they could pretty well run me down any time they wanted.

I turned a corner, scaled a pile of rubble and slipped and slid my way down the other side.

Someone threw what must have been a brick at me. Then another. I got hit on the back of the neck, right at the top of the spine, causing reverberations all the way down, but I still managed to lumber on. I guess they just wanted to get as much fun out of the situation as they could, to run me 'til I could run no more, 'til I dropped and offered them no resistance.

I turned another corner, skirted round a jumble of walls and rubble, and found myself in the main square. Already it felt as if my heaving chest was being torn apart, my legs disintegrating beneath me. Still I forced myself on, blundering headlong into the fog.

They kept closing in and dropping back again, screaming, taunting, hitting me and moving away. This boy with heavily matted long fair hair, who once might've laughed the same way if he'd pushed a friend into a pool or something, came up behind me and gave a squeal of delight as he hit me on the back. I felt the pain of the blow and something else, more incisive, more penetrating, and I realised I'd been stabbed.

In the end I simply couldn't go any further. No matter what the situation, when you reach that point there's nothing you can do. I staggered to a halt, collapsing forward, hands on knees, helplessly watching as they surrounded me, holding their baseball bats and bricks aloft, getting ready for the kill.

I didn't notice it and nor did they, but there must've been a slight thinning in the fog. The moonlight briefly edged through and instantly one of the satellites took a shot. It didn't hit anyone – it was closer to me than them – but it sure brought things to a halt.

We were frozen there, staring into each other's faces, too scared to move. I tell you, they were practically licking their lips, their eyes burning, bodies twitching, with the urge to mash sinew and bone.

God knows how long it lasted, it could only have been a few seconds, but then, just as suddenly as the gap in the fog had opened, it closed again; the moon was lost and they started jeering once more. The absurd thing was, it didn't just close, it moved on, and seconds later there was another moonlit patch a few yards away. I barged through, running to stand in that spotlight as if it could take me out of there.

Again they circled me, weapons raised, falling back when the satellite took another shot. It had to be right on the edge of its performance, able to see but not calibrate its response.

The moonlit patch, my most fragile of sanctuaries, slipped away again and once more I ran after it. But as I did so, the fog closed right in and extinguished it altogether and I was left foolishly chasing after nothing. The kids whooped with delight. I hesitated for a moment, then turned and ran into the ruins, fearing my last chance had gone and I was merely seeking a place to die.

I managed to jump over a collapsed section of wall and stumble along an alleyway, but found my path blocked by one of the largest mounds of rubble I've ever seen. I ran at it as hard as I could, took half-a-dozen or so strides upwards, then lost my footing and slipped back down. I tried again. And again. But no matter how far I got, I always slid back down. The kids didn't even bother following me. Just waited at the bottom, mocking my efforts, taunting this lumbering old prehistoric beast, this sad ex-king of the jungle.

'*Go! Go! Go!*' they kept crying.

'He'll have a heart attack,' I heard one complain. 'We won't get to kill him!'

I was struck on the head so hard it felt as if blood was welling up in my brain. Again I attempted to scramble up that precarious mountain, my hands ripped and bleeding, my legs capitulating to pain. Still I forced myself on. Stumble by stumble, slip by slip, 'til I managed to reach the top. However, no sooner had I, than dizziness engulfed me, whirling me round and round 'til I plunged forward into a deep pool of darkness.

I don't know whether I was hit with a brick or just passed out, but it gets kind of vague after that. I remember falling, my forehead colliding with something, and a dull pain . . . the sensation that somebody had grabbed hold of me and was dragging me along. The sharp edges of bricks dug into my back, the fog closed in and out as I gained and lost consciousness. At first I thought it was them, the kids, but after a while I began to realise it was someone else. I even wondered if it might be Mr Meltoni. I mean, he's the only one who's ever looked out for me. I swear at one point I saw him looking down, those big brown eyes of his deep in the shadow of his famous fedora.

'It's okay, Big Guy,' he said. 'We'll get you out of this.'

I felt so weak. I couldn't speak. I wanted to thank him for looking out for me again, to tell him how happy I was to see him once more. I also thought I should apologise for getting old, for losing all of my strength and muscle, all the things he'd once valued me for.

But do you know something? It wasn't Mr Meltoni. It was someone else. Someone I couldn't have even dreamed existed and who was about to change my life forever.

CHAPTER FOUR

A small part of me came to – a solitary candle deep inside spluttering back into life whilst everything else remained dazed and dormant. For a long while I just lay there, trying to build on that small flame, knowing I was hurt and allowing my body time to assess the damage. It was only when my consciousness reached a certain level that it informed me there was something wrong: I couldn't see.

I blinked a few times and turned my head from side to side, panic sweeping through me. I was blind! Those little bastards had beaten me so hard I'd lost my sight. Or maybe they'd done something to me while I was unconscious. I gave an involuntary low moan then stopped, forced to think again. The sound of my own voice, sharp-edged and echoey, made me realise what normally would've occurred to me right away. I wasn't blind. I was *inside*.

At first I assumed it was a lean-to, but there were no draughts and not the slightest glimmer of light. I closed and opened my eyes, squinting as hard as I could, trying to make something out of the darkness. A shape. A shadow. But everything was lost to me.

I stretched my hand out, further and further, as if willing it to disconnect from my body, 'til my fingertips scraped up against a brick wall. Jesus, I was in a building.

You have no idea what that meant. I hadn't been in a building for years. Never even thought I would again. I immediately stuck my other hand out, sweeping it from side to side, trying to touch something else, to give myself another clue as to where I might be. Back and forth, digging deeper and deeper into the darkness, 'til suddenly I brushed up against someone's face.

If I hadn't been in so much pain, I would've leapt six inches into the air. As it was, all I could do was to try to scrabble away.

'It's okay,' a woman's voice said. 'Calm down.'

'What the hell's going on?' I shouted, my words sounding like they belonged to someone else.

'Nothing.'

'What do you mean "nothing"? Where am I?'

'You were chased. I hid you. Don't you remember?'

I paused. No, I didn't remember. Not clearly. 'Where am I?' I repeated, the dark now so threatening it felt like it was rearing up all around me, getting ready to pounce.

'I can't tell you.'

'What do you mean you can't tell me?'

'*I can't tell you,*' the voice said, now with more than a touch of impatience.

Again I paused. 'Why ain't there any light?'

'I don't need it.'

I stuttered and spluttered for a moment. What was going on here? Total darkness, total nothing, and who was I sharing it with?

'Who are you?'

'No one,' she replied.

That was it. That was as much as I could take. I tried to get to my feet, ready to bust my way out of there, but soon crumpled back to the ground.

'Oh, for chrissake!' she cried angrily. 'Look, I've got some candles somewhere. If I light one do you promise to stay where you are?'

I grunted my agreement and she began rummaging around.

'Don't know what makes you think you can go anywhere anyway,' she complained, seemingly more to herself than to me.

A match flared and I finally saw who I was talking to. It should've put my mind at rest, but it didn't. You've never seen such a sight in all your life. I said a lot of us were reverting to animals, but she's gone much further than anyone I know. I wouldn't like to say how old she is. Fortyish maybe. With long dark bushy hair that doesn't look like it's ever been on any terms with a comb, a kind of broad and primitive face, and nothing in the way of attire you'd recognise as clothing. Just remnants and rags loosely tied about her grimy body.

I just stared. I mean, I know it was rude, but I couldn't help myself. She looked like something that had crawled up out of the ground.

'Better?' she asked, slightly begrudgingly.

I nodded my head, continuing to gape, and it was the fact that she didn't return my stare or complain about it that eventually made me realise I'd missed maybe the most important thing about her: she's blind.

Human nature being what it is I couldn't help but amend my attitude, especially as only moments before I'd been spooked because I thought that was my condition. 'I'm sorry,' I said. 'I . . . I was a little confused.'

'But you're not anymore?' she asked, with some surprise.

I stopped for a moment, looking round, realising what she was getting at. We weren't in a building at all. We were in a tunnel. 'Well . . . yes. Guess I am. Where is this?'

She paused, taking a deep breath, obviously deciding how much she was going to tell me. 'It's one of the old subway tunnels,' she eventually said.

'But . . . I thought they were all filled in during the riots? Too much of a security risk.'

'Just the approaches to the City, on the other side. They couldn't fill in the whole system. There's miles of it.'

I paused. 'You live here?'

She didn't answer. Maybe 'cuz all her things were around us and she didn't think it was necessary. I was about to ask her why scrabbling round in the dark all the time didn't frighten her when I realised what a stupid remark that would be, that everywhere she went she was in the dark.

Both of us fell silent. My initial panic petered out and I realised just how weak I was. I sank back down onto a bed of plastic packaging softened by a few layers of rags, aware that somewhere something was hurting me more than any other part of my body. I knew that she'd bandaged me, but I was too tired and nauseous to ask any more questions.

For a while I just lay there, staring at the blackened roof of the tunnel. I didn't feel so good. Everything was slipping away from me as if I was too weak to hang onto it. Presently the candle went out, everything went black, and I lost consciousness again.

I kept waking and falling back to sleep for what seemed like forever. Darkness and blackness, the boundaries blurring over and over 'til they weren't there anymore. Sometimes I couldn't bring myself to say anything, other times I'd call out into the dark to see if she was still there and for a few minutes we'd exchange a slurred and broken conversation. Then I'd slip away again.

'Why did you bandage me?'

'You were stabbed.'

'What?'

'One of the kids. Remember?'

'Oh, yeah.'

'Does it hurt?'

'A little.'

'What's your name? . . . Hey, are you there?'

'Lena. What's yours?'

'Clancy. Most people call me Big Guy though.'

'Oh.'

'Have you got any more candles?'

'Yes.'

'Why don't you light one?'

''Cuz you been asleep.'

'Not anymore . . .'

But even as the match flared, even as I saw that strange broad face with the pale sightless eyes before me again, everything was starting to go black once more.

Turned out the main reason I was like that was 'cuz I'd lost a lot of blood. My body needed to shut down to get its strength back. All I can remember is that endless sporadic awareness of self, swaying back and forth between this world and another. But eventually the time came when I awoke, and instead of drifting off, began to sigh and stretch and she, hearing me, lit another candle.

'You okay?' she asked.

For a long time I didn't answer. No, I wasn't okay. I felt as if death had sucked me in and spat me out again, though only after a great deal of deliberation.

'How long have I been here?' I asked.

'Three days.'

'Oh,' I grunted, a little surprised. I thought it was more like a couple of weeks.

With considerable effort I managed to prop myself up against the wall, the pain in my back that had haunted me all throughout my unconsciousness, turning out to be all too real. I winced. More and more things coming back to me.

'How did I get away?'

'You fell down a pile of rubble. By the time they'd climbed up the other side I managed to hide you. After they left I got you down here.'

I stared at her. Was she serious? Not only is she blind, she ain't much more than half my size. How could she have dragged me all the way down here? Under normal circumstances I would've thanked her for what she did. As it was, I was starting to wonder if maybe I was being set up for something.

'Are you alone?' I couldn't stop myself asking.

'Yes.'

I shook my head in disbelief, already taking liberties with the fact that she couldn't see me. And yet, if there were others, why didn't they show themselves?

'I'd better change that bandage now you're awake,' she said, moving towards me.

Don't ask me why, but I backed away. 'No, no, it's okay. I can do it.'

She hesitated for a moment, as if she didn't quite believe my stupidity. 'For chrissakes – it's your back! What are you, a contortionist or something?'

I grunted, realising she was right, that I didn't really have a choice. 'Oh. Yeah, right.'

It's funny, she hadn't appeared to register my doubts about how she got me down here, but she must have, 'cuz as she came up behind me to unfold the bandage she grabbed hold of me under the arms, lifted me up and moved me away from the overhanging arch of the tunnel.

'That's better,' she said.

I couldn't believe it. I mean, okay, she struggled a bit, but she's a helluva lot stronger than she looks.

'Oh, and by the way,' she said pointedly, 'I believe it's considered good manners to thank someone who saved your life.'

I could hardly get it out quick enough. 'Yeah, right. Sorry. Haven't quite got myself together yet,' I said lamely. 'I'm really grateful.'

The point made, she didn't linger over it, just silently carried on with her bandaging, finishing up by wrapping it round me several times and then securing it.

When she was in front of me, only inches away, I found myself helplessly staring into her face. Up close it's even more remarkable. She's got this really broad nose, turned up at the end, like she uses it for digging or something. Her complexion's sallow, almost yellow, like a suntan that's gone bad, and on her cheeks and neck there are clusters of freckly moles. Course, I probably wouldn't have noticed half of this if she hadn't been blind. But it's like, without the eyes, there's nothing to hold onto, no feature to communicate with, so you find yourself searching for somewhere else to address yourself.

For a few moments, she was that close I could actually smell her. To be honest, it wasn't the way I imagined. There *was* a strong odour but it wasn't that unpleasant. In fact, it reminded me of when I was a kid, visiting my grandfather, playing in the garden – it was that smell you get when you've been rolling in damp leaves.

When she finished, she asked me if I wanted something to eat. I looked at her for a moment and it crossed my mind that maybe her notions on food might be a little different to mine, but I was hungry enough to try anything. 'Yeah . . . Sure.'

I was in for one helluva shock. She set off down the tunnel, into the darkness, and presently returned with several small white eggs and a handful of mushrooms.

'Where d'you get those?' I asked.

She ignored the question, as if she couldn't be bothered, concentrating on getting the fire going.

I tell you, watching her going about her business, being somehow clumsy and adept at the same time, is truly something to behold. Everything's down to touch, smell, sound. The proximity of the fire, the evenness of the flame, the noise and aroma of what's cooking. And the most amazing thing of all is that it was the best meal I've had in years. Mushroom omelette. Can you believe that? Here, underground, under the Old City – mushroom omelette.

Afterwards I felt much better, more relaxed, and I had this strong urge to try to get to know her, to be on more friendly terms.

'So, how d'you end up down here?' I asked.

She paused for a long time and I sensed she was once again wondering how much to tell me. In the end I think her caution was overwhelmed by the novelty of having someone to talk to. Which, I guess, proves she's telling the truth: she *is* down there alone.

'It's a long story,' she told me.

'I'm not going anywhere,' I commented.

At first it came out a little fragmented, like she'd lost the knack of constructing a conversation, but I soon got the gist. She was born on the Mainland, to parents who later abandoned her when they hit hard times and decided they couldn't afford her any longer (there ain't nothing unusual about that. People'll do anything rather than risk being made an Economic Detainee). Course she got shipped out here, aged fourteen, which is older than most, and soon started working the tips for this guy De Grew, the number-one Wastelord on the Island. (I know him by reputation only, everyone does, and if only ten per cent of what I heard is true, he is one evil sonofabitch. Rumour has it he was one of those on the first boat over, which makes me think someone was trying to get rid of him, and others like him, and saw this as the perfect opportunity.)

For a while she managed okay, picking through the garbage, living the miserable life they do. Then one hot summer's day, she and a group of other kids got caught in a blowout. Two were killed, several maimed, and she ended up losing her sight.

'Volatiles' are one of the main hazards of Island life – methane *and* the more modern ones, the supercombustibles. In the old days, when the place was properly managed, they would've been burnt off, but since we been out here, no one bothers to check them. Some days, all you gotta do is cause the slightest spark, kick metal against metal or let the sun heat up a piece of glass, and you'll get a 'blowout'. Or even a 'chain blowout', when the explosion from one pocket of gas ignites another, and the whole ground erupts around you like Hell's bursting up out of it.

People get killed or injured all the time. Mainly kids, of course, 'cuz they're the ones who spend most time out there. It ain't nothing to see a garbage urchin scrabbling up and down the tips missing an arm or leg. They're usually on the outer, picking up what the others leave behind, but they got an incredible will to survive. Lena's problem was that, from then on, she got picked on; teased, abused, as if it was the only use they still had for her.

'But how did you end up in the tunnels?' I asked.

'Before the blowout, I used to spend a lot of time up here. It fascinated me. I just couldn't believe that people ever lived here and I guess I was forever looking for proof. One day I found this grille. I could see a big opening underneath and knew it must have something to do with the subway. It took me a while, but I got up the nerve to smuggle a rope over and find my way down.'

'Jesus. That must've been something,' I commented, my respect for her escalating by the minute.

'Nothing ever seemed so dark.' She paused for a moment, as if she knew there was something she had to pay deference to. 'Well, not then . . . Soon I was spending every moment I could down here. I don't know why. I guess I just had this feeling that one day I might need it.

I started stealing from the Camp. Stocking up. Canned food, tools, even medical stuff.'

'Canned food?'

'Comes over from the Mainland. You'd be surprised. I've still got most of it. Just in case of emergencies.'

'Wasn't it difficult – stealing stuff? I thought De Grew and his boys kept that place screwed down pretty tight.'

She went quiet for a moment, a look of concern flitting across her face as if she'd just spotted a circling demon looking for somewhere to settle.

'It's okay,' she eventually replied. 'If you know what you're doing.'

I didn't like that pause. Something about her expression made me think I wasn't getting the full story, that there was a short cut somewhere back to an open wound.

'Course, after the blowout, I couldn't come up here anymore. It was over a year before I finally managed. One night I just decided I'd had enough. I grabbed everything I could and made my way over.'

She said it so matter-of-factly that it could almost pass you by. It was only when you stopped and thought about it that you realised how difficult that must've been. Can you imagine? Stumbling all the way over from the Camp? Through all those endless mounds of garbage, wondering if you've got the right direction, if you've been seen or someone's following you. Maybe tripping over now and then, hurting yourself, crying tears of pain and frustration. But she still managed to locate the entrance, slip inside and disappear down into this underground world. She's not even sure how long ago it was. Only by counting the winters, by running back through the seasons, did she finally arrive at what she thought was four years.

I mean, what can you say? All that time down there on her own. And yet, when you think about it, she's safer there than anywhere else. Without light she's the equal of anyone. More than an equal.

When I first came round in the dark I was helpless. But not her. It's her element and you'd have to back her against anyone else in it.

'Wow,' was all I could manage to utter, but she just shrugged, as if it was nothing, as if everyone has a similar tale to tell.

Later that night, lying on my makeshift bed, I started going back over her story, thinking about it in more detail. I don't know why but it hadn't really occurred to me that she might be from the Camp. The way she looks, it's pretty easy to imagine she's been down in the tunnels all her life. To discover that she was once one of those kids who consider our deaths an amusement left me feeling decidedly uneasy. On the other hand, she did save my life, and it was the kids she saved me from.

I guess the truth of the matter is, I'm more inclined to trust her because she's blind. I know that's not logical, maybe even patronising – blind people can be as evil as anyone else – but for some reason, her condition slackens the normal rules a little, and I found myself simply ignoring that part of her story as if it didn't exist.

The next day she took me on a tour of the tunnels. With no use for them herself she still has any number of boxes of candles so I was able to light the way wherever we went. I still felt a bit weak and dizzy and it was pretty slow progress, but astonishing for all that. There's miles of it down there. The Island wasn't only a junction for two mainland lines but also one of the maintenance depots for the entire system. There are main tunnels, service tunnels, inspection tunnels. Some starting to collapse a little, in need of attention, whilst others look pretty much the way they must've the day they were sealed off.

Not that that was my biggest surprise. The most impressive thing is what she's achieved down there. In one place daylight shines down (through the grille that first alerted her to the existence of this place that she spent months disguising with blackthorns and rubble) on an area where she's created a garden. She's got all kinds of stuff growing: potatoes, peas, beans, even a few flowers. Water gets channelled down from the surface, flowing into neatly lined-up containers, whilst a mob of nesting pigeons, that she manages to keep away from the garden with some homemade netting, are her source of eggs.

Excuse the indelicacy, but she's also got what must be the largest flushing toilet in the world. It's on the lower level, where some of the tunnels are flooded. The water's tidal, which means it's seawater, and that it rises and falls twice a day. You can go down there, do whatever you gotta do, and a few hours later it's gone, taken away by the tide. Don't ask me how she discovered it. By accident, I guess. It's not the sort of thing I care to discuss. Once she directed me there I never raised the subject again, but it sure is convenient.

Anyways, the whole thing is so well set up – with her stores and fresh food and everything – she doesn't want for a thing. Well, apart from the obvious: company.

Perhaps that was why, on the way back to the living area, I started worrying about her. Was she getting so lonely she was taking chances? By helping me she'd plainly made herself vulnerable. Secrecy's everything to her existence. If someone like De Grew ever found the place, I wouldn't want to guess at her fate. It's the perfect hideout for them: below ground, away from the eyes of the satellites (strange how the one person on the Island who can't see is the one person who can't be seen, as if one cancels the other out). She's risked it all, and I couldn't help but wonder if she'd do the same for *anyone* who might alleviate her loneliness.

'Why did you trust me?' I asked her.

She hesitated for a moment, a little surprised by the suddenness of the question. 'What do you mean?'

'You brought me in here. Your secret world.'

'So?'

'You don't know me. I could've been anyone.'

She grunted. 'I know you.'

'What do you mean?'

'I know you,' she repeated.

We reached the living area and I sagged gratefully back down onto my bed. 'I don't understand.'

'I've known you for some time. You're always scavenging in one of the old apartment blocks over on Parkside. Sometimes you sit for hours down in the square.'

I stared at her. How the hell did she know that? For a moment the absurd notion went through my head that maybe she wasn't blind after all.

She turned my way, as if she'd sensed my confusion. 'I smell you,' she told me.

'You what?'

'I smell you.'

I didn't want to say nothing, 'specially as she saved my life and all, but I wasn't taking that from anyone. 'Listen, lady, it ain't that easy,' I said. 'I look after myself as best as I can. You want to talk about personal hygiene, take a look at yourself sometime.'

'I can't, *can I*?' she replied, as if she'd waited a long time to deliver that line.

She said it like it was a real put-down, like my conscience was going to kick my ass so hard I'd be somersaulting for a week, but I was feeling far too indignant.

'What do you mean, you "smell" me? How the hell do I smell?' I demanded.

'Of salt, which means you either come from the rocks side of the Village or perhaps you do a lot of fishing; of smoked meat, which *must* mean you've been trading with the Mainland, and, just occasionally, of hooch. That, and the fact that you're always alone, gives me the impression that you're not just a loner but a pretty discontented one at that.'

I paused for a moment. I mean, she'd kind of mocked me with it, like she was talking to the village idiot or something, but I do have to admit, it was pretty impressive.

'Never saw you,' I conceded.

'I know you didn't.'

It was only then that it occurred to me – I hadn't seen her, but I had *heard* her. 'The footsteps!' I cried.

She didn't say anything.

'Jeez! You damn near drove me insane!' I told her.

'I'm sorry.'

'I never told a soul 'cuz I was sure they'd think I was crazy. *I* thought I was crazy!'

'Some days I just used to tag along to see what you were up to . . . See where you were going. Sometimes I even imagined us having conversations . . . I know you,' she repeated.

I chuckled to myself. There was something about that I quite liked. As if I'd just discovered we were childhood friends or something. 'And what else could you tell about me?'

'I don't know,' she shrugged. 'You're old.'

It was like a bomb being dropped into the conversation, only it exploded with silence. I looked at her to see if she realised what she'd just said, but if she did, it didn't register.

'I smell old?' I asked.

She shrugged, as if to indicate it was just a fact of life.

For a long time I didn't speak. I felt really angry and I wasn't altogether sure why. Suddenly I wanted to be away from the tunnels, from this strange young woman and all her darkness.

'I'm going back to the Village tomorrow,' I announced.

She paused, a slightly startled expression on her face. She knew I was upset, but not the reason. 'Why?'

'Time's come,' I replied, in a way that forbade any further discussion.

There was a long and painful silence. I could see some fresh emotion beginning to flow through her, like a river starting to change colour, but I had no idea what it was. It must've been getting on for five minutes before she spoke again.

'I'm sorry,' she said, almost in a whisper.

For some reason it was the last thing I wanted to hear. I mean, I didn't think it was an apology or anything, more an admission of what stood between us. I was old and she was young and that was an end to it. Too much had happened between us, too many terrible things, and we could never forgive each other.

I turned and looked at her, cross-legged on the ground, her back almost statuesquely straight, her sightless brown eyes directed at the wall. I was a fool to think it could be ignored. No matter what had happened, how estranged from her peers or reformed she might be, the truth was, I was down there in the company of the enemy.

CHAPTER FIVE

The following morning the atmosphere between us continued to be awkward and uncertain, potentially even hostile. Over breakfast she asked if I was still leaving and I told her I was. I don't know why, but nothing mattered more to me than getting back to the Village and being with the rest of the old people, where I belonged.

When we finished eating, the two of us sat there in silence for a few moments, knowing that the next words, the next move, would be away from each other.

'Well,' I eventually sighed, struggling to my feet, still a long way from full recovery.

She hesitated, almost as if she was going to stay where she was, but finally stood. 'I'll show you the way.'

There was an awkward pause.

'You want to blindfold me or something?' I asked.

'What?'

'Well, you know, take me up-top, walk me round a bit then take it off. So I won't be able to find my way back down again.'

She went quiet for a moment. 'Don't you want to come back down again?'

I turned to her, a little surprised. 'You mean like . . . calling in?'

'Yeah.'

She said it kind of carelessly, like she really didn't mind one way or the other, but I was beginning to appreciate just how much she did.

'I dunno,' I said, shrugging to myself, if not her.

'You're welcome. As long as you're careful.'

'Oh yeah. No problem.'

She stood there waiting for me to answer, her whole face reflecting what her eyes couldn't. The only problem was, I didn't know what to say. Part of me was thinking *stay away*, that to have anything more to do with her was unnatural and could only result in trouble. Whilst, on another level, I could sense her need that strongly I didn't see how I could possibly refuse.

'S'pose I could,' I eventually said, and for probably only the second or third time since I'd been down there, she broke into a smile.

It was one helluvan improvement, believe me. Sometimes I wonder if it's only the unhappiness of her isolation, of being down there alone, that makes her so hard on the eye. As if she's forgotten some of her expressions, particularly those of joy and happiness. The few times she has smiled, she's seemed that much more human, that much more redeemable.

A little later she led me up-top and showed me the entrance. I tell you, it's a piece of modern art. You'd never find it unless it was pointed out to you. It looks like a pile of rubble, in the middle of dozens of other piles of rubble, but in that particular pile is a door made out of bricks woven together with heavy wire. Mind you, it's one helluva weight. No wonder she's so strong. But the most important thing about it was, even if I gave you directions, even if I drew you a map, you'd probably still spend all day searching and not find it.

She didn't open it straight away. Instead she squatted down and pressed her face to the gaps in the bricks, sniffing and listening. It confused me for a moment 'til I realised she was checking if there was anyone outside. Finally satisfied, she heaved the door back and motioned me through.

I'd been rehearsing something to say all the way up the tunnel. I mean, no matter who, or what, she is, she *did* save my life. I hesitated for a moment, trying to get it out, but she didn't give me the chance.

'*Go!*' she hissed and gave me a real hard shove.

I got some fifty or sixty yards away before I finally dared look back. I'd been that way hundreds of times before, but it would never have occurred to me that there was anything unusual about it. The fact that there'd been someone watching me (or *smelling* me, if you must), that an entrance to another world had been so close, wouldn't have even made it into my dreams.

A little bit of advice for you: if you ever want to find out who your real friends are, try coming back from the dead sometime. Jimmy just about had a heart attack when he saw me approaching. He was up on this box, tinkering around with one of his roof-mounted windmills. He took a quick glance down the row, in my direction, then turned back to what he was doing. I don't think it really registered. Then his gaze suddenly whirled back my way, his mouth falling open so far I couldn't help but laugh. In fact, he was that shocked he lost his balance and fell off the box, scrambled up, hopped-and-stepped in my direction and threw his arms around me.

'Big Guy!' he cried. 'I don't believe it!'

Delilah wasn't a lot better. The moment I entered their lean-to, she shrieked loud enough for the whole island to hear and threw herself at me, helplessly laughing and crying at the same time. At one point I actually had them both hanging off me. Tell the truth, it was a little painful, but I wasn't about to draw their attention to my wound nor the fresh bandage Lena had put on me that morning.

Jimmy went and rummaged in the back of their lean-to and returned with a prime bottle of hooch he'd been saving and we all sat round toasting my return.

That being said, I got a bit stuck when they asked me for an explanation. I've never been that good at making up stories. I hesitated for a moment, swallowed my words a couple of times, then muddled out a combination of fact and fiction – taking them up to the point where I passed out and fell down the pile of rubble – then claiming to know nothing from then on. Maybe the kids left me for dead? Maybe the fog suddenly cleared and they had to back off? All I knew was I'd regained consciousness that morning in exactly the same spot.

'Jesus,' Jimmy uttered, topping up my hooch. 'Lying there all that time. You were lucky, Big Guy.'

It wasn't the most plausible of stories and I guess if they hadn't been so pleased to see me they would've realised, but as it was, neither of them seemed to give it much thought. Their only concern was that I was back, that I was alive and well, and to tell you the truth, I was kind of enjoying the fuss. I've never had that many friends, and to see people so obviously caring about me was nice. The only thing that spoilt it was, later – still celebrating in their lean-to – my eyes suddenly fell on my kerosene lamp in the corner.

'Jimmy?'

'What?'

'What's my stuff doing here?' I asked, now noticing one or two other items.

He looked around as if it was the first he knew about it, his mouth getting wider and wider but never looking like it was going to give any kind of explanation. Meanwhile, Delilah started sniggering to herself.

'*Jimmy!*' I protested.

'No, no, I was just looking after it, Big Guy!' he reassured me. 'You know what they're like round here.'

'Yeah, I know what they're like!' I told him. 'They'll help themselves to a guy's personal effects even before they know he's dead.'

'Exactly!' he agreed. 'And I didn't want that happening to you.'

The following few days found me doing more thinking than I had in a long time, or maybe a different kind of thinking. Living on the Island dries up your brain. Once you get used to it they may as well stick your head in a can and seal it off. From then on, nothing changes until you die. A brain needs stimulation, especially an old one like mine. And this woman who lives beneath us, this ex-kid from the Camp who wants to be my friend, is it. My mind's suddenly bursting back into life, resuming operations, doing its best to get back up to speed. I tell you, it disturbs me, but it excites me, too.

When I walked away from the tunnel entrance that day I wasn't sure I'd ever go back. But as the days went by I thought of little else. I mean, no matter how fraught, how uncertain the situation, it is *something*. And, Jesus, I need that. We all do. However, the longer I put it off, the less confident I became. Did she really want me down there? An old person? And a grouchy one at that? Or was it just a case of anything being better than isolation and loneliness?

I guess I've been putting the brakes on, not letting the situation get away from me, but it's become more and more difficult. It's been over a week now, and finally I've acknowledged that I really don't have a choice, that even if she rejects me, I have to go back.

It was one of those cold but mercifully blowy mornings when you could almost kid yourself you're not living on a stinking mound of rotting crap. Flocks of seagulls wheeled round and round overhead, screeching and calling, the strength of the wind enabling them to stand in mid-air like snowflakes frozen in their fall. In the distance I could see one of the garbage boats coming over from the Mainland, the weight of its load dragging it deep in the water. Down by the pier the kids would be starting to gather, thousands of them, all pushing and shoving each other, jostling for position.

I ain't ever seen it myself but I'm told that when the stuff's unloaded they go crazy; throwing themselves in amongst it even before it hits the ground, so that it falls on them like shit raining out of the sky. Not that they care. All that matters is getting your hands on the plum items – anything of value. Inevitably fights break out, kids knocking each other over, wrenching things out of each other's hands. Can you imagine? Filthy, ragged little urchins – somebody's children, somebody's son or daughter – having to fight each other over garbage.

Several times on my way over I found my pace slackening. In fact, the whole journey was punctuated by milestones of doubt and indecision. I had this idea she might've changed her mind – that I'd be intruding somehow.

I approached the entrance with all the care of a bird returning to its nest. Watching and waiting, going forwards a few steps, hesitating, forwards a few steps more, 'til I was finally satisfied no one was around and I could dart over.

I had a bad moment or two thinking I'd come to the wrong pile of rubble, unable to locate the door, then spotted the wire handle and wrenched it open.

It made me feel a whole lot better to see the candles she'd promised to leave me just inside the door. Lord knows what I would've done if they hadn't been there – slipped back out again, I reckon.

I lit one and slowly began to make my way down the long slope to the main hall (it's weird, you can still see the direction signs: 'South Side – Through to the shops, Exit to Aquarium-Land', that kind of thing), then down a further tunnel to the living area. But, she wasn't there. I started to feel really uncomfortable, to wonder if maybe I should leave. But I'd come this far, and anyway, you never know with her. I wasn't looking for light, I was looking for darkness. I'd have hated to start blundering my way out of there and walk straight into her.

The only other place I could think to look was the garden. There's a long, straight stretch of tunnel that leads to it, with a sudden swell of light at the end, like the garden's an altar or something, and as I got nearer, I could see her squatting down, digging vigorously. I started to scuff my feet, to walk a little heavier, anything to let her know I was coming. But the closer I got, the more I understood that she already knew, that she'd probably been listening to my clumsy approach for some time.

'Hi,' she called.

'How you doing?'

'I was beginning to wonder if you were going to come,' she smiled, standing up to meet me.

'Oh . . . Well, you know . . .'

For some reason, I couldn't finish the sentence. I guess in part 'cuz she was obviously so delighted to see me, but also 'cuz, well, she hadn't exactly undergone a transformation, but she had done something about her appearance. Oh, don't get me wrong, I'm not talking about 'girlie' stuff, that ain't her at all. She probably just did it out of politeness. Prior to me she hadn't seen anyone in years, it's no wonder she stopped bothering. But there she was in clothes which, though a rough mixture of men's and women's, were still recognisable as such. She'd also bathed, brushed her hair and tied it back, and looked altogether more wholesome and human.

The only problem was, by doing that she made me realise she's considerably younger than I first thought. More like thirty than forty, and, as if I needed reminding, a damn sight closer to the kids' age than mine. Which was probably why I felt so thrown. Already I was telling myself that coming here had been a mistake.

'Oh er . . . don't worry,' I blurted out. 'I was real careful coming in.'

She shrugged. 'I wasn't worried.'

Again we fell silent. I felt so uncertain of what I was doing here it was almost hurting. 'Can I help you with anything?' I offered.

I think she was on the point of saying no, when she changed her mind. 'Yes, okay,' she said, and handed me a shovel to dig out some potatoes.

I don't know whether it was what she had in mind, but having something to do made me feel a whole lot better. Soon I began to relax and the words started coming out naturally rather than having to be watched and weighed over. Nothing that deep, mind. Just everyday stuff: the garden, the weather, but it helped us to create a common foundation from where we could start to build.

A little later I scooped up the potatoes and we ambled back to the living area. Things were slowly becoming that bit more personal, more meaningful, as if we both knew we had an awful lot of ground to cover.

For sure I wasn't the only one who'd been doing a lot of thinking. She'd come up with a number of questions, most of them prompted by the novelty of having an old person to talk to. She had a real thirst to know how Villagers felt about everything – their perspective and history.

'You never saw it coming?' she said.

'Well, kind of, but . . . you know, human nature ain't it. We got this blind faith in the future – or we used to. Even after the Meltdown, when so many lost everything and were blowing their brains out, or making bonfires out of everything they owned rather than let it be repossessed, most of us still thought it would turn around. I mean, queues for jobs, people begging, soup lines – most generations have seen that at one point or another. On the other hand,' I added, sighing, 'when they introduced punishment satellites . . .'

'That was when you knew?'

I paused for a moment, then gave this little grunt. 'You wanna know something? Even when they told me they were sending me out here, I still thought it might be okay. I was actually fool enough to believe that "self-sufficiency" shit they gave us. I remember coming over on the boat feeling more optimistic than I had in years, excited at the prospect of making a new start. Lots of us were. It was only when we got here, when we saw the place and realised we'd never be allowed off, that it finally struck home.'

The odd thing is, normally I'm not much of one for talking about myself. I'm more comfortable listening to others. But something about the tunnels, the dark, the candles, yeah, if I must admit it, even her blindness and lack of scrutiny, prompts me into honesty. Mind you, I was a little taken aback when she asked me if I had a partner in the Village. I mean, I know it's one of those questions, but I still wasn't expecting it.

'Nah. Not me,' I replied.

'What happened?'

'Nothing. Never had one.'

'Really?'

'No one serious.'

She thought about that for a moment. 'Don't you want anyone?'

I took so long to answer that eventually I think she sensed my discomfort and took pity on me. 'Never the right one at the right time, huh?'

'Something like that.'

There was a pause whilst she sought a new topic, but for some reason I felt compelled to repay her enquiry. 'What about you?' I asked. 'Wasn't there anyone in the Camp?'

She hesitated for a moment, this slightly haunted expression coming to her face. 'No. You can't have a relationship down there.'

At that moment, almost as if our mutual discomfort had created it, one of the winds that occasionally get up in the tunnels began to howl down upon us. I don't understand the scientific principle. Apart from the grille above the garden, and the entrance up-top, as far as I know the whole complex is more or less sealed. So how come we periodically get these winds hurtling through? First time I experienced it (when I was in and out of consciousness), I didn't know what the hell was going on. It got into my head, it got into my dreams. I thought it was a train pounding round. I mean, you get used to it, apart from when it whips up smoke and ash from the fire, or blows out a candle or something, but I still don't understand what causes it.

For several seconds it buffeted and swore at us, then, like some retreating stampede, it swept off into the distance. My eyes hadn't left Lena for a moment, no more than that disturbed expression had left her face. Suddenly everything had stopped; all our unchecked outpouring and confessional honesty had ground to a halt. The raising of the subject of relationships had meant that, for the first time, both of us had something we preferred to hang on to.

I don't know what it was for her, but I knew all too well what it was for me. I know it's going to sound pathetic, maybe you'll even laugh, but just once I wanted to tell someone how lonely I am; that I've been this way most of my life, that barely a night goes by when I don't reach across my bed and wonder what it would be like to have someone there. Okay, I know it's not exactly what you expect from a big guy. We're supposed to have axes for hearts and bullets for brains, but we got our emotional needs, too. I mean, they tell you there's someone for everyone, right? No one ever says: 'No, sorry, what we mean is, there's someone for everyone 'cept big guys.' So where is she, for chrissake? Dead of some incurable disease? Run over by a cab? Or did she just get tired of waiting and marry someone else? And if she did, how's that going to work out when she was meant for me? I mean, I don't want to complain, but this whole relationship thing could've been arranged a whole lot better.

Finally, we diverted onto something else, went round the obstruction rather than through it, and the atmosphere between us returned to what it had been.

I told her all sorts of stuff: childhood memories, things about my parents, about Mr Meltoni and his wife and daughters. And she filled in a lot of space around her. In total she was on the tips for about twelve years. Can you believe that? Most of the time sorting, but for a while she was also on other details. Like cooking or gardening, or, as her father had given her a good grounding in mathematics, supervising the warehouses.

I mean, to look at the Camp from up in the Old City, it appears to be utter chaos, but greed is a great organiser. Over the years De Grew and his Wastelords have found the most efficient ways of extracting everything of value from that place – no matter what the cost.

'Don't you have any friends?' I asked. 'Wasn't there anyone you trusted enough to tell them about this place?'

She shook her head. 'Some days, yes. Other days, no.'

I took her to mean that drugs were the problem – with that kind of inducement you wouldn't be able to rely on anyone.

'When I first arrived from the Mainland I was desperate to make friends. You soon learn though. Life is unbelievably cheap. Those here today might not be tomorrow.'

'What do you mean?'

'Kids die all the time.'

'How?' I asked.

'Accidents, mostly. But fights, too. Run-ins with the Wastelords.'

'Jesus. No wonder you don't miss the place.'

For hour after hour we exchanged views about almost every aspect of our lives, old and new. And yet, the one thing neither of us chose to discuss – a topic so carefully avoided you might've thought it was mined – was what happened in the Village on foggy nights. Several times one of us said something that looked like it might lead that way, but the moment they did the other took off in the opposite direction, as if they were rebounding off the discomfort. In any case, the more I get to know her, the less I believe her capable of doing something like that. But I still don't want to discuss it.

I stayed as late as I could. I've never had a conversation like that before – certainly not with a woman – and it was a hard thing to leave. However, I knew the light must be fading up-top and there was no way I was going to risk being out at night again. This time I told her I'd come back a lot sooner, within a day or two, and I meant it.

It's totally irrational, but when I came to say goodbye I felt guilty that I was leaving her that way – alone down there in the dark. It don't make any difference to her, but all the way up to the entrance I kept wanting to go back, as if I was taking away life rather than light.

Even when I got outside I couldn't stop thinking about it. Those miles of tunnels – that whole world in complete darkness. Jeez, it would frighten most sighted people out of their minds. I mean, I realise it's simply a case of someone adapting to their circumstances, but I can't help but feel a certain admiration for her. In fact, despite her age, I'm beginning to really like her. I feel good down there. Comfortable. Something else, too. Something I never would've expected, not from her, not from anyone – she inspires me. If she can triumph over her problems, then maybe I can still triumph over mine.

I don't know if that was why I did it. It was certainly out of character, but on my way back to the Village I suddenly ran to the top of the nearest mound of garbage and let out the loudest, longest yell you could imagine. It must've gone right across the Island, skimmed over the water, and ended up on the Mainland. My voice, my cry, my echo, over there. And maybe, you know, just maybe, one day I'd be back over there, too.

Again I shouted, even louder this time. I wanted them to hear me on the Mainland. I wanted them to hear me down in the Camp. This big old bastard yelling at the top of his voice, giving it everything he'd got in an act of wholesale defiance. *I want to go free!* The flame may be weaker, it may occasionally flicker or threaten to go out, but sure as hell it still burns, and I guess I owe that to Lena.

Which made it something of an irony that, as I approached the Village, I glanced out towards the ocean and saw this huge bank of fog moving in on us.

CHAPTER SIX

All throughout the Village people were battening down in that grim resigned manner they have when a fog's coming. Like they know it has to be done and the effort made, but only 'cuz it's in everyone's best interest to perpetuate the myth that we have some kind of control. Which, of course, is a joke. We might as well knit ourselves bulletproof vests, or staple together a cardboard fort. The only thing available is hope, prayer maybe – that it ain't going to be you they come for this time – anything else is just keeping busy. But people still do it. Reinforcing this, wedging that, working themselves into tiny fortified corners 'til the whole village looks deserted. When in fact, behind the shored-up timber and plastic, thousands of old folks are silently sitting there holding their breaths.

As usual, Jimmy was out covering up or dismantling his inventions, worried they might make him a target. He called out to me as I passed by.

'Hey, Big Guy! Wait up!'

But I just waved and walked on, as if I had to get busy the same as everyone else.

Truth was, I was feeling sick to the depths of my stomach. Something about meeting Lena, this sense that we were almost friends, had lulled me into thinking that this wouldn't happen again. I don't know why. I mean, she's as detached from the kids as we are now. What difference could it possibly make?

I took one last look out to sea, at the slow, tumbling avalanche of fog bearing down upon us, then ducked into my lean-to. I didn't bother to drag the bricks and boards across the doorway. What was the point? If they wanted to get in, they could. Instead I just carried on as normal, fixing myself something to eat, trying to pretend none of this was happening.

An hour or so later that became impossible. I took a peep out in the hope that maybe things had improved and ended up sticking my face into one of the thickest fogs I've ever seen. You could've cut it into slabs or carved it into statues. Shortly after, any hopes we had that they might not come were dismissed by the sound of the drums starting up. It was slow and muffled at first, a couple of lazy beats, but soon drum after drum was joining in, pounding a rhythm so loud, so insistent, it shook the entire island.

Don't ask me why, but as I sat there waiting for them to arrive, this image slipped into my mind that I just couldn't get out: the kids streaming up the hill, hundreds of them, dressed and painted to kill, machetes raised, moonlight in their eyes, but the worst bit was who was leading them.

She looked the way she did when I first regained consciousness in the tunnels, but wilder, dirtier, as if she hadn't so much come out of the ground, but was made of it. Lipstick was smeared around her mouth as if she'd been eating something you'd rather not know about, and those sightless eyes, no longer vacant, glinted in a way that frightened the hell out of me. Like she was the true keeper of moonlight on the Island, locked away down there, summoned when they wanted the devil to take form.

It was crazy. Lena wasn't on her way to the Village, she was down in the tunnels. And in any case, she'd never be a party to this. But try as I might, I couldn't shift the image from my mind.

Somewhere in the distance I heard the first screams of the night and knew they'd arrived. It was more than I could bear. I jammed my fingers into my ears, closed my eyes and began humming to myself – some dumb kids' song from long ago, trying to block out what kids were doing now. I hummed louder and louder, reinforcing it by rocking back and forth, doing anything I could to prevent the sounds penetrating.

A bright orange glow pierced my tightly closed eyes and, when I opened them, I saw a flickering light that soared through the air and landed with a thud on my roof. My lean-to was on fire.

I rushed out and found myself in the middle of a scene straight out of Hell. They were all over. Hundreds and hundreds of them. Screaming out of the fog, torching everything they came across. I mean, Jesus, insanity is so often something we don't recognise, but I didn't even recognise this as insanity. Kids dressed in ball gowns, boots and feather boas, thick with make-up, armed with machetes, chopping at everyone and everything they saw, their costumes drenched in blood. Another group kitted out in football gear, shirts, shorts, everything, 'cept they wore vivid pink and lime-green wigs and were tossing round a human head as if it was a practice ball. Others were naked from head to toe, every part shaved, their heads, genitals, everything. But they'd painted themselves in something that made them glow, like grotesque and ghostly worms. It was as if they were trying to outdo one another. Not only in dress, but also in brutality.

Old people were screaming and wailing; cries of terror, death and pleading. Occasionally there was an explosion as someone's kerosene store went up. It was bedlam. I heard Delilah yelling and looked over to see their lean-to in the full grip of a blaze. She was cursing this gang of kids in a way few had the courage to do, and Jimmy was trying to drag her away. One little punk in a tiger skin shoved her to the ground and then raised his machete. I started to run over but Jimmy threw himself on top of her, his bald-headed splayed-limbed frame acting like a sea creature trying to play host to too big a body. I swear they both would've been killed then and there, but at that moment an old man who'd been hiding in his burning lean-to came rushing out, his hair and clothing alight, screaming with pain as the kids shrieked with laughter and ran after him into the fog.

Immediately I helped Jimmy drag Delilah into the shadow of one of the few lean-tos that wasn't burning. She was obviously in some pain, but still all for giving them a piece of her mind. We dragged her further out of sight, just as the kid wearing the tiger skin came rushing back out of the fog. He looked round kind of dazedly, like he wasn't sure if this was the right place or not. Or maybe he was so high he couldn't even recall why he'd come back. Either way, he knew he was there to kill and, turning to the nearest person, he hacked a woman cowering on the ground across the neck, her head detaching so effortlessly from her body you couldn't believe life had ever been there.

People were running this way and that, begging to be spared, doing everything they could to get away. Whilst – and I'd heard but never believed it – others just stood calmly in front of the kids, like trees waiting to be felled. They even offered themselves: kneeling down, placing their bodies in the arc of the machete, the swish of the knife. They wanted to die. They wanted to be put out of their misery. And I saw some obliged, and I saw others just laughed at. As if the kids knew that the cruellest thing of all was to let them live.

Finally, with the Villagers that were able scattered, and barely a lean-to left standing, they moved on: disappearing into the fog, taking out another row, doing to others what they'd done to us. You could tell which way they were heading merely by the sound of the screams, going further and further into the night, like ripples of terror.

Round about three it stopped altogether and we realised they'd had enough. Lord knows how many they killed, how many lean-tos were destroyed. All I can say is that it was the worst night they'd ever put us through. So much so, I wondered if De Grew and his Wastelords had got hold of some new drug, an even bigger thrill, an even surer way of achieving madness.

The silence they left behind was unlike any I've ever known. All of us just standing or sitting around, shivering and shaking, in many cases too stunned to even react to the moans of the wounded.

I'd lost everything. As had Jimmy and Delilah. The little guy was heartbroken. All his inventions, his little bits of cleverness, his reasons to live and hope, now gone.

We stayed that way 'til dawn, and then, with the light somehow charging us with energy, someone started clearing up and others followed suit. But not me. I had something else to do. Something that simply couldn't wait, and the moment I saw my chance, I slipped away. Down the long row of burnt-out lean-tos, out of the Village, and over to the Old City.

I found her in the living area, sitting motionless on her bed, staring into nothing. I don't know how, but she knew why I was there. For a long time neither of us could bring ourselves to say a word.

'Did you used to do that?' I eventually asked, in little more than a whisper. Still she didn't speak. 'Did you?'

She tried to give this long sad sigh, but it came out all broken and chopped into little pieces.

'Tell me!'

It took a long time. Too long. Finally she nodded through the distance of a quarter of an inch or so, as if it was all she could manage.

'Jesus!' I groaned.

'Clancy!' she cried. 'What can I say? I can't believe it now, but then I didn't know any different.'

She went quiet again, lengthening a pause into a silence.

'How could you?' I asked.

'I don't know! We thought of it . . . almost as a treat.'

'*A what?*'

'Foggy nights, take drugs, go and terrorise the old people. It was what we did. They encouraged us to do it. Told us we had every right. You weren't people. It wasn't wrong.'

'It *is* wrong!' I shouted.

'I know that now!' she shouted, tears coming to her eyes. 'But I didn't know it then! It was just the way it was . . . I can't explain.'

For several moments I stood there staring at her. I didn't understand this any better than what I'd just witnessed in the Village.

'What we think is so often a matter of circumstance,' she said helplessly. 'Like you and your "Mr Meltoni". Are you so sure he was such a great guy?'

'For chrissake!' I protested, angry at the comparison. 'He'd never do anything like that – never!'

She paused in frustration, as if she feared I simply wasn't capable of understanding. 'De Grew and the Wastelords are so good at creating this idea that they're looking out for you. I mean, when you first arrive they seem so bad, so brutal, but after a while they kind of pull you in. They're family. Or the only one you got. They feed you, give you shelter, a sense of community, and every now and then encourage you to go crazy. Like you got to do it 'cuz it's good for you. Good for everyone.'

'Jesus!' I moaned.

'I *know*!' she cried. 'I know! . . . I guess they're manipulating you, but you don't know it. You're too young. You gotta believe in something, and they're all there is.'

For a long while neither of us spoke. Blind she might be, but I could tell how acutely aware she was of my stare. I hated the fact that I'd begun to see her as a source of hope, of possible change in my life, and now she was part of the very worst of it.

A wind got up, sweeping down the tunnel, blowing out the candle. I fumbled for my matches and relit it.

'Clancy,' came a whisper from behind me.

I turned around. She was sitting on the edge of her bed, leaning forward, reaching out towards me.

I just stared at her. What the hell did she want?

'Please!' she begged.

It took a while, but I forced myself to take a pace forward, then another, 'til I dropped to my knees in front of her. I was that nervous, the only sound you could hear was my breathing. No way could I make the first move. No way. She leant further forward, put her arms around me and pulled me towards her.

I can't describe how that felt. There just aren't the words. Not in any language. She was so warm and soft, I was so big and clumsy – I was scared I might squeeze too hard and hurt her. 'Cuz I got to tell you, despite what happened in the Village, despite what she just told me, the only thing I could think of in that moment was that no woman had held me like that for almost twenty years. Even then it had been a hooker who I'd paid extra to do it. I stayed where I was, not daring to move, even to breathe, in case it had happened by accident and she might suddenly realise. I mean, it might not have meant much to some, but for me it was nothing short of a miracle.

Eventually she kind of shifted her body a little, in an awkward way, leaning back and pulling me with her, and I realised what she had in mind. Nothing could've shocked me more. My first reaction was to stop her. I even tried. When she started to take off her clothes, I kept saying, 'No, no!' over and over, but she wouldn't listen. She just carried on, removing item after item, 'til she lay naked beside me.

I couldn't look. It wouldn't have been right. Not with her being blind and all. I just hugged her tighter and tighter, as if to squeeze away our mutual embarrassment. She wasn't done though, 'cuz then I felt her fumbling at my belt.

Again I tried to stop her, even more urgently this time, but she wouldn't have it. Shushing my protests, ignoring my struggling, pushing and directing me 'til I was as naked as she was.

It's a terrible, terrible thing to say, and, please, God, forgive me, but just at that moment I was almost glad she was blind. I couldn't bear for her to see that old bag of bones stretched out beside her. Over and over she tried to embrace me but I kept squirming away. I didn't want her to touch me. I didn't want her to know what I felt like. In the end she forced herself upon me, insisting I let her put her hands wherever she wanted.

I hated the way her fingers probed deep into my giving flesh. How she kneaded biceps that once wouldn't have given an eighth of an inch. I wanted to tell her that she should've known me when I was in my twenties or thirties, before the parting of the flesh and bone, before the flaps on my back and the creases across my chest appeared, but do you know something? After a while I began to realise that she didn't care. In fact, I don't think it even occurred to her. It didn't matter *who* I once was, or *how* I'd once felt, she wanted to make love to the man I was *now*. And once I realised that, once I got it into my thick head, I don't know why, and it's a helluva thing to have to confess, but I started to cry.

For literally the first time in my adult life, tears rolled down my cheeks. I was that embarrassed, I did everything I could to keep her from knowing, but she felt them fall upon her bare shoulder and hugged me and kissed them away with lips so warm they felt like they were burning off my dulled old skin and exposing something more sensitive underneath.

And finally we made love. Yes, we did. We made love so beautifully I never even imagined I was capable of such a thing. But don't ask me about it, 'cuz I ain't ever going to tell you. I don't agree with that sort of thing being talked about. It ain't respectful. Not to a lady. You're just going to have to believe me. Down in the dank underground depths of Shit Island, we made love like angels, and come what may, wherever this madness leads us, I tell you, I'll never forget.

I stayed with her for another couple of hours, and then, remembering what had happened, that I, along with many others, had to rebuild my lean-to, I told her I had to get back to the Village.

She walked me up to the entrance and I stood there with her for a few moments, feeling awkward, not sure what had just happened, what it meant. Eventually I gave her a quick clumsy kiss and turned to go, but before I could push the door open, she grabbed me and hugged me for all she was worth. Which made me feel a whole lot better about everything.

When I got outside I was met by a surprisingly bright and warm day. At any other time I would've been really grateful for the first real promise of another season, but as I began to make my way over to the Village, all I could think about was Lena.

I couldn't believe it. 'Big guys never get the girl!' Didn't I tell you? It's a universal understanding, written in nods and grunts. But here I was walking away from having made love to her.

Why had she done that? *Why*? Had I just participated in making love? Or something completely different? . . . Need? Desperation? I mean, when was the last time she had contact with any man? Or maybe – Jesus Christ – maybe she felt it was the least she could do. That it was her way of making up for what the kids had done to us.

Not for one moment had it occurred to me that anything like that would happen. For chrissake, I could give her thirty years at least. Already I was starting to worry what it might mean, that it would change everything, that I might lose her 'cuz of it.

I trudged slowly on across the garbage, anxiety following pleasure as surely as night does day. I guess all I could do was appreciate it for what it was and expect no more. If the next time I saw her she was all cool and flinty with me, just to make certain I hadn't got the wrong impression, that I wasn't fooling myself about anything, well, it would hurt, but I'd take it. I mean, no matter what she said or did, she could never take the memory away from me. Nor the fact that I'll treasure it for the rest of my life.

CHAPTER SEVEN

Arriving back in the Village was a bit like whistling down an alleyway and having someone lay one on you from behind. Reality hit me so hard all the joy so recently in my heart ended up spilled out across the floor. The rows of burnt-out lean-tos were a wound, a black scab, running through our community. But do you know something? There were those already fixing themselves up with new shelters. Nothing special – in some cases nothing more than freshly found plastic stretched over holes they'd scraped out of the ground – but you still got to admire them.

Not that everyone was of the same mind. The one thing that's getting harder and harder to repair is the human spirit. I saw several villagers in exactly the same places I'd left them that morning. Sitting dazedly on the ground, staring into space, ignoring everything going on around them as if they simply couldn't do it anymore.

All the bodies had been dragged away, the chopped flesh, the ruptured sinew, but the stains of blood linger forever. Someone had tried to improve things, splashing a lot of water around, but it just meant that sinister-looking red puddles had formed everywhere; the earth itself looked like it was bleeding.

Jimmy was still sorting through the remains of his lean-to, digging stuff out, cleaning ash off it, seeing if it was worth keeping. One look was enough to know I was in his bad books.

'Where you been, Big Guy?' he asked, wincing a little as he straightened up.

'Oh . . . nowhere,' I said, immediately feeling guilty.

He looked me up and down. 'I thought you'd gone out searching for materials? To rebuild?'

I shook my head. It's not often I'm intimidated by Jimmy. Or maybe it was my conscience that was beating up on me. 'Sorry,' I eventually muttered.

He paused for a moment, then sighed, long, white and shaky, and I realised just how upset he was.

'I don't know what I'm going to do,' he whined. 'I lost everything. The lean-to. My stuff. I mean, how can I rebuild? *Everyone's* out there looking. What chance do I have with this leg?'

'Where's Delilah?'

'Aw, she's gone out, but she ain't as strong as she likes to think she is. No way is she going to be able to fight that lot and bring us back enough to build a new lean-to.'

I put my hand on his shoulder. 'Hey, Jimmy. Come on. When she gets back, the three of us'll go out.'

He gave this kind of involuntary shudder, a real stunned look about him. 'Thanks, Big Guy. I just feel a bit lost, you know.'

A little later we saw Delilah approaching, slowly picking her way through the line of blackened lean-tos; empty-handed, heavy-limbed, her proud face looking like it was carved from dark, depressed stone.

I made her rest a bit before going back out. I still had some salted meat from my coat pocket, and the three of us sat there, in the middle of all that charred chaos and weary industry, chewing away in silence.

It was more torture than anything that the weather was so beautiful.

You wanted it to be overcast, dull, expressing affinity, not teasing us with ideas of a better life. But with each passing hour the temperature continued to rise. It was the kind of freakish spell that makes you think the world might be coming to an end, slipping off its axis, heading off in the direction of the sun.

And the oddest thing about it was, after a while, this seasonal buzz started to go round the Village. As if, no matter how dark the circumstances, the optimism of the sun, the promise of spring, is just too big an influence to deny. Again it went through my head how like animals we are; as cumbersome mounds of clothing came tottering out into the sunshine, wandering aimlessly around, stretching and shaking out their stiff old bodies like bears coming out of hibernation. Winter's silence was discarded. People started chatting to each other, calling across the flattened and blackened rows, there was even a little cackling laughter. I mean, you can't figure it, but that's how it was.

Though not for Jimmy, Delilah and me. We had to get out and find enough stuff for not one, but two lean-tos, and rebuild them both before nightfall. With materials so scarce and competition so great, we'd have to fight for every scrap.

The first place we tried was the tip out on the Head that everyone else seemed to be ignoring. It didn't take long to work out why. The corrosives were starting to ooze right on through there, breaking it all down, blending everything from garbage to rock into a putrefying puree, and we quickly moved on.

God knows what prompted me to head over towards the Old City. I guess I just had this urge to be as near Lena as I could. Not that it mattered which way we went; we were as likely to find building materials there as anywhere else.

It was a helluva weird feeling, I can tell you; knowing she was somewhere beneath us. I kept trying to figure out how things up here related to her world. The living quarters, the garden – where she might be at this moment.

At one point I even led Jimmy and Delilah into sight of the tunnel entrance just so I could hang round for a little while, stealing glances, feeling that familiar excitement percolating away inside me. Not that I went any closer. I didn't want Lena misunderstanding what was going on.

After an hour or so of scrabbling and scratching and finding nothing more useful than a handful of nails and a rusty old sheet of corrugate, it began to occur to me, as I'm sure it was Jimmy and Delilah, that there was a real possibility of us having to spend the night in the open. Worse still, that the chances of another fog after how warm the day had been were uncomfortably high. Why this should move Delilah to sing, I don't know, but it did. She suddenly burst out with this real chilly old blues number that echoed round the ruins of the Old City like a requiem. I guess it's just her way of coping, a refuge, a place to take herself when things start to look really bad. Whatever, for however long it lasted, it was a delight to hear.

A little later, and without anyone actually saying anything, we started to work our way out of the city. At one point I glanced over to the spot where I'd decided the living area might be, smiling to myself, and Jimmy turned and caught me.

'What?' he asked.

I shrugged, like I didn't even know myself. 'Nothing.'

He stared at me for a moment, then bustled impatiently on, plainly of the opinion that there was nothing to smile about, nor worthy of discussion, other than the building of a new lean-to.

Taking one final look back, I followed along behind him. I mean, what could I say? How could I explain that, just at that moment, I really didn't give a damn about our situation or prospects? That all I cared about was this young woman living beneath us and what the two of us had got up to that morning. Let's face it, sometimes what happens fast has to be let in slow. I needed time to go over it, to savour in minutes what had happened in a split second, stretch it out into endless fine detail, and every time I did it made me smile.

As soon as we got back out onto the tips, I was reminded of one of the major disadvantages of warm weather. I mean, I hate winter. Especially out here, it never leaves without extracting a cruel sacrifice. People die all the time. We just ain't no match for it. But the one thing it does do for us is to freeze up some of the smell of this place. With all this sunshine the process of decomposition was starting up again in earnest. You could sense it oozing back into life, rising up out of the ground, like the spirit of decay: stale, flatulent, rotting. Every year I forget how bad it is. How sick it makes me feel. There were flies, too. Millions of them coming out of nowhere, buzzing excitedly around. Delilah tied a handkerchief round her face and pretty soon Jimmy and me copied her. I mean, it didn't do a great deal of good, but it did make us feel a little better.

We still hadn't found much. A couple of lengths of wet and bowed timber, some fresh sheets of plastic (always the easiest thing to come by) to add to the corrugate we found earlier, but not enough to build *one* lean-to, let alone two. Delilah dug out the broken side of a wooden crate we could use, but Jimmy kept getting distracted by other things – junk to fill a lean-to that hadn't as yet been built – and she was getting angry.

'Look at him,' she grumbled, as he started tugging on this length of corroded wire poking out of the garbage. 'Another name for useless.'

As if to prove the point, the piece of wire suddenly came free and Jimmy fell backwards onto his ass.

'See! See what I mean?'

I immediately pretended to notice something a little ways off, anxious not to find myself in the position of being a reluctant arbiter in yet another of their disputes.

'Tell you something, Jimmy, I ain't sleeping in the open tonight,' she hollered across. 'Even if it means sleeping with someone else.'

'We'll find something,' he told her, more embarrassed than intimidated by her threat.

'You ain't even looking!' she challenged.

'Sure I am.'

I tried to calm things down, to remind them of the urgency of our situation, but even though they stopped arguing, their silence was no less hostile than their words had been, and in the end, Delilah lost it altogether. Storming off to a spot thirty or forty yards off, plopping herself down, idly picking up bits and pieces and angrily tossing them down in front of her, saying she wasn't gonna bother if no one else was.

Jimmy kept calling her to come back, promising he'd keep his mind on lean-tos and not junk, and then made great play of digging out another sheet of plastic packing.

'Hey! Cool! Lile, look at this!'

It was a game, the kind all couples play. He was attempting to win her back, acting the fool, trying to make her smile, and she was equally determined not to let that heavy scowl off her face.

I just didn't see it coming. Everything seemed so normal, so familiar. I remember poking about in one of those huge industrial waste-bags that you sort through at your peril. Someone had already slashed it open and taken a look, but I was hoping they might've missed something. I tossed some of the contents out, squatting down to sift through it, and just as I leant forward there was this almighty explosion behind me and I was blown off my feet.

Next thing I knew I was face down in crap, the back of my head feeling like a flame-thrower had just scorched the hair and skin off me.

It was only as I looked up, in that split second when I thanked God for sparing me, that I realised we were in one of those awful vacuums where time has stopped and won't begin again until tragedy takes its form. I didn't have long to wait. There was an awful wail, a high-pitched scream behind me, and I knew it was Delilah.

For a moment I thought it must've been a satellite malfunction, that she'd been taken out by mistake, but when I looked, when I saw the scattering of flames around her, I knew immediately what it was. There's always a lot of gas on the first warm days of the year. More than at any other time. The sun unlocks it, just like it does the smell. We should've kept that in mind. Something Delilah had thrown had caused a spark and ignited a blowout.

Jimmy let out a cry and scrambled across to her, losing his stick on the way, reaching her almost on all fours.

'Lile! . . . Lile!' he shrieked.

I slid and tripped my way up behind him, the first sight of her taking my breath away. She was covered from head to toe in blood; barely a spot on her was free of red. Most of her clothes had been blown off, and though there were no obvious major injuries, judging by her screams she was in a helluva lot of pain.

Jimmy kept crying her name, over and over, telling her it was going to be all right, but you could see he didn't have a clue what to do. He just squatted down next to her, trying to take hold of some part of her that wasn't bleeding.

'Big Guy!' he screamed, turning to me, his face so white I thought he was going to pass out. 'What are we going to do?'

Time and time again he asked me, 'til it became almost meaningless. What could we do? Violent death and injury are just things you get used to on the Island. There are no emergency services. No doctors.

Certainly not for anyone outside the Camp. That's just the way it is. Until it happens to someone you care about.

'Big Guy!' Jimmy pleaded again, his voice barely audible above Delilah's shrieking.

I looked at him, looked at her, and realised I had no choice. There was only one place I knew where she could get any kind of medical attention, and even though I'd sworn I'd never tell anyone about it, this was different. Immediately I scooped Delilah up and started to run.

'Where you going?' Jimmy yelled after me, but still started to follow.

Delilah might be a thin old stick, but she was still a helluva weight to carry that distance. Especially with her screaming and writhing, her blood making everything all slippery and sticky at the same time. I kept saying the same thing to her Jimmy had, that it was going to be all right. As if she couldn't feel the pain searing through her body, as if she wasn't aware she was bleeding to death.

I reached the tunnel entrance, had a quick look round, juggled Delilah into one arm, then threw back the door and got her and Jimmy inside. The little guy didn't say a word, just kind of gaped, like the whole day was now one big shock to him and all he could do was to helplessly follow along behind it. I lit a candle, got him to hold it, then led him down to the living area.

There was no sign of Lena. I called out to her, knowing she had to be hiding, that she must've heard Delilah's screams and was wondering what the hell was going on.

'Lena! . . . It's okay, it's me!'

She came out of the shadows, her face frightened and confused.

'My friend's been caught in a blowout,' I told her. 'I didn't know what to do. I'm sorry, this is all I could think of.'

The situation explained, she immediately took control in that way somebody always does, digging out bandages and antiseptic cream from her stores, getting me to boil up some water.

Delilah was passing in and out of consciousness, screaming and moaning, then slipping away again as if the pain was just too much for her to bear. Lena knelt next to her and set about trying to assess the damage, touching her as gently as she could, but Delilah still couldn't take it.

'I've got some hooch over there,' Lena said. 'It might help deaden the pain.'

I fetched the bottle and gave it to Jimmy to pour down Delilah's throat. Presently the screaming began to subside and Lena was able to start cleaning the wounds; slowly, tenderly, letting the water do most of the work. Occasionally Delilah would cry out and Lena would shush her like a baby, waiting a few moments then carrying on with what she was doing.

In one place on the upper arm, you could actually see the bone poking through a flap of torn flesh. There was also a piece of metal jutting out of her hip that we had to ease out as gently as we could. I tell you, it made you wince just to see it. I mean, I know Delilah, I know how tough she is. If she's screaming, there's a damn good reason.

As for Jimmy, the poor little guy was cradling her head in his arms, tears streaming down his face and all that love you always knew was there was out and swirling around them.

It took a couple of hours and the best part of a full bottle of hooch to get through the bandaging. I spent most of my time building up the fire, making sure Delilah was warm. I mean, she's hurt really bad, no doubt about that, but shock's the first thing you gotta worry about. I seen it before. Really tough guys, who didn't care about pain, who treated their bodies like inefficient forms of armour. But that tiny spark we call life can be so frail. You'd see it in their eyes, the shock, the realisation that the plug was being pulled inside them. That somewhere in there was a weakness that didn't care how tough they were; it just wanted to die.

A little after midnight, Lena was so exhausted she went to bed. I sat with Jimmy for a while, almost as worried about him as I was Delilah. He'd barely said a word since we arrived. At one point he did ask about Lena, how I knew her, what she was doing down here, but I just brushed it aside. He wasn't listening anyway.

Later, with the warmth of the fire and the long silences, I started to get a bit sleepy myself and, telling him to wake me when he wanted a break, I dragged the bed Lena had made up for me down the tunnel a little and settled down. It went through my head that I would've liked to have slept with her, that she was just what I needed to soothe the terrible sadness I was feeling, but I didn't want her to think I was presuming in any way. However, no sooner had I fallen asleep than I was awakened by her crawling in beside me.

If you already know it, I guess I don't have to tell you what a wonderful feeling that is: having a cold bed turned into a warm one. There ain't a dream in the whole world better than that. I woke to find this soft and drowsy woman next to me, my arms about her even before I realised, and this time I *will* tell you what happened. We made love. And I'll tell you the details, too. We made love by hugging and kissing and caressing and making each other feel a whole lot better and braver about this world. But nothing else. It ain't always necessary, you know. To be honest, at times I just think the sex thing confuses us.

Later, Delilah started moaning and I slipped away from Lena to see how she was doing. Jimmy was still holding her, his face registering every moment of her pain. He poured some more hooch into her mouth, said what he could to calm her down, though I doubt she could hear him. Eventually she passed out mid-wail so that for a moment, until she caught her breath again, we both feared the worst.

'Big Guy,' Jimmy whispered, stroking her forehead, 'what am I going to do?'

'What do you mean?'

'Look at her.'

'She'll be okay,' I reassured him, though not entirely convincingly.

'But if she's not . . .' He stopped and shook his head. 'If she's not . . .'

'Jimmy. It ain't going to come to that.'

'There'd be no point. You know that, don't you? Not without her.'

What could I say? I knew he meant it, and just at that moment, I wouldn't presume to argue.

I turned to Delilah. She's one helluva tough old bird, but she'll have to be to get through this. And you wanna know something? Something that shames me? Sitting there, with that tortured body of hers spread out before me, that proud but pained face so racked and wrinkled by life, it momentarily flitted through my mind that maybe death was her best option. I mean, I wouldn't choose it for her myself, not in a million years, but sometimes you think, the way things are, what this life has to offer, maybe this is a battle that just ain't worth fighting.

I shook the thought off, briefly resting a reassuring hand on Jimmy's shoulder before going to build up the fire again.

I don't know whether you know this or not, but in case you don't, it's not a fair world. When you're a kid you got all these dumb-ass ideas about life. What you're entitled to, what you're going to get, but the overriding notion is that it's going to be fifty-fifty – part good, part bad. Well, I'll tell you, that ain't nothing but shit, and I hope by now you know it. There ain't no equal rights when it comes to good and bad fortune, no more than we all got an equal amount of money in the bank or live for the same amount of years. It don't work that way. Maybe there are equal portions of good and bad luck slopping around out there somewhere, but that don't mean you're going to get your share. Some get equal bad and good, some get nearly all good and very little bad, while others get nothing but shit all their lives. And if you've always been unlucky, right from the moment you were born and you're still sitting there, scanning the horizon, waiting for your great gleaming silver-plated ship to come sailing on in, then I hate to tell you this, but maybe that sonofabitch has sunk somewhere.

You're a fool if you're living life that way, 'cuz the truth is, in the real world, some slide on silk while others constantly get their asses dragged across rocky ground.

Delilah had it tough right from the moment she was found one freezing night amongst the garbage in some alleyway; squeezed out by some anonymous fleshy sac and then just left to die in the blood and afterbirth. I guess she was crying, but she likes to tell it as if she was singing and that's why she's been singing ever since. In the hope that someone else'll come along and pull her out of the crap. And if you're thinking that only goes to prove she's a 'survivor', and that eventually she'll go on to better things, well, you just ain't listening, are you? She was rewarded for her obstinate refusal to die by being put in an orphanage and being physically and mentally abused almost every day of her childhood. She lost a lung to TB when she was in her early twenties, became a whore and was repeatedly beaten up 'cuz she couldn't afford to be that fussy about her customers, and finally, the one great love of her life, who apparently was her pimp, was cut to pieces before her for getting a little careless on the subject of geography and straying onto someone else's patch.

When I first saw her she was this brash and ballsy figure who used to strut round the Village in rags twenty years too young for her, still turning the occasional trick for food or whatever. But she was losing it and knew it all too well, no longer tragic, nor pretty enough, to keep the sniggers at bay. Jimmy heard her hacking away outside his lean-to one night and invited her in. She left the next morning, but returned a week later. This time she stayed for a few days. Then a few weeks. Then months. Even now she'll leave him, wandering off without so much as saying a word. He worries and frets over her, terrified she ain't going to return, that something's happened, but when she finally does return he acts as if nothing's amiss, like she's just been out for a walk or something.

But now Delilah lies here, lacerated, erupting with pain, as if every scar life's ever put on her has suddenly opened up again. And really, is it any wonder that the prospect of death, of wrapping her up in that great grey blanket, appears in your mind? Maybe she's somewhere at this very moment making that self-same decision, with exactly the same thoughts going through her head? Should she let go, release her gnarled, bony old grip on life, or maybe try singing one last time?

She hung on throughout the next day, not getting any better or worse, but staying unconscious for longer periods. Lena and Jimmy were constantly at her side, tending to her, watching over her, while I did all the fetching and carrying, keeping things turning over. But the following morning, when I came back from the garden, Lena was sitting next to Delilah with a really worried look on her face.

She heard me returning and motioned for me and Jimmy to join her a few steps along the tunnel.

'We got a problem,' she said.

'What?' I asked.

Lena hesitated for a moment, as if she wasn't sure if Jimmy could take this. 'She's deteriorating,' she eventually said.

I hesitated for a moment, not wanting to admit it, though I knew it was true. I'd been looking on Delilah's unconsciousness as a friend that occasionally came to relieve her of pain, but now I was beginning to fear it might take her away.

I glanced at Jimmy but he didn't say a word. He's been like that ever since we came down here. This old man suddenly becoming a lost child, turning from one adult face to another, waiting for us to decide his fate.

'She's pretty tough,' I said, in that dumb way people always have when they think they gotta come up with something positive.

Lena shook her head. 'Clancy, this island is made of crap. The whole damn thing's toxic. People die of infections they get from cuts or grazes. Can you imagine what she must have inside her?'

I paused and looked back down the tunnel to the long stick of Delilah. I hadn't really thought of that. She'd been opened up from head to toe. Any virus, any germ, any foul damn creeping evil parasite that we got round here could've crawled inside her. Jesus, if it hadn't seemed hopeless before, it did then.

'She needs antibiotics,' Lena said.

'A doctor?'

'Medicine.'

'Same thing.'

She paused for a moment. 'Not necessarily.'

I turned to her. The way she said it, I knew she had something in mind. 'What?'

Lena hesitated for a few moments, then sighed, like she was about to say something she knew she shouldn't.

'Where do you think I got all these creams and bandages?' I didn't answer. Tell the truth, I hadn't really thought about it. 'I told you, I used to work in the warehouses. A lot of Mainlanders don't finish a course of tablets when they're ill. As soon as they start to feel better they throw what's left away.' She paused for a moment. 'There's a warehouse down there stuffed full of medical stuff.'

For a moment I just stared at her, barely able to believe where this was heading. 'What are you saying?'

'I'm just telling you what's there, that's all.'

'Go down to the Camp? Steal from the Wastelords?' I asked.

There was another silence that no one seemed inclined to break, then, almost like a stranger walked in, Jimmy finally piped up.

'Is she going to die if she doesn't get antibiotics?' he asked.

Lena sighed. 'I think so.'

'Then I have to go,' he said simply.

I turned on him. '*Jimmy!* For chrissake! You can't go down there!'

'I don't have a choice,' he told me.

'Are you crazy? What good's it going to do for *you* to die?' I asked, the thought of what he said before momentarily occurring to me, that without Delilah he wouldn't want to live anyway.

There was another long silence. Both of them seemed to want something from me and I wasn't exactly sure what.

'We wouldn't stand a chance,' I told them. 'We don't know a thing about the place. The layout, the security, nothing.'

There was another pause, then finally Lena spoke. 'I do,' she said.

CHAPTER EIGHT

If Mr Meltoni knew what I was planning, if he was gazing out from his huge, ornate Gothic pink marble mausoleum over on the Mainland, I reckon he'd probably pull the lid shut on his coffin and go back to being dead. A blind woman, a little bent old guy with a stick and a spent heavy intending to go down into what must surely be one of the most dangerous places on Earth. The heartland of thousands of drug-taking kids who've all been indoctrinated with the notion that the murder of old folk is a fine recreation. To maybe confront the Wastelords, those who've attained an almost legendary status for being the source of everything evil upon this island. I tell you, it's insanity gone mad.

And you wanna know something else? Maybe the craziest thing of all? The one time Lena thinks we might just get away with it is on a dark foggy night. Okay, so I can see there's a certain logic there. If it's foggy we got a chance of not being seen, right? And if the kids are getting themselves up on the notion of paying the Village a visit, sure as hell the last thing they're going to expect is for us to repay the compliment. But that don't ease my mind none. No way. I mean, if I had to nominate the number-one place I would least like to visit on a dark foggy night – or any other time come to that – it would be that Camp.

Trouble is, we don't look to have a choice. Delilah's getting worse by the hour, her face draining of colour as if it's an indicator of life, the rasping of her one lung echoing away down the tunnel. Like it or not, if we want to save her we have to go down there – and as soon as we can.

Which means that we actually find ourselves in the unique position of praying for fog, that this freak spell of weather, with its warm days and cold nights, might allow us a further dark pocket of anonymity in which to hide.

Lena's been over the whole complex with us. Not just the Camp, but the warehouses, De Grew and his Wastelords – everything. Tell the truth, it makes me feel a little uneasy – the amount of detail she knows. Maybe it's 'cuz they're amongst the last of her sighted memories? Like the final model off the line of a superseded car, kept by the company, forever shiny and new.

Apparently there ain't a lot of security (who's going to rob them, for chrissake, and where would they go if they did?). The only place they bother to put a guard on is – yeah, you guessed it – the medical warehouse. At any one time there's enough stuff down there to stock a couple of hospitals. Pills, creams and potions, thrown away by the sick, the dying, or merely the hypochondriacs of the Mainland. The reason it's guarded is 'cuz everything medical is there – including 'recreational' drugs – and the enemy they really got to watch for is the one within, the child addicts who can't wait for the next hay day.

Tell the truth, twenty–thirty years ago, with some good boys and decent hardware, I might've fancied it. We could've blasted in there, kicked the ass of anyone who got in our way and been home in time for the big game. Now though, and with what we got available, I don't think we stand a chance. I tried to persuade them to let me go alone.

At least that way there might be a scrap of hope, but Lena wouldn't even hear me out. She told me she's the only one who knows her way round down there, who can get us where we want to go, *what on earth was I thinking?*

Which kind of irked me in the same way Jimmy used to when I played chess with him and was about to make a move and he'd start all this tutting and shaking his head. Which was probably why I turned on the little guy, telling him he should stay and look after Delilah, he'd do more good that way. He got all prickly with me, saying no one was going to stop him doing his 'bit' and that at some stage we might well need his 'specialised knowledge'.

I guess he just can't cope with the idea of sitting around waiting to see if Delilah's going to make it or not. Or maybe the possibility of losing her means he's got that rush of wayward courage that those who find they have no interest left in life sometimes get. Either way, it don't matter. I'm stuck with both of them, and there's nothing I can do about it.

A little before eight I went up to check yet again on the weather and found that, since I'd last looked, the night had returned and brought an old familiar enemy with it. I turned and walked back down to tell the others, cursing myself all the way for not being able to think of another way to do this.

Jimmy and Lena never said a word, just started to get ready, and even though I'd promised myself I'd have one last try at changing their minds, they looked so determined, I didn't bother.

Fifteen minutes or so later, we made a final check on Delilah, then left. She never heard our reassurances that we'd be back soon, that we'd be bringing something to make her better, and to tell you the truth, I think we were all a little grateful for it.

Believe me, it was one helluva disturbing feeling pushing back that entrance door and being met by nothing but a dark, hanging grey wall of moist silence. I mean, Lena was right, for once it might be on our side, but that didn't make me feel any more comfortable about going out there.

She pushed past me as if she didn't understand my hesitation and Jimmy and me followed her out into a world as alien now as any distant planet.

I tell you, it's amazing how she gets along. In the tunnels I've come to expect it. I figure that over the years she's drawn a map of that place in her head and couldn't lose herself if she wanted. But outside? That's something else. For the first couple of hundred yards I kept telling her to mind out for this, and mind out for that, 'til eventually she lost patience and told me to shut up. From then on all I could do was to watch helplessly as she walked straight at obstacle after obstacle. It was nerve-racking, but after a while I began to appreciate how she's adapted to her disability. She's like one of those all-terrain vehicles that immediately responds to whatever conditions it strikes. If it was you or me walking into a pile of rubble we'd fall flat onto our faces, but she instantly brings her foot up a little higher, or swivels one way or another, managing to somehow keep her balance and carry on. It took me a while to relax. She did stumble now and then, and occasionally, if she was faced with something really big, I couldn't help but tell her, but it didn't take me long to realise she was nowhere near as vulnerable as I thought.

Soon the ground began to slope away and we realised we'd found our way to what was once 'Chinatown', and the hill that, were the weather clear, would overlook the Camp. As soon as we began our descent the sound we'd been dreading and anticipating in equal measures started up somewhere in front of us. The beating of their drums vibrating out of the fog, warning us how close we were getting, what penalty we'd have to pay if we got any nearer.

Jimmy froze in mid-stride. Even in the dull light I could see how pale his face was.

'Jesus, Big Guy,' he whispered, as if it was only now the full impact of what we were doing was getting through to him.

I nodded. I mean, no matter how well-intentioned this might be, it still didn't stop it from being suicide. There were thousands of them down there, whipping themselves up into a killing frenzy, and we were going to walk smack dab into the middle of it all.

'Clancy!' Lena hissed back at us impatiently. 'Let's go!'

We hurried after her, concerned she might disappear into the grey murk locked about us, that we'd never find each other again.

I kept trying to relate where we were to the diagram she'd scratched on the tunnel wall. The Camp had to be slightly over to our right, the sorting area for new garbage in front of us and the warehouses behind that, then De Grew and his Wastelords up on the hill. Not that it really helped. The fog was so thick we might as well all have been blind. Mind you, if we had been, we wouldn't have coped as well as Lena. At times she was taking us along at such a pace Jimmy was starting to get a bit puffed.

'You okay?' I whispered to him.

'Yeah, yeah,' he muttered, taking yet another nervous look around. 'Worry about yourself.'

We descended another couple of hundred yards or so, the drums getting progressively louder, more threatening, joined by the occasional mad scream, when suddenly something so weird happened that for a few moments it made us forget everything.

I don't even know how to describe it. It was like being mugged from inside. Set upon. Beat up. As if a thousand sleeping memories suddenly reared up inside me and went screaming through my head, colliding with each other and shooting into the air. Out of nowhere I saw my kid brother, Don, the one who died drinking bleach when the babysitter was supposed to be looking after him. It was a hot summer's day and him and me were searching through some long grass for a ball I'd just hit. Then I saw my mother on her hands and knees, washing the kitchen floor, that sweaty piece of hair that used to hang in front of her eyes rocking back and forth. Mr Meltoni puffing out his chest the way he used to when he was having his photo taken, standing next to his freshly polished limo. My father painting the bedroom ceiling. The girl who used to work in the flower shop on the corner. I saw them all in a kind of rapid-fire attack, so quick it literally left me gasping. I mean, despite my situation, where I was, what I was doing, it was all I could do not to cry out. All of it was so vivid.

I turned to Jimmy and found the same stunned, almost horrified look on his face.

'What the—?' he gasped, his voice trailing away.

Before I could answer Lena walked back out of the fog. 'What are you two doing?' she asked.

She grabbed my arm and yanked me on and I finally realised what it was about. We were on the edge of the sorting area, near the fresh garbage, and suddenly it wasn't one smell we were faced with, not the melded old rotten one we've known for the past God knows how many years, but a whole lot of different new ones.

It was those smells that were dragging our memories up. I was getting wafts of all kinds of stuff. To my right there was a heap of dying flowers, hundreds and hundreds of them. I don't know where they came from. Maybe a wedding or a funeral or something. Some of them were still fresh, still innocently giving off perfume long after they'd been discarded. A few paces on I started homing in on something else. The synthesised freshness of polish. Detergent. Cellulose paint, motor oil, cut grass. It was like a smorgasbord of scents and all you had to do to get a different one was to take a couple more strides and face in another direction.

Suddenly my nose was invaded by a smell so strong it seemed to barge all the others out of the way. Jeez, I could smell food! Meat, vegetables, spices – *goddammit, garlic*!

I tell you, I couldn't stop myself, I struck out for it like some snuffling pig, letting my nose guide me to the spot, sifting through bags, squelching through discarded vegetables, digging through all sorts of crap 'til I found what I was looking for. A big fat steak cooked in garlic butter; medium-rare, almost untouched, just a little bit cut out of the middle and then thrown away.

Jimmy came up behind me and grabbed some, too. There was so much food it was obscene. People up in the Village could've lived for a whole year on what had been thrown away in one day. I practically jammed the whole damn steak into my mouth. Lena hung back, looking away, almost embarrassed, as if we were taking a pee or something. Or maybe 'cuz she knew what was about to happen.

See, you're probably thinking we were about to go through all sorts of mouth-watering convolutions, finding ourselves with 'real' food in our mouths again, but we didn't. Something really weird happened. No matter how long Jimmy and me chewed on those steaks, how much we got our jaws chomping, we just couldn't swallow. It was as if it wasn't our food anymore and even if we did manage to swallow some, we'd just throw it back up.

In the end we both spat it out. As if we'd just learnt we'd been reprogrammed. And when Lena urged us to move on we followed along without a word of complaint, a little ashamed of what we'd just done.

Jimmy might've been worried sick about Delilah, he might've been scared stiff at where we were and what we were doing, but that didn't stop him from realising his long-treasured dream had finally come true: we were on the fresh garbage. A couple of times I noticed him hesitate for a moment, peering down at stuff on the ground, pushing and prodding with his foot, then squatting to take a better look.

'Jimmy!' I hissed.

'Do you know what this is?'

'No! And I don't care either. Now, come on! You'll lose us.'

'It's an old TX motherboard!'

I grabbed him by the arm, pulling him to his feet, resuming our journey, but within moments I'd turn round to see him crouched over something else. I went back and was about to go mad when suddenly I noticed Lena had stopped a few paces in front of us, her head kind of cocked, listening intently. I clamped my hand over Jimmy's mouth, just in case he was about to say something.

The two of us remained there, crouching low, breathlessly watching as Lena slowly turned her head from side to side, like she had antennae. All the way down from the Old City I'd been aware she was working off a different map to us. Different coordinates. And I ain't just talking about hearing either. I mean smell, too. Searching through places our eyes didn't have a chance of piercing, cross-referencing her senses, plotting out the whole thing in her head.

I released my grip on Jimmy and silently made my way over.

'There's someone over there,' she whispered, gesturing into nothingness.

I turned and strained to see in the direction she'd indicated, to somehow pierce the grey milky murk, the noise of the drums, the chorus of screams around us, suddenly seemed much louder.

During the next few moments a dozen or so people came out of that fog – not one of them proved to be of any substance.

'Can't see anyone,' I whispered.

For several moments neither of us spoke or moved, just waited for something to happen. Eventually she gave a sigh of relief. 'It's okay. They've gone.'

She moved on, noticeably much slower and more watchful now, pausing every few seconds. A door slammed somewhere over to our right. No more than thirty yards away. Probably on one of the warehouses. Someone called out, 'Where?'

'I dunno!' someone else shouted back. 'It was there this morning.'

Kids. Both of them. And if that fog lifted, if that curtain went up, I tell you, it'd be on a scene of total massacre.

Lena paused again, like she was checking her internal bearings. Every now and then I noticed her touch something, maybe a post, a stack of old drums, and she'd nod to herself like she'd reached a milestone. 'It should be over there,' she whispered.

Both Jimmy and I looked in the direction she was indicating but couldn't make out a thing.

'There's nothing,' Jimmy whined, the growing cacophony of noise around us, the knowledge that we were right in amongst them really getting to him.

'It's there,' she repeated, taking a step forward. 'Mind out for the guards. They won't expect anything. Especially not tonight. The kids'll have taken everything they need. If we're discovered just run for it. We'll have a better chance separately.'

Jimmy grunted to himself. I knew what he was thinking; that if it came to making a run for it, with his stick and bad leg, he was at something of a disadvantage. But I could see Lena's point. One person could easily disappear into this fog, but three would be a different matter.

Slowly we began to inch our way forward, step by step, crouching low, ready for anything that might come our way. I was starting to worry, to think maybe she had it wrong, when the big black slab of the warehouse loomed up before us.

'We're here,' I told her.

Lena went right up to it, touched the wall, then directed Jimmy and me to follow as she began to work her way along it.

Every step of the way I was expecting someone to come out of the fog, a sudden shout, a cry of discovery. There was a tension in my body I hadn't felt in years, pulsing through me like it was searching for any weaknesses I might've developed.

When we reached the corner of the building, Lena hesitated, her head raised, listening, sniffing, then she turned and moved slowly on, further into the fog and darkness.

It was only when she paused again that I realised she'd brought us to our destination, that we were standing outside the warehouse door. I immediately gave it the once-over. It wasn't exactly what I'd been expecting. If Jimmy had any ideas about his expertise in the field of hi-tech coming into its own, he could forget them. It was an old-fashioned solidly padlocked door, and what we needed wasn't specialised knowledge, but brute force.

I cursed to myself. I'd brought a few tools, just in case, but nothing that was going to bust that open without alerting everyone in a fifty-yard radius.

'Shit,' I groaned.

For several moments I stood there helplessly, feeling like it was my turn, that Lena had delivered us here and now I should be taking over, but how exactly?

But do you know something? I was way behind on this one. Way, way behind. I mean, big guys, what do we know? 'Cuz Lena just stuck her hand in her pocket, pulled out some keys and unlocked the damn thing.

'Where'd'ya get those?' I asked, but she was already disappearing inside.

The moment Jimmy and I closed the door behind us, the darkness became so complete I couldn't move. I just stood there, wondering what to do, whether it was okay to call out to Lena or not. Then I heard her rummaging round somewhere, a couple of items falling to the floor in her wake.

Soon she returned with some boxes, dividing them amongst us, giving half to Jimmy and half to me. Which wasn't that reassuring, 'cuz I realised why she'd done it, that she was making provision in case one of us didn't get back.

Again she disappeared into the darkness, and again we could hear her rummaging around.

'Come on!' Jimmy begged her, but she shushed him angrily.

Soon she returned with another armful of stuff, this time sharing it out amongst the three of us.

'Let's go,' she said.

Jimmy gave a perceptible sigh of relief, turned and pushed the door open, then froze. There was someone standing there. Blocking our way. Not a kid, or certainly not a young one judging by how much of his bulk filled the doorway. I guessed it was one of the guards.

It was pure instinct. Suddenly it was yesterday and I was doing what I always used to. I saw him, realised we were in the dark and that it would be a split second before he could focus, then I dropped what I was carrying and hit him as hard as I could.

Okay, so in the moment that my fist was flying through the air it did occur to me that maybe the bones in my hand weren't up to this anymore, that they were old and brittle and might break on impact. But they didn't. I got him right on the point of the jaw, and I'll tell you, it must be like riding a bike or something, 'cuz I hadn't forgotten a thing. I pivoted from the waist so I got all my weight into the shot, kept the punch short and full of momentum and he went crashing back against the door frame, slowly collapsing to the ground like paint dripping down a wall.

'*Go!*' hissed Lena. 'There's another one somewhere.'

We ran out of that place and sprinted headlong into the fog, not having a clue where we were going, just praying we wouldn't run into anyone.

Lena was in the lead, with me a little way behind and Jimmy pegging along at the back. But all that changed when she lost her footing and tumbled over, and I fell heavily on top of her.

She was hurt quite bad. For a moment I thought I was going to have to carry her. But she got to her feet and massaged her leg, trying to ease the pain.

'It's okay, it's okay!' she assured me.

It was only then I realised that Jimmy had run straight past us. I could just about make him out, scuttling across the garbage, the three-legged spider making surprisingly rapid progress. Lena tried her leg, limped a little, then started to run after him.

I heard a voice yell out from behind, furiously and repeatedly, and guessed they'd found the unconscious guard. Mind you, we had an even bigger problem to deal with.

'Where's he going?' Lena suddenly cried.

'What do you mean?'

'Jimmy,' she said. 'He's heading in the direction of the kids!'

I couldn't believe it. That mad little bastard was in such a state of panic he was just blindly running anywhere. I wanted to shout after him, warn him, but if I did, everyone would know where we were.

'*Jimmy!*' I hissed as loudly as I could. 'Jimmy!'

I ran after him but suddenly those drums seemed to be exploding all around us, bombarding us, beating us down, and I was almost as panicked as he was.

I just couldn't understand why he didn't realise. I gained a little, thought I might have a chance of catching him, but then, and I tell you, I couldn't believe it, their fire suddenly loomed in front of us. Not just their fire, but the kids dancing round it.

This time I did scream out. '*Jimmy! For chrissake!*'

He stopped, looked kind of lost for a moment, then finally realised what he'd done and turned around. It was the craziest thing you ever saw. He ran straight down their throats, hundreds of them whooping and dancing in a mad frenzy, getting ready to kill, but none of them reacted 'cuz they just couldn't believe it. A little old guy with a stick running into the middle of their camp. Jesus, why would they?

He must've got thirty or forty yards before the first scream went up. Then another, and another, until suddenly the whole night was filled with nothing but their baying and crying. Lena shouted for us to separate, to just get out of there any way we could.

I turned and looked back. Jimmy was some way behind, pegging it away, and I fell back a few steps to try and drag him on.

'Leave me, Big Guy!' he shouted. 'Get the stuff to Delilah!'

'Come on!' I cried.

'*No!*'

I tried to pull him along, but he shook himself free of my grip and lurched off to the side into these piles of garbage.

I was going to follow him, but he disappeared so successfully I thought maybe it was best to just keep going, to distract them.

I looked for Lena, my eyes straining into the fog, but I couldn't see her either. This mob of kids came at me from the side. I didn't see them 'til the last moment. Still I managed to swerve around them and run on, but it's like I told you, I ain't any sort of runner. Just to get this great bulk up and moving is one helluvan achievement, let alone to keep it going. It wasn't long before I realised they were gaining on me. Closer and closer, 'til one of them jumped on my back. From then on it was like a pack of wild dogs. They threw themselves at me, one after the other, 'til they dragged me to the ground.

I knocked one away, then another, but they just got up and leapt back on me, more and more piling in. They were just little kids. Most of them no more than eleven or twelve. Once it might've been a high-spirited game. I might've been their grandfather or something. But not anymore. You have to take this seriously. No matter what you might think, you can't hold back, otherwise they're just going to swarm all over you.

I knocked the biggest of them down, hit him as hard as I could, then tried to drag myself to my feet. But before I could get properly up, I received a blow to the back of my knees from a baseball bat and tumbled down again. Immediately they jumped on top of me again, kicking and punching; no one blow really hurting, just an accumulation. These little fists and feet pummelling you from all directions, harder and harder, 'til you feel yourself starting to weaken.

I lashed out and sent one flying through the air, but the moment he hit the ground he was up and back at me. There were even girls amongst them. Can you believe that? Little girls doing that sort of thing? One kept trying to kick me in the groin as if it was the spot to slay the dragon; giggling all the time, like it was a skill she hadn't quite mastered.

I got hit again by the baseball bat, on the side of the head, surprisingly hard, and felt myself starting to slip away. I lashed out blindly, but they were so quick I was missing most of the time. The little girl caught me where she'd been aiming, squealing with pleasure when she saw me grimace. She was as bad as any of them. I made a lunge and grabbed the leg of the nearest one, pulling him down, then just kind of threw him broadside at the others. It stopped them for a moment, and gave me the chance to struggle to my knees, but then they were back, hanging off me everywhere, punching me in the back, doing everything they could to get the finishing blow in.

I felt like a sea creature emerging out of the water, covered in wriggling parasites. Somehow I got my legs beneath me, pushed with all my strength, and despite buckling for a moment, got to my feet with a defiant roar. I threw one child in one direction, one in another, then grabbed one of their fallen baseball bats and threatened them with it until they ran off into the night.

I didn't hang around. I knew it wouldn't be long before they returned with bigger and probably heavier-armed kids. I could already hear them yelling out to someone for help, giving directions to where I was. Instead I turned and lumbered off into the fog. Calling out to Jimmy, calling out to Lena . . . but there was no reply.

CHAPTER NINE

Getting back to the tunnels took me over an hour. I was forever ducking and diving, getting lost, finding myself where I shouldn't be. It was difficult enough negotiating the fog with Lena showing us the way. On my own, I only had the benefit of my senses, and they were playing some pretty weird tricks on me, I can tell you.

On several occasions I almost bumped into gangs on their way over to the Village. Thank God they were making lots of noise, whooping and shouting, so I had plenty of time to hide. One group – there must've been close onto forty or fifty of them – passed so close to the pile of crap I threw myself into that one of them actually trod on my foot as he went by.

Up close they're one helluva bizarre sight, I can tell you. All dressed and made up, carrying flaming torches, their eyes strangled and popping with drugs. As they went by, I could hear them going on about what they were going to do over in the Village; how many they were going to kill, how they'd go about it. Kids boasting, the way kids always have done, but not about this.

I guess I was hoping that when I did get back underground, I'd find Lena and Jimmy already there, but I was to be disappointed. Leastways about the little guy; Lena had made it. As I neared the living area, she was already administering to Delilah; removing old bandages, applying some of the organi-plasters she brought back. But there was no sign of Jimmy.

'You okay, Clancy?' she called, pausing for a moment to listen to my approach, as if the way I was walking would tell her if I was hurt or not.

'Yeah. I'm fine.'

I knew she would've heard that I was alone, that Jimmy wasn't with me, but she didn't say anything. Probably 'cuz she was worried that, no matter how much Delilah seemed out of it, she might be able to understand.

'I've given her some antibiotics. They should start to act pretty fast.'

I just slid down the tunnel wall and sat silently watching as she tended to Delilah: bathing her, applying ointment, then putting on new dressings. There was something about the way she did it, so deliberate, so tender, it was really soothing. Almost as if it was you she was taking care of.

When she'd finished, she led me off down the tunnel a little way; giving me a grateful hug, squeezing really hard, evoking our special world even then.

'What happened?' she whispered.

'I don't know. I got set on by some kids.' She immediately began to check me out; feeling my face, my head, my body. 'No, I'm fine, but . . . I don't know about Jimmy. He just disappeared.'

She went quiet for a moment, as if gauging his chances, but obviously decided to remain positive. 'He'll be fine.'

'You reckon?'

'Yeah. Course,' she said emphatically.

'I don't know. There are hundreds of them out there. If they do come across him, after what he did – running into their camp – Jesus.'

'He's probably just found himself a good hiding place and decided to stay there 'til they return to the Camp.'

Come the early hours, and still with no sign of him, she was saying the same thing, only she didn't sound quite so convincing, and I was starting to get a really bad feeling about it. As if witnessing the further exercising of some inevitable law of tragedy. Delilah never had anything go right. Maybe the fact that we had a chance of saving her life meant she was going to have to pay for it with Jimmy's.

I did consider going back out to look for him, but with the way things were, the fog and everything, there didn't seem to be a great deal of point. He could be anywhere. Lying low, taking the long way home, or maybe just hopelessly lost. I mean, after what we'd witnessed earlier, I didn't have a great deal of faith in his sense of direction.

All night I lay there keeping an ear out for his return, hoping to hear that familiar hoppity-tap coming down the tunnel. I even wandered up to the entrance at one point, but it was so quiet out there you wouldn't have thought there was a living soul on the Island.

Come dawn there was still no sign and my grip on hope was beginning to loosen. To make matters more complicated, the stuff Lena had given Delilah was working miracles. She regained consciousness and became quite lucid for a while and we had to explain where she was and how she got here. When she asked about Jimmy, both Lena and me fell silent.

'He's dead, ain't he?' Delilah croaked, managing to get herself up on one elbow.

'Course he ain't!' I cried dismissively. 'What d'you think?'

'I think he's dead,' she told me.

'Delilah! He's probably just lost. Hey, come on, the satellites'll be back on by now. You ain't going to get rid of Jimmy that easy.'

She glared at me long and hard, like she knew I was lying and thought I should know better, and then, worn out by the effort, fell back and immediately closed her eyes.

I turned to Lena. 'I'd better go and look,' I sighed.

She didn't say a word. Maybe 'cuz she'd searched down inside herself and found there wasn't even a drop of optimism left.

I lit a fresh candle and made my way up to the entrance, a sense of foreboding dragging at my every stride, beginning to fear that I was no longer looking for Jimmy, but his corpse.

There was just a little early-morning light, soft and colourless, oozing in through the gaps at the entrance. I momentarily glanced out, not expecting to see anyone at such an hour, and then heaved the door open.

My next move would've normally been to slip out and be smartly on my way, but I found my path blocked by such a large pile of junk I couldn't even squeeze round it.

For a moment I just stared stupidly. There were all sorts of things there. Circuit boards – broken and otherwise – hard disks, a couple of old monitors. Where the hell had it come from? Then, of course, the obvious hit me.

'*Jimmy!*' I growled.

And, as if he'd been waiting for his cue, he came into view, struggling over a nearby mound of rubble, almost buckling under the weight of another load.

'What the hell are you doing?' I shouted, grabbing some of the junk and tossing it inside.

'Careful, Big Guy!' he said, his lack of stick causing him to totter a little. 'Some of that's fragile.'

'I don't care what it is! Why d'you leave it here? Talk about drawing attention!'

'Ah! No one's about yet,' he said, taking a quick look round to be sure. 'I been going back and forth all night. Didn't have time to put it inside.'

I completely lost it with him. Grabbing hold of him and his junk and throwing the lot inside.

'Big Guy!' he protested.

'For chrissake!' I shouted, heaving the door shut behind us. 'Delilah thinks you're dead!'

He stopped and stared at me as if he'd come out of a coma and I realised what this was all about. OD'ing on junk had just been his way of distracting himself from her.

'She's okay?' he asked.

'Looks like it.'

'Really?' he cried, this lost light suddenly sparking back up in his eyes.

I nodded and he let go this huge sigh of relief. 'I gotta go see her!' he cried, turning to hurry away.

'Hey!' I shouted after him, indicating the large pile of junk he'd left behind.

'Oh yeah. Bring that, will you, Big Guy?'

I tell you, that was about as much as I could take. I promptly swivelled around and kicked the whole lot as hard as I could, sending it crashing into the wall, the sound rippling all the way down the tunnel.

Jimmy stopped and turned to gape at me, a look of complete mystification on his face, but I marched past him and away. I mean, it's like I told you; sometimes I let him get away with it, sometimes I don't.

For the last few days we've all been laying low, licking our wounds, living our memories. Delilah looks awful, like a badly bruised piece of fruit, but, in fact, has little in the way of serious injuries. The organi-plasters on her arm and hip are working so well you can practically see her healing. Mind you, I think it's having the will that's really cured her. Seeing Jimmy come back, knowing they're still all right, made all the difference.

Course, it was a bit awkward at first: everyone suddenly finding themselves living with someone they didn't really know. A lot of hanging around went on, looking uncomfortable, not knowing what to do next. Jimmy mentioned going back to the Village as soon as Delilah was fully recovered, but I could tell he didn't really want to, and Lena wouldn't hear of it.

With her help, the two of them have set up in an alcove a little further down the tunnel. They put up a makeshift wall of blue plastic draped over a stack of barrels to grant them some privacy, stuffed sacks with anything soft they could find to make a double bed, added crates for a table, and used the ubiquitous plastic packing for something to sit on. Lena even brought them a few of the flowers from the garden. Okay, so you wouldn't exactly describe it as a palace, but compared with what we've known – with a lean-to – it's a damn close thing. When Delilah was first installed in there, she was that grateful she didn't know whether to cry or sing, and ended up doing both.

As for Jimmy, well, you ain't going to believe this, but the moment he realised Delilah didn't need him anymore, his attention turned to the junk he brought back. Sorting it through, seeing what he had, making up an inventory. He just can't help himself. We've already had one morning when Lena and me were lying in bed, enjoying one last cuddle, and were blasted to the vertical by the sound of him smashing something apart, cannibalising it for the part he needed. I tell you, moments like those, I start wondering if maybe I might end up regretting inviting him to live down here.

To be fair, he did bring back some pretty amazing stuff. Not just the circuit boards and monitors, but a box of disks he's hoping might have something interesting on, and – maybe in an attempt to placate Delilah – an old microwave and an almost brand-new irradia-fry. Course, none of it works, but he seems pretty confident he'll be able to get it going somehow.

The only problem is, I need him for other things. There's a lot of work involved in keeping the tunnels going. Not just day-to-day stuff, but actual structural work. Lena's done a certain amount of shoring up since she's been down here, but more's needed. Jimmy just doesn't see it as a priority, not compared with the miracles he reckons he's about to perform, and it's already causing a degree of friction. Delilah, who's not that happy at finding her new life consists of being surrounded by even more junk than her old, told him that as soon as she's strong enough, she's going to drag the whole lot up-top and throw it out.

In the end, after several more frank and heated exchanges, and him whining on about 'brains being made to do the work of brawn', I had to introduce a work rota to make sure he did his fair share.

The thing I don't understand, the thing that I keep asking him about but he just ignores, is what's the use of all this electrical stuff when there's no power for it? He got so pleased with himself one afternoon 'cuz he reckoned he'd fixed this radio. But how the hell could we tell? Anyone could've pointed at anything and said they'd repaired it. I could've mended the whole damn lot and got it doing twice what it was before. With no juice, it's a waste of time, surely?

Thank the Lord irritations were soothed when the two of us were out one morning inspecting tunnels and came across a workshop of one of the old maintenance crews. There were still tools hanging up there; building materials, conduits, sheet metal, electrical cable.

To see the look on Jimmy's face you would've thought we'd stumbled on Aladdin's cave. He went from one shelf to another, holding up his candle, giggling away like some demented miser counting his money.

With everyone's full blessing he immediately moved all his stuff down there. Since then, whenever he goes missing, we know exactly where to find him.

I did wander down a couple of times. Just to see what he was up to. I got no idea if he knows what he's doing or not, but he's certainly got a real enthusiasm for tinkering around. It's almost an act of worship. A study in a meticulous nature. He'll spend the whole day taking something apart, piece by piece, analysing it, deciding how it works, then, as if giving it his blessing, carefully putting it all back together again. And after thinking it through, I decided I really don't mind. Screw the rota. If Jimmy's got some idea that I don't truly understand, that might benefit us in some way, then I'm more than happy to occasionally take over his chores.

A couple of times I had to warn him about the amount of noise he's making, tell him that he's hammering so loud he might be able to be heard up-top, but the truth is, it's a real pleasure to see someone looking and acting so positive and passionate for a change, and I'm all in favour of it.

I don't know how long it was before the subject of going out again was raised. I do know that, for some time, everyone avoided it in such a way that you'd swear 'up-top' didn't exist anymore. Until one evening over dinner Jimmy started harping on about this favourite wrench of his, that he couldn't do without and reckoned might still be in the ashes of their lean-to.

I knew what he was after; he wanted me to suggest we both went over, but since our excursion down into the Camp, the idea of going out filled me with apprehension, and I wasn't exactly sure why. Maybe 'cuz I had this fear that, by doing what we did – sneaking down there and stealing from them – we might've made things a whole lot worse.

In the end, that was exactly the reason why I decided to go. 'Cuz I wanted to reassure myself I was wrong, that nothing more sinister than usual was going on over there.

Delilah was up on her feet full-time by that point. A little frail and uncertain in a way I didn't associate with her, but strong enough for giving Jimmy a good haranguing now and then, and also for the occasional song.

Like I said, that voice of hers is something else at any time – in the Village, out on the tips – but down here, with the acoustics, to hear it echoing along the tunnel is like the Song of the Earth. Or maybe her singing's got better? Maybe she's expressing her gratitude in the only way she can for being hauled out of the shit once more.

Course, she wasn't happy about the idea of Jimmy and me going out. I think Delilah's got it into her head that if we stay down here long enough, everything up there's going to disappear. No more Village. No more satellites. No kids, no foggy nights, no mountains of garbage or suffocating stench. And for us to go up there and open the door again is to risk letting it all back in.

Lena was even less happy about it. She went all quiet when I first told her, as if it was something she'd been expecting but still hadn't found a way of dealing with. On the actual morning that Jimmy and I stood there ready to go, you could see her thoughts churning away inside so much it was as if she was slowly imploding. I put my arm around her, told her not to worry, that we'd be fine, though the truth was, her unease was only serving to enhance mine. The moment I swung that heavy brick door back, the moment Jimmy and me stepped outside, I knew we had good reason. There was just something in the air, a sense of disturbance I've never known on the Island before. At first I tried to tell myself it was just 'cuz I'd been so long underground, that in the same way I had to learn to relax down there, now I was having to tense myself again up here, but I knew it wasn't true.

As we made our way across the square, portents were sticking out of me like fired arrows. As usual, the sky was filled with seagulls, but even they seemed distracted. Normally they spend most of their time over towards the pier and sorting area, whirling round like some great snow twister, but they were darting all over the place, screeching at the tops of their voices as if in a continuous state of panic.

Jimmy didn't say anything, but I knew he had to be feeling it, too. A couple of times he almost shuffled to a halt, seemingly on the point of turning around and scuttling back to the tunnels.

'You okay?' I asked.

'Yes,' he replied, though it was obvious he wasn't. 'Just feels a bit strange to be out again, that's all.'

I nodded and without another word we forced ourselves on. I was pretty sure he was having as much difficulty as me convincing himself his fears were irrational. Mind you, if that was the case, then both of our fragile self-deceptions were about to be blown away.

As we emerged from the ruins of the Old City we saw this huge bow of black smoke arcing across the Island like a satanic rainbow. At first we assumed it was a blowout that had got out of control. It's not that unusual. There are fires all over certain times of year. But as we got closer, we realised it was the Village.

Jimmy turned to me, his face fading of colour. 'What the hell's going on?'

I didn't reply, just broke into this clumsy jog and he did his best to keep up; over one mound of garbage, down the other side, then onto another. The nearer we got, the more we began to appreciate the sheer scale of it. I mean, we're not talking about a row or two here, not a small area, more like as far as your eye could see.

I tried to go faster, stretching ahead of Jimmy, ignoring his cries to wait up, desperate to know what had happened.

After all the terrible things I seen out here, I didn't think there was anything left that could shock me, but I was wrong, and I wish to God I hadn't been. More than half the Village was burnt down. Everyone and everything covered in ash, as if the Island had erupted. Bodies lay all over; blackened, beaten, hacked to death. Those who'd been killed with a single blow, those who'd been tortured so long and so badly their own pain must've finally spared them. Some had tried to run away and were now sprawled out on the ground with ugly gashes to the backs of their heads. Others so old they'd attempted to crawl away on their hands and knees and been butchered in their arthritic flight. It was an abomination. An indelible stain on humanity and human life.

Where those who survived had gone, I don't know. I mean, there were a few people around, but presumably most of them were hiding somewhere. Maybe amongst the rocks? Or out on the Head? Whatever, the overriding sensation was that everything that had happened on the Island up 'til now, all the things we've been so sickened by, are as nothing. 'Cuz I got to tell you something: that wasn't the work of kids. It was someone else, someone of far more evil intent, and it didn't take a lot to work out who it had been and why they did it.

It was the Wastelords. De Grew and his boys must've gone up there as a punishment for what we did. Our little excursion into the Camp, the stealing of a few medical supplies, had resulted in wholesale blood-letting, in these terrible scenes of genocide.

I don't know how long Jimmy and me wandered dazedly around, stunned by the horror, the sickening extent of what had been done, but if what we'd seen up 'til then hadn't been bad enough, we still had one more shock to go.

We reached this area where everything had been razed to the ground and cleared away, as if it had been turned into a meeting place where the Villagers had to gather (which made me realise that whatever had happened had taken place over several nights). Suspended across it, hanging from a couple of ropes strung between the remains of lean-tos, was a line of ten Villagers; stripped naked, mutilated and murdered.

They were just hanging there like bleeding leaves, each of their contorted bodies and faces reflecting different methods of torture.

'Jesus!' Jimmy moaned.

For several seconds we just stood there, appalled, not only by what we were looking at, but also by the fact that, in all probability, we were the cause. Then slowly something else dawned on me.

There was something odd about their wounds, about the way they'd been mutilated. I looked along them, one by one, trying to work it out, 'til finally I realised.

'Oh no!' I moaned.

I turned to Jimmy. He gave this kind of *urging* sound and I knew he'd seen it, too. They hadn't been randomly mutilated, they'd had letters carved into their flesh so crudely it took you a while to work out that's what they were. Together they formed the words:

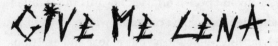

The little guy grabbed my arm. 'Let's get out of here!' he cried.

'I don't get it.' I said. 'What the hell's going on?'

'It don't matter! Let's go!'

I didn't need any further bidding. The two of us turned and started to run, blundering through smouldering ruins and butchered bodies, atrocity after atrocity that left you wondering if you were losing your mind.

A chopper suddenly appeared overhead, spotted us and swooped down. I could make out the familiar two-eyed symbol of Infinity International on its side, Mainland media, which gives you some idea how serious an incident it was. They started chasing after us, buzzing around, the whirl of their blades whipping up ash, pounding it into our bodies and faces. I mean, I guess they were filming, but they were getting so close it was as if they wanted to add to our distress.

I heard Jimmy cry out behind me and turned to see him sprawled on the ground, tangled in the ribcage of a dismembered body. He was screaming, trying to drag himself free, but his bad leg, numbed by fear, kept collapsing over and over. I grabbed hold of him, dragged him up, ran on, that damn chopper still following.

I ain't going to lie to you: for probably the first time in my life, I completely lost it. It was such madness, such an assault on the senses, fear took a hold and wouldn't let go. I felt as if my bones were turning to liquid, like I was going to start peeing and just piss myself away. Everywhere you looked there was evidence of what one human being has the capability of doing to another, of behaviour that laughed at our notions of civilisation. I leapt over stuff without bearing to look what it might be, almost fell a couple of times, had to pick up Jimmy once more, but didn't stop 'til we were away from the Village, 'til that chopper gave up and peeled off back towards the Mainland.

Jimmy and me more or less collapsed where we were, squatting on the ground, puffing and panting out of fear and exertion.

'What the hell's going on, Big Guy?' he whined.

I didn't reply, just shook my head.

'Why do they want Lena?'

'*Jimmy!* I don't know!' I shouted.

We stayed there for a while, getting our breath back, trying to calm ourselves, then slowly moved on. Along the way, he started up again, putting into words what I was thinking.

'She used to be one of them, didn't she?'

'Yeah.'

He paused for a moment. 'Did she go on raids?'

I shrugged, not really wanting to tell him but feeling I had no choice.

'Did she kill?' he persisted.

'I don't know, Jimmy,' I told him honestly. 'Maybe.' For a while we walked in silence, then I turned and looked at him. His face was black apart from a network of fine white lines where his wrinkles were, and I guessed mine was the same. 'She's got a past, I've got a past. I don't care.'

'But why do they want her?' he asked.

I sighed, long and hard, feeling so dumb, so stupid, so much the lumbering Big Guy. I should know this. I know I should. There *is* a reason. I just can't think what it is.

'I don't know,' I eventually confessed.

CHAPTER TEN

I told Jimmy not to mention the 'message' to Lena, it could keep for another time, but when we got back to the tunnels and related a slightly censored version of what we'd witnessed, she didn't react quite the way I expected.

She went all quiet on us, no longer even listening to what we were saying, staring into the fire the way she sometimes does, as if she really can see after all. Or maybe she's just feeling the warmth.

When our story was finally exhausted, everyone fell into a kind of stunned and horrified silence. However, after a few moments Lena turned to me as if expecting more.

'And what else?'

'What do you mean?' I replied.

'What else, Clancy?' she repeated, with a touch of impatience, and I knew I had no choice.

I made it sound as matter-of-fact as I could, as if bodies got strung up and people's names carved into them almost every day of the week, but it didn't do a lot of good. Again she fell silent, only this time the rest of us could do nothing but wait in agony for what we feared she was about to say.

'I should've known he'd look for me,' she eventually moaned.

'Who?' I asked, though I had a fair idea.

'De Grew.'

Jimmy glanced at me, Delilah looked even more worried. I mean, just the mention of his name's enough to make you feel uneasy.

'Why does he want you?' Delilah asked.

'Stealing from the warehouse.'

Delilah frowned. 'But . . . how does he know it was you?'

'Yeah!' I agreed, seizing on the point. 'It could've been anyone. And you were the only one of us who wasn't seen that night.'

Again she went silent, but not for long. 'The keys,' she reminded us.

I just gaped at her. Jesus, no wonder I never made it past the rank of big guy. Amongst everything else that'd been going on, I'd completely forgotten about her having the keys that night.

'Where d'you get them?' I asked.

'They're duplicates. Someone in the Camp made them for me. A provision for what I always feared might be a difficult future.'

'Anyone can make duplicates. How does he know it's you?'

'Oh . . . he does,' she replied, with a level of certainty I didn't care for at all.

'So all this is because of me?' Delilah groaned.

'No!' Lena protested. 'It's because of me!'

'Hey, come on,' I told them. 'It ain't you up there burning and killing.'

But even though Delilah gave a slight nod, as if acknowledging my point, Lena didn't even seem to hear me. And as I gazed at her, frustrated that she obviously intended to say no more, I wasn't altogether surprised to see that familiar haunted expression form on her face.

I didn't press her. For the rest of the day I tried to carry on as normal.

Making a point of agreeing with Jimmy and Delilah when they said there was no way De Grew could be sure it was her – especially after her having left the Camp so long ago – dismissing any notion of him ever being able to find us in the tunnels, but still allowing Lena her silence and space.

Yet later, in bed, as if it had been building up all day, tears suddenly breached that obstruction, flowing over it and everywhere.

It's strange, but tears coming out of her eyes, welling up from within her blindness, is like a terrible miracle and hurts all the more for it. I wished to God there was something I could say. But how could I? I didn't have a clue what it was all about, and to be honest, I wasn't even sure I wanted to. Trouble is, sometimes you don't get a choice. And when she finally did start to speak, I knew my heart was about to be broken.

We don't know much about what happens in the Camp. We know the results in terms of us: that as soon as we're unprotected a deranged and desensitised mob comes over to terrorise and kill, but I guess they have a life over there, too. There have to be people and problems and getting-by. They ain't just robots. Well, that night Lena well and truly educated me in their ways, and it turns out it ain't quite as simple as I thought. I mean, we've always regarded that place as evil and that was an end to it, but there are varying degrees of evil and they got their victims, too. The other thing I found out was, well, she didn't exactly lie to me that day she told me her story, but she had left a lot out.

Not all the kids go on raids. In fact, according to her, it's very much the minority. In a strange way, most of them are like us: stuck in a society they didn't create and doing what they can to survive it. They do their work and get paid with food, shelter, and occasionally drugs. That's all there is. All they'll probably ever know. Meanwhile, De Grew's making a fortune out of that place. Apparently that home of his on the hill overlooking the Camp, has everything. Swimming pool, cinema, every damn luxury item you can think of. He's even got outdoor extractors so he don't have to suffer the smell of the Island. Up there he can be in a pine forest, a spring meadow, anything he chooses. Can you imagine how that must make the kids feel? Every day living in shit, thigh deep in it, then looking up there and seeing what he's got. They'd do anything for a piece of it.

Which brings me to the part of Lena's story that really hurts. I mean, I knew there was something, I just didn't know how bad. Like I said, the kids've got a pretty distorted sense of values, it ain't hard to corrupt them. If De Grew sees someone on the tips who takes his fancy, girl or boy, he gets them sent up to the house, cleaned up and given a room. It don't matter how young they are. Some of them apparently ain't much more than babes. From then on he pretty well does whatever he wants with them. I ain't going to go into details. I didn't even want to hear it myself. All I will say is that most of them don't last long. Some, the less 'compliant' or 'enthusiastic', that ain't 'no fun', don't scream in the right way or whatever, are lucky if they get through the night. Afterwards they get passed on to the other Wastelords, and pretty soon disappear altogether. As if their death is the final thrill they have to offer.

Like I said . . . they got their victims, too. What I hadn't expected was that Lena was one of them. 'Cuz the sorry truth is, she was one of those who got transferred up to the house for 'special duties'. I mean, she's not exactly your conventional idea of pretty, and apparently she was out here some years before it happened, but one day, after a chance meeting with De Grew, she got the 'invitation'.

At first she just did what she was told and nothing more, so grateful to be out of the shit and stench, that wretched existence, she didn't care about anything else. But as time went by, and she began to see the way it worked – how everyone was eventually tired of and dispensed with – she realised that if she was going to survive, she had to do that bit extra. So she did. Everything they wanted, everything she could think of, and a bit more. And apparently she was really good at it, too. So good that, despite not being as pretty as some, she lasted a whole lot longer. For almost five years, in fact. Still, in the end, De Grew tired of her, just like he tired of everyone else. The one concession he made to her long-standing servitude was to let her go back to the tips rather than be handed on to another Wastelord and disappear.

It never occurred to him that she might have her own agenda whilst living with him. That she might be spying in case it ever came in useful, studying his operation, even making a set of duplicate keys. If she hadn't got caught in a blowout, if she hadn't taken refuge in the tunnels, he probably would never have known. For sure it would've never crossed his mind that she'd come back to haunt him the way she has. No wonder he's so angry, so determined to find her and pay her back for what she's done.

It's shit to admit, but as sad as I felt for Lena, the more she told me, the more detail she went into, the more it felt like something blunt and rusty was whittling away at my insides. When she finally finished, I couldn't bring myself to say a thing. I knew she wanted me to, that she was waiting, but for some reason it just wouldn't come. I felt as if my life had been broken into and all the best parts stolen.

For a long while we lay there, an aching silence gaping ever wider between us. Eventually she turned to me, demanding I said something. 'Well?'

I paused for a long time. 'What?'

'Say something.'

'What can I say?'

'I don't know.'

Again I paused. 'Just a bit shocked, I guess.'

Immediately she lost her temper with me. 'Don't you judge me, Clancy!'

'I'm not!'

'Not by your standards. They don't apply anymore. Not round here.'

I don't know why, but that hurt me more than anything she said. Or maybe I let it hurt me more, I don't know. With that one accusation I suddenly felt lost – old, tired and obsolete. As if any pain caused was of my own making.

Eventually I couldn't take it anymore. I got up and went to find myself somewhere else to sleep further up the tunnel. I mean, I felt bad for her, I really did, I could've so easily wept, but it was just too painful to lie there any longer.

The next morning I woke full of blood and bile. I was fermenting away most of the night, tossing and turning, and the conclusion I came to was that suddenly I felt embarrassed by my relationship with Lena. I mean, who the hell am I trying to kid? The only reason it happened was 'cuz of circumstances, 'cuz she's blind and can't see what she's been getting herself into. Inevitably the age gap had finally yawned and my tired old carcass had slipped straight through, there to lie buried forever.

I spent the whole day refusing to speak to anyone. Not a word. Compared with my mood now, my disposition over in the Village had been positively sunny. To make matters even more pointed, Jimmy came up from his workshop later that morning all flushed and excited, saying he had a surprise for us all. I just shrugged and stalked past him on my way down to the garden, ignoring his yelping protests to come back, that I'd 'miss it'. The only thing I wanted from this world was to be left alone.

It's funny how we are about nature, about green stuff. I can remember, even as a kid, when things went wrong, when my old lady was after me or something, I always retreated somewhere like the park. 'Sanctuary', that's what Father Donald used to call it. Course, he would've preferred me to come to church, but he didn't get to see that very often. Not that there was anything wrong with Father Donald. He was a good guy. Outside of Mr Meltoni, maybe the only one who'd ever looked out for me. But at that age there are some professions you're just never going to take to, no matter who's representing them.

I remember after my old man's funeral, at the family get-together, he went round and spoke to everyone, even us kids. Real words, too. Stuff he'd thought about. None of this 'Thanks for the glass of cheap sherry and you'd better all be in church next Sunday otherwise God's gonna take another one of yours out.' He took me aside and explained that God had probably called my father to Heaven 'cuz he needed some good work doing. However, I told him it was more likely that God had got fed up with seeing him beating up on my old lady and was taking him up there to give him a good whopping.

I guess priests ain't supposed to laugh at stuff like that, but Father Donald practically choked on his cake. After that, whenever he saw me he would burst out into this smile and I knew he was thinking about what I said. At first it used to irritate me, but after a while it made me smile, too. It's nice I brought him a little happiness all those years. Even now I can still see him: standing on the steps of the church, a big fringe of grey hair whipping round his forehead, looking all serious and reproachful at his errant flock, then seeing me coming and getting jumped on by that smile. Not that I stopped for him. Even when he called me over I just pretended I didn't hear him and hurried by on the other side of the street.

Looking back on it, I guess Father Donald was a bit like me: a man out of his time, swimming against a drowning tide. The more the Church updated itself, the more I had this sense of him barricading himself in, piling pews up against the door. I mean, maybe if they'd stuck to what *he* believed, to what we'd come to trust them for, they might've made a difference. All those who got so lost might've found themselves in God, but the Church decided to embrace the enterprise economy like everyone else. They got into real estate, selling off their land, charging for services, leasing the franchises of churches to priests. It was crazy: Holy Trinity Inc. People thought they had to hold stock to be sure of a place in Heaven. Naturally, everyone wanted to do business with them. They had prime sites, ones never considered available for commercial purposes, and, by inference, an unblemished reputation. Then they got themselves into a couple of scandals. Things started to slide. And finally the stock market managed to do what two thousand years, numerous wars, and countless heads of state hadn't: bring down Christianity.

I'd been digging for a couple of hours and my back was starting to tell me how it used to be able to do this sort of thing all day but now couldn't, when suddenly I heard a distant cry from what I guessed to be the living area. I stopped for a moment, wondering if I'd imagined it – I mean, it's a fair distance – when there it was again.

It wasn't a cry of alarm, more like joy or excitement, and I'll tell you, the mood I was in, it irritated the hell out of me. I couldn't imagine what was worth making so much noise over. I hesitated for a moment, deciding whether to ignore it or not, but then it started up again.

For chrissake, how could they be so stupid? If I could hear them in the garden, then it was possible they could be heard up-top. I tossed down my shovel and stormed off in their direction, determined to give someone a piece of my mind. However, as I approached the living area, as I began to turn that long bend in the tunnel, I got such a shock it blew all thoughts of reprimand away.

I could see the glow of a light up ahead. Not a candle or a fire, an *electric* light. I was that confused I started to run, all sorts of thoughts ricocheting round my mind. Had someone got in? Had they found us somehow? But as the living area came fully into sight I saw no strangers, no invaders, just a proud and excited little guy jigging around in front of Delilah and Lena.

He's fixed up an electric light. Down here in the tunnels. There it was hanging from the roof, solitary and glowing white, like some guiding star. Jimmy turned as I approached, so delighted when he saw my astonished face.

'What d'you think, Big Guy?'

I gaped for a moment, the others eagerly awaiting my reaction.

'How the hell d'you do that?' I asked.

He pointed above his head. There was a windmill thing attached to the roof of the tunnel, like the ones he used to have on his lean-to, only made out of metal. It was rotating away, driven by the tunnel winds and presumably – though please don't ask me how – generating electricity.

'I told you I could change the world if I had the right materials!' he cried.

'Ain't it great, Clancy?' Delilah shouted, more proud of her bald-headed little hero than I ever could've imagined.

'Sure is,' I said, staring at that single light as if it was the eighth wonder of the world.

It was some time before it occurred to me how little it meant to Lena. I turned to her and, as she often seems to do, she sensed me looking.

'What kind of light is it?' she asked.

I paused for a moment. I mean, shit to admit, but despite all the excitement, I still didn't feel like talking to her. Thankfully, Delilah got in before it became obvious.

'Aw. Just a light, I guess,' she said, deliberately playing it down. 'Just a whitish kind of everyday light.'

But it wasn't true and we all knew it, even Lena. It wasn't an 'everyday light'. It was the first one to illuminate our darkness, and, as such, a symbol of hope. As if the human race was starting to fight back, regaining some small measure of control over its environment. We already had fire in our cave, now we had light as well.

For the rest of the day none of us was able to leave it for any great length of time. It was a miracle. Electricity, taken for granted for so many generations, was a wonder again and we were left breathless by it. When the time finally came for us to go to bed, Jimmy, who hadn't managed to wire in a switch, went to disconnect it, but we wouldn't let him. We wanted to look at it a bit longer. To wake up at night and find it shining there.

Despite all the excitement, I still have to admit, it was a solitary bed I went to that night. Lena and I barely exchanged a word all day. I mean, not that that's so unusual. Some days we don't speak that much. The way we see it, if you got something worth saying, say it, if you haven't, keep your mouth shut. Whereas Jimmy and Delilah like to have a constant babble going, as if to reassure themselves the other one's still there. Nor does it seem to matter if it's happy talk, bitching, or whatever, just as long as that signal's getting passed back and forth.

But even when you're not talking, it's surprising how many moods silence can have. You'd think silence was like a glass of water waiting for a flavour – but it ain't. It can be far more potent than any conversation. The silence between Lena and me felt like a slab of stone waiting for a chisel. The only trouble was, neither of us was of a mind to do the carving. I knew I wasn't behaving that well. Not for a grown-up. That I'd gone off on some mad-assed emotional tangent. But I was into a lot of lonely old thinking. I felt lost and rejected, humiliated somehow, and I wasn't able to do anything about it.

It was a bit like the time Mr Meltoni took on this new heavy – Thomas. He wasn't like me. He was younger and smarter and could talk about all sorts of things I knew nothing about. Like books, foreign movies, even wine and food. Him and Mr Meltoni had conversations about that sort of stuff all day and I'd just stand there, smiling, nodding, trying to look like I knew what they were talking about when I really didn't have a clue. It never occurred to me that Mr Meltoni would want to talk to one of his boys. It wasn't my place. Still, after a while I thought I'd give it a try. One morning I went in early, when I knew we'd be alone, and asked him what he thought about last night's big game. He just brushed it aside, like it was nothing. Matter of fact, I don't even think he knew there'd been a big game.

The problem is, sometimes I think that having muscles is a bit like being beautiful: it's so obvious what you are, no one expects you to be anything else. Nor are they going to give you the chance to try. It's only since I been out on the Island that I actually started to read properly. And d'you know something? I'm nowhere near as stupid as I thought. Okay, I'm not telling you I'm super-intelligent or nothing, but I reckon I've read just about every book that's circulated round the Village – fact and fiction. Which I guess makes me sort of self-educated. I even had a dictionary for a while. I used to make myself learn three new words a day. Walking around, repeating them to myself over and over. 'Ideology . . . Idiosyncratic'. Course I'm too embarrassed to actually say them most of the time, but I don't mind writing them down occasionally. Maybe you noticed the odd one?

Anyways, that period, when Thomas first arrived and Mr Meltoni and him were forever exchanging jokes and conversation, being all smart and sophisticated, hurt me more than anyone can ever know. I felt like one of Mr Meltoni's old limos getting driven away while he proudly stood before the new one. I even put the word out that I was looking for another job. Then one day, when Thomas tried to talk to Mr Meltoni about French wines and Swedish films, he was too busy. A week later Thomas disappeared. Not from the neighbourhood, I don't mean, but from everything. From existence, maybe. I never asked why or what had gone on. Like I said, I never thought it was my place to start a conversation.

But if I felt lonely and obsolete then, it ain't nothing to how I feel now. I've always had this concern that I was far too old for Lena, that she's only been doing these things with me 'cuz there's no one else around, but I didn't want to believe it. You gotta take other people's feelings into account in this life. It's been a long time since I held anyone like I hold her. In fact, I don't think I've ever held anyone that way. It's okay for her. She's young. No matter how things turn out she's still got a chance of meeting someone else one day. But I won't. I know that. After her, there'll be nothing. And as a matter of fact, I wouldn't want there to be.

CHAPTER ELEVEN

The following morning I got up before everyone else and again slunk off down to the garden. More people mean a need for more food and more work and just at that moment I was happy to be doing it.

Everything was going fine, I was absorbing my daily quota of daylight, feeling it reinvigorate me and chase away the dark, when around mid-morning Delilah sidled in; all languid and slow, like it was a hot day and she was an old cat seeking out some shelter.

She stood there silently for a while, waiting for me to speak. When I didn't take the opportunity, she sighed and plopped herself down on one of the water barrels.

'What's your problem, Clancy?' she asked.

'I ain't got a problem,' I told her.

'Why aren't you speaking to Lena?'

'I'm speaking to her.'

'Huh. When you have to,' she commented. For a moment she paused and gazed out through the grille at the clouds colliding noiselessly overhead. 'It's funny, you can know someone for years, but until you seen them in love, you don't know them at all. I would've thought you'd handle this better.'

'Handle what?' I asked, stopping what I was doing and giving her the look.

The way she shrugged made me suspect she probably knew as much about Lena's past as I did, that amongst those many conversations the two of them have been having, the subject of Lena's life in the Camp had inevitably come up. It made me even more angry. I don't agree with these things getting discussed with everyone. It's not right.

'None of us have been angels,' Delilah said, a rusty little chuckle scraping out of her throat. 'Certainly not me. Jimmy don't care. Oh, but that's me, innit? That don't matter.'

'I don't know what you're talking about.'

'Like hell you don't.'

I started to feel all hot at the back of my neck, like I was glowing red. 'It's none of my business what Lena got up to before I met her.'

'So that *is* the problem?'

'No! I told you, there ain't no problem,' I said, jamming my spade so hard into the ground I had to struggle to pull it out again. 'I just thought it was time we both stopped this play-acting, that's all.'

'What play-acting?' she asked.

'You know.'

She just stared at me as if she didn't have a clue what I was talking about.

'Like we're a couple,' I told her. 'Partners. We both know that ain't true.'

'Aw, Clancy!' she groaned, like she was dealing with a very small child.

I glared at her again, daring her to say another word, then turned back to what I was doing. 'One day, God willing, she'll find someone her own age. That's right and proper. That's the way it should be.'

Delilah just snorted and shook her head, as if the whole thing was quite pitiful, making me feel even more uncomfortable.

'We just ain't suited. That's all there is to it.'

'Yeah, you're right,' she replied. 'She's brave and honest and quite special.'

'And half my age,' I reminded her.

'Yeah. Like that matters.'

'Course it matters!' I snapped.

For several minutes we simmered away in that ripening silence. I could feel her gaze upon me as surely as if she had me in the sights of a gun, but I wasn't about to acknowledge it. Finally, with me refusing to say another word, she sighed long and hard and stood up to go.

Just before she went back up the tunnel, she paused. 'You know something, Clancy? You're disappointing me with this. You really are.'

Still I ignored her, carrying on with my digging as if I hadn't heard a word.

As soon as the shuffle of her footsteps faded, once her candle dimmed into the distance, I tossed my spade down and ambled over to where she'd been sitting on the water barrel, gazing up at the overhead grille and the thin slices of bramble and distant sky.

I thought Delilah would've understood. She's more my generation. It ain't so much that I disapproved of what Lena'd done, it's what she'd said about my standards not applying anymore. As if the main reason I was upset is 'cuz I was old and past it.

I mean, I guess we all reach an age when we start to feel that people don't think like us, that we're the keepers of dying values, but what makes life really difficult is when you find yourself involved with someone on the other side of that divide.

Not that I was thinking that clearly. I had all sorts of stuff sparring away in my head. One moment I was going to walk up to Lena and hug her so tightly every bit of the last two days would drain out of her and we'd be back the way we were; the next I got so mad I was convinced she was the most callous and unfeeling woman I'd met in my life. Not that you would've known, of course. No matter what I'm thinking, I'm still the Big Guy. And silence is what I do best.

I guess it made life in the tunnels pretty difficult: twenty-five per cent of the population refusing to talk to another twenty-five. Especially for Jimmy and Delilah, who appear to see other people's arguments as rivals to their own. No doubt that was why, the following day, when I told Jimmy we urgently needed to get out and do some shoring up, he came up with this story about his leg hurting really badly.

I know it is worse some days than others, but since he's been down here, it's almost gone into remission. I haven't seen him use his stick in ages. But he insisted that he was in a lot of pain, which put me in an awkward position. I mean, Lena's stronger than him anyway, and as I'd made such a big thing about it needing doing, I didn't have much choice but to take her with me. Which, I guess, was what Jimmy had been planning all along.

No wind has ever blown colder through the tunnels than the one that day. We loaded ourselves up with tools and materials and trudged off down to the lower level, not saying a word to each other. The whole morning the only time we spoke was for work reasons: to be passed a tool, or for someone to take the weight of something. I hated it. I really did. But you get so locked into those things sometimes you forget where to find the key.

Eventually we finished that particular section and moved on to find somewhere else where we might be needed. I mean, we're just patching things up, trying to arrest the rate of decay, knowing it's hopeless but kidding ourselves that one day the time we're buying might prove important.

We came to a flooded stretch, I don't know, maybe twenty or thirty yards of it. For a moment I hesitated, but holding my candle up and seeing dry land further on, I entered the water.

'Might be deep,' Lena said, her sudden words almost alarming me.

I just ignored her; wading on, splashing through. I mean, if it followed the line of the tunnel floor, I didn't see how it could be.

What I didn't know, and she unquestionably did, was there was an old inspection pit looming up in front of me. I took about ten paces and my world suddenly changed from air to water. I was so shocked it took me a moment to realise what had happened. I floundered round in the depths of that rancid pool, my feet repeatedly slipping on the slimy bottom, then finally managed to find some grip and propel myself back to the surface.

As I broke through I was met by Lena's shrieking laughter. I never heard her laugh that way before. The candle she was carrying to give me a little light had fallen to the ground in front of her and was spluttering away with her doubled-up shadow rocking back and forth on the wall behind her.

I grabbed the side of the pit, amused her no end by falling back a couple of times, then managed to haul myself out. I was that furious I could barely get the words out.

'You knew!' I shouted, but she was laughing so much she couldn't even reply. 'For chrissake! I gotta go change now!'

'Oh, come on!' she cried, urging me to see the funny side of it.

'No!'

I turned to stomp off, so angry, maybe irrationally so. But I didn't get very far.

'*Clancy!*' she shouted, a more impatient tone coming to her voice.

I hesitated. 'What?'

There was a very long pause, as if she thought I should be able to guess every bit of the conversation that was about to follow, that it was unnecessary. 'I don't understand this,' she said.

'What?'

'Why are you acting this way?'

I couldn't think of a thing to say, so just shrugged. A small act of defiance, of estrangement, 'cuz I knew she couldn't see it.

'What right have you got to judge me?' she demanded, repeating the same question as the other day.

'I'm not judging you.'

'What then?'

I sighed, 'I don't know. I just need to sort a few things out in my head, that's all.'

'What do you mean?' she asked, walking right up to me, her big, broad face demanding answers.

I tell you, sometimes she gets so much expression about her. If eyes really are the windows of the soul, then the act of seeing must be a layer of glass, 'cuz with her, when you look into that face, there's nothing between you and pure emotion.

'What were you confused about?' she asked.

'Nothing . . . It don't matter.'

She sighed. Again there was a pause. A whole conversation of silences, one after the other.

'I don't understand you,' she said.

'Different generation,' I shot back immediately.

'What's that got to do with anything?'

'Everything,' I replied, the words coming out so quickly it was like they were on a spring.

'Why do you have this thing about age?'

'I don't.'

'Do you know how many times you mention it?'

'No.'

'It's boring.'

'Oh, pardon me,' I sneered.

'Do you really think I care? Do you? . . . I'm blind, Clancy! *Blind!*'

'Oh, right. So one disability for another?'

She hit me so hard, I could barely believe it. Once more, I reckon I might've even gone down. I also realised that part of me had wanted her to, that I was pushing her in an effort to get this thing out of me.

'Listen to me, will you!' she shouted. 'You stupid old bastard! We are prisoners on this filthy stinking rat-infested pile of crap in the middle of nowhere. Garbage thrown out with garbage. Wastelords feed kids drugs and send them out to murder and the kids don't know any better than to do it. Disease is everywhere. Blowouts. Flies. This place is hell, Clancy. The human race has never sunk any lower. And you really think that amongst all this, it matters that you've been on this Earth longer than I have? . . . *Do you?*' she screamed.

I went silent for a moment. She was crying tears of anger, brushing them away as soon as they formed, and I tell you, they were hurting me a damn sight more than that shot to the jaw. I felt embarrassed and stupid, and yet I had something inside me that I just had to get out, and I reckoned this would be my only opportunity.

'You don't know what it's like,' I told her.

'What?'

'Getting old.' She groaned with frustration, started to protest, but I talked over her. 'Day by day watching your body rot. Feeling where it's starting to go, the wear and tear, the opportunities for pain. I mean, I ain't nothing. I ain't ever been nothing. I know that. Just a big lug with muscles. But it got me respect. When I walked into a room people used to stop and look. You think there's any other reason why someone like me's going to be respected now? You think they stop and look?' I paused and grunted to myself. 'All they see is an old man.'

'Clancy!'

'If they see anything at all.'

She hesitated for a moment, just to make sure there was nothing more, then sighed. 'Does it matter?'

I gazed into her face. I wanted to tell her that it did, that at times it felt like everything, but I couldn't. I wasn't even sure I could live with what I just said. But if I was hoping for some kind of reward for my painful honesty, for rolling over and exposing my soft underbelly, I wasn't about to get it.

'You know something,' she said, 'I don't think you're anywhere near as old as you are sorry for yourself.'

'What!'

'You've given up, "*Big Guy*",' she said, sneering at the nickname.

'What the hell do you know?' I exploded, my voice echoing all along the tunnel. 'You ain't much more than a kid!'

'So what?' she asked.

'It's important!'

'Not to me.'

There was a long pause. I don't know what I expected, but it hadn't been this.

'I know there's an aging process,' she said. 'Course there is. But you sound like some dumb film star or something. Just because you lived off your physique most of your life, you can't cope with losing it.'

I don't know whether I felt angry, humiliated, or what. I wish to God I hadn't said anything. She had no right. Not at her age. Though to be fair, she did know how to soften the blow.

'Now, if that's really what this is all about, if there's nothing more, then, please . . . please, will you stop? I don't give a damn how old you are. Not now or ever. And, Clancy,' she said, her voice suddenly softening, 'I been missing you so much.'

I just don't understand how someone so much younger than me can make me feel like a badly behaved child. Suddenly I was filled with unreserved apologies. I reached out, grabbed her, gave her such a squeeze she cried out in pain, which made me feel even more dumb and useless.

I know I'm a fool. You don't have to tell me that. But sometimes it just seems like you gotta prove it to yourself. That you got to keep doing something over and over 'til it hurts so much you realise you can't do it anymore. As if pain was only invented to teach us how far we can go in one direction.

Maybe she's right. Maybe I do get a bit carried away with this 'age thing'. I know I do keep mentioning it all the time. As if I don't want either of us to ever forget. But I hadn't realised how much it was irritating her.

That night, reinstated in her bed, holding her, listening to her gentle breathing, I started turning it over – the time on the clock, the wear on the body and how much influence your mind has on these things anyway. I ran a hand over my body. One clammy mass of flaccid flesh, sagging muscles and jutting bones. I hate it. I really do. But does that mean I've given in? I'm still stronger than most. Stronger than anyone of my age I know, that's for sure. Maybe she's got a point? Maybe I have given up too soon? And yet, what else can I do?

The following morning, almost as soon as I opened my eyes, I got it into my head that I had to go back up-top to see what was happening. I mean, we've been trying to ignore it, to pretend it's no longer our concern, but I think we all know that's not true, that at some point we're going to have to deal with what's going on up there. I wanted to know if the Village had been attacked again. If there'd been any more atrocities. And most of all, how great the threat to Lena is. Is De Grew really searching for her? Or has he merely been exorcising some old insecurity?

I decided not to tell the others. As far as they knew I was off inspecting tunnels for the morning. But when I got up to the main hall I hid my tools, and instead of turning down, turned up; towards the entrance and the light.

The number of fears that had been burning away in my head, it was reassuring to emerge out into a day where nothing presented an immediate threat; no sense of broken humanity, of shattered time or universal outrage. The gulls were going about their business in their usual manner, screeching and wheeling across a cloudy sky, and as I came into sight of the Village, I was relieved to see no sign of any fires.

I wasn't in the least bit surprised to see that people were starting to rebuild. I mean, it may seem courageous, or tenacious, or whatever; that no matter what happens they still pick themselves up and keep going, but when you stop and think about it, what other choice do they have? The only other option would be to simply lie out in the open and wait to die.

A small group's decided to break away from the others, a new village springing up near the top of the Head, but I don't give a lot for their chances. Like it or not, there is a kind of strength in numbers. It's best to find yourself a spot as close as you can to the centre of everything. That way you'll know when the kids are coming and from what direction. Also, there's always the chance that they'll get bored before they reach you. Up there they're going to be as vulnerable as hell. Just a light snack before the main meal.

Don't ask me why, probably just force of habit, but for some reason I found myself heading over to where my lean-to used to be. It didn't take long to remember that the destruction of that part of the Village had been so total I couldn't even be sure where it was.

In a way I guess that says everything; Villagers can come and go without a trace. Non-people, non-existences, so much dry dust to be blown away.

I ambled slowly on, past half-constructed dwellings, their owners using more and more imagination to create them. Tepees made out of wire mesh interwoven with garbage; the now-familiar holes in the ground covered with plastic, anything that afforded a little warmth and protection. I nodded at a couple of familiar faces, both of whom ignored me, then, seeing nothing else of note, decided to return to the tunnels with, if not good news, then thankfully not bad.

Just as I was leaving the Village, I heard a lot of shouting and yelling going on over by the water. This crowd was gathering, mostly old people, but as I got closer, there was a gang of kids on the other side of the inlet as well.

It didn't take long to work out what they were looking at, nor to guess what the situation was. There was an old couple in the sea, about forty or fifty yards out from the shore, sitting atop what I suspect was the remains of their lean-to; half-a-dozen lengths of burnt and battered timber they'd somehow managed to lash together.

I guess they just couldn't take it anymore. No matter what, they were going to try to make it to the Mainland. But, Lord, I gotta tell you, it was pitiful. There ain't no way. Day or night, the satellites are gonna get you. And on those odd occasions when they're not functioning, and presuming you don't get lost in the fog, there's a welcome party waiting with orders to shoot on sight. Why that should persuade these two to try at this time of day, I don't know. For sure they couldn't have imagined they'd be cheered on by gangs of spectators. The man was frantically paddling with a broken length of plastic padding, whilst the woman was screaming at everyone to go away, not to draw attention to them. One or two of the old folks did, more out of respect than anything, but the kids thought it was a great joke. They were baying out to the sky for the satellites to take a shot, get a bead on them, blow them out of the water.

It was awful. Mainly 'cuz you knew that was exactly what was going to happen. That somewhere up there, their coordinates were being locked onto, the charge of 'Crime Against the State' proven, and any moment now the appropriate punishment would be dispensed.

As much as I couldn't bear it, as much as I felt as if I was intruding on private grief, like everyone else, I wasn't able to walk away. All of us were just standing there holding our breaths, hushed apart from the kids, waiting for it to happen. To make matters worse, whatever they'd used to bind the raft together started to give way and one by one the timbers began drifting apart.

Soon, both the man and woman were in the water, not going anywhere. They floundered round for a while, like they were thinking they might just try swimming for it, then, already beginning to tire, turned and reluctantly headed back towards the shore.

Don't ask me why the satellite chose that moment to blast them. Maybe it had been referred to a higher authority and they decided that, no matter what, they had to make an example of them. But suddenly it happened, a laser spat down its fatal stream of light and both of them kind of disappeared under the water, leaving it crackling and steaming with dissipating energy.

The kids shrieked at the top of their voices. They loved it. You'd think they'd been watching a game and someone just scored. The rest of us turned and silently walked away. What we'd always known confirmed; that the boundary is still drawn as violently as ever.

That aside, the only other thing of note that happened was another Infinity chopper – maybe even the same one – nosing round for a while. Maybe it's just me, but when they hover there like that, stationary in the sky for minutes on end, it always gets my imagination going. I guess they were just checking things had died down, and after a while they did leave, which only went to reinforce my belief that I was returning to the tunnels with encouraging news. The Village was being rebuilt, there was no sign of any further Wastelord activity, nor a search for Lena. And maybe it was this mood of relief, of rekindled optimism, that caused my mind to return to what she'd said the previous day; about me having 'given up'.

I didn't see what I could do about it. I'd felt that way for so long, surely now it *was* too late? Or maybe that's her whole point? That I wasn't even prepared to give it a try. I quickened my stride a little, wanting to make that extra effort, to feel my legs breaking their normal slow and weary rhythm.

When it finally occurred to me, it was like having a private joke with myself. The way you do sometimes. When you smile quietly and hope no one asks you why. I mean, it's crazy. I couldn't possibly be serious . . . could I?

Again I lifted my pace a little, stretching muscle and sinew that further millimetre. On the other hand, what did I have to lose? And, almost without realising it, I broke into a clumsy jog. I had to get back to the tunnels. There was something I badly needed to do.

After I told them what I'd seen, or rather, what I *hadn't* seen, the atmosphere over lunch became noticeably more relaxed. Lena had a little dig at me for not letting her know I was going out, but you could see how relieved she was that there was no further sign of De Grew and his Wastelords. Course, I never said anything about the couple who got zapped. What's the point? It's just a fact of life, a power beyond us, like a force of nature or something.

I did mention to Jimmy and Delilah about the site of our lean-tos having disappeared. Neither of them seemed that concerned. The little guy didn't even mention his favourite wrench. I guess in a way it only confirmed what we already knew: our life over there's gone. This is what we have now. And I think we're all pretty well agreed, it's one helluvan improvement.

With what I had in my head, it wasn't easy to sit there and act normal. I kept agreeing with everything that was being said, trying to ease the conversation along, to make sure no one got into any kind of debate. Thankfully, I can always rely on Jimmy not to ignore the call of his workshop for too long.

'Well . . . gotta go,' he eventually said, in that way that makes it sound like he's off to his downtown office.

'Yeah, I'd better inspect those tunnels,' I told them.

'Make sure you do this time,' Lena warned.

It's a terrible thing. I don't hold with telling lies, especially not to someone you care about, but damned if I wasn't about to do it for the second time that day. I reassured Lena that inspecting the tunnels was all I had in mind for the afternoon, that she knew she could trust me, then sidled off. Her and Delilah were far too engrossed in their conversation to notice me grabbing a box of candles before heading to the lower levels.

It took me almost an hour. The first time round I didn't notice the service tunnel linking the two main ones. By cutting through I could form a circuit of some half a mile or so. Ideal for what I wanted. I retraced my footsteps, putting up a lighted candle every thirty or forty yards, 'til finally the whole stretch was illuminated.

Don't ask me why, but I still got a watch. If it ever stops, I guess that'll be an end to it. I'll throw it away and it can take time with it, but until that happens I continue to strap it on and live a little by what it tells me. It shows seconds as well as minutes, which I was hoping might come in useful. On the other hand, maybe I was being a little ambitious? Maybe that amount of detail wasn't gonna be necessary?

I think I already told you, I ain't that good at running. Weights are my thing. I can clean and jerk a couple of hundred pounds all day. But as a means of assessing general fitness, running's a pretty good place to start. It took me precisely three minutes and fifty-seven seconds to heave and huff my way round that circuit. I intended to carry on, maybe do several laps, but there was no way. I had to take a break, get my breath back, wait for the pain to subside so I could check myself out for any permanent damage. Ten minutes or so later I set off again, taking it easy this time but still ending up doubled over and gasping.

It was discouraging. I couldn't believe how heavy my limbs felt, how much effort was needed to drag them along. I went around a further three occasions, the final time walking the last few hundred yards. I was that exhausted I thought I was going to throw up, though it was my heart that was really worrying me. I had this mental picture of it being asked to suddenly thrash and pound away after years of peacefully ticking over. In the end, I just had to tell myself to stop worrying, that if it was going to blow there was nothing I could do.

I thought it over for a while, then reluctantly decided to go and see Jimmy in his workshop. I mean, I'd promised myself I wouldn't tell anyone – not yet – but I needed help. Running wasn't going to be enough. I needed to make me up some weights as well. Mind you, the way he looked at me when I first broached the subject I damn near gave up the idea then and there.

'You what?' he said, as if he hadn't heard me properly.

'I'm going back into training.'

He paused, still gaping, a frown puckering up his whole wrinkled little face. 'You're kidding, right?'

'No!'

'Big Guy! People our age . . . You know. Not a good idea.'

I can't tell you how much that annoys me. The gap between our ages might not be that great, but one day it could be the difference between life and death – mine and his.

'I ain't your age, Jimmy,' I told him. 'Now, are you going to help me or not?'

'You going to tell Lena?'

'Not for the moment.'

'So I'm going to be left to explain why you had a heart attack?'

'Jimmy!'

In the end, and despite endless tutting and shaking his head, he gave a very long resigned sigh, like a croupier being forced to take the bet of a bankrupt man. 'Okay.'

He started hunting round his workshop 'til he came up with this idea of securing drums to the end of a length of metal pipe and filling them with sand.

'How much sand do you want?' he asked, as if he thought a cupful would be most advisable.

'Try half full,' I told him.

Again he gave a long sigh, but still commenced pouring the sand into the two drums. The moment he finished, I grabbed the metal pipe, ignored the slight pull in my back as I lifted the whole apparatus, and without another word struggled out the door.

'Your funeral,' he called after me.

'Shut up, Jimmy!'

That evening, Lena was so convinced I was sick she insisted on putting me to bed. I had no colour, my muscles were repeatedly going into spasm and my limbs were shaking like they were in a state of shock.

'Probably just a cold,' I told her.

'Clancy, you can hardly move.'

'I'm fine,' I said. 'It'll be gone by morning.'

The following day, when I woke up, I was that stiff it was all I could do to stand up. I tried exercising it off, but I was in such pain I had no choice but to delay getting fit for a while.

Lena wanted me to go back to bed, to sleep off whatever it was, but I stubbornly insisted on getting round; tottering from one place to another, my limbs so rigid I was like a wooden marionette.

A few days later, I started again. Taking it slower this time. Bit by bit, day by day, 'til several weeks on, it does seem to be getting a little easier.

I swear my muscles are firmer. I mean, I think there's a limit to what you can do. Sixty-three-year-old unflexed muscle seems to flop no matter what; but flexed, there does seem to be an improvement. I can manage five laps of the circuit without stopping. Plodding through those tunnels, sweat pouring off me, puffing and panting like some recommissioned old steam train.

When I was sure I could keep it up, that it wasn't going to be a five-minute wonder, I told Lena. As a matter of fact, I think she was pretty impressed. So much so that some days she comes with me. The two of us jogging that candlelit circuit far underground, her tagging along behind using the sound of my footsteps as a guide.

It's her who's done it, of course. She made me take a long hard look at myself. I'd become all grouchy and bitter about losing something that, to some degree, I still have. I owe her. But do you know something? It ain't just her. There's something else too, that I don't really know how to put into words. See, I got this feeling that the situation on the Island's changing. There's always been a kind of terrible balance here – us, the kids, the Wastelords, satellites and fog – but now, the existence of Lena and the tunnels seems to have altered all that.

I guess I'm not making much sense. But every time I press another weight, or run another circuit, I get this feeling that I'm not so much trying to get fit again, as training up for something. Not that I have the slightest notion what it might be. All I do know is that with each passing day, I can feel it coming closer and closer.

CHAPTER TWELVE

Despite this vague sense that there was a small tear in the fabric of our lives that was getting ever bigger, our existence in the tunnels continued in a fashion that, certainly for Jimmy, Delilah and me, has been far more agreeable than anything we've known since we came to the Island. We're safer, warmer and better fed than we've been in years. Sure we miss the daylight, the sun, the sea breeze (that being the only time the air ain't stuffed full of crap), but that's a small price to pay for what we've gained down here.

I went up-top again one afternoon, just for a quick look round, but nothing seemed to be happening, and even Lena was beginning to think that maybe De Grew came to the conclusion that he had it wrong, that she wasn't involved in the break-in on the warehouse after all.

Jimmy put a switch on his light. As if to prove that we hadn't only recaptured electricity, we were also in control of it again. He also tried hooking up a second one, a bit further down the tunnel, but it must've been too much of a drain on his 'generator', 'cuz both of them went so dim he had to disconnect it and go back to the original arrangement.

Mind you, I gotta say, the one thing that never gets drained is the little guy's enthusiasm. He's working flat out on some new secret project down there, and every day comes up smirking to himself, barely able to wait to show us what it is. As for Delilah, she's become a lot more forgiving of him and his junk since she realised he actually can do some of the things he always claimed. She's never going to fuss over the little guy – Delilah's never going to fuss over anybody – but I noticed she's become that bit more attentive of him and his needs.

Once everyone knew about my jogging and working out, I didn't have to stick to the lower tunnels anymore. It gets kind of tedious going round and round the same circuit. You quit 'cuz you're bored rather than tired, so I began to run the main tunnel: starting down the other side of the garden, up through the living area, then on to the main hall and back down again. It was a kind of a 'warmer and stretcher', to ease out the aches, get everything moving so I could get on with what I saw as the main business of the day – lifting weights.

In fact, I was feeling so much healthier, so much stronger, that one morning I thought I'd give myself a real test and take on the slope up to the entrance.

You get a false idea of your fitness when you go jogging. You can go for miles and you feel so easy, so comfortable, you're convinced you can run forever. Then one day you gotta sprint fifty yards for a bus or something, and after thirty you start wondering if it really matters, and what time's the next one.

It turned out a bit like that. I started off up the slope, sure it would be no trouble and that I was just going to glide up there on the back of my newly regained fitness. About halfway, I felt as if my lungs were starting to tear; at three-quarters, like they were being wrenched out of me through my nostrils. I just about made it and no more. One further stride I reckon might've been my last. I collapsed onto the ground on my hands and knees, gasping and wheezing fit to bust.

It was only when I started to get my breath back, when I straightened up and glanced out through the gaps in the bricks, that I realised someone was outside.

I threw myself back into the darkness, my need for breath gone in a gasp. There was a kid out there. So near I could've almost leant out and touched him. I crouched in the corner, not daring to move, expecting him to start scrabbling at the rubble at any moment, looking for a way in. I mean, he must've heard me. Surely. All the noise I was making.

But after a couple of minutes, and with no sign of any reaction, I began to slowly inch my way back to take another look. He was still there, in exactly the same position: facing away from me, hunched over something. I could see the freckles on the back of his neck, the lank and greasy tails of his coppery hair. I froze, too scared to make the slightest movement in case my old bones creaked or groaned.

Finally he shifted position a little, half turning, and I got a better look at him. I guess he was about sixteen or so, unnaturally tall, like he'd been force-fed something; a few wispy ambitions to a beard, a night sky of zits, and this real red and raw look about him, as if he'd been exposed to too much too soon. I also got a chance to see what he was so closely studying. He had this apparatus slung round his neck with a small screen, a set of headphones (which was obviously why he hadn't heard my puffing and wheezing), and in his right hand was holding a long handle with a kind of dish on the end of it.

It was a bit like a more complex version of those old-fashioned metal detectors. In fact, at first that's what I thought he was: an elaborately equipped scavenger. Then it hit me. It wasn't a metal detector at all. It was something else. A thermal plotter or sound detector and, *Jesus* we're in a lot of trouble.

He started sweeping the dish back and forth, his eyes never leaving the screen, repeatedly, and rather angrily, punching buttons, as if the apparatus wasn't working properly. I felt sick. They hadn't given up, they'd just been closing in. Another kid came into view over in the direction of the square, using exactly the same equipment. They must've divided up the city and were going through it section by section, looking for us.

'Come on, you piece of shit,' I heard the red-haired kid mutter at his detector. 'What the hell's wrong with you?'

He altered the angle of the dish to the ground, sweeping from side to side again, then suddenly stopped, a frown appearing on his face. He repeated the action, now concentrating on just the one area, slightly turning his wrist from side to side, starting to look that bit excited. Oh Jesus, no! *Lena and Delilah!*

I watched in horror as he locked onto what he'd located, as he squinted at the screen, desperately trying to clean up the image. He punched a few more buttons, was about to cry out to his companion, but then stopped himself. At that moment the other kid shouted something across that I couldn't quite hear.

'Nah! It's a piece of crap,' the tall kid replied, his voice sounding so strange spilling down into the tunnel.

He repeated his actions yet again. Squinting even harder at the screen. Did he have something? His dish was certainly pointing in the direction of the living area. I thought about running down there, hushing Lena and Delilah up – before he was sure, before he could pinpoint them – but surely he'd pick me up if I did?

I was just about to take the chance, to tiptoe down there as best I could, when he came out with a whole mouthful of curses, spat on the bricks next to the door and, removing his headphones, started to make his way over to his companion.

'I told you, no one's going to throw anything away that works,' he complained.

I gave a long, drawn-out sigh of relief, panting to myself as if I'd been holding my breath for the last few minutes – which I might well have been. Thank God, the immediate threat was over. But at that moment, this loud hammering began somewhere deep in the innards of the tunnels.

At first I couldn't think what it was. I was that confused I thought there must be more of them, that they were breaking in somewhere. The vent over the garden maybe. Then, of course, I realised. It was Jimmy. Down in his workshop.

I stared across at the two kids. By now they were some way off, but I could still see them stop and look around, as if they could just about hear something but couldn't quite make out what it was.

I didn't wait for their reactions, I took off as fast as I could. I had to get to Jimmy before they worked out what that noise was and where it was coming from.

The candles were at the bottom of the slope, but I was in too much of a rush to stop and take one. It would only blow out anyway. I knew the route well enough. Or so I thought. Turning a corner a little too sharply, I ran straight into the wall. There were a couple of bright flashes somewhere, a real sickening thud, and the next thing I knew I was flat on my back. Such was my urgency I was up and running again almost before I knew it. Staggering a little, down through the main hall, plunging darker and deeper, then having to slow, to use my hands for the less familiar tunnel approaching the workshop.

The closer I got, the louder the noise became. I couldn't imagine what he was doing. It was more like thunder than hammering. I could just see those two kids up there, putting their headphones back on, adjusting their dials, making their way over to the entrance.

Finally the glow of the workshop loomed up before me and I rushed in to find the little guy furiously beating this huge sheet of metal into shape. 'Jimmy!' I hissed.

He was making that much noise he didn't hear me. I ran over, grabbed the hammer he was using and tore it from his grasp.

He turned towards me, an astonished look on his face. 'What the hell's up with you?'

'Shhhhh!'

'What?'

'Shut up!' I hissed angrily.

He paused for a moment, utterly confused by my behaviour. 'What is it?' he whispered.

'They're up-top looking for us.'

'Who?'

'Kids.'

'Oh no!' he groaned, letting the sheet of metal fall from his grasp and collide with the wall.

'For chrissake!' I whispered.

'Big Guy, they ain't going to hear that all the way up there,' he sneered.

'They got detectors,' I told him.

He paused for a moment, a rather different expression coming to his face. 'What sort?'

'Warmth, sound, infrared, I don't know! Sort of a metal box with headphones,' I informed him. 'And this, like a big triple-coned vacuum-cleaner thing they keep sweeping across the ground.'

Jimmy's face suddenly drained of all colour. 'Shit!' he moaned. 'Sound detectors.'

'Maybe,' I said, his reaction convincing me this was every bit as serious as I thought. Both of us went silent for a moment, not really knowing what to do or say.

'Wonder what kind,' he muttered, more to himself than to me.

'Does it matter?'

'Yeah. Some ain't much better than a hearing aid. Others could almost pick up what we're saying now.'

We turned and stared at each other, momentarily too afraid to even speak.

'I think they found them in the garbage,' I whispered.

He nodded, far from comforted. 'Where are Delilah and Lena?'

'In the living area. You go find them. I'll go back up.'

Jimmy took a candle and the two of us set off almost on tiptoe, not speaking, communicating through gestures, finally separating at the main hall.

It took me the best part of ten minutes to get back up to the entrance. All the way up I expected to meet those kids coming down. But when I reached the top and peered out, there wasn't a soul to be seen.

It should've brought relief, but it didn't. I checked out the door really closely, as if I'd be able to tell if someone had discovered it or not. Nothing had been disturbed, not as far as I could see, but I still had this awful fear that we'd been breached in some way, that everything we'd gained was now in jeopardy.

When I got back down to the living area I found the others all silent and grave-faced, waiting to hear what I had to say. Delilah actually had tears in her eyes. I mean, she's been a different person since she's been down here, like she's found an old spark of herself and polished it up. The thought of someone taking that away from her was just too much.

'They've gone,' I said, putting them out of their misery.

'You sure?' Lena asked.

I shrugged. 'Sure as I can be.'

Jimmy gave a long sigh of relief. 'See!' he said to Delilah, and very much for her benefit. 'They don't have a clue where we are.'

Delilah didn't answer, just shook her head. She wasn't any more comforted by that than I was.

The real problem, that no one knew the answer to, was how efficient those sound detectors were. What precautions should we be taking? We were already talking in whispers – you couldn't help yourself – but we had no idea if it was necessary or not. One thing was for sure, like it or not, it meant changes around the tunnels, and big ones, too.

From then on we've had to keep all noise to a minimum. Jimmy was told he'd have to give up his workshop, that it was just too much of a risk. The little guy went crazy. Apparently what he'd been working on down there was a much bigger generator, that'd give us enough juice for not only more lighting, but a few other things, too.

It presented us with one helluva dilemma. I mean, I agreed with him, it's too good a thing to miss out on. On the other hand, nothing's worth losing what we got.

In the end, after a great deal of hushed and heated discussion, it was decided that as long as Lena was prepared to act as lookout he could carry on. After all, with her sense of smell and acuteness of hearing, I'd back her against sound detectors any time.

But no matter how great or how little the threat, all of us have been left with this undeniable sense of loss. It's as if those dense yards of moist earth that separate us from the surface, that have kept us safe and unseen for so long, have suddenly been blown away. We're vulnerable again, open to attack, and it ain't a nice feeling, I can tell you.

For the rest of that day every little sound was a cause for alarm, even a cough or sneeze. And if a serious noise was made, someone dropping something, or knocking stuff over, well, we just held our breath and stared upwards, wondering whether we'd been overheard or not. It was a bit like one of those old-time submarines: engines stopped, lying on the bottom, waiting for the depth charges to come drifting on down.

The only place I felt at all comfortable was up at the entrance, staring out, keeping an eye on things. I spent the rest of the day up there, endlessly running my gaze along the horizon, 'til it got dark and I had to give up and return to the living area.

The following morning I was back up at first light, squatting down, peering out through the gaps, my old knees locking up every now and then. I mean, it ain't exactly my idea of fun, but anything's better than not knowing.

Couple of hours later Lena came up and joined me. Jimmy wanted to make some noise in his workshop and had asked if she'd be his lookout.

'Everything okay?' she asked.

'Haven't seen a soul.'

However, when she squatted down and pressed her nose to the gaps, she caught the scent of someone almost immediately. 'Over there,' she said, pointing in the direction of the ocean.

It took me a while, but I saw them way over in the distance, almost hidden by piles of rubble. Maybe the same two kids as yesterday, scouring round, still using the sound detectors.

'Yeah. You're right,' I told her, feeling a little embarrassed.

For a while I watched them, reporting everything I saw as they wandered up and down piles of rubble, went this way and that, not seeming to have a plan after all. Then they began to drift further away 'til finally they were lost from sight.

I sighed and stood up, straightening out my legs and back.

'Gone?' Lena asked.

'Yeah.'

She nodded her head thoughtfully. 'Maybe they don't know where we are after all.'

'Yeah,' I sighed. 'Maybe not.'

Several days later and Jimmy was ready to install his new generator. I tell you, it's huge, like some old turbo-prop engine. Just getting it up to the living area took one helluvan effort. He fixed up this bench for us to climb up on, and while I took the weight, attempted to attach it to the roof of the tunnel; plugging the brickwork, getting a good fixing, having to stop every now and then 'cuz we thought we heard Delilah relaying messages from Lena that someone was about.

I couldn't believe how heavy it was. Not the blades so much, but the huge j-bracket they were attached to. I had to prop it a couple of times with lengths of timber while I got my strength back. Sweat was pouring off me, forming this little pool at my feet. Thank God I was back in training. Jimmy kept telling me to 'move it this way a bit', or 'move it that way a touch', and 'hold it steady, will you, Big Guy'. Tell the truth, it got pretty heated a couple of times. He also forgot to secure the propeller, which meant that when a sudden gust of wind swept down the tunnel, it started rotating and damn near took my arm off.

And yet, when we finally finished, when it was fixed there, looking all big and purposeful and starting to spin, I almost got as excited about it as he was. The only miscalculation he's made is that the blades are a little too long. The length of the bracket's right, they clear the tunnel roof okay – and it ain't going to be a problem for the others, they ain't tall enough – but if I'm not careful when I walk under that thing, I'm going to get one helluva haircut. Jimmy says he'll adjust them, but he's so excited about getting it all working, I can't see it being a priority and I reckon I'll be best advised not to walk too tall in that particular part of the tunnel from now on.

That evening, after several hours of connecting stuff up, he threw the switch on a length of the old subway emergency lighting circuit (I'd seen him messing about with it, but I'd just assumed he'd been taking parts), and we had lighting almost as far as you could see.

If it hadn't been for the possibility of being overheard I reckon we would've let out a whoop that would've echoed through every inch of the tunnels. After all that time in the dark, suddenly to be able to see so far was almost beyond belief. Delilah ran up and kissed one of the lights, as if it was a relative she hadn't seen in a long while.

Jimmy was gone even before we had a chance to congratulate him.

Limping off down to his workshop, soon returning with a selection of those electrical items he once claimed he'd fixed. And, do you know something? They are fixed. The mixer, the micro-centre, the irradia-fry, all of them. The only trouble is, by working, they make a noise, which means we can't use them.

The little guy was so disappointed it almost broke your heart. Delilah gave him a big hug, told him not to worry. I mean, as far as we're concerned he couldn't be a bigger hero than he is already. More lighting makes us feel braver. As if we can only cope with what we can see, and if we're able to see more, then we're pushing back the boundaries of fear.

Again it occurred to us that lighting didn't mean a great deal to Lena. You'd suddenly feel embarrassed by your enthusiasm, stifle it like it meant nothing, but the moment she got the idea that was what you were doing she'd beat up on you with some real full-frontal honesty. She wasn't having any of it. If we were celebrating 'cuz we had lighting in the main tunnel, then so was she and that was an end to it.

That night we all went a little crazy. We had this real urge to celebrate, to shout into the night the same way we'd lit up the dark, and once Lena produced a couple of bottles of hooch, well, that was what we did. There was a lot of fooling around went on, racing up and down the tunnel. Several times we said we should be more careful, that someone might be listening, but we were making more of a joke of it than anything. We hadn't seen a soul since that glimpse the other morning, and even then they'd been some way off. No one was going to be out with a sound detector at that time of night. Anyways, sometimes you just get an urge that won't let go 'til you give into it. You gotta be a little reckless now and then. It's in the human spirit.

Later, Lena and I made love. I mean, I already told you I ain't one for giving out details about this sort of thing, but in this case, I don't know. Tell the truth, it almost frightened me. I'm a down-to-earth, body-functioning big guy. I never held with anything else. But somehow we instinctively found this slow sliding rhythm that seemed to pass back and forth between us and induce a kind of trance. At first it was just acute pleasure, but then, something else. I could still feel my hands on her body, our nakedness where we touched, but it was like going into a different dimension. As if the physical was just too cumbersome, too restrictive, for us. I don't know. It's beyond me to explain. I've lived sixty-three years and no one's ever told me two people could create such a thing.

When the moment finally came it was almost more than we could bear. I had to stifle a scream. Partly 'cuz of the pleasure, but also 'cuz it was such agony to have to let go of what we created. Afterwards we hugged each other as tightly as we could, as though it was a frustration, a sadness, to find we were separate bodies again.

I might know a few fancy words, but I'm not very good with them, leastways, not when it matters. But that night I finally said the three words I been waiting to say all my life. The first time kind of tentatively, almost losing my nerve, but then over and over. Like I knew it was only small change now, but one day it was going to amount to something a whole lot bigger.

Later that night, God knows what time, Lena nudged me from a deep, satisfying sleep.

'Clancy! . . . Clancy, wake up!'

'What? What's the matter?' I managed to mumble, though I was too dazed to really know what I was saying.

'Clancy!'

'What?' I asked again.

She paused for a moment, like she was waiting for confirmation of what she was about to say.

'There's someone in the tunnels.'

CHAPTER THIRTEEN

It's amazing how the body can bypass the normally slow process of recovering consciousness when it has to. The moment Lena told me someone was in the tunnels I was up and on my feet.

'Where?' I asked.

'Main hall. Coming this way.'

'Shit!' I hissed, immediately realising we must've been pinpointed by those detectors after all.

I stumbled over to rouse Jimmy and Delilah, hesitating momentarily by the light switch, not having time to think it through, but instinctively deciding it was best we were left in the dark. Delilah woke instantly, but we had to physically drag Jimmy to his feet.

'What's going on?' he whined.

'For chrissake, Jimmy!' I hissed. 'They got in!'

'What?'

Just at that moment we heard a crash. Someone knocked something over, by the sound of it an old oil drum; you could hear it rolling over and over and then slamming up against a wall. Instantly Jimmy went through the same rapid process of recovery I had.

'Jesus! What are we going to do?' he whispered.

Which was one helluva good question. The only direction open to us led down to the garden, but it's a dead end really; the tunnel dips away after that and becomes flooded.

'I don't know,' I said, still joining everyone in a general movement in that direction.

Whatever doubts I had, Lena didn't seem to share them. She immediately took the lead, urging us on, and when we didn't move quickly enough in the dark, got us all to hold hands: Delilah grasping onto her, then Jimmy, and me at the back.

I felt kind of stupid hanging onto the little guy's bony mitt. I could feel this real tension flowing through him, like it was being conducted from one person to another, getting stronger as it went along the line, but it did mean we made faster progress. Behind there were raised voices, a couple of excited cries, and we knew they'd reached the living area.

'*Come on!*' I hissed. But I knew I was just saying it for the sake of it, that we were already going as fast as we could, and anyway, where the hell were we going?

Someone gave a little panicky moan – I don't know, I think it was Delilah, though it could've just as easily been Jimmy. I glanced behind and realised why. We were on the long straight stretch approaching the garden and you could just make out the faint glow of pursuing light. It wasn't candles. More like flaming torches which, in case we had any doubts about who got in and was pursuing us, immediately confirmed our worst fears.

When we reached the garden, a glimpse of the night sky, the stars twinkling away like they knew we'd never be able to afford them, seemed to release our panic and we broke into a sprint. Almost instantly, Jimmy and I managed to go sprawling over.

I can't tell you how loud that sounded, the two of us dragging each other to the ground, knocking a stack of empty cans over in the process. Behind there was another shout, the pounding of their footsteps noticeably increasing in tempo.

We scrambled up, rejoining hands with the others as we got dragged into the black mouth of the continuing tunnel.

'Where we going?' whined Jimmy, the way the ground was falling away beneath our feet obviously worrying him as much as it was me.

But Lena just kept tugging us on. Down and down into absolute darkness and a tunnel no one knew but her. I was starting to panic, wondering if maybe she was so scared she was just leading us anywhere, when suddenly I heard splashing in front of me and found myself in water. Just a few inches at first, then a few more, 'til soon we were up to our knees and wading. Delilah was making these little protesting noises, like it was a cold day at the beach and someone was forcing her to go in for a swim, but Lena wasn't having any of it.

'Delilah!' she hissed impatiently, and I felt the jolt of her anxious tug transmitted down the line.

Someone slipped, there was a wrench on the chain, then they righted themselves and we staggered on. We were up to our thighs now, doing that kind of jumpy little walk you do when you're trying to hurry through water, lurching one way then the other. But there were no reference points for your senses, no way for your body to know what to do. We had to keep moving, but everything was screaming that it had no information, that all it could feel or see was darkness and water. It slowed us so much the kids began to catch up, their yelling becoming more and more eager as they scented blood.

We were on this long gradual bend when the glow of the first of their torches began to come round it and suddenly we were immersed in orange light, flickering and tossing our shadows into a state of panic.

Whoever it was gave a cry of triumph, calling back to the others.

'We got 'em!' he screamed. 'We got 'em!'

I glanced back. Even at this distance, and with the glow of only one torch, there was no mistaking the big lanky kid who'd been outside that day. Nor the fact that he was carrying a machete.

'Go!' I screamed at the others, the need for silence now gone.

There was a splash behind us and I realised the tall kid was already in the water. Behind him another torch appeared. Then another. Jesus, we were going to be slaughtered.

I don't know what it was at the bottom of that water, but it was slippery as hell. Everyone was sliding all over the place. Twice I held on to Jimmy to prevent him from going under. But I couldn't stop myself. My foot shot out from beneath me like someone had wrenched it away. I tugged at the little guy, hoping he could save me, but the next thing I knew I was underwater. I tried to right myself, fell over again, then managed to regain my footing with the aid of the others.

'Keep going!' I shouted, not able to bear the thought of us losing ground 'cuz of me. But it was too late. The tall kid was almost upon us, his torch in one hand, his machete in the other, swinging it back and forth, chuckling to himself, like he couldn't wait to slice somebody open.

The tunnel took another bend, a much sharper one; we couldn't see the pursuing group, only him. Mind you, he was enough. By virtue of being that much taller than anyone else he was nowhere near as deep in the water and found it that much easier to get along.

I thought about stopping and trying to take him out. He might've been tall but he wasn't that solid. But with a machete, and that reach of his, I didn't fancy my chances. Certainly not unarmed and slipping and sliding all over the place. I looked round for something I might use. A length of timber, even a brick to throw, but there was nothing.

Then, to my astonishment – Jesus, I could hardly believe what I was seeing – Lena suddenly stopped and turned to face him. I mean, I would've prevented her, but I was so surprised she was past me before I realised. Even the kid looked puzzled, like there was something he might've missed. Then he smiled, raised his machete and stepped forward to cut her down.

'*Lena!*' somebody screamed – I think it was me – but I needn't have worried.

She didn't fight. She did something far more sensible, that maybe I would've thought of if I wasn't so dumb. She swept her hand across the water and drenched his torch. The flame died and everything changed. Apart from the faintest glow from the pursuing group we were in darkness again.

The tall kid stopped in his tracks, screaming for the others to catch up. '*Come on!* Get here, will ya!'

Before they could arrive, Lena pushed us through a small unnoticed opening in the wall and we slipped away.

I found myself in this narrow service tunnel, no more than a couple of feet wide; stumbling along behind Jimmy, giving him the occasional push, aware of this sudden mustiness, that dank odour you get at the crotch of a building. I slipped again and had to reach out for the wall to steady myself. It felt all soft and slimy, like it was alive, and from then on I did my best to avoid touching it.

Behind us the tall kid was still shouting to the others to catch up, that he had us trapped. I heard them arrive, their cries of frustration when their torches revealed nothing, but they soon spotted where we'd gone and began to follow.

I gave Jimmy another shove, told him to move it, but he was going as fast as he could. A few moments later I felt the ground beneath me beginning to rise, the water growing shallower. There was a splashing up front. It sounded as if Lena got out. Then Delilah, then Jimmy. I fumbled round, found some steps, and followed the others up and through a doorway.

'Wait,' I said, tugging back on Jimmy's hand.

'What is it?' Lena whispered.

'Keep going,' I told her.

I gave her a nudge, the three of them moving on, though after a few moments I heard them stop. I guess to wait for me. Jimmy whispered to Lena, asked her what I was up to, but she told him to shush.

Slowly the light of the flickering torches grew nearer. I crouched behind the door, listening to them getting out of the water, starting to climb the steps. It was only when someone's shape actually filled the doorway, when his torchlight spilled through, that I finally swung the door, hitting him with every bit of strength a half-fit old big guy could muster.

Whoever it was, and it wasn't the tall kid, got it full smack in the face, and I'll tell you, the way that door rebounded off him, he must've been made of rubberised rock. He fell back against the others, bounced off them and ended up in a twisted heap across the doorway. But his machete, that I'd been hoping to get my hands on, clattered down the steps.

I cursed to myself, but at least had the presence of mind to learn from Lena. I grabbed his fallen torch and tossed it into the water. I then turned and hurried after the others, taking Jimmy's hand, rejoining the human chain.

Lena led us this way and that, through an endless maze of confusion and darkness. Along tunnels narrow and wide, through more flooded areas, across some kind of metal walkway, then back into another tunnel. The kids got left way behind. Tell the truth, I didn't have a clue where we were myself. Not 'til I heard a greater depth to our echo, felt a certain familiar sense of spaciousness, even a familiar smell, and realised we were back at the main hall.

'Let's go,' urged Jimmy, who'd also worked it out.

'Where?' I asked.

'Up-top!'

He started towards the entrance, but I called him back. 'Jimmy! Wait!'

'What?' he asked. 'Big Guy! They ain't that far behind!'

'We can't leave,' I told him.

'What?'

'We can't leave,' I repeated.

'Why not?'

''Cuz if we do, it's all over. We're back the way it was.'

There was a momentary pause, then Delilah's voice came out of the dark. 'Shit,' she muttered, obviously having taken my point.

'What else can we do?' Jimmy asked.

I fumbled in my pocket, unwrapped my matches and struck one. For some reason I needed to see their faces to say this. 'We can't leave . . . and we can't let them leave either.'

There was a long pause.

'What are you saying?' Delilah asked.

'I don't know. But we can't let them go.'

They paused, weighing it up in their minds, a white-faced grimness descending upon us all. Lena turned away, like she didn't want to participate in this conversation. My match went out and I struck another.

'You don't mean kill them?' Jimmy said.

I didn't answer, just shrugged, and he turned and stared into Delilah's face, like they were searching for something from each other. The little guy started to shake his head, as if the idea of the hunted becoming the hunter was just too much for him.

'We can't,' he said.

'There aren't that many of them,' I told him. 'Half-a-dozen at the most.'

'Three,' Lena announced, speaking for the first time since the subject had been raised.

I turned to her. 'You sure?'

She nodded. 'Yeah. But, Clancy . . . no killing, huh?'

I sighed. I hadn't really had it in mind to do anything, just stop them leaving, but at least that made one decision for us.

Again the match I was holding went out and this time I didn't bother to strike another. We all knew the decision had been made. We also knew it was one we could never have imagined making: to turn on the kids, to go after them, we wouldn't even have dared dream about it.

The one advantage we had was that we knew the tunnels. Or most of them. All of us could just about find our way round in the dark. The kids had only one torch left, one final source of light; if we could extinguish that, it might give us a chance.

Mind you, up against that was the fact that they were armed with machetes: razor-sharp, deadly, that could slice through anything with just one swish. I thought about sneaking down to Jimmy's workshop, looking out some tools we could maybe use to defend ourselves, but it was too close to where we last saw them. In the end, Lena took Jimmy with her to the garden to see what they could find there, whilst Delilah and I kept watch over the tunnel up to the entrance.

If it was going to come to a fight I couldn't imagine Delilah being much use, but she was as determined as anyone that those kids wouldn't leave. In fact, sitting there in that alcove, whispering to one another, listening out for the sound of footsteps or an unfamiliar voice, I realised she shared none of the little guy's reservations.

'They ain't getting past me,' she croaked determinedly. 'No matter what.'

'Delilah. I don't want you getting involved in any fighting,' I told her, mindful of the fact that she hadn't fully recovered from the blowout. 'Leave this to me.'

She grunted a little louder than she meant to. 'You really think it matters?'

'What?'

'I'd rather be killed *here* than go back up *there*.'

I never said anything, but I knew what she meant. She didn't want to live without tunnels, and I didn't want to live without Lena; and both of us were prepared to do anything, pay any price, for what meant so much.

'It ain't going to come to that,' I reassured her.

Lena and Jimmy returned laden down with a lot of stuff I wouldn't normally associate with combat. Two shovels, a rake, a bundle of pea sticks, a roll of twine and a couple of plastic containers full of water. Can you believe that? But the thing was, when they explained it to me, it made perfect sense. Water to douse the torch, sticks and tools to fight with, and twine to tie the kids up afterwards. Well, that was the theory. The practice might prove a little different.

Jimmy briefly argued the point, but we decided that he and Delilah should stay and guard the way up to the entrance while Lena and I went in search of the three kids. I mean, Lena has to go, no one knows the tunnels better than her, and I was the closest thing to a fighting force we had, so as far as I could see, it more or less decided itself.

No sooner had the little guy accepted the idea than he started to think up their 'battle plan', the best way he and Delilah could defend the exit. When we left they were cutting off lengths of twine and stringing them across the tunnel. The idea being that when the kids tripped over the twine, our two crack troops would rush out and pulverise the hell out of them with gardening equipment. I mean, I never said nothing, I didn't want to hurt Jimmy's feelings, but I hoped to hell it wasn't going to come to that.

Slowly and silently Lena and me made our way back down to where we'd last seen the kids; her carrying a container of water, me a shovel raised and ready. Despite it just being the two of us, she still insisted on taking my hand and I have to admit, entombed in all that darkness, knowing how at home in it she was, I was pretty glad of it.

God knows how long it took. Every now and then she'd stop, sniffing, listening, then venture forward again. We didn't say anything to each other, or not in the conventional sense. Just a squeeze of the hand now and then, a twist of the fingers, a nudge, a grip on the upper arm. Strange how we've developed that since I've known her. How all those gestures human beings make – the smile, the frown, the shrug, the wink, whatever – have been translated into a language of touching. Really, we don't need to say a word to each other anymore.

We descended some steps, turned into a service tunnel, then slowed right down and I realised we were back where we'd last seen the kids: near the door. Lena stopped. I could hear her quietly sniffing the air and I knew she could smell someone. I squeezed her hand to ask where and she pointed in front of us.

I raised my shovel higher, getting ready to swipe at anyone that came at us, but Lena slipped from my grasp and moved forward. I tried to stay with her, but before I knew it, she was gone. I fumbled around, reached for her and touched nothing but wall. What the hell was she doing? Then her voice came to me from out of the darkness.

'Clancy,' she whispered.

I inched my way forward, waving my hand in front of me, eventually finding her squatting down over something. I soon realised it was the kid I'd hit earlier, that he was still unconscious. The others must've just left him.

We thought about it for a while, then decided to take him over to one of the storerooms near Jimmy's workshop, where we could lock him away and he could come round in his own sweet time.

I got him up on my shoulder, no trouble, he wasn't any size at all, but it still felt a bit odd having a kid draped over me. I couldn't actually see him, but sure as hell I could smell him. It was like a mixture of wild animal and garbage. He reeked: his clothes, his body, his hair. I'd already searched him once, just in case he had a knife or something, but on my way over to the storeroom I started to feel a little uneasy and stopped to frisk him again, just to be sure.

When we got him locked up, Lena and I gave each other a quick hug. One down, two to go. The only trouble was, where were they? Where was the tall kid? The one who worried me the most.

'Maybe we should go back up,' Lena said.

I muttered my agreement. I mean, those kids could've been anywhere, but it was hard not to worry about Jimmy and Delilah all on their own, maybe having to face them.

This time Lena took me down a long service tunnel that intersected many of the main ones, including my original running track. Course it was all just black to me. Everything's black. Jimmy reckons he's starting to see something, that his eyes are adjusting and he can pick out faint shapes, but I think he's imagining it. You do start to hear things differently though. To get these notions on size and shape. I mean, I could tell we were approaching another intersection with a main tunnel. There's just this sense of impending space, of freedom opening up to sound.

I was about to mention it, to tell Lena what I could now 'see', when I suddenly noticed this faint orange glow in front of us. I grabbed her and pulled her back before she could step out into the main tunnel, though actually, I think she'd been about to do the same to me.

We retreated a couple of paces, the glow starting to grow on the wall opposite, the sound of muffled footsteps and whispering coming our way.

Lena tapped me on the shoulder, passing me the container of water. I mean, can you imagine? Two vicious little drugheads approaching, armed with machetes, looking to hack us to pieces, and there I was lying in wait for them with a garden tool and a container of water. What sort of big guy was I, for chrissake? Krusty the Clown?

Lena stepped back a pace so I had a good swing. I mean, as dumb as it might sound I had to get it just right. Miss that torch of theirs and it'd probably be the last thing I ever did.

I waited 'til the very final moment, just as the light of their flame began to swing down the service tunnel, then leapt out and threw everything at them.

I had an instant to see the look of alarm, of astonishment, on their faces as the water arced through the air and then hit the flame. For a moment it crackled, it spluttered, it even flared back into life, but then finally it went out.

'Get him!' the tall kid screamed.

It was crazy. I was so intent on making sure I had the right angle for my throw that I lost my bearings, and when I turned to leap back into the service tunnel I cannoned straight into the wall and ended up on the ground. Someone must've taken a swing at me with a machete, 'cuz I heard it smash against the brickwork only inches above my head. Again the tall kid yelled for the other to get me, but they became confused who was where and the second kid kept screaming to the tall one not to hit him by mistake. I stayed where I was, prostrate on the ground, wondering what the hell to do, when suddenly I felt Lena tugging at my arm. I was just about to follow her when the second kid lit a match.

They saw us, raised their machetes and advanced our way, but a gust of wind blew the match out. Both of them cursed, the tall one shouting for another match to be lit and I took the chance to leap at them.

There was a confused struggle, legs and arms going everywhere, a lot of yelling and screaming, and I heard the box of matches fall to the ground. Then someone ran off, and whoever I had hold of, I guess it was the smaller kid, broke free and backed away. However, in the brief instant that the match had been lit, I'd seen enough of the tunnel to know he was backing himself into an alcove.

He started shouting at me from out of the darkness.

'Come on! Come on!' he screamed, daring me to come closer, the sound of his machete swishing back and forth. *'Come on!'*

I hesitated for a moment, wondering what the hell to do, one step nearer I could be cut in two, then Lena's voice came to me from out of the dark.

'Left . . . Right . . . Left.'

I didn't know what the hell she was talking about. It didn't make no sense. But she kept saying it over and over.

'Left . . . Right . . . Left.'

And finally I realised. It was the swing of his machete. She was telling me what direction it was going in.

'Now, Clancy. Now!'

And I knew what she meant. It was the moment when the machete reached the end of its sweep, that split second when I had a chance to jump him. I stood there, listening to its swish through the air, hearing her words. Jesus, I had to trust her. Get it wrong and I was about to dive straight into the wild slash of that fearsome blade.

'Left . . . Right . . . Left . . . Right. *Now, Clancy!*'

I just leapt forward as hard and low as I could, my eyes closed, expecting at any moment to feel that machete slice straight across my face, or take the top of my head off or something. But I hit the kid so hard I slammed him up against the wall, crushing the air out of him like a burst paper bag, and he collapsed to the ground.

I jumped up, lit one of my matches, retrieved his machete and thrust it into his face. Not that he was in any shape to be concerned. He was just lying there, a look of real panic on his face, trying to get some air back into his crushed lungs. Before he could, I grabbed some twine and with Lena's help, tied him up.

'We'll put him with his friend. Then we'd better go back up,' I said, concerned about where the tall kid might've gone.

When we got to the storeroom and unlocked the door the first kid was starting to come round. We didn't hang about. I just threw the other one on top of him and left them to it. Thank the Lord, both door and lock are solid and secure. The last thing we needed was for the tall kid to find them and let them out.

You could hear the fear in Jimmy and Delilah's voices when they challenged our approach. And the relief when they realised it was us.

'What happened?' the little guy asked.

'Two of them are locked up in one of the storerooms,' I told them. 'We lost the tall one though.'

There was a pause.

'So what do we do?' Delilah asked, the thought of him lurking down there, waiting to spring out when you least expected it, unsettling her as much as it did the rest of us.

'I don't know,' I sighed.

'Maybe we should just wait him out,' Lena suggested. 'He can't stay down there forever.'

In the end, and in the absence of any other suggestions, we agreed with her. I mean, looking for him down there, on his own, that lanky vicious sonofabitch, I really didn't fancy it.

For some time we stayed there in the dark at the foot of the exit tunnel, speaking little and in whispers, occasionally spooking each other by hearing all kinds of sounds, 'til finally Jimmy asked the question that maybe should've been asked long ago.

'Why don't we put the lights on?'

I stopped for a moment. Yeah, why didn't we put the lights on? There was no advantage to being in the dark anymore. It might even make us feel a bit more comfortable.

'Lena?' I asked, knowing she was the one person it might put at a disadvantage.

'Why not? I'll go and do it if you like. I can bring us back something to eat. We could be here for a while.' She set off, her soft footsteps soon fading into the darkness.

'What are we going to do with the two you locked up?' Delilah asked.

'I don't know. Keep them, I s'pose.'

'Forever?'

'For the moment,' I replied.

Jimmy sighed, 'How do we know they haven't told other kids they were coming here?'

'We don't. But I kind of figure that if others had known, they would be with them, so maybe these three had a good reason for coming alone.'

There was a pause. Delilah sighed. 'We should kill them,' she said.

'*What?*' Jimmy gasped.

'You heard!' she cried angrily.

I guess you couldn't blame her. There are plenty of old folk who, given the chance, would take revenge for all the years we've been terrorised, all the horrendous things that've been done. And it would've solved our problem. But it's like I said before, Mother Nature plants this idea deep down inside that no matter what children say or do, we share a common responsibility. Or maybe a common guilt, I don't know. Either way, I knew I couldn't kill them in cold blood. And Jimmy was appalled by the idea.

'Jesus, Lile!' he cried. 'That is so uncool!'

'What did they come to do?' she spat. 'Why did they break in here, if it wasn't to kill us?'

In the face of such intense rage, the little guy went quiet. It was hard to put up an argument in their defence at any time, let alone now. He sighed and tried to change the subject. 'I wish Lena would get the lights on,' he muttered. 'I can't stand this much more.'

It was only when he said it that I realised how long she'd been. I mean, I wasn't worried or anything. The tall kid was way down below; she was off in the living area. It was just weird not having her there, not being able to account for her for a few minutes.

'I'll go see what she's up to,' I said.

I made my way down the tunnel, expecting to hear her voice at any moment, that she would suddenly come to me out of the darkness the way she does, but I arrived there without a sign of her.

I paused for a moment, now feeling just that little bit uneasy. Maybe she'd gone down to the garden for something to eat? I was just about to head off in that direction when I remembered about turning on the lights. As I moved towards the switch, a voice suddenly came to me from out of the darkness.

'Clancy!' Lena whispered.

I tell you, it frightened the very life out of me. Not 'cuz it had been so sudden, not 'cuz it had come out of the darkness in front of me, but the tone in her voice. It didn't sound like her at all.

'Lena! . . . *Jesus!*' I cried. 'You frightened the hell out of me.'

There was a disturbingly long pause.

'Strike a match, Clancy.'

'Why?' I asked, but I was already doing it, fumbling with the box, dropping one or two on the ground. I mean, I knew something was wrong, I just didn't know what.

The match flared and I saw her in a moment of brilliance. Up against the wall, next to the light switch, the tall kid behind her wrenching back her head by her hair, his machete pressed against her throat.

I can't describe how that felt. I mean, this . . . *thing* was in front of me. This grotesque tangle of human limbs. Parts I knew and loved, parts that were strange and repelled me. And two pairs of eyes. One sighted with blood and a need for senseless slaughter, the other lost and helpless, as if gazing at some faraway horizon where she wanted to be.

I been in a lot of bad situations in my life. Ones where people I cared about were under threat. I once saved Mr Meltoni's life, and his wife's, and took a couple of bullets for my trouble, but this was something else. I'm a man of action. That's what I do. I act. I'm physical. I barely got a brain in my head. *You* do the thinking, then you set *me* in motion. But my first reaction when I saw her like that was to want to just stand there and scream. That machete shoved up against her neck, pushing into her flesh, a fine edge of blood seeping round its blade. That woman is everything to me. There has never been, and never will be, another one like her; and now this worthless punk, who ain't even fit to belong to the same species, could just jerk his hand across her throat and she's gone.

And you want to know something? Something truly sickening? He read it in my eyes. He saw what the situation was and started to laugh. Taunting me, pretending to do it, building up to that moment, that flick of the wrist as he sliced her open and her life gushed out onto the ground. And there was nothing I could do. Nothing. And suddenly I found myself pleading with him. Tears streaming down my face . . . *Me! The Big Guy!* Weeping and begging this little punk. Lena called out to me, told me not to, as if, no matter what the circumstances, she couldn't bear to see me that way, but I couldn't help myself.

The match I was holding burnt my fingers and I fumbled to strike another. I died in those few seconds. Over and over. When I finally got it lit he was starting to inch away in the direction of the main hall, still holding Lena as tightly as ever, a trickle of blood now sliding down her neck.

I've never been so scared in all my life. I mean, I could threaten, I could tell him what I'd do if he hurt her, I could cause him more pain than he'd ever known, but what good would that be if Lena lay dead?

'Put it down,' he said, indicating the machete I was still carrying.

I just let it fall from my hand. Tell the truth, I forgot I had it. I couldn't believe how stupid I'd been. It had never even occurred to me he might be able to find his way back through the flooded tunnels to the garden and the living area. Especially without a torch.

He backed away a little further, kicking a couple of cooking pots out of his way, still pulling on Lena's hair.

'Get back!' he shouted, and even though I hadn't moved an inch, I took a couple of steps away.

I was trying to calm myself, to think what I could do, but with Lena in that position, I just couldn't. I thought about Jimmy and Delilah, how I could attract their attention without him knowing. I thought about the lighting switch behind him – it was something he didn't know – but I couldn't see an advantage in any of it.

He shuffled a few more steps away, the light from my match making his eyes glow red. I made a slight movement to follow, but he cursed me and wrenched Lena's head to one side, the cut on her neck bleeding that bit more freely.

'No! Please!' I begged again. 'Don't hurt her! Please!'

I mean, I hated myself for doing it, but I couldn't stop. He was taking Lena away from me, with every stride threatening to end her life. Again my match went out and I struck another.

'*Please!*' I cried.

He shook his head, a really mean smile coming to his face. 'Don't you know what she's worth?'

I didn't know what he meant at first. I wasn't thinking that straight. Eventually it hit me. De Grew had put a price on her head. Money or drugs. That's why there were only three of them. They wanted it all for themselves.

He went to back away again and slightly stumbled on some uneven ground, almost losing his balance. Lena had a split second to attempt to wriggle free. She half turned and tried to drive her knee into his groin, but he was so much taller than her that she missed and in an instant he had hold of her again.

I screamed out. I knew that was it. You can see it in someone's eyes when they're about to kill. He snarled at her, like it just wasn't worth the trouble of keeping her alive, then jerked her head back, lay her throat open and went to drag his machete across it.

'No!'

In that precise moment a gust of wind swept down the tunnel and blew out my match.

'Lena!'

There was an awful slicing sound, of a blade cutting through flesh, and I knew it meant death. I went crazy. Rushing forward, calling out over and over, fumbling for her in the darkness. Someone tried to grab hold of me, to grip me around my neck, and I lashed out. Then a voice spoke.

'Clancy, it's all right! It's all right!'

I was so confused all I could do was hold on to her, wrap my body around her and protect her from whatever further blow was about to fall.

It was only the sudden flickering light of their candle that alerted me to Jimmy and Delilah arriving. I looked around, trying to work out what the hell had happened, where the tall kid was, and saw his body lying on the ground. Still I didn't know what happened. Not 'til Jimmy turned on the lights.

I was right, there had been a death, but it hadn't been Lena's. The kid was laying there, his head sliced open, part of his insides oozing out. I looked at Lena, thinking she must've done it, but she looked as confused as me.

It was Jimmy's slightly guilty look upwards that finally alerted us to what happened.

'Shit!' he muttered, staring at his generator.

It was that damn propeller. Those long whirling blades. The kid was so tall that as he'd been backing away, the same wind that had blown out my match had sent the blades spinning and he'd walked straight into them.

Jesus, what a way to go. To some degree, it was almost appropriate: his death was every bit as sad and senseless as his life.

We buried him down below, in one of the collapsing tunnels, right at the very end, so that, as the bricks fell, they'd cover him. I even put up a little cross. God knows why. I'm sure he wouldn't have wanted it, but it just seemed right.

Not that anyone grieved, not for him, even if he was little more than a child. Maybe we reflected a little. Maybe we wondered where he came from, who his parents had been, why he ended up that way. But we've done all that before. A long time ago. Now I'm not sure there's any point.

As for the two we got locked up down below, well, they're another matter. What the hell are we going to do with them? No way can we let them go, but does that mean we have to keep them forever? I'm pretty sure no one's going to come looking for them, that what I said was right; they were bounty hunters who wanted to keep all the reward for themselves. But having them down there, no matter how securely locked away, ain't going to do a great deal for our peace of mind. And who wants to be their jailers, anyway? Feeding them, looking after them, it don't make any sense. And yet, the way things are, what other choice do we have?

CHAPTER FOURTEEN

It wasn't until late in the afternoon, after something to eat and a little sleep, that Jimmy and me went down to take a look at our two captives. We weren't expecting any trouble, but the little guy insisted on carrying one of their machetes – more, I suspect, for his peace of mind than anything else.

I felt kind of nervous as I was unlocking that door, like we'd set a trap and didn't know what we'd caught. I kicked it right back on its hinges, holding my candle up to give the maximum amount of light in case they tried anything, but both of them were just slumped motionless on the floor. My first impression was that they looked a little pale, maybe even a touch scared. I guess what I'm trying to say is, they looked a bit like children.

It wasn't hard to work out which one I hit with the door. He had a bump on his forehead so big you could've used it for advertising. I guess it was that, and the fact that he was younger and smaller than the other one, that made him look the sorrier of the two. He was also quite normal-looking for an Island kid. I s'pose it's the life they lead, but they tend to have really hard little faces, even the very young ones, but he was slightly different. Mixed race, of course, like most of them;

his brown eyes peering out through long, matted hair giving him the look of a stray mongrel.

His companion on the other hand was more typical; his acne-covered face as sharp and pointed as the machete he'd wielded. He also had half an ear missing and just behind it a bald patch where his close-cropped mousey-brown hair refused to regrow, which must've been the legacy of some fight or other. Both of them were dressed in rags, had dirt ingrained so heavily it seemed to be in the actual pigment of their skin, and like I said before, reeked of the tips so strongly it was as much as you could do to share that confined space with them.

And yet, I don't know, seeing them there like that, kind of lost and forlorn, almost made me feel embarrassed. The little one couldn't have been any more than eleven or twelve, and the other, well, maybe a couple of years older. You couldn't imagine them doing anyone harm; you couldn't imagine why we had to lock them up. But I'd have bet you these two had killed and many times.

For a long while there was silence. For the life of me I couldn't think what to say to them. 'D'you want something to eat?' I eventually asked.

Neither of them replied. In fact, you would've sworn I hadn't spoken, that I didn't even exist.

'Well?' I said. Again they didn't reply. I turned to Jimmy. 'Not big on conversation.'

While my back was turned the little one suddenly leapt to his feet and ran at me, trying to push and wriggle his way through and out the door. Jimmy slammed it shut and stood there with his machete raised, looking more frightened than threatening, but I managed to get a hold on the kid and toss him back.

'For chrissake!' I shouted, more indignant than angry – I mean, we're old, not senile, dammit. 'Get back.'

He slumped back down with his companion and for what seemed like an awfully long time we were on the receiving end of a very hostile silence. I tell you, it's weird. We're only a couple of generations or so apart, but you'd swear they were of a totally different species. I couldn't think of one thing they might respond to. I gestured to Jimmy that maybe we should go, and the two of us left them still sitting on the floor gazing at nothing.

The one thing that had been obvious to Jimmy and me while we were in there was that we needed somewhere more suitable to hold them. Something resembling a proper cell. A little further down the tunnel there was another, slightly larger storeroom, full of sand and cement, planks and scaffolding, that we immediately set about clearing and converting. We put up a wall of heavy-gauge wire mesh from floor to ceiling, cutting and welding in a padlocked door and a hatch for serving food. A couple of plastic containers took care of the need for water and a toilet, and we finished up by fitting extra locks on the outside of the door.

The following evening we transferred them over, insisting on giving them food, though they still didn't show the slightest sign of an appetite.

It took us a foolish amount of time to work out why. If Lena hadn't said something we'd probably still be wondering. I returned to the living area with their dishes, the food again untouched, and Delilah started grumbling.

'What a waste,' she complained.

'We can reheat it,' I told her.

'Yeah, yeah. We can do a lot of things.'

Lena threw some wood on the fire, sighing heavily. 'Clancy, they're not going to eat anything.'

'Why not?'

'It's not food they want.'

Delilah chuckled to herself, as if she knew that all along.

I stared at Lena, suddenly feeling that familiar old-age obsolescence – that I was out of my depth again. 'Drugs?' I eventually asked.

'Course.'

'So what do we do?'

She shook her head and sighed again, as if I had no idea what I was getting into. 'Nail them to the floor,' she replied.

Couple of days later I began to see what she meant. At last the two kids started talking to us, but in such a way we could've well done without it. They screamed abuse, frothing at the mouth, demanding we let them go, and when we wouldn't they went even more crazy. Throwing themselves at the wire mesh, hanging off it like frenzied animals, baring their teeth, making all sorts of vicious threats. You wouldn't believe it. Even though they were just little kids, even though they were locked up, it still left you feeling decidedly unnerved. All you wanted was for them to stop, be quiet, act in a way that was recognisably human.

One day, when they were particularly bad and Jimmy went in to change their crap container, they grabbed him and a scuffle broke out. I had to get in there and give the older one a real clout before I could drag Jimmy away. Even then they managed to tip the entire contents of the container over him.

When Delilah saw him, smelling and stinking and looking all sorry for himself, she went crazy.

'Jesus Christ!' she ranted. 'Why are we carrying on with this? We all know what's gotta be done. Let's do it!'

There was a long pause. I hadn't heard Delilah lose her temper that way for a long time.

'Delilah,' Lena said soothingly, but she wouldn't listen to anyone.

'*No!* We can't keep them forever! You know we can't!'

'We can't just kill them,' Lena said.

'Why not? What other choice have we got?' Delilah challenged. 'You gonna look after them for the rest of your life?' Jimmy turned and skulked off down to the garden to clean himself up. 'Kill the little bastards!' she screamed, turning to hurry away after him.

Neither Lena nor me could find it in ourselves to speak. I mean, I knew Delilah hated them, I just hadn't appreciated how much.

Lena lowered herself down to sit cross-legged in front of the fire. 'We can't kill them,' she repeated.

I went and squatted down behind her, wrapping my arms around her so far it was like they went round twice. I knew why it was so important to her, that there was still enough of the Camp in her to identify with those two, but I was also afraid that after this long period of happiness and harmony in the tunnels, this situation just might tear us apart.

Day after day it went on. Going down there was like entering the forbidden wing of an asylum, sometimes they started screaming at you even before you unlocked the door. Spitting through the wire mesh, throwing food at you, coming out with stuff so sick it made you think something else must be speaking through them. A couple of times, I gotta be honest with you, it even went through my head that maybe Delilah was right. Maybe putting them out of their torment and misery was the kindest thing we could do. Then one morning I went down and everything had changed. They were utterly exhausted, their fury spent, and instead of screaming at me, they started to beg for their freedom.

The little one came over to the mesh on his hands and knees, pulling himself up by the wire, pleading with me, again reminding me of a stray dog.

'Please, let us go!' he begged. 'Please! Please!'

I just shook my head. 'Sorry.'

'Come on!' the other one howled at the ceiling. 'Let us out!'

'We can't let you out and you know it,' I told them.

'We won't tell anyone!'

'Honest! Honest, we won't!' the little one confirmed.

'We won't go to the Village again. Ever,' his sharp-faced companion added.

'Look! You're not going anywhere, so get used to it,' I told them.

And you know something? When they realised, when they saw how adamant I was, that there was no chance of changing my mind, they both burst into tears. I tell you, I just stood there and stared at them, their behaviour no more believable, no less extreme than it'd been before. I couldn't take any more. I walked out, leaving them to their wailing, the sound echoing all the way down the tunnel. It almost pulled at your heartstrings . . . until you remembered what it was they were really weeping for.

Couple of days later they both started to run a fever; doubled up with stomach cramps, vomiting, sweating so much that they left watery imprints on everything they touched. I had to keep taking them water. Gallons and gallons of it. Then they started hallucinating. Seeing all sorts of stuff. Calling you the names of people you didn't know, shouting at things and folk that weren't there, pulling demons out of their heads like pieces of glass from an accident victim.

Sure as hell it wasn't what we intended, but we didn't have a choice. Somehow we had to help them purge the crap from their systems. Thank the Lord, Lena knows something about it. Apparently De Grew mostly gives them 'bubbles' and 'flames'. I mean, shit, I don't know what that means to you, but it didn't mean a helluva lot to me. But that's what they were full of when they went up to the Village, when they did their killing and stuff, which, as far as I'm concerned, makes it a transfusion straight out of the Devil's veins.

Day after day it went on. Every time you unlocked that door you never knew what you'd find. Sometimes they were so spent they were almost comatose, lying on their sacks, staring out into some far dark corner of the universe. Other times they couldn't sit still for a moment, leaping all over the place, shouting at the top of their lungs.

The older one had a habit of headbutting the walls. It was nothing for me to walk in there and find blood pouring from his forehead, a line of impact points around the room. Both of them got in such a state racking body and mind that it even went through my head to go out and try to get them a little of what they so craved. The stuff their bodies had been deceived by – the drugs that they would willingly administer to themselves 'til it destroyed them.

Eventually, just when I think everyone – and that included Lena – was starting to despair, to wonder if we'd bitten off more than we could chew, their madness began to be interspersed with something else. Something more familiar. And at last there came the odd moment when you could see the slow rising of the human face.

I went down there one night to pick up their dishes and stuff and as I turned to leave the little kid spoke to me, normally, like I was a human being or something.

'What's your name?' he asked.

Before I could answer the other one turned and sneered, 'Big Guy!', probably 'cuz he heard Jimmy say it a few times.

'It ain't exactly my name,' I said, feeling a bit of a fake, like a champ who lost his crown years ago. Still, it was the first bit of normal conversation we had and I was eager to build on it. 'And you?'

'Arturo,' the little one told me, and when his companion refused to say anything, filled in for him. 'He's Gordie.'

'Hi, Arturo. Hi, Gordie,' I said, but the latter wasn't having any of it.

'Shut it!' he said to Arturo. 'We ain't talking to no old people.'

I went silent for a moment, not quite knowing where to go from there, but fortunately Arturo was his own little man.

'How old are you?' he asked, for the first time his big brown eyes reflected rather than absorbed the candlelight.

I hesitated for a moment, then decided to come straight out with it. 'Sixty-three.'

I tell you, they practically wet themselves. You'd have thought I just told them the funniest joke ever known to the human race. They simply couldn't believe anyone could live that long.

'*Sixty-three!*' Arturo cried, throwing himself round the cell, shrieking at the top of his voice, falling helplessly to the floor and rolling over and over. Gordie was more restrained, laughing partly at me and partly at the antics of Arturo.

I just stood there, not saying a word, waiting for them to calm down. When they did you could tell it wasn't going to be for long.

'You smell,' Arturo informed me.

'I smell?' I said, immediately opting to meet him on his own level. 'Ever smelled yourself? A skunk wouldn't keep you company.'

'I don't smell!' he replied, surprisingly indignant.

'Matter of opinion.'

'I don't!'

'How old are the others?' Gordie asked, more aware of where the real serious mocking lay here.

'Ask them.'

'That little old guy must be a hundred,' he sneered.

'Two hundred!' Arturo cried.

I stood there for a while, listening to their rekindled shrieking, Arturo upping and upping Jimmy's age and squealing louder each time. They might've calmed down a bit, but they still seemed crazy to me. I wanted to try to relate to them somehow. To prove we weren't so very different. But maybe that was my first mistake.

*

Despite the difficulties, the friction the kids were creating, Delilah still occasionally threatening to take a machete and go down there and 'solve the problem', life in the tunnels gradually settled into a new routine. In fact, it wasn't so very different from the old one, just a few extra duties.

Jimmy went back to playing with his power supply, running a lead all the way down to his workshop. I think he had it in mind to go through all those computer bits he brought back and see if he could build one working unit. Which sounded like a pretty tall order to me, but according to him he was one of the last great computer prodigies. He could hack in anywhere. At the age of thirteen he was headhunted by the government after leaving messages with every major head of state in the world announcing his birthday. There ain't nothing he don't know about those things. Or so he says. And these days, I'm more of a mind to believe him.

As for me, well, if Lena don't need me, if there's no fetching or carrying or shoring up of tunnels to be done, I divide my time between lifting weights, running and going down to see those kids. Don't ask me why. They don't exactly make me feel welcome. Some days it's just plain uncomfortable, what with them either refusing to speak, or making stupid personal comments that end up with them shrieking and giggling and falling all over the place.

Couple of times Arturo has tried to get a more normal conversation going, but Gordie just tells him to shut up. He's a real mean little sonofabitch. Everything's confrontation; all language is war. Trying to have a conversation with him's like blowing up balloons for a knife thrower.

Nevertheless, I still sit there, hour after hour, hoping that somehow I'll win Arturo over a little and maybe Gordie'll follow. Not that I'd put money on it. Not on either count. I mean, they couldn't be more blunt and barefaced about how they feel about old people; how they deserve to die and should've been exterminated long ago. And if it's not that, if it's not the irrational hate, the blind prejudice, then, as I say, it's the endless teasing and laughter.

One afternoon Lena walked in and caught them at it and decided to intervene.

'What did you say?' she asked Arturo, hearing the tail end of yet another bout of merciless mocking.

He hesitated for a moment, a little taken aback by her obvious anger. 'He smells. Can't you smell him? I think he might be dying.'

'More like he's dead,' Gordie chipped in. 'Starting to rot.'

The two of them squealed with laughter, jostling each other from side to side, but they were in for a real shock. For a few moments Lena stood there silently, as if letting the irritation build up inside her, then she erupted. 'If anyone smells round here, it's you two! You're damn near stinking out the whole place!'

There was a momentary pause. They both stared at each other, then back at her, as if one of their own had committed an act of treachery.

'You reek of the tips,' she continued. 'And you know what? It's time we did something about it.' She turned to me. 'Clancy, go and get Jimmy, will you?'

I paused for a moment, as curious as the kids to know what she had in mind, then went off to fetch the little guy.

Course, he wasn't happy about it. I had to practically drag him away from that barricade of boards and chips he'd built up around him. On the other hand, maybe he just had a premonition about what we were letting ourselves in for.

As soon as we got back to the storeroom Lena unlocked the cell. 'Come on,' she said. The kids immediately backed away.

With Jimmy and me on escort duty, both of them were marched

up to the garden, forcibly stripped of their clothing and made to take a bath in one of the water barrels.

I tell you, I been in a few wrestling matches in my time, but never anything like that. Little Arturo cursed and swore and wriggled like some hydrophobic cat, spreading his limbs out, gripping onto the sides of the barrel, arching his back and refusing to be pushed into the water. But that was as nothing compared with Gordie. He saw the whole process as a direct attack on his manhood and went crazy, taking a couple of swings at me, almost wrenching off Jimmy's ponytail, only ending up inside the barrel when we enlisted Delilah's help. Her and Jimmy holding his legs, me his arms and Lena just washing whatever she could.

It was the first time Delilah had seen either of them since the day they broke in, and no matter how aggressive Gordie was, how much he cursed us, she was his equal.

'Shut your foul little mouth!' she told him. 'I ain't taking that from you.'

'You old bitch!' he shouted. 'I'll kill you!'

'Yeah, well, if it was left to me, that's what we would've done with you long ago,' she replied.

They went at it hammer and tongs the whole time. I never heard such talk, and I wouldn't want to say who came out on top. And yet, I'll tell you something, when it was all over, when Gordie stopped fighting, when he was sitting there in that water barrel, shivering from the cold, for all his toughness, for all he knew and had done, he was just a child and Delilah saw that as clearly as anyone.

Why that one forced act of familiarity, bathing those kids, seeing them naked, should start to change things, I don't know, but it did. 'Cuz I gotta tell you, from that day on, the strangest thing happened. Gradually, what we saw as a terrible intrusion, as a threat to our lives, has begun to seem more like one of its attractions. I've been going down there more and more. So has Lena. Sitting on the floor, coaxing and calling to them, doing our best to get some kind of conversation going. Even Delilah's softened a little. I mean, she don't visit them or nothing, but she did stop talking about killing them, or getting all aggressive every time they're mentioned. Which, I gotta tell you, these days is pretty often.

I still think Lena's the only one they feel comfortable with. Probably 'cuz of her age, 'cuz they can identify with her background. Mind you, she did take one helluva dive in their opinion when they worked out her and me were a couple. They went on about it for days. Describing me to her at great length, saying how saggy and wrinkled my face was, how grey and thin my hair, in the belief that it could only be 'cuz she couldn't see me that she was participating in such a sick arrangement.

Tell the truth, a couple of times I got a bit upset about it. But she always answered them in exactly the same manner, by telling them that none of that mattered, not in the least, not when she loved me as much as she did. Which might make you feel a degree queasy, but I tell you, it made me feel a whole lot better. As if, no matter what they threw at me, she'd always be there to make sure it didn't hit.

How long it would've gone on like that, one day better, two days worse, and vice versa, I don't know. But eventually I had a real breakthrough with them. And the irony was, it was through the thing they most despised me for: my age. I was down there one day – I don't even remember how it got started, I think I mentioned Mr Meltoni – and the fact that his name had come up a couple of times before prompted Arturo to ask me who he was. I mean, I think they'd worked out he was my boss, but they just assumed in a factory or a shop or something. When they realised the nature of the business I was involved in, they suddenly got a whole lot more interested.

'Were you a gangster?' Arturo asked, a little wide-eyed.

I shrugged. 'If that's what you want to call it.'

'Yah!' Gordie sneered dismissively, though not with complete conviction.

'Tell us about it,' Arturo said.

'What's to tell? I worked for a guy called Mr Meltoni. Don't mean a lot to you, I guess, but on the Mainland it'd probably still get a reaction. Even now.'

'Bet you never killed anyone,' Gordie said, in a way I didn't altogether care for.

I hesitated for a moment. It was the last question I wanted to answer, but the first I knew would be asked. 'Unfortunately, I did.'

'How many?' he asked, as if we were in competition.

'I don't know. Never kept score. Not exactly proud of it. But then . . . I guess I didn't know any better.'

They went quiet for a moment, like they were digesting that, like they weren't sure how they felt about it.

'Did you have a gun?' Arturo asked.

'Yeah. Didn't use it very often though. Mr Meltoni didn't like violence any more than I did. Only to show we meant business. To put someone in their place.'

'Who?' Arturo asked. 'Who did you put in their place?'

I really didn't want to dwell on the violence, but I knew they would, that I had to get it out of the way. Mind you, once I did exhaust the subject, once I'd gone through every last detail, at least it would make it easier to go on to other things.

I spent the whole afternoon down there. In fact, if it hadn't been for Jimmy being sent down to remind me it was dinner time I'd probably still be there. I told them all sorts of tales of the Mainland – or the Mainland as it used to be. The various larger-than-life characters, the different nationalities that dominated the neighbourhoods. What we did, what we stood for and believed in. I even explained about old people being the victims of circumstance, of propaganda, and not the cause of everything that had gone wrong. Though, to tell the truth, they didn't seem that interested. Maybe they don't know the story. Or maybe they've just inherited their attitudes from others and never bothered to question them. All I do know is that, by some means or other, I managed to connect with those kids.

And you wanna know something else? Maybe the most amazing thing of all? After I'd been talking to them for a while I saw this light starting to come into their eyes. This expression that I haven't seen for God knows how long. They were getting the look about them. Honestly. I know it when I see it and they were getting the look all right. But this was *kids*! Kids getting the look about *me*! I tell you, I couldn't believe it. But yeah, as far as they were concerned, I was someone again. Someone to look up to. I guess what I'm trying to say is: I'm the Big Guy.

CHAPTER FIFTEEN

It never really occurred to me how obsessed I'd become with those kids. How an urge to make their intrusion sit more comfortably with everyone had been completely preoccupying me, 'til that unlikely transformation looked like it might take place. The moment it did, my thoughts turned to other things. In particular to something that probably shouldn't have been neglected for so long: what was going on up-top?

Yet again that familiar concern resumed its nagging, and when one night over dinner Lena mentioned that the only food she missed in the tunnels was fish, I saw my opportunity.

I volunteered to go out the next morning and see if I could catch her some. I mean, I tried to keep it low-key, like that was the priority, but the others saw straight through me.

'Clancy!' Lena and Delilah chorused, as if they didn't have to put their fears into any more words than that.

'Yeah, Big Guy,' Jimmy agreed. 'Give me another week or so with this computer, I'll come with you.'

'Look, I'm just going fishing, that's all. Just a regular guy going fishing. What's wrong with that?'

Course, none of them believed me, but I think they were all in need of the same reassurance I was, and for that reason, though they made a lot of warning noises, no one actually said I shouldn't go.

Early next morning, I reluctantly eased Lena's warm grip away from me, shushed her sleepy words of caution and made my way up to the entrance and out into the growing light of day.

Even with the sun barely up, after a prolonged period in the tunnels, the light could still damn near fry the eyes out of your sockets. It took a good five minutes for them to stop hurting and the tears to stop streaming down my face. I stumbled away from the entrance as quickly as I could, grateful that my few working senses were informing me nothing was amiss, and made my way over to the old jetty.

I'd already decided I wasn't going to go looking for trouble. In fact, I was going to do exactly what I promised: sit down by the water, try to catch a fish or two, but at the same time keep an eye out for anything untoward going on.

Fishing always has had a reputation for being a thankless pursuit, but I tell you, out there, it'd be easier to try hooking the stars out of the sky. Apparently it was a prime spot years ago – bass, fluke, blackfish, bluefish – but now the water's become so polluted that even if you are lucky enough to catch something, it's going to have a couple of heads or no eyes or something. I mean, when I was first on the Island, a length of fishing line was seen as standard equipment, but now, even with the amount of time we got on our hands, fishing's seen as a terrible waste of it.

As I approached the jetty, I noticed the trench I dug all those weeks ago was still there. Not the cable, of course, that was long gone. Over to the Mainland, proceeds to the coffers of the Wastelords. Not that I give a damn. I mean, I don't know what they got for it, but what it inadvertently brought me was priceless and always will be.

The winter storms had certainly taken their toll on the old jetty.

As I walked out on its rotting and twisted planks I could feel it swaying away beneath my feet. Nevertheless, I found a comfortable spot leaning up against one of the more secure-looking support posts, and taking out a bagful of maggots I extracted from a dead pigeon in the garden, I baited my hook and dropped it into the dull grey ocean gently swelling beneath me.

I mean, I already said, fishing ain't my idea of recreation and never will be, but just at that moment the Island seemed so quiet and unchallenging that I was kind of melting into it. And, of course, it was quite special to be outside again.

Couple of hours later, with no fish nor activity to interrupt a peace I was getting a little bored by, I became a bit drowsy. After that, I guess I must've nodded off.

Next thing I knew I was jolted awake by the crashing of an earthquake, by the whole world vibrating around me. Took me a while to realise where I was and that it wasn't the world that was moving, but just the old jetty, vibrating to the pounding of heavy footsteps.

I turned to see five big guys – in their twenties, mean-looking, wearing those city-council regulation red overalls Wastelords were so fond of – marching down on me. I tell you, my heart damn near burst out my ribs.

'You!' one of them shouted. 'What you doing?'

'Fishing,' I mumbled, for some reason feeling obliged to get to my feet.

'There ain't no fish here,' he told me.

'Can be. If you're lucky.'

He paused, looking me up and down. I don't know, maybe it's still there, no matter how old I'm getting. For sure there was something about me that made him uneasy.

'D'you know Lena?' he suddenly asked.

My stomach seemed to shrivel and freeze. Just for a fleeting moment our eyes met. I mean, I wouldn't advise it, not if you want to stay healthy, but I couldn't help myself.

'No,' I answered.

Still he glared. He wasn't as tall as some of his companions, but heavier-built and thick-necked, of Oriental extraction by the look of him.

'I don't like you,' he told me.

'I don't like him either,' agreed this shaven-headed thug behind him.

'I'm just fishing,' I told them, innocently.

Five pairs of eyes continued to burn into me, wishing me all manner of ill, and I'll tell you, if it wasn't for those things up there I reckon I would've been beaten to a pulp and sold off as fish bait.

'You don't know her?' the Oriental one persisted, as if he didn't believe a word I said.

'Who?'

'Lena.'

'No. Who is she?'

He took a couple of paces closer, so near, in fact, I could actually smell his fetid breath. 'Don't you fuck with us,' he said. 'Right?'

'I'm not.'

'You're as good as dead. And so is she.'

I just lowered my gaze to my feet. Nothing I said here was going to improve the situation.

There was another pause, I could feel them glaring still, wondering what to do about me, until the Oriental guy turned and began to saunter slowly back down the jetty and the others followed.

I thought that was it, that they'd leave me in peace, but when they reached dry land they stopped, talking amongst themselves, looking back at me.

I did my best to ignore them, going back to my fishing, resuming my seat, pretending all I cared about was urging some fish to slurp up the big fat maggot on the end of my hook, but it wasn't easy. Not with what I had going through my head. They were still looking for Lena. Still scouring this small island inch by inch. Jesus, how long could it take? Gordie and Arturo had found us. Who was going to be next?

I turned and stole a quick glance over, the five of them still lurking at the end of the jetty, still shooting the occasional glare. God help us if it's these guys.

As I was sitting there, trying to look all peaceful yet preoccupied, the now almost familiar Infinity Dragonfly made its way over from the Mainland. Jesus, what do they want? What do they know? I watched as it flew slowly around the Island, grateful for the interruption, for something else to look at. However, when it reached the Old City, it suddenly stopped, hovering in mid-air as if looking for something. A few moments later it moved on, but only to stop again, hanging there, slowly rotating through three hundred and sixty degrees.

Infinity had been at the forefront of the propaganda that circulated before we got sent out here. Doing specials about selfish old people with no money who were determined to drag hard-working families down. A lot of folk thought they were in collusion with the government, that there was something sinister about them. For sure they wielded an unhealthy amount of influence, and now, apparently, even more.

Eventually, whoever was flying that thing decided they'd seen enough and headed back towards the Mainland, leaving me to my bobbing line and hostile spectators. For almost an hour it went on, both of us pretending we weren't in a stand-off, 'til I realised they weren't going to leave, that I had no choice but to pack up my things and make my way back along the jetty.

Just for a moment, the Oriental-looking guy blocked my path. 'You're dead, and so is she,' he repeated.

I just shrugged, even half smiled, like I didn't have a clue what he was talking about, or maybe was a little simple or something, then continued on my way.

It was only then I realised why they'd hung around: they wanted to know which direction I was going to take. I had no choice but to head off towards the Village, to pretend I still lived there. I hadn't gone more than twenty or thirty paces before I realised they were following. Shit. Now what was I going to do?

I kept walking, trying to look as relaxed as possible, slowing a couple of times to look at something in the ocean, giving them every chance to walk by, but they didn't take it. I mean, they weren't making a big thing of it, you'd almost think it was coincidence we were on the same path, but I knew they were as aware of me as I was of them.

When I reached the Village I turned down one of the rows and once again they followed. Now I really was in trouble. Where the hell was I going to go? I wandered slowly on, glancing behind me every now and then, checking they were still there. I saw this group of villagers ahead of me and took the opportunity to stop and see what was going on. Problem was, no sooner had I stopped, than they noticed the approaching Wastelords and immediately scattered.

For a moment I was left awkwardly hanging there. I pretended I knew this couple that were heading off and tagged along behind them, immediately arousing their suspicions. The woman didn't say anything, but you could see she didn't like it, especially when she looked behind and saw the following Wastelords. She started walking quicker, her partner doing the same, but I stuck with them.

For the life of me, I couldn't see what I was going to do. The moment these two reached their lean-to and went inside, I was lost. Still, I kept with them, saying stuff they ignored, reacting and smiling every now and then as if they'd answered me.

In the end, it was the Wastelords themselves who saved me. Or rather, their reputation. The sight of those five guys swaggering through the Village created considerable panic. When I turned down another row and the Villagers saw them following along behind me, they all staggered to their feet, running this way and that, eager to get away. Amongst all the confusion I was able to slip between two lean-tos, through to the next row and scamper away.

I mean, I don't think they know anything. They were just out to scare me. The way they scare everyone. And to some degree, I gotta admit, they were successful. It was my first real close-up face-to-face confrontation with Wastelords, and I can see why they put the fear of God into people. Those guys practically ooze evil, as if they been majoring in it all their lives, as if they've never known anything else. Which, I guess, ain't that far off the truth.

It took me forever to get back to the tunnels. I had to keep scurrying and hiding, lying low for minutes at a time, checking my surroundings over and over before I made a further move. I mean, let's face it, there would be nothing more unforgivable than leading those bastards to Lena.

God knows how long I hung around near the entrance, too scared to make that final dash. It was only when I realised how late it was getting that I scuttled over and heaved the door open, stepping through to find Lena waiting for me.

'Where you been?' she demanded.

'Told you. Fishing,' I attempted to lie. 'Didn't catch a thing.'

'Clancy, you been waiting over there for a couple of hours. I been imagining all sorts of stuff. Now, where you been?'

I sighed to myself, knowing I didn't have much choice but to tell her. 'De Grew's still looking for you,' I admitted. 'I had a run-in with some of his boys.' She gave out with this little tortured groan, like a weight returned to her shoulders had pushed it out of her. 'It was nothing. Just them trying to frighten up whoever they met. They don't know anything.'

She never replied, just fell silent, staying that way all down the tunnel, as if she was thinking of something she'd prefer not to. It wasn't 'til we got to the main hall that she told me what.

'Clancy . . . It's only me they want. If I gave myself up, they'd never find all this. Nor you, or Jimmy and Delilah.'

I tell you, if I thought those Wastelords put the fear of God into me, it was nothing compared with what those few quiet words did.

'Lena!' I cried, my voice slightly trembling. 'You're not going anywhere! Not without me! And if you try, I tell you, I'll just follow. No matter where it might be.'

'Okay, Clancy. Okay,' she said, the soothing tone in her voice making me realise just how upset I must've sounded.

'That is not an option.'

'Okay!' she repeated.

'No way.'

I paused for a moment, shocked she'd even think such a thing, that there was such unpredictability in someone I knew so well. Then I grabbed hold of her, hugging her as tightly as I could, letting her know I would never ever let go.

I think it was probably that brush with the Wastelords that convinced me I needed to try even harder, to be that much more forgiving with Gordie and Arturo. I mean, when you consider that those are the sort of guys who've been bossing them most of their lives, their only role models, for chrissake, is it any wonder they've turned out as they have?

With every day I was continuing their education in the Mainland, of life as we knew it, as we thought it would always be. No longer just tales of the man 'Big Guy', but more and more of the boy Clancy. A couple of times I doubled them up talking about Ma and the minor acts of revenge she perpetrated on the old man. Like when she put a laxative in his favourite meal and he spent the evening, not watching the big game as he planned, but on the john; or hid an iron under the blanket for when he got home all drunk and aggressive and he threw a punch at her and ended up breaking his fist. Other times their reaction's been one of wonder at how different our young lives were to theirs. But apart from the odd mood when they don't seem to want to know, when they repeatedly go into their giggling fits over nothing and I end up shrugging and walking out, it seems as if they can't get enough. Almost as if I'm filling in blank spaces they've got somewhere inside them.

Course, they got their stories, too. Both of them have had short but brutal lives. Arturo was born out here, to a twelve-year-old mother who did her best to look after him but was careless with herself and ended up dying of pneumonia. After that he just hung on: to life, to the edge of the Camp, to anyone who didn't wish him harm. Gordie, on the other hand, came out from the Mainland. Yet another set of parents whose changing circumstances made them decide that a child wasn't worth jeopardising Mainland Status for. Course he talks tough about it, says he can't remember them and doesn't want to, and for once I believe him. Out here it's the ones who've got the most to remember who find it hardest to cope.

I mean, it's been painfully slow progress, sporadic at best. For a while they'd start to resemble children, you'd get up your hopes, then suddenly they'd revert back to being garbage urchins again. And yet, it almost seemed as if it was completed in one final night.

Jimmy took them their meal, but didn't return, and after a while I started to worry about him, that something had happened. I hurried on down there, wondering what the hell it could be, and walked in to find him telling the kids about when he was their age and used to spend all his time on a computer.

I tell you, he loves those damn things so much, and the more he talks about them, the brighter his eyes get, the more he becomes a kid himself. Arturo and Gordie were just sitting there, staring at him, as much in awe of his passion as what he was saying.

'I never seen a computer,' Arturo told him.

'I have,' Gordie said, in that slightly boastful way that always sets you wondering if he's telling the truth or not.

'I got one!' Jimmy told them. 'Got one here. Made it up from bits. Maybe, once I get it working properly, I'll show it to you.'

I didn't interrupt them, just found myself a place and sat down, enjoying the open-mouthed looks on Arturo and Gordie's faces. They were feeding on his life the same way they had mine. Presently, Lena appeared, also wondering what was going on, promptly placing herself down next to me. Twenty minutes later, and much to everyone's amazement, Delilah followed.

She was the only one they didn't know anything about, and after a while they asked her to tell them her story. At first she just shook her head, clamming up, refusing to say anything, but eventually, with us urging her on, she let go.

In a room full of sad tales, I guess hers was the saddest; and though she didn't linger over things, or talk about how much they hurt, you knew they must have.

When she finished this awful silence locked in on us, like it was going to stain us forever, but then, right out of the blue, Arturo said he wanted to play a game.

Tell the truth, I couldn't imagine anything less likely, but Delilah was all for it.

'Okay!' she croaked. 'Clancy, come on, open this door.'

'We're playing games?' I asked.

'Yeah! Why not?'

She came up with all sorts of suggestions – demons and dragons, hopscotch, musical chairs (or 'musical sacks', with her doing the singing) – stuff I thought was stupid even when I was a kid.

At first Gordie and me wouldn't have anything to do with it. Just sitting in the corner, feeling uncomfortable, making snide comments about the others as they scooted up and down and round the cell, but eventually they dragged us in.

I gotta say, that was one of the most enjoyable nights of my life. We played games, giggled and laughed, sang songs, everyone just mixing in. When the time came to leave, to go back up to the living area, it was one helluva jolt to be confronted by the prospect of locking those two in again.

I turned to Jimmy, to Lena, but they both avoided my gaze, like they didn't want any part of my dilemma. In the end, I just did it, without saying nothing, as if it was my duty and that was an end to it.

On the way back up through the tunnels the conversation inevitably turned to what we were going to do with them. With every day it was becoming more obvious that we couldn't keep them prisoners forever, but what alternatives did we have? Let them go free? Go back to the Camp? We might be able to trust them now, but a few weeks or months down the line – who knows? The only other possibility seemed to be to just unlock them, let them live down here with us and maybe keep a guard on the entrance or something.

'So they can go wherever they like?' Delilah asked.

'I don't know. What d'you think?'

She shrugged. 'I dunno either.'

'I trust Arturo,' Jimmy said, 'but I don't know about Gordie. He's a real tough kid. I'd hate to think what he's done.'

I nodded my head. I didn't say anything, but the day I told Arturo and Gordie about my life with Mr Meltoni, some of the things I'd done, they came back with a lot of stuff about raids on the Village. I guess Gordie said it to impress me. That's just the way he is. But for every story he had, Arturo almost matched it.

'What d'you think?' I asked Lena, realising she hadn't spoken for a while.

She paused for a moment, then sighed. 'I don't think we have a choice.'

'What do you mean?'

She tilted her head back, the way she sometimes does, as if she's somehow looking up at the sky, to her spiritual home. 'If we're going to go forward, if things are going to improve . . . we've got to trust them.'

I guess I don't do it very often when Jimmy and Delilah are around, but I gave her a hug and kissed her, too. She was right, and the fact that no one spoke, that we all fell to a nervous silence, only went to confirm it.

Not another word was said 'til we got back to the living area and bid each other goodnight. A little later Lena and I made love. It was as if we needed it to give us courage, to pass strength back and forth between us. Afterwards we lay in silence, our arms locked about each other, both too afraid to put into words what we could see coming at us from out of our individual darknesses.

The following morning, after a brief conversation with Lena and Delilah, I went down to tell the kids what we decided. I guess I was feeling pretty pleased with myself in a way. It's always nice to be the bringer of good news. I kept imagining what their reactions were going to be: little Arturo's excited face, Gordie's inevitable suspicion. But when I got to the cell I found it open and both of them gone.

'Shit!' I cursed, the irony that I'd been about to tell them we were letting them out immediately striking me.

I turned and started to run back up to the living area, cursing myself for having missed the fact that they'd been planning an escape, that maybe they'd used last night's games to gain some sort of advantage.

'Dammit! Dammit!' I shouted, already imagining them back over in the Camp, telling others about us.

I turned a corner, was about to shout a warning to Jimmy as I passed his workshop, when I heard laughter coming from inside.

I changed direction, shoved the workshop door open and found him and the kids sitting in front of his computer.

'What's going on?' I demanded.

'Hey, Big Guy!' Jimmy cried, apparently oblivious to the tone in my voice. 'I got it going!'

I paused for a moment, my anger subsiding, then sidled over to stand behind him. It wasn't exactly a thing of beauty, what with wires and bits and pieces hanging off all over, but he was right: he had got it working. There was some game on there he was trying to teach the kids how to play.

'Cool, huh?' he said.

'Jimmy!' I muttered, out of the corner of my mouth. 'What about them?'

He glanced up at me, a little surprised. 'We're letting them out . . . Aren't we?'

'Yes, but . . . I thought . . .'

I stopped in mid-sentence, not wanting Arturo and Gordie to begin their freedom on such an obvious note of distrust. Though to be honest, I don't think they'd even noticed I entered the room, so excited were they by the computer. Jimmy was going through it with them, step by step, giving them a basic lesson, and they were picking it up real fast. Playing the game in no time at all, destroying everything in sight, the irony of them committing such wanton destruction in a cyber world apparently lost on the three of them.

I don't suppose I'll ever get any use out of it, but I gotta say, I could still appreciate the achievement. A computer working in the tunnels. I wouldn't have thought it was possible. For a while I just stood there, staring at this further miracle, smiling at the miracle-maker and occasionally acting out the role of diplomat when the kids started to fight about whose turn it was.

'I got these to go through yet,' Jimmy told me, indicating a box beside him.

I peered inside. 'What are they?'

'Hard disks, cards, flash drives. Found a whole load of them. No label on them for some reason.'

I nodded my head. I mean, it might as well have been a pile of kindling for all I knew, but I didn't have the heart to turn down the heat on his enthusiasm.

'Have you told them what the deal is?' I asked.

'Yeah, yeah,' Gordie said, rather dismissively, his eyes glued to Arturo's efforts on-screen.

I sighed to myself. 'Okay then. I'll go and work out some kind of rota.'

I stood there for a few more moments, then, feeling a touch redundant, left them to it.

I mean, I had it in mind to strike the fear of God into them before releasing them. Leastways to try. Mr Meltoni always used to say: 'Mankind understands the concept of fear far better than that of morality.' He reckoned that was what was wrong with the Ten Commandments: Moses got so loaded down with the tablets, he forgot the big stick.

So, yet again, life in the tunnels has changed. The idea of having someone up there, guarding the entrance, making sure the kids didn't try to escape, was abandoned almost immediately. Sitting up there for hours on end – it just ain't practical. All we can do is keep an eye on them, never let them out of our sight. Mind you, I gotta say, that first week or two was far from comfortable. No one slept that well.

You had the distinct feeling that you were living life on two levels and the top one was decidedly fragile. There were a couple of false alarms; everyone rushing round one day, going crazy, convinced they'd got out, only to find them down in one of the flooded tunnels skimming stones across the water.

Yet slowly we've begun to relax, to hope we can trust them. Okay, so Gordie's pretty difficult at times. You ask him to do a chore, and if he thinks it's below his dignity, he'll tell you to go and screw yourself or something. But we get around it. As for Arturo, well, I gotta say, the little guy's developing a way about him that's pretty hard to resist. You can't believe what he's been through, he seems that unaffected. He's starting to capture a few hearts, and none more so than Delilah's. She's lost all hostility towards them and now treats them like family. Gordie won't have a bar of it, but she loves to get her arms around Arturo and give him a hug. Tell the truth, I don't think they got any more interest in leaving this place than we have. Life in the Camp's pretty tough. They told us a lot of stories; about De Grew, how he went crazy when the medical warehouse was raided. Lena wasn't the only suspect. All sorts of people were questioned, tortured and killed. Wastelords as well as kids.

They also came up with some stuff even Lena was surprised by. Apparently, one of the reasons De Grew gets away with so much, why those on the Mainland turn a blind eye, is 'cuz he's in league with them. He don't run this place in *spite* of the Mainland, but *for* them, with them creaming off the major portion of the profits.

Ever since we freed them we keep the lights on all the time. Even when we're sleeping. Originally for security reasons, but now just 'cuz we prefer it that way. The only real setback we had, the only occasion when I wondered if we really knew what we were doing, was the night I caught Gordie up at the entrance looking like he might be on his way out.

You get a kind of sixth sense about somebody trying not to make any noise. If he'd walked past Lena and me normally instead of creeping I probably wouldn't have heard him. As it was, I not only woke up, but had the presence of mind not to move or alert whoever it was.

I waited 'til the footsteps were some way off, 'til I judged they were almost at the end of the lit section of the tunnel, then turned to see Gordie making his way up towards the main hall.

I gave it a couple of moments, managed to extricate myself from Lena without waking her, then went to follow. I mean, I could've stopped him then and there, but I wanted to see where his free will would take him.

Fortunately for me he was carrying a candle, which made it easy to follow. All I had to do was stay in the dark and creep along behind that flame. He went through the main hall and then, just as I feared, up towards the entrance.

I waited 'til he was actually at the door, then snuck up behind him. 'What you doing, Gordie?' I asked.

He turned to me, at first a little taken aback, but then got this expression of real defiance about him. 'Just looking.'

'This time of night?'

There was a long pause. I didn't want to know this, not after everything we'd been through. I bent down to take a quick look out through the cracks and got a real shock. There was a fog out there. For the first time in ages. Somehow he'd known, he'd been woken by its call, like a werewolf being summoned by the full moon.

'You want to go out? Is that it?' I asked.

He shrugged, but didn't answer.

'You could be over there right now, huh? Full of that stuff De Grew gives you? Burning and killing? Is that what you want?'

Still he didn't answer, but he had a look about him that damn near frightened me to death. As if bubbles and flames hadn't been his only addiction, that it was the pleasures of blood and carnage he was really missing.

'Why go over there, Gordie? We can make it easy for you. There are old folks here. Why don't you go down and chop up Jimmy or Delilah? Or me? I mean, why not? We're just the same as them.'

He looked at me and for the first time I saw that kid with real hurt in his eyes. As if he couldn't believe I'd think that of him.

'We're just the same, Gordie,' I repeated. 'If you got to know some of them, they're just like us.'

I don't know if I imagined it or not, maybe I did, but as I stood there staring into his face, I swear I saw that moonlight in his eyes finally disappear. Something else triumphed over it. And I tell you, I pray to God it never ever burns again.

I put my arm round his shoulder and led him back down the tunnel, and for once he didn't seem to mind; the two of us returning to our beds without saying another word.

I never told anyone. Not even Lena. I kind of figure it's our secret. I know it hasn't been easy for him, that he's probably still got a few more demons to show the door. But ever since that night, the disappearance of that look in his eyes, I've felt I could trust Gordie. That he'll be there for us. Which is just as well, 'cuz the way things are, I got this feeling that we're going to need every little bit of help we can get.

CHAPTER SIXTEEN

In the light of the sheer malevolence of those searching for us, I guess it sounds pathetic, but I've started to increase the difficulty of my workout. I mean, I don't think I'm imagining it, I do feel better. There seems to be a difference in the amount of breath I can get into my lungs, in how long my limbs take to tire, in my overall stamina. Mind you, how fit this renovated old body can get, I just don't know.

Occasionally the kids make their way down and ask if they can join in. Gordie tries to show off, to prove how strong he is, putting too much sand in the drums and barely being able to scrape them off the ground. Whilst Arturo merely talks a good game, without ever doing anything. I guess the thing is, weightlifting's too disciplined for kids of their age. They need to let their energy off all over, like bees darting from flower to flower.

Jimmy's still letting them play with his computer, but since he started to go through that box of disks, they've had to pick their moments. Games are starting to take a back seat. The little guy's getting that look about him again, like he's becoming filled with the colour of obsession. One night I was awakened by this rumbling beneath us, deep down in the bowels of the tunnels, even a bit of vibration. I knew at once what it was, that a major stretch of tunnel had gone down, and the following morning I went down to ask him if he'd give me a hand making good.

The moment I walked into his workshop I knew I had no chance. He was crouched over his computer like some crazed gnome, a look of furious concentration on his face, punching the keys so fast you could barely see his fingers.

'Jimmy—' I started to say, but he immediately told me to shush, which I didn't altogether care for.

He continued to patter all over that keyboard, changing sequence, backtracking, sighing, starting all over again, then eventually slumped back and gave a cry of frustration. '*Dammit!*'

'What's the matter?' I asked. He didn't answer, just sat there glaring at the screen as if he was about to punch it and I began to get a little irritated. 'Jimmy?'

He shook his head, making that little clicking noise with his tongue he's so fond of. 'Look!' he said, indicating the blank screen.

For a few moments I stared, not sure what I was supposed to be seeing. 'Yeah. Nice colour,' I commented. 'Bit like the sky.'

'No, Big Guy! . . . Watch this.'

He started hitting keys again, over and over, and for a while nothing happened, then he got this screen full of endless code and finally a sign saying: 'Access Denied'. I nodded my head, trying to look impressed. I mean, like I told you, this stuff don't mean a lot to me.

'What is it?' I asked.

'I don't know!' he shouted, throwing his hands in the air.

'Oh,' I said, finding it impossible to keep the disinterest out of my voice.

'No, no, Big Guy! Don't you understand?' he groaned. '*I* don't know! . . . *Me!* There's nothing I don't know about computers. I mean, they get more and more sophisticated, but the basic principles remain the same. But this . . .' he paused, again shaking his head. 'I never seen anything like it. I been trying to get into it for days.'

I shrugged, still not seeing the significance of what he was saying.

'The only thing I do know . . .' he continued, ejecting the disk and holding it up for me. 'See that small mark there?'

I squinted, just about able to make something out, then nodded; more to please him than anything else.

'That's government issue,' he said, looking at me, expecting some kind of reaction, though for the life of me I didn't know what.

'You mean . . . some kind of . . . classified information?' I ventured, suspecting I was making a fool of myself.

'Could be,' he nodded, much to my relief.

'In the garbage?'

'Wouldn't be the first time. Stuff gets stored, departments get reorganised; before you know where you are someone has a clear-out and things that shouldn't go missing disappear.'

I turned and frowned at the screen. 'What could it be?'

'I don't have the slightest idea,' he sighed.

For several minutes I stood watching his fingers chattering away with those keys, trying this, trying that, cursing at whoever had programmed the thing. It was like a fight, only one of the contestants had long left the ring.

'No good?' I asked, some of his frustration beginning to rub off on me.

'I got to try to break it down somehow but . . . I don't know if I've got the necessary technology.'

He jumped up, starting to search through all his various bits and pieces for inspiration, and at that moment, Arturo and Gordie entered.

'Sorry, guys,' Jimmy said. 'No games today.'

But for once the two of them weren't interested in playing on the computer. Instead, Gordie kind of nodded towards the door, indicating he and Arturo wanted a word out in the tunnel.

'What's up?' I asked.

'There are others,' he said.

I paused for a moment, having no idea what he was talking about. 'What?'

'There are others in the Camp who want to get out. Lots of them.'

For several seconds all I could do was to stare at their anxious little faces as they waited for my reaction. Before I could recover, Arturo started to reel off a lot of names, mostly boys, occasionally girls, and one person who Gordie had to remind him was dead.

'You want them to come and live here?' I asked.

'Yes,' Gordie told me.

'You're kidding, right?'

'Why not?'

I made those kind of huffy-puffy noises people do when they think the answer to a question's so obvious it doesn't need verbalising. 'Any number of reasons! It's too much of a risk. Especially the way things are. We don't have enough food,' I said, like that was just for starters.

'Lena said we had enough for an army!' Arturo protested.

So that was what this was about. Lena and Delilah have been reorganising the garden, creating tiers to increase the growing space; obviously it had set these two thinking.

'She didn't mean it!' I told them.

And then something happened that, fortunately, doesn't happen very often, 'cuz when it does, it tends to mean Arturo gets his own way. The little guy burst into tears. 'I want my friends!' he whined.

Gordie turned on him, telling him to shut up or he'd whack him one, but I could tell his real anger was directed at me.

'Why not?' he demanded.

'I just told you! It's too much of a risk!'

There was a long pause. What with Gordie's anger and Arturo's tears, I was feeling pretty ganged up on. In the end, I had to agree to put it to the others, to discuss it over dinner that night. I mean, I knew what they'd say, but at least that way betrayal would be split four ways, rather than just the one.

The only thing was, it didn't quite work out that way. None of them rejected the idea immediately. In fact, they started discussing it in all seriousness: talking about numbers, practicalities, how many more the tunnels could feasibly support.

'You're not serious?' I said, interrupting a conversation between Lena and Delilah about how they could maybe reorganise the garden further.

'Why not?' Lena asked.

'Jesus!' I cried, again finding myself floundering round for words that seemed wholly unnecessary. ''Coz of everything we've said in the past!'

She just shrugged, as if that wasn't important now.

'I don't believe this! What the hell's got into you people?'

'We'd have the same troubles again,' Jimmy warned. 'They'll all be on drugs.'

'Damn right,' I said. 'What are you going to do – rehabilitate the whole camp?'

'We wouldn't bring anyone who was on drugs,' Gordie interrupted.

I paused for a moment. I mean, I could see everyone had the best intentions, I really could, but we had more than enough problems already.

'What about De Grew?' I asked, directing my question at Lena. 'The Wastelords?'

'They wouldn't notice,' Gordie said dismissively. 'We're all the same to them.'

Lena paused for a moment, obviously thinking it through. 'Few kids on the outer . . . might not be a problem.'

'Hey, now, wait a moment.'

I'd deliberately withheld a lot of what I'd seen on my last trip up-top, but the way this conversation was going, I thought it was time to enlighten a few people. I told them about the gang down at the jetty, how the Villagers were more scared than I'd ever seen them, the way the Island was crawling with Wastelords. I told them everything. And you know something? It didn't make a blind bit of difference.

'They'd still want to come,' Gordie said. 'Anything's better than being in the Camp.'

For a while we all sat in uneasy silence, the impasse obvious to everyone, then Arturo kind of whined that he wanted his friends. Not to anyone in particular, but Delilah, as she does all the time now, used it as an excuse to drag him over and give him a cuddle. It was cute. It really was. I mean, sitting there, looking round me, it was like an extended family, and I tell you, I wasn't going to do anything to risk it.

'Sorry. It's out of the question,' I told them.

The silence continued, heavy and ominous. I turned and looked from one face to another, aware that no one would meet my gaze. I couldn't understand it. I knew I was right, they knew I was right, but I could feel the tide starting to run up against me.

'I guess if we just took a couple. See how it went,' Jimmy ventured.

'Jimmy!' I shouted. I'd assumed he was on my side. 'You wanna lose all this? Your workshop, your computer, everything?'

There was another pause, this time a decidedly more uncomfortable one, I guess I'd been a bit more forceful than I intended.

Delilah was sitting there, playing with Arturo's hair. She hadn't said a lot and I hoped it meant that she, at least, agreed with me – but I was wrong again.

'Clancy, we can't go on like this,' she said.

'Why not?' I demanded.

''Cuz it's impossible and it's selfish.'

Once more silence descended, only this time I was beginning to understand. Delilah had said the one thing I thought none of us would ever be brave enough to say. All of us might have thought it at one time or another, that we were just hoarding ourselves away down here and damn those left suffering up-top, but I never imagined anyone would come out with it. Least of all her. But she's been totally different since the kids joined us, like a lot of the walls she's built up in her life have come crumbling down.

'Maybe we should vote on it,' Lena suggested.

I took in a whole chestful of tunnel air, then gave out with a very long sigh. 'Nah . . . No need.'

Don't get me wrong, a dumb old big guy I may be, but I knew what I was saying. I wasn't just agreeing to allow some more kids into the tunnels. I was signing up to a whole new philosophy – one that verged on suicide. Up until then all we'd cared about was us. Preserving our wrinkled old hides. And maybe that's the whole point. If Gordie and Arturo hadn't come along, that's all we would've ever done. And at some point in the future, one by one, we would've died down here. Until, chances are, only Lena would've remained. Patrolling these tunnels with just three skeletons for company. Or maybe those who survived the longest would drag the dead down to be buried in the same place as the tall kid. Four graves for her to pay occasional homage to, knowing that, when her turn came, she'd just have to rot wherever death took her.

In the end, that thought alone was enough to persuade me. Her on her own down here, Jimmy's generator broken, the lights gone, shuffling round in the darkness 'til one day she would stop shuffling, stop breathing, and there'd be nothing left but silence and black.

But whatever our individual reasons for going along with this, we all know we're taking one helluva risk. Letting the kids go out? Back to the Camp? I mean, we have come to trust them, but that's down here, in the tunnels. Once they're back with their friends and got access to drugs and everything, who knows?

But the most worrying thing of all is – at least as far as I'm concerned – by allowing them to leave, we're relinquishing our control of this situation. Down here our world is clearly defined and we can keep a pretty tight lid on it, but as soon as those kids go out, anything can happen. And just at this moment, it feels like there's any number of ways this can go wrong, and not too many it can go right.

The morning Gordie and Arturo left, they promised us over and over they'd be back as soon as they could. I mean, those kids ain't stupid, they knew how nervous we were about this. All four of us accompanied them to the entrance, reminding them again to speak only to those they were absolutely sure of, not to let even a whisper get out to anyone else.

It was like the parting of a family; the kids off on their first vacation, the parents left worrying behind. Delilah kept hugging and kissing Arturo. Gordie sneered at them, gave the little guy a push in the back, and when Delilah said he was just jealous and tried to kiss him, shot off so fast you would've sworn his ass was on fire.

Sometimes that kid reminds me so much of me at his age it's uncanny. I'd rather have taken a bat across the face than have some woman plant one on me. It was an affront; an invasion of my masculine cool. Kind of funny when you think that later in life there are times when you'd do anything for the touch of a pair of warm lips.

As soon as we closed the door behind them, all of us, bar Lena, jostled to get a look out through the gaps. Two kids heading off in the direction of the Camp, picking their way over the rubble, Arturo already looking so small you wouldn't send him anywhere, 'cept perhaps off to bed. I watched for a few moments, scanning the distance for any sign of Wastelords, then, pretending not to notice the tears in Delilah's eyes, turned and headed off down the tunnel. We were gambling everything and we knew it. If those kids let us down, if they were seduced away somehow, it'd be the end of us all.

For the rest of the day we tried to carry on as normal, but it wasn't easy. I kept thinking about the night I caught Gordie up at the entrance; that expression on his face. What if a fog got up? Would it mean anything to him? Would he be able to resist it? Or would the moonlight get caught in his eyes once more and he'd go and search out his make-up and machete?

I went down to see Jimmy in his workshop, hoping for a little distracting conversation, but he was still immersed in his siege of the 'secret' disks.

'How's it going?' I asked.

He sighed and paused for a moment, like replying to me had been queued somewhere in his head – round about priority one hundred and forty-seven.

'As far as I can work out,' he said absently, 'there's some kind of three-dimensional password: numerical, light and maybe impulse.'

I grunted. He'd lost me already. 'Sounds complicated.'

He nodded, which was the last acknowledgement I had from him until I got fed up and left. As much as I was trying to resist it, I knew there was only one place I'd be remotely comfortable under these circumstances, and soon I was making my way back up to the entrance.

When I got there, I found Lena had beaten me to it.

'You too, huh?' I said.

'I'm so scared, Clancy.'

'Hey. They'll be all right.'

I sat down behind her, so she could lean back against me and I could get my arms around her, but I didn't bother taking a look out. I trusted her senses far more than my own.

'I love you, Clancy,' she said, and I gave her a real hug, so grateful for those words even if I was concerned at her motive for saying them, that perhaps she was worrying our time together might not last much longer.

'Whatever happens, that'll never change,' I told her.

I leant forward, twisting round the side of her to kiss her on the cheek, but in that moment, this terrible sequence of quick-fire expressions played across her face. First confusion, then panic, 'til there was so much fear there it damn near repulsed me.

'What is it?' I asked.

She started panting, gasping for breath.

'*Lena!*'

'Someone's out there!'

'Who? '

'Oh shit! No!'

I scrambled over on my hands and knees to take a look. She was frightening the life out of me. It was as if what she was thinking was so bad just the thought alone might kill her.

'Can you see anyone?' she asked.

I swivelled my head from side to side, crouching right down in the corner so I could take in as much as possible. 'No.'

'You sure?' she said, still panicked.

'There's no one,' I told her. 'No one at all.'

She sniffed the air repeatedly, her breathing slowly subsiding, then gave a long sigh, so relieved that whatever she thought she'd caught a hint of wasn't there.

I took one final look, then resumed my place behind her, not daring to ask what had frightened her so. In fact, not daring to speak at all in case my voice gave me away; in case it let her know that for the first time ever I'd lied to her about what I'd seen, that by trusting me to be her eyes, she'd been deceived.

See, over in the distance there was a big gang of guys, some wearing those tell-tale red overalls, searching their way through the ruins. Not that it was that that worried me so much – though it was reason enough. It was the fact that, amongst them was someone else. Someone who, even from this distance, you could tell they were all deferring to. I gave Lena a comforting squeeze, begging my body to stay relaxed, not to betray my tension. If he was over here looking, we really were in trouble. I mean, distant though it might've been, I was left in no doubt that I'd just caught my first glimpse of the evil Island legend De Grew.

Not long after that, and with some persuasion from me, Lena went down to reheat some of the stew I cooked up the night before, and I told her I'd follow in a few minutes. The moment her footsteps faded away I leapt back to the entrance to see if anyone was still out there, but they'd gone.

Not that it made me feel any better. I mean, Jesus, you have no idea how disturbing that was. What the hell was going on? In my heart I was sure I could trust those kids, but seeing De Grew over here, obviously searching the city, was deeply worrying. Maybe he tortured it out of them? Maybe they'd been betrayed by other kids?

I stayed there for another hour or more, waiting to see if De Grew reappeared, 'til round about eight, with the light almost gone, Lena returned.

'Clancy! I thought you were hungry.'

'Yeah. Sorry.'

'Are you coming?'

'Yeah, yeah. I'll be there in a minute.'

'Not in a minute. Now!'

In the end she had to literally drag me away. I was convinced something had happened to Gordie and Arturo, that De Grew and his Wastelords had got to them and would soon be coming for us. Not that I said anything. Not to her or anyone else.

That night I barely slept a wink. I kept hearing these sounds. Distant thumps and groans I was sure I'd never heard in the tunnels before. Even the wind was panicked, rushing everywhere, searching for places where our defences might be breached. The only time I did nod off, just for a few minutes, I had this dream I used to get over in the Village, about Mr Meltoni's funeral.

I guess that was one of the saddest days of my life. Cancer got him in the end. A peaceful death if not a painless one. I mean, it had to be something like that, I wouldn't have allowed anything else. People came from all over, all types, all callings, to say their final goodbyes. Every yard of the way from his home to the church was lined two or three deep. Some throwing flowers, some openly weeping, and others just looking like they were too shocked to know what to do.

I don't know why such men create so many ripples on this Earth. I mean, he did a lot of bad things – I did some of them for him – but when he died, it was as if we all lost the faith that had held us together. We were children again, not knowing what to do, how to make our way.

Course, it didn't take long for the fighting to begin. Men not fit to brush his hat trying to step into his shoes. Killing for no reason other than to build a reputation, bragging themselves big: the king is dead, long live the king. Even though no one was in the mood for any kind of coronation.

But the thing about my dream is, in it, Mr Meltoni don't die. Well, not really. One day I go to visit his mausoleum, to pay my respects, talk with him for a while, and while I'm there this limo draws up. For a moment nothing happens. I start to get a little nervous, the windows are heavily tinted and I can't see who's inside. Maybe someone's come to settle an old score? Or one of the new pretenders don't want any reminders of the old regime? Slowly the back window slides down and I see a familiar face. It's him! Mr Meltoni! You have no idea how much better it makes me feel. As if the whole thing was just a joke, that there's no such thing as death at all. He leans towards me, as if he wants to take my hand. Only at the last moment do I see his antique revolver. His smile gets even broader as he pulls the trigger. I take it in the chest, bang, to the heart, and as I go down I hear him say, 'That's it, Big Guy, go to sleep now. Everything's gonna be all right.'

And the funny thing was, when I used to have the dream over in the Village, I thought it *was* going to be all right. Almost as if he was the doctor come to administer my medicine. But now, with Lena by my side, when I saw that solid silver barrel coming for me, I shouted for him not to do it. I even tried to run, to get my old legs going, but for some reason, despite all my exercising, they just couldn't move fast enough. And you want to know something? That even in my dream I could barely believe. It didn't make the blindest bit of difference. Mr Meltoni just went ahead and shot me in the back.

With sleep so elusive I was up and back at the entrance a little after eight. There was still no sign of anyone; no kids, nor Wastelords. In fact, I didn't see a living soul until Delilah came wandering up a couple of hours later.

'Lena said I'd find you up here,' she said, breathing a little heavy from the climb. She bent down and took a look out, the pale light of the morning turning her face a touch purple.

'Crazy world, huh?' she said. 'Not so long ago I would've done anything to be rid of them, now I'm praying for their return.'

'They'll be okay,' I said, not entirely convincingly.

'I hope so.'

We both stayed there, taking it in turns to peer out, conversation becoming progressively more sparing as our anxiety grew. I didn't say anything, but I was starting to get a really bad feeling about this. What could be taking so long? All they had to do was grab a couple of kids and come back.

'Uh-oh. Company,' Delilah said, squinting into the distance.

I knelt down next to her just in time to see a couple of Wastelords making their way towards the square.

'Was that who I think it was?' she asked.

I nodded my head. 'Yeah. They're everywhere.'

She shook her head, like she couldn't imagine how we could've allowed Gordie and Arturo to go out there, and again tears filled her eyes.

'They'll be okay,' I repeated. 'They're good kids.'

In the end, when she started complaining about her old bones aching, wanting to go to the toilet, I encouraged her to go back down. She just wasn't helping. As she faded into the darkness of the tunnel I could hear her stifling her sobs; the further she went, the less successful she became, and, to be honest, I could've damn near joined in with her. Never in my wildest dreams would I have imagined how precious those kids would become to us. I mean, we're worried about ourselves, course we are – life in the tunnels and all that – but really, just at that moment, nothing mattered more than the safe return of Gordie and Arturo.

By mid-afternoon, my worst fears were giving me a real going-over. They weren't coming back. Something had gone terribly wrong. Maybe they'd been betrayed, or maybe they'd betrayed us? Either way, I felt so weighed down by guilt I could've thrown up. Why had we taken such a chance? Why, when we had everything, had we risked it all?

I was about to make my way down to the others, to confront them with a few difficult home truths, when I took one last habitual, rather than hopeful, look out.

God knows how long it was before I registered what I was looking at. There was a group of four kids making their way towards me through the afternoon heat haze: Gordie, Arturo, plus a sort of roly-poly kid and a tall slim girl.

I wanted to shout out, to run down and tell the others, but I couldn't. Instead, I just stayed where I was, transfixed by their hesitant approach, nervously scanning the horizon behind them in case anyone was following.

You could see Gordie was giving out the orders. At one point the plump kid looked in my direction, as if trying to make out the entrance, and got a mouthful for his curiosity. They took this altogether erratic approach, going from one pile of rubble to another, like they were just messing around with no particular purpose in mind. As they got nearer, I could see the two new kids looked kind of bulky, as if they had things stuffed inside their shirts, and I guessed Gordie had persuaded them that was all they could bring. Or maybe it was everything they had?

Finally they made the last twenty yards or so and were standing outside. Gordie took one last look round, then leant down to grab the door, but I heaved it open for him.

'You okay?' I asked, as the four of them scrambled in.

'Wastelords are everywhere,' he said, by way of an explanation. 'You can't do a thing.'

He promptly introduced the two newcomers: the girl being Hannah, and the boy, Luxurious. Both of them never said a word, just kind of gaped, like they thought they were going to be the victims of a practical joke and were now rapidly having to rethink.

Immediately Arturo started to show off, leading them down to the living area, acting like he was in charge of the whole set-up.

I tell you, if they weren't pop-eyed enough walking down the tunnel, taking in all there was to see, when they got to the bottom and Delilah screamed and squealed, hugging and kissing Arturo, they sure were then. Gordie backed away, huddling up against a wall with the two newcomers, making a face as if to say that he fully understood how nauseous they must be feeling.

Standing there, in the electric light, I had a chance to see both of them in a bit more detail. Hannah's tall, dark, kind of graceful in a way, but has this odd, permanently startled expression about her. If Arturo gives you the impression that he's oblivious to everything that's ever happened to him, then she makes you feel she's been touched by every drop. Not a word crosses her lips, but if you ever get the chance to unravel the stories in her eyes, I reckon you could knit quite a tale. As for Luxurious, well, he's about the closest thing to a human bowling ball you're ever going to see. There's no gap between his shoulders and chin, no light between his fat little thighs. Everything about his stature says 'Don't knock me over 'cuz I'm never going to be able to get up again.'

The thing that really shook them – more than secret doorways, underground worlds, or electric lighting – was to see their friends on such good terms with old people. I guess Arturo and Gordie must've told them, but obviously it hadn't sunk in. They had this appalled look on their faces, as if they were in the reptile house at the zoo and someone was asking them to handle one of the exhibits. I could've almost taken offence. But we decided not to mention it, to just act as natural as we could and wait for them to come around.

Whether deliberately or not, Arturo gave the situation a real kick-start by taking them off on a guided tour. When they returned an hour or so later, they were a lot more relaxed; Luxurious acting like he'd been in the tunnels almost as long as the other two. He's got this real high-pitched voice, like he's been taught to speak by an insect or something.

'They do understand, don't they?' I said to Gordie. 'I mean, this is it. They can never go back.'

He nodded. 'They never want to see that place again. Not for any reason.'

He said it with such feeling, I knew something else had happened and asked him what. He turned to Luxurious, waiting, but the bowling-ball made this face like he didn't want to talk about it.

'Kids are disappearing,' Gordie eventually said.

I shrugged. I knew that. Lena already told me kids disappeared sometimes. 'More than usual?'

'Yeah,' he said, pausing for a moment. 'We know what's happening to them.'

'What?' I asked, a little fearfully.

Gordie gave that little sneer and shrug he's so fond of, as if something doesn't really matter, even though you know it really does. 'They're taking them for organs.'

I just stood there, gaping at him.

'What?' Delilah croaked.

Luxurious nodded. 'They installed this cold store in one of the warehouses. Someone saw bodies hanging up in there.'

There was a long shocked pause, as if no one wanted to pass comment, to admit they were even part of this conversation.

'We're an organ farm,' Gordie whispered, like it was a joke he couldn't quite bring himself to say out loud.

It was only when I realised how hard she was squeezing that I noticed Lena had taken my hand. I turned and stared into her face. There was so much pain there it hurt you just to look.

'Oh, Clancy!' she moaned.

None of us knew what to do. We just stood there like we'd been hit or something. As if by shutting down, by going all cold and hard, we just might be able to cope with it. Forcing kids to live and work in shit, physically and sexually abusing them, then snuffing them out when their organs were ready to be sold, like they were just plants bearing fruit. How could any of us live in this world knowing that?

'I want to go back for two more,' Gordie said, like he wasn't sure if we would allow it or not.

'Two!' Delilah moaned, as if any number was going to be futile.

And then, I don't know what happened, but I guess I lost it. In the way that everyone imagines a big guy eventually will. I turned and punched the wall of the tunnel so hard it's a wonder I didn't go right through. The others just gaped at me, like something they'd always been a little frightened of had finally happened. Over and over I hit it, only the many times in the past my knuckles had broken and mended stronger protecting them from breaking again. A smear of blood appeared on the wall, growing with every blow, like I was painting with my fists. I felt such rage, such fury, but most of all, such shame. All my life I've followed orders. Never making a judgement or a decision. But I've roughed people up, broken legs and arms, and more. And for what? No one had ever done anything. Just got in someone's way, or been too stupid or greedy or something. And occasionally, thank God, not that often, I've even killed people. I actually took a life. I didn't enjoy it, but I didn't hate it either. It was never personal. But can't you see what I'm saying? All that fear, that force, that pain, it should've at least been for a good reason. Maybe I could've changed something? Maybe this great useless mass of dulled muscle could've made a difference?

'*Clancy!* Stop it!' Lena screamed, grabbing hold of me and trapping my arms.

I stood there, puffing and panting, letting her hold me, blood dripping from my fists to the ground.

'It's okay,' she kept repeating. 'It's okay.' As if pleading with me not to frighten her anymore.

But it wasn't okay. Not one bit of it. And we all knew it. Ever since

I been on the Island, I stood back and watched things happen that, if Mr Meltoni had told me to do something about them, I would've done my best to stop. But I accepted them as if it was none of my business. Day after day retreating more and more into myself, resignation chewing its way through me whilst I did nothing but wait for it to take a terminal hold.

Well, no more. I may be old, I may be weak, I may be useless – I don't know – but I'm still alive. And if I never do another damn thing on this Earth, I'm going to do whatever I can to stop what's happening on this Island.

CHAPTER SEVENTEEN

So now I know what all this working out's been for, what the challenge is to be. I always had a sense there was a reason, that destiny was lurking somewhere, I just didn't expect the task to be quite this great.

The moment I made my decision, I marched straight down to the lower tunnel and started to, not jog, but run as fast as I possibly could. As if I had a need to exhaust myself until it hurt, to draw out some of the pain. Pounding round and round that circuit 'til I literally collapsed to the ground; my legs going into spasm, my lungs screaming like baby birds. But still I wasn't finished. I poured extra sand into the drums, more than I ever would've imagined lifting again, and forced my old body to jerk and push that cumbersome weight into the air. Over and over, 'til my muscles told me they couldn't do it anymore and yet still I coaxed and cursed them till they finally did.

I'd been putting limits on myself. I said I wanted to get fit and no more, that it was crazy asking an old heart to take the strain of a young one, but now it's different. I got something to aim at: enemies I think about every step of the way, every time that I need the motivation to drive a heavy weight into the air.

Course, once Lena calmed me down and the others thought I was approachable again, they started voicing their doubts about the whole thing, Jimmy and the kids warning me that we didn't stand a chance. But the way I see it, the way I managed to convince them, it's not a chance we don't have – it's a choice. Even if we could ignore what was going on over in the Camp – and sure as hell we can't – even if, for some miraculous reason, De Grew and his Wastelords never find us, we're still finished here, and we're fools if we think otherwise.

We ain't moles, no more than we're rats. We're human beings. We got to have the scent of the season in our faces, the sun and the stars sweeping across our sky. And if there's any hope at all of that happening again, it's in us dismantling and destroying everything that's sprung up round here. Blowing the whole damn place apart and hoping that, when the pieces fall back to earth, they'll form something far more conducive to humanity.

Lena started coming with me more and more when I worked out. Not just running, but weightlifting, too. I tell you, she's surprisingly strong. No wonder it hurt so much that time she laid one on me. We take it in turns, helping each other out, shouting encouragement to make that last limb-trembling lift. I like it. It makes me feel we're, not just a couple, but a team; a unit joined by sweat and strain, by our mutual rendezvous with fate.

The only problem is, I have no idea how I'm going to go about this. Not the slightest. Everyone assumes I'll come up with something, that it's my territory, but that's just adding to the pressure. I mean, I don't want to disillusion them or anything, but I thought they would've known: I don't come up with ideas, I carry them out.

The one thing I do know is that the balance of power on the Island revolves around drugs. That's how the kids are kept in check, how they're being manipulated. If you stop them, you got a chance of stopping everything. Which means that somehow we gotta get down to that warehouse again and put it out of business.

Course, there's a lot more to it than that. Drugs ain't bad, no more than they're good; in themselves, they're nothing. It's those who exploit the weaknesses they create who are evil. And the real challenge is on the hill overlooking the Camp, with De Grew and his Wastelords.

All the years I been hearing about this guy, what a sick, sadistic sonofabitch he is, I never imagined I'd ever have to go up against him. It must be getting on for fifteen years since I did anything like that. And more since I actually killed anyone. I don't even know if I've still got it in me. For so long I avoided asking myself the question. When I finally did, I knew it was all over. Killing's wrong. No discussion. The irony is, that maybe, just this once and for the first time in my life, I got an idea it might be right.

It's the one subject Lena and me have gone out of our way to avoid. Mind you, I know she's brooding over it all the time. One night I woke up and found her lying next to me with the kind of expression that tells you someone hasn't slept at all. I put my arms around her, too tired to talk, but as I started to doze off, she spoke.

'He thrives on pain and fear.'

'What?' I said, with a slight start.

'As a species we need food and water to survive. He needs to torture and kill.'

Immediately I knew who she was talking about. 'Yeah . . . I know,' I sighed.

'You can't make allowances for that. It's madness.'

She fell silent and I wondered if that was all it was going to be, if we'd continue this another time, but she got herself into such a state, worrying away next to me like a sheet of ice slowly cracking.

'It's the ultimate weapon because no one knows what it's capable of.'

Again she went silent, as if she hadn't spoken at all, as if it had just been a thought that had escaped from her head, and by doing so been transformed into words.

'It's okay,' I said sleepily, giving her a hug. 'Don't worry.'

I guess the thing is, in her mind she can't put us both together: the meanest murderous bastard on the Island and the tired spent old heavy coming out of retirement to face him. And when you think about it like that, is it any wonder she's worrying?

Presently her breathing became deeper and I realised she'd fallen asleep. She was lying on my arm, cutting off the circulation, but I couldn't bear to move her. I took a deep breath and held it as long as I could in that dusty old cathedral of my chest. I have to come up with something. Everyone's waiting on me, relying upon me to know what to do, and it means everything to me that I don't let them down.

In the end, I realised that was the problem. I was more worried about convincing people I wasn't stupid than coming up with a plan that might work. Sometimes you just got to go with what you know, the tried-and-tested stuff you seen succeed over and over.

I remember Mr Meltoni sending me and a couple of the boys down to settle with the D'Anno kid. He had great teeth, so white and even, nicest smile you ever saw. Women loved him. I never saw the kid without a 'model' or 'actress' hanging off his arm looking all serious and sulky, probably 'cuz they knew there was no way to compete with that smile. The only trouble with the kid was he was lazy. He wanted all the rewards, but took short cuts with the work: telling lies, getting careless about whose pocket the dough should be going in. Mr Meltoni gave him chance after chance, but he never had the savvy to take one. I guess what I'm trying to say is, the kid might've been great to look at, but he wasn't that bright.

Eventually, Mr Meltoni lost patience with him. The kid and his gang used to operate out of this huge fruit warehouse down on the docks.

They thought it was impregnable, that no one could touch them in there. One night we sent this old tub straight into the wharf, smashing it to pieces and bringing down the front of the warehouse with it. That harbour looked like a great big floating fruit salad. Everyone came out, gawping and laughing. Meanwhile, Frankie sneaked round the back and blew the kid away. Tell the truth, I got real angry about it. Frankie was the ugliest sonofabitch you ever seen in your life, he had a face that looked like he'd been rummaging through a cosmetic surgeon's trash-can, and you know where he shot the kid? Why, straight in the mouth, of course. Shattering all those lovely white teeth like broken china. I mean, can you believe that? He was dead, for chrissake. What kind of guy's jealous of the smile on a corpse?

Anyways, I reckon that's what I need to get me to De Grew: a distraction. The bigger the better. And the more I think about it, the more I realise the destruction of the drugs warehouse fits the bill perfectly – somehow we gotta blow that damn place into the sea. If we can manage that, then maybe, in the ensuing confusion, I can find my way to De Grew.

The only thing is, by solving that problem, by coming up with a plan at last, I've presented myself with another. I'm going to need more people. A whole lot more. And there's only one place I can think of to find them.

Life's thrown me some pretty juicy ironies over the years, but none that dripped more than this: me and Jimmy going back to the Village to see if we could recruit people to help us fight the Wastelords. God help us all. We had a better chance of gathering up an army of rats, or training an airborne squadron of seagulls.

As we turned down one of the rows, an old familiar feeling began to weigh heavily upon me, but we really didn't have a choice. It was them or no one.

'Jesus,' I muttered to Jimmy. 'We gotta be kidding.'

'Give them a chance, Big Guy. Maybe, when they're presented with a real opportunity to change things, they'll surprise you.'

'You reckon?'

He shrugged. 'Maybe.'

I took a glance through the door of a lean-to. An open-mouthed couple stared dully out at us, looking so ready for death they seemed almost disappointed we hadn't brought it with us.

It went through my head to just turn around then and there, to go back to the tunnels and come up with another plan, but Jimmy, maybe 'cuz he sensed my mood, saw this small group sitting nearby and pitched in amongst them.

We'd already decided it was best for him do the talking. I might be a changed man in many ways, but I've no doubt that any Villagers who know me still see me as an insular bad-tempered individual they'd rather avoid. And though I didn't recognise any of the group, I still felt Jimmy was a much more likely source of persuasion.

Course, he didn't come straight out with it. That would be asking for trouble. Who knows who might be listening? He just got into a bit of general chatter; the weather, Island life, everyday stuff. And to tell the truth, I reckon they would've been happy to have kept that up all day. But the moment he began to slide towards what he really wanted to say you could feel their suspicions being aroused. And soon I was reminded of why I despise Villagers so much. They're so resigned: fate is their prison and nothing's going to persuade them to escape. The little guy did his best, but as soon as they got an idea where this crazy talk was leading they practically fell over themselves to get away.

That being said, the morning didn't turn out quite as I expected. We made our way over to the general area where we used to live and, boosted by several familiar faces, managed to involve ourselves in a much larger gathering.

The conversation more or less went the same way as before: lots of jawing about nothing very much, then Jimmy started to turn it towards the Wastelords and how no one had ever tried standing up to them. Immediately there was a general melting away, but for some reason, one or two of them got really upset. Not irritated, not impatient, but what was, to me, irrational anger.

'Screw you, you fucker!' this little fat guy said, turning and storming away.

'Thank you for the discussion, sir,' Jimmy called after him.

'There ain't nothing to discuss, prick!' the guy shouted, and disappeared into his lean-to, still shouting away in there, maybe to his partner, maybe to himself.

But that was nothing compared with Jimmy's next encounter. This bearded guy – I don't know, somewhere between my age and Jimmy's, dressed only in shorts, a flurry of white hair falling down his brown and parched back – appeared out of nowhere and looked like he was about to put one on the little guy.

'Get out of here! Go on!' he snarled, waving his arms around.

Jimmy backed off three paces, then came back one. 'Hey! What's your problem?'

'You! You're my problem!'

'Why?'

'Talking shit! That's why!'

'I'm not allowed to express an opinion?' Jimmy asked, smirking at the remains of his audience, futilely trying to get them on side.

'When it's shit, no. Now just go, will you?'

Jimmy's not the bravest guy in the world, but, I tell you, sometimes he's close to being the most stubborn. 'What's so wrong with talking about standing up to the Wastelords?

'Jesus!' The bearded man snarled, now clenching and unclenching his fists. 'What a fucking imbecile.'

'What a fucking coward,' Jimmy responded ill-advisedly, his annoyance making him revert to the schoolyard.

It's funny, but whatever the bearded guy was, I knew it wasn't that, and I was over there in seconds, standing between the two of them. Judging by the look on his face, the glare he was giving Jimmy, it was just as well I did.

'You call me that again, I don't give a damn about those things up there,' he spat at Jimmy. 'Stamping on your empty head'll be worth getting fried for.'

I had to practically escort Jimmy away. Even a couple of those he'd known, who he once might've thought of as friends, were jeering and cursing him. I've never seen Villagers get so agitated. Nor did I understand why. Whatever the reason, it was a real disappointment. All the way back to the tunnels, neither Jimmy nor me said a word. We had to have more people. Without them, we couldn't do a thing.

Later that day, Gordie and Luxurious asked me if they could go back over to the Camp for a couple more kids. They don't exactly pick their moments. I was so disillusioned by what happened earlier that I wasn't really listening to what they were saying, but no matter what sort they might be, they're still kids, and they nagged me so much that, in the end, and after making them promise they'd be really careful, I gave in. I mean, what difference is two more kids going to make to us anyway?

I don't know if I thought it would help in some way, or if it was merely frustration, but I decided to go up-top and make my way over to the hill that leads down to the Camp. Maybe if I studied it for a while, it'd help me to come up with a new plan.

The first thing that strikes you about that place is that it's not exactly easy on the eye. Just one big ugly sprawl of human necessity and waste, filling the half-basin from the hill to the ocean like the cold leftovers of a meal.

Way over to my left, almost at the same height as me, was the Wastelords' complex. A litter of wooden shacks with one proper brick-built house – De Grew's, of course – looking down on them. Leading up to it there's a steep slope with lots of junk scattered all round and, slightly to the left, the largest patch of green on the Island, the plots where they grow their fruit and vegetables.

There are several ways up there. The only problem being, just like before, we gotta go on a foggy night and I don't like my chances of getting lost. In fact, the more I look at it, the more I realise that, whoever I did, or didn't, get to help me, the one person I couldn't do without was Lena.

It don't exactly make me happy. I've been hoping to keep her out of this, that I'd take all the risks. And yet, thinking about it, I couldn't identify De Grew from that one glimpse. Call it another irony from a very long list, but she's the only one of us who's ever seen him up close, who can help me identify the guy, though I'm not entirely sure how we're going to go about it. I guess she's got to hear his voice, or maybe even smell him.

I don't know how long I sat there. Maybe three-quarters of an hour or so. Desperately trying to come up with another option, a way of doing this with fewer people, but having no luck.

Maybe it was that, the fact that I was so engrossed in what I was thinking, that made it possible for them to sneak up on me. For sure, it was one helluva shock when this voice rang out right behind me.

'Well, well, well. Look who's here.'

I turned around and was confronted by the same group I'd seen down at the old jetty, with the same Oriental-looking guy as their leader.

'What are you doing?' he demanded.

'Nothing.'

He paused for a moment, shaking his head. 'You know, I think that's too much of a coincidence. Doing nothing down at the jetty and now doing nothing up here.'

'I do nothing all over,' I said, trying to smile, to win him over, but getting no response.

As one, he and his companions began to circle around me.

'I told you before,' he said. 'I don't like you.'

'Yeah,' his shaven-headed companion agreed. 'Remember how he left the other day? Without even saying goodbye?'

'That was rude,' the Oriental one said. 'Why do you suppose he did that?'

'Maybe he's embarrassed about where he lives?'

I just stared at them, my stomach feeling like it was being force-fed iced pebbles. What exactly was going on here? What did they know?

'Well, we can't have that,' the Oriental guy teased. 'Let's go there now and show him we don't care what sort of place he lives in.'

I looked from one face to another, each one an image of stony and impassive malevolence. 'I'm not going home,' I eventually muttered, rather stupidly.

'Not doing anything here. You just told us.'

'I'm scavenging.'

'Let's go!' the Oriental guy growled, shoving me forward.

I knew I was in a lot of trouble. What I didn't know was exactly how much. I started to walk in the direction of the Village, any hopes I had of being able to get away dashed as soon as they hemmed me in.

As I walked, I did my best to think it through. Did they know anything? Had one of the Villagers talked? Or was it just that they wanted me to show them my lean-to so they could mark it out for the next foggy night? Whatever, once they knew I didn't have one, they were going to have an awful lot of questions.

For the second time that day I entered the rows, though on this occasion I got a very different reception. The moment people saw us they panicked and disappeared, rushing into their lean-tos. You could actually smell the fear coming off them, as if they'd wet themselves and were steaming. Mind you, their discomfort was as nothing compared with mine. What the hell was I going to do? I didn't live in the Village, I had no lean-to, and I couldn't keep walking them round for much longer.

'Where you taking us?' the Oriental guy demanded, already frustrated by my slow progress.

'You wanna see my lean-to,' I answered.

'I hope you ain't screwing me around,' he warned.

Another ten minutes or so, he started to get really angry. 'D'you think we're fools?' he said, stretching up to fill my face. 'We're going round in circles!'

I stopped, looking around as if I'd temporarily lost my bearings, which, in fact, I had. I mean, what did it matter which way I went? There was no way out of this. I thought about picking the nearest lean-to and entering, praying there was no one in there, or they'd be too surprised to say anything. But if they did, if they kicked up a fuss, I'd never see Lena again.

The Oriental guy continued to glare in my face, waiting for me to say something.

'*Where do you live?*' he shouted.

I really didn't see I had any other alternative. I'd just have to take a good swing at him, hope he went down, maybe get a couple of his friends, then make a run for it. I didn't give a lot for my chances, but what else could I do?

I was just about to do it, twisting my body into position to take a good hard shot, when at that very moment, the bearded guy from the morning, the one with long white hair, who got so angry with Jimmy, emerged from a nearby lean-to.

I tell you, it was the proverbial nightmare; all my worst fears rushing me at once. If anyone was going to take huge delight in dropping me into the shit with the Wastelords, it would be this guy.

He took one look at me, one look at them, and summed up the situation immediately. 'I hope you're not expecting me to feed them as well,' he said.

For a second I just gaped. I mean, it was far too quick for me.

'Thank you, gentlemen, for escorting my friend,' he continued, and with that, lifted the plastic on the door of his lean-to, and without a word, I allowed myself to be shepherded inside.

The Wastelords just stood there for a moment. They knew something didn't feel quite right, but not exactly what it was. The bearded guy promptly dropped the plastic so they were lost from sight.

There was a slight pause, then the Oriental one spoke outside. 'See you later,' he said threateningly.

There was some laughter, a couple of words of reinforcement from the others, then they left.

I turned to the bearded guy, astonished he should help. 'Jesus. Thanks,' I muttered.

'Not a pleasure.'

'You'll have to move. I think they were marking me out.'

'Won't be the first time,' he told me. There was an awkward pause. He was studying me closely, as if he wasn't quite sure what he was dealing with. 'So . . . what the hell is this about?'

'What do you mean?'

'This morning. And now this.' I paused for a moment, not sure how much I could tell him, but he made my mind up for me.

He gave a very long sigh. 'You know, I can take the bars; it's the patches of sky in between that break you.'

'What?'

'Hope,' he said. 'That's what really gets you. When someone starts trying to give you hope and then can't deliver.'

And finally I understood. Not just him, but some of the other Villagers as well. In a way, it was quite a shock. Deep down they howled for freedom as much as I did. Only they been ignoring those feelings for so long they've almost forgotten them. Which was why they'd got so angry when someone tried to stir them up again.

'To be honest, I don't know how much hope we got to offer,' I told him, 'but if it's only a speck, it's a damn sight more than we've had round here before.'

Again he paused, meeting my gaze as if reaching right down inside me, probing around, looking for something. 'So, tell me,' he eventually said.

The habits of a lifetime told me not to say anything. But something about that formidable stare, his forthright manner, made me think I could trust him.

'You wanna go for a walk?'

It felt kind of strange to take someone into the tunnels, but it just seemed like the easiest way to explain. Mind you, it gave the others a bit of a start. Especially when he walked into the living area and was nearly knocked over by Arturo. He made this instinctive grab for the little guy, like he was going to strangle him or something. Delilah went crazy, threatening to do all kinds of stuff if he so much as touched a hair on Arturo's head. I s'pose it was as much that as anything that convinced him things are a little different down here.

Turns out his name's Bailey, ex-army, which might come in useful. A member of one of the old mercenary battalions that, years ago, the government used to hire out to foreign powers to fight their battles. He got out when a lot of soldiers got out; when they found themselves killing allies on behalf of a foreign dictator who just happened to have more money. For years he survived on his own in the wilderness, but one day fell and broke his leg. Somehow he managed to get himself to hospital, but when he couldn't pay his bill, they tipped off the authorities. He was means-tested and sent out here. Something about him told you self-sufficiency came natural, that he loved freedom and solitude, and living on the Island was more painful for him than most.

I introduced him to everyone: Delilah and Arturo – the former who still hadn't forgiven him, the latter who couldn't give a damn – the still mostly silent Hannah, and finally, when she returned from the garden, Lena.

He studied her for a moment – on the way over I'd told him something of her story. 'You're the one they're looking for?' he said.

'Yes,' she replied. 'I'm sorry.'

'Not your fault,' he said. He took a pace nearer, staring into her face as if frustrated he couldn't search out her worth through her eyes. 'You lived down here on your own all that time?'

'Yes.'

He nodded, as if finally satisfied. 'Maybe they're right to be worried about you.'

Afterwards I showed him round. He didn't say much but you could see he was impressed. When I finally told him what we were planning, why we needed help, he got all excited, mentioning a list of Villagers he was sure would join us. Mostly ex-soldiers, like him, who could still remember how to handle themselves. I mean, we're not talking great numbers here, but with what we got so far, us, the kids, who knows?

Actually, I was in something of a dilemma concerning the kids. In a perfect world I wouldn't have involved them – they've had enough violence to last them a lifetime – but so much of what we're planning is dependent upon those in the Camp seeing them with us and not attacking. Who knows, maybe even joining our side. You gotta remember, there's thousands of them down there. If this goes wrong, there's going to be one helluva massacre, and we're going to be the first ones they turn on.

Later, I took Bailey down to the lower tunnels. I had it in mind for him to meet Jimmy under rather more favourable circumstances, working in his workshop, maybe on his computer, but on our way down we met the little guy running up.

I tell you, I've never seen him move so fast, not even when that crazy was after him in the Village. He must've run the whole distance, how puffed he was.

He hesitated when he saw Bailey, wondering why he was there, but only for a moment. He had something on his mind and was bursting to get it out.

'Big Guy! Big Guy!' he panted.

'What's the matter?' I said, gripping hold of him, scared he was going to give himself a heart attack or something.

'I got into those disks!' he cried. 'Or part way. Jesus, Big Guy, it's gonna change everything!'

CHAPTER EIGHTEEN

Jimmy took my arm and tugged me in the direction of his workshop. He was exhausted and all of a shake, but still started to run again, calling back for me to keep up. Bailey got left a few steps behind, mainly, I think, 'cuz he was so bemused by what was going on. I kept telling the little guy to wait up, not to get so excited, but he wasn't listening to a word I was saying. Eventually, with him still calling my name over and over, I followed him into his workshop. I just couldn't imagine what was so important.

I found him standing there, open-mouthed and trembling, jabbing his finger at the computer screen. There was a lot of information on there, headings and subheadings, I don't know, I guess that was as far into it as he'd managed to get. Most of it seemed to be details about something called '4S'. Whatever that might be.

Jimmy continued to gape at me, waiting for my reaction, almost imploding in agony when he didn't get one. Bailey followed us in, immediately stopping when he saw the screen. Initially, I think, just at seeing a computer, but then 'cuz he obviously realised something I hadn't.

'Jesus!' he gasped. 'Where the hell did you get that?'

'What? What is it?' I cried, not caring whether it made me look the dumb big guy or not.

'4S!' he told me.

'What?'

'Don't you know what 4S is?'

'Just tell me!' I said, getting a little annoyed.

'Satellite Surveillance Security System. By the look of it, you got the whole damn thing there. A complete breakdown.'

There was an astonished pause. Jimmy was so excited he had tears in his eyes. 'Big Guy! Don't you see? If I can get into this, maybe I *can* change the world!'

I gaped at him like I'd been hit real hard and was too stupid to go to the floor. 'How?' I finally blurted out.

He waved his arms about helplessly. 'I don't know! I got to get into it properly,' he said, studying the screen. 'Maybe I could fix up an antenna, some kind of transmitter.'

'Send it commands?' Bailey asked.

'Maybe . . . In time,' Jimmy replied, though not with complete conviction. 'It's just so damn difficult. One locked door after another and the key's always hidden in a different place. Even if I break all the way in there's got to be security codes on the actual system.'

'How long?' I asked.

The little guy made a face like maybe it would be next week, maybe next year, but more likely sometime after the world's gone bang. I sighed, unable to hide my disappointment. He really had me going there for a moment. Now we were back to firing pea-shooters at the sun.

'I need time!' he cried.

The only trouble is, we don't have it. Or certainly not in the quantities he requires. I mean, I can see why he's so excited by the possibility of finding out about the satellites, maybe even discovering something that might prove invaluable in the future. But the trouble with Jimmy is, he gets so swept away on these tidal waves of enthusiasm it can take days before he gets his feet back on firm ground again. We have other, far more pressing, problems, and now, thanks to Bailey, maybe the means of confronting them. When I told Jimmy the news about the Villagers who might want to join us, ex-soldiers, he wasn't in the slightest bit interested. In fact, he was so intent on getting back to that damn computer, I don't think he even registered what I said.

'Did you hear me?' I asked.

He nodded his head. 'Yeah, yeah.'

'Jimmy!' I groaned, but this time he didn't even answer.

In the end we left him to it. I mean, I have a fair idea what's gonna happen, that at some stage I'll be forced into dragging him away from that thing, that I'll be accused of all manner of tactical and mental shortcomings, but I don't care. He isn't the only one on a mission round here.

Bailey and me returned to the living area to find Gordie and Luxurious back with a couple more friends. Little guys, I think they were brothers, I don't know, Johnny and someone. As we arrived they were telling Lena and Delilah about more kids disappearing, that they'd seen a refrigerated container being loaded onto the night garbage boat.

There was a long silence. I could feel Delilah looking at me, but I refused to meet her gaze. I mean, I don't know if it's my imagination or what, but I hate this idea that everyone's waiting for me to do something. The intention's there, they know that, it's just that I haven't quite got my head round the logistics yet.

'I got two more lined up for tomorrow,' Gordie told us.

I turned to Lena. 'What d'ya think?'

She shrugged, plainly a little concerned. 'I don't know. That would make eight. It's unlikely to be noticed but . . .'

Gordie gave such a howl of protest, his disappointment in us so obvious it was just the final push I needed. 'Gordie! Gordie!' I cried, calming him, putting my hand on his shoulder.

'What?' he moaned.

'I want you to do something else for me.'

'What?' he repeated, even more begrudgingly.

I paused for a moment, taking a deep breath. 'Instead of persuading kids to come up here, I want you to get them to help us down there.'

He just stared at me, as if I wasn't making any sense. 'Doing what?'

'Next time there's a fog, we're going to attack the Camp.'

Silence fell like a pebble into a pond, and Johnny, or whatever his name is, whispered, 'Shit!' as if he just realised he'd been tricked into joining the funny farm.

'Are you serious?' Gordie asked.

'Yeah. But be careful. Better ten kids you can trust than fifty you can't.'

'But what are we going to do?' he persisted.

I shrugged, as if making the most matter-of-fact of decisions. 'We're going to blow that damn place, De Grew and all his Wastelords into the sea.'

Later, when I went down to Jimmy's workshop to inform him of the plan, that we were going down into the Camp as soon as the fog allowed and Bailey's contingent of Villagers was confirmed, his reaction was, well, about what I would've expected.

'You're kidding me?' he said, for once unlocking his gaze from his computer screen.

'No.'

'Big Guy!'

'Why not?'

'Wait for me to go through these disks!'

'Jimmy! We haven't got the time! Can you guarantee me that what's in there's going to help?'

'Yeah . . .' he said, with a slight hesitation.

'People are dying!'

'People are always dying,' he said, almost dismissively.

I tell you, that really got me. Obsession's such a selfish thing and I understand it normally, I really do. It's people like him who get things done in this world, who make the discoveries, illuminate our darkness. I'm just one of the dull masses who go to make up the demand. But this is something else.

'Can't you see how short-sighted you're being?' he said. 'What difference is a few days, a week or two, going to make to the overall situation?'

'To those kids being killed and chopped up for spare parts, quite a lot,' I growled. 'Still, as long as you get to play with your toys.'

There wasn't a lot of going back from that. I mean, we'd never had a proper argument before and I don't think either of us knew how to handle it. In the end, he just said I could do whatever I liked, but it would be without him. Which was a bit of a problem, 'cuz the main reason I'd gone to see him was to ask for his help. With no weapons on the Island apart from waste workers' machetes, I was hoping he might come up with a few ideas to even up the odds. It was the first time Jimmy ever let me down. He wouldn't even answer me. Just sat there hunched over his computer, tapping away at the keys, sulking like some shrivelled-up old man-child.

Thank God that Bailey returned from the Village with more encouraging news. He's managed to talk thirty-two people into joining us and, to be honest, when he told me it made me feel kind of humbled. I've always been so critical of Villagers, to find I'd misjudged them by that much came as quite a shock. All but two are ex-soldiers, some

nen, some women, and just like with the kids, we're going to bring
hem over a few at a time.

The other thing he's proved invaluable for is coming up with
nakeshift armaments. There's kerosene in one of the storerooms,
allons of it, and after collecting up every suitable container, he started
o make up some Molotov cocktails.

Course, when Jimmy got to hear, he was even more put out; sneering
t Molotovs, saying they were crude, only for 'kids and backstreet
ioters'. I guess he was just peeved at someone else taking over his
ole of inventor. In the end, and despite still being pissed at me, he
ouldn't resist showing Bailey how it 'ought to be done'. He knows
vhere he can get some weed-killer – that must've been used to keep
he concourses clear on the old stations or something – and has
egrudgingly abandoned his computer for the shortest of whiles to
et about making us up some 'real explosives'.

The following day, Gordie and Luxurious returned from the Camp
eally pleased with themselves. They've spoken to a lot of kids, those
hey're sure they can trust, and reckon they got twenty or so who are
vith us, and maybe twice that number who'll join in once they're
ure we're serious.

It's almost beyond belief. After everything that's happened, the
ids, who once hunted us, who treated our destruction like one of
hose old computer games, are now ready to fight alongside us. Maybe
iordie's oft-repeated boast that he's got a real reputation in the Camp
in't bravado after all. Either that or he's one helluva persuasive
peaker.

Later, Bailey's going to bring over the first of his old soldiers. I mean,
razy, harebrained, whatever this plan is, it's actually starting to fall
nto place. There's a real buzz going round the tunnels, a sense that
hese old arteries are starting to pulse with life again.

*

That afternoon I went up to the entrance to wait for Bailey. I knew he wouldn't take any risks bringing them in, I wasn't worried about that, it was more wanting to be there to greet them, to maybe make up for my past sins. And also, if I'm really honest about it, I was feeling pretty excited at the prospect of their arrival.

The only problem was, they didn't come. Not that day, nor the following one.

It completely threw me. I would've staked my life on that guy. It wasn't 'cuz of Wastelords, I knew that. All the times I'd looked out over those few days, I barely seen more than the odd one in the distance. In fact, I'd been wondering where they'd gone. So what the hell was keeping them?

I waited 'til the next morning, and still with no sign, decided to go over and see what the problem was. The moment the Village came into sight I got my answer. No wonder I hadn't seen many Wastelords in the Old City, they were all over there. I never seen that many. Every direction you looked there were gangs of red overalls bleeding from one row into another. And as I got that bit closer, I saw something that was even more of an unpleasant surprise.

It wasn't only Wastelords. Not just Islanders. There were others too. Men and women, casually dressed in civilian clothing, and yet something about them made you think they were a proper trained and disciplined force. I turned to look down to the pier. There was an unfamiliar boat tied up down there – I don't know, I'm not an expert, it wasn't painted in military colours or anything, but it was some kind of patrol boat. Over in the distance, up near the Head, not one, but two Infinity Dragonflies suddenly chattered into the air. Jesus, they must've thought that whatever was going on was interesting.

I stood there for a while, tempted to go into the Village, try to find out what was going on, but in the end decided it was too risky. Instead

I made my way back to the tunnels. All of the others, with the exception of Jimmy who was still spending his time down in his workshop (and presumably away from me), were waiting in the living area.

'Well, that's it,' Delilah said, on hearing my news. 'They'll be over here next.'

'We can trust Bailey,' I reassured her.

'And what about the other thirty-two?' Delilah asked.

There was a pause, Gordie made this kind of sneering grunt, like it was my fault for involving Villagers in the first place.

'Who the hell are those other guys?' I asked, for maybe the tenth time.

'Mainland police?' Lena suggested.

'Is there such a thing?'

'Some kind of security maybe?'

'But what are they doing here?'

'I don't know!'

I sighed, knowing she was getting a little irritated. 'I gotta go back over. Speak to Bailey.'

'How?' Lena asked. 'If there's that many?'

I hesitated, but only for a moment. 'At night.'

'Clancy!'

'What choice have I got?'

'I'll come,' Gordie volunteered.

'Me, too!' Arturo chimed in, with Luxurious only a fraction behind.

'I don't think so,' I said.

'Why not?' Gordie asked, though he swallowed the question almost as soon as he said it. 'Oh.'

'What?' Arturo asked.

'Nothing.'

'What?' Arturo asked again.

Gordie kind of headed him away, the other kids following. 'They don't want us going over to the Village at night,' he muttered. 'Frightening old people.'

All of them went quiet and drifted off down the tunnel, their heads slightly bowed, like they'd just been reminded of a misdemeanour they'd almost forgotten.

Lena sighed. 'I'll come with you.'

'No, dammit!' I said, wishing I'd never said anything. 'I know the way better than you do. And, Delilah, before you say anything, no, I don't want your help either!'

It's funny how nights can vary in terms of darkness, with or without the moon. This one seemed a lot denser than the time I went out to dig up the cable, like I was having to actually push its folds aside to get through. I knew I couldn't do what I did before: assume there'd be no one around and go wherever I liked. Island rules have changed. Anything's possible now. I needed to skulk in the shadows, slip from one pile of rubble to the next, constantly on the lookout.

When the pier came into view, the boat had gone and presumably its passengers with it, so that was one worry I didn't have to deal with. Mind you, I still didn't have a clue what I was up against, nor what to expect.

It took me the best part of three-quarters of an hour to get over there. Ducking down, leaping in and out of mounds of garbage, forever disturbing protesting rats. The way the weather's been, with no fog in a while, I was hoping Bailey wouldn't have moved his lean-to yet. If he had, God knew what I was going to do.

I turned into the rows, walking as quietly as I could, aware I was probably alarming Villagers, that they had to be wondering who the hell was out at this time of night. One lean-to I passed, this woman must've been on the final strand of a whole lotta torture, 'cuz she started to scream, over and over, like she just couldn't bear it anymore.

I heard this female voice trying to pacify her, telling her it was all right, but I hurried on, anxious to be gone before any Wastelords came to investigate.

Villagers don't normally sleep that well, just endlessly doze, but there inevitably comes a time when they're so exhausted they almost fall into a coma. Which must've been the case with Bailey, 'cuz I was able to slip into his lean-to without so much as the slightest alteration to his long, low snoring. I locked my arm around his neck, my hand across his mouth and he instantly awoke.

'It's me!' I hissed, as he tried to wrench himself free. His eyes kind of gaped, like he was furious with me, or maybe himself, then he went all limp, as if to indicate submission. 'We need to talk. And I hope for your sake you haven't been talking to anyone else,' I warned.

He nodded his head slowly to show he understood and I removed my hand from over his mouth.

'They're searching the Village,' he told me. 'Going through every single lean-to. No one's being allowed to leave.'

'Who is?'

'The Wastelords. And others. From the Mainland.'

I sighed and released my grip fully, knowing instantly it was true. 'Who?'

'Infinity?' he suggested.

'Nah, they're just media.'

'Only name I've seen. Whoever they are, De Grew seems pretty grateful for their assistance.'

'He's been here?'

'Every day.' Bailey gave this kind of low whistle, as if he'd come face to face with the devil. 'One helluva nasty piece of work.'

I paused for a moment, trying to take it all in. 'Is this still about Jena?'

Bailey shook his head. 'I don't think so. Somebody's talked

somewhere. They're going through the whole place inch by inch. Searching for weapons, anything that might be used in a fight. The Old City'll probably be next.'

'I don't get it.' I sighed. 'What about these volunteers of yours?'

'We're still with you, but . . . what can we do?'

I thought for a moment. 'Can you round them up now?'

'In the dark?'

I nodded. Bailey made this face like it wasn't going to be easy, but still agreed.

'We can't do nothing without you,' I told him. 'Thirty or so people are going to make all the difference.'

'Twenty-seven,' he said, sounding a little apologetic. 'Including me.' I looked at him, waiting for an explanation. 'He frightens the hell out of everyone.'

I nodded my head, again feeling that plunging in my stomach I'd got so used to over the last few days; he was talking about the man I was planning to kill.

As quietly as we possibly could, Bailey and me went from lean-to to lean-to, gathering up our little army, their ages and shortcomings all too obvious as they stumbled sleepily out into the night. Several times one of them fell over something as we made our way along the row. You could hear people inside muttering away, wondering what the hell was going on. A couple of plastics were pulled back a finger or two, but we just kept moving.

It was even worse when got out on the tips. Scampering from one mound of garbage to another was almost comic. God knows how long it'd been since they'd been out at night. I mean, each society creates its own culture and in ours you simply didn't do it. They were tripping over, wandering off in the wrong direction, getting lost all the time. It was all I could do to ensure we ended up with the same number we started off with.

Mind you, to be fair, by the time we reached the tunnel entrance they were starting to get the hang of it. But any hope they had of regaining their composure was lost when I suddenly leant into a pile of rubble and magically opened a door. There were a couple of gasps, one or two muttered curses, and though they tried to take it in their stride, what they were met with inside, what they saw on their way down, made it impossible.

You should've seen their faces when they first confronted the kids. They were like age-old natural enemies, cats and dogs, hackles raised, eyes blazing, circling round, getting ready for a fight. Course, we had to explain to them that it ain't like that down here, but they only really got it when they saw Arturo cuddling up to Delilah, Luxurious jealously trying to slide in between them. Even Gordie became aware enough of the situation to soften his act a little, cutting down on his usual attitude and aggression.

As for Hannah, well, in a way she's the biggest miracle of them all. She still hasn't spoken more than the odd word, but I tell you, I gotta helluva shock the day I found her dancing in the garden. I went down to see if she wanted any help digging up some vegetables. As I was approaching, I could hear these skippy little footsteps, someone softly humming. Course, she stopped as soon as she realised I was watching, but do you know something? Even though I only caught a moment of it, even though she pretended like it never happened, it was long enough for me to see what she was doing. Out here, in all this shit and violence, and after the ugly and despairing life she's known, that kid was dancing ballet. Pirouetting and skipping across the garden, leaping into the air, and I tell you, it was something quite beautiful to behold.

Anyways, small and disparate though we might be, our little army is finally assembled. Thirty-one adults and six kids (plus the promise of at least another twenty, maybe more, to rendezvous with us on the way down). Which probably doesn't sound like that many under the circumstances, but in the few days that we've all been down here, it sometimes feels like a good old-fashioned rush hour. Everywhere you look there are people. Stretched out along the living area, sleeping in every alcove, wandering round wondering what to do. All of them living in this kind of limbo state, not used to this underground world the way we are, and not planning to get that way either. Life for them is up-top and won't begin again until we go up there and fight for it.

Lena's had to break out the last of her canned food. Even allowing for what people brought with them, I reckon we haven't got much more than a week or so. The garden's almost stripped bare already. On the other hand, our stockpile of armaments is growing by the day. Home-made explosives, Molotovs, a handful of machetes, clubs and various other sundry weapons (mostly adapted tools Jimmy reluctantly allowed us to take from his workshop). Not exactly hi-tech, but it still makes you feel good to see it all stacked up there.

The only thing for me is, I don't fancy any of it. Maybe it says a lot about the *new* me, but these days there's something about a machete I find just too personal. It only has one function, to cleave, slice, stab, and inflict as much physical damage as possible, and I don't want that anymore. I decided to make myself something I feel more comfortable with: a length of heavy metal pipe, with a block of wood in one end and a blade embedded in the other. I guess it sounds a bit odd, but it gives me options that a machete can't. A little on the heavy side, maybe. Arturo can barely lift it. Six months ago, it would've had me puffing. But do you know something? While I been working out with that thing, whirling it round, thrashing it back and forth, something's started to reawaken in me. Maybe it's the actual feeling, maybe it's just the memory, but I got this notion of being formidable again, of being able to stand in everyone's way, and that nothing and no one is going to move me.

Course, the frustration is, will I get the chance to prove it? The weather's set fair, without the slightest hint of fog, and already people are starting to get on edge. Pacing up and down to the entrance, peering out, frightened the enemy are going to begin their search of the Old City before we get a chance to go down into the Camp.

Delilah had a bit of a spat with one of the old soldiers; someone she had a problem with from the Village. The kids got a little too boisterous and got shouted at in terms that make you realise this is still an extremely fragile alliance. But the person worrying me the most is Lena. With each day she's been withdrawing, as if she was no longer sure she wanted any part of this. I've asked her a couple of times what the problem is and she's reassured me there ain't one, but I get the feeling that I just picked the wrong moment.

One night, lying in bed, the hands of the clock finally hit the mark and she said one of the nicest things anyone's ever said to me. Only later did I realise it wasn't quite what I first imagined.

'You know something?' she whispered. 'Lying in your arms is the only place I feel comfortable.'

I squeezed her. 'Me too.'

There was a long pause in which, at some point, I realised the weight of silence was doubling by the second. 'How am I going to cope, Clancy?'

'What d'ya mean?'

'I've fallen over twice in the last couple of days.'

I half chuckled, half grunted, remembering how she'd been caught out by someone shifting the pots and pans and went sprawling over them.

'This isn't my home anymore,' she told me.

And finally I saw what was getting to her. She was comfortable only in my arms 'cuz it was the one place she knew hadn't changed. Everywhere else there were new people, their possessions, all manner of things, getting ready to trap her. It was sucking on her confidence. Outside she expected to have to live with such problems, but this was her base, her security, the certainty from which she stretched out.

'It's okay,' she eventually sighed, as if she thought I had worries enough. 'I just got to get used to the idea of leaving this place.'

I kissed her on the forehead. 'Maybe you won't have to?'

'We're not doing this so we can come back. You know that as well as I do.'

I hugged her so hard, like I was trying to tell her that, no matter where we were, I was always going to have my arms around her.

It's shit to admit but, the truth is, I don't know how this is going to turn out any more than she does. I've been promising everyone a new life, but really, what do I know? If we do manage to get rid of De Grew and his Wastelords – and that's got to be the biggest 'if' since our ancestors flippered their way out of the ocean – and they aren't running the Island anymore, I haven't got a clue what's going to replace them. Just a blind faith that, whatever it is, it's gotta be better than what we have now.

The following afternoon I couldn't take it anymore. We been going crazy cooped up down here. I slipped out to get a better look at the incoming weather, finding myself a spot down in the square, sitting atop a pile of rubble, watching the sun descend slowly through yet another unpromising sky. Below it, getting ready to catch that flaming ball, waited the Mainland, the City stretching all the way up the coast 'til it gives way to a distant smudge of something else. We haven't given a thought to what they might do. Plainly the rumours are true: De Grew is in league with the Mainland, but how far does it go? These 'helpers' or 'advisors' or whatever they are come over every day, but then go back at night. So at least we don't have to worry about meeting them in the Camp. But what's going to happen afterwards? That's one of the things about punishment satellites: they never dispense retrospective justice. If they don't get you at the time, that's it. There ain't the programming, or maybe the manpower, to do it later. But maybe this is different?

I was just sitting there, trying to weave strands of cloud, or hints of haze, into the beginnings of a fog, when I saw a group of Wastelords emerging out of the ruins. I rolled to my side and fell back behind a pile of rubble, waiting there a few seconds, then peering back over. There must've been eight or nine of them. None that I'd come across before but equally as threatening. And a kid, too. A boy, no bigger than Arturo. They were all grouped around him, shouting at the little guy, and though I couldn't make out what was being said, I could hear him crying.

One of them pushed him on, gave him a real shove, like they wanted him to lead them somewhere and it hit me. *Oh Jesus, that kid knows something!* Somehow he got to hear about what was going on and the Wastelords found out. Now they were forcing him to show them where we were!

As I watched them prod and push him forward, the kid reluctantly heading in the direction of the entrance, my heart was pounding so hard it felt as if it might smash out through my ribs. *No! Not now!* And the worst thing of all was, I couldn't warn the others. A gang of Wastelords was advancing upon them, about to come bursting in, and there was nothing I could do.

It was only when the kid started to take a slightly different direction, to veer away from the entrance, that I realised. What the hell was I talking about? He couldn't know where it was. The new kids had all been led up there. He must've just heard a whisper, maybe indulged in some idle boasting and they thought he knew more than he did.

Again he stopped, again they shouted at him and again he started to cry. They jostled him a bit, threw him from one to another, and he became so disorientated that when they pushed him on again, he started to lead them back the way they came. This time they completely lost their tempers. One of them shoved him to the ground. I mean, they were taking a chance with those things up there, but they obviously had a fair idea how far they could go. The little guy tried to get up, to scramble away, but another one trod on his arm, pinning him down.

It was all I could do not to go over there and stop them. And yet, how could I? Not only would I not stand a chance, but I'd be jeopardising everything and everyone in the tunnels. There was nothing for it but to remain hidden, listening to those cries, knowing that at least they couldn't go too far without being punished.

There was another shout, a much angrier one – maybe they worked out that he didn't know as much as they'd hoped – and suddenly they were going crazy at him; snarling and threatening, abusing him at the tops of their voices. The little guy was just lying there, in the middle of them, rolled up in a ball wailing and sobbing, having to soak up everything they threw at him.

In the end they just walked away and left him where he was. And d'you know something? Something that may surprise you? They hadn't got more than thirty or forty yards before he picked himself up and chased after them. You couldn't believe it. If it hadn't been for the satellites they probably would've killed him. First chance they get, they probably still will. But he ran after them, begging and pleading for forgiveness, just like they were his family or something.

As soon as they were out of sight, I slipped back over to the entrance and got myself inside. I was worried to hell, but didn't know if it was justified or not. How much could that kid conceivably know? Was he one of Gordie's wavering recruits? Or just someone who picked up on a rumour? Whatever, I couldn't help but feel that they had a pretty good idea where we were.

*

The following morning I made sure I was the first one out of bed, immediately making my way up to the entrance. I'd had a really difficult night, unable to tell anyone, not even Lena, what I knew and not sure what it meant anyway. I mean, there must be rumours all over. At times like this, when something's brewing, it's only human nature. Why would anyone pay another rumour any more mind? Unless they knew exactly where we were, they were going to have to go through the Old City the same way they did the Village, inch by inch, which hopefully meant we had weeks before they'd find us. Surely there'd be a fog in that time? Surely we'd get the chance to call on them before they called on us?

I don't know whether I believed that or not. To be honest, I didn't know what I expected to find when I reached the entrance. I just wanted to be able to put my, and everyone else's, minds at rest. I didn't even reach the top before I heard a kind of resonant thumping echoing down the tunnel, then this dull grating, the roar of an engine, a slight shaking of the ground. *What the hell?*

I ran the rest of the way, falling to my knees, jamming my face to the cracks in the door, having my worst fears realised and even bettered. There was a small army advancing upon us, dozens of them spread across the horizon, with all kinds of equipment and machinery. Trucks, a couple of bulldozers, drills, picks and shovels. I guess it had all been brought over on that boat. Most of those following along behind, appearing out of the haze and dust, were Wastelords – tidying up what was being smashed down, putting some of the heavier stuff onto trucks – but again there were others and this time they were wearing uniforms.

'Jesus, no!' I groaned, immediately realising they were heading straight for us.

To my left, no more than twenty or thirty metres away, a small advance guard came into view. A man and woman, both using some kind of imaging equipment, seeking out the most likely places for people to hide. When the guy turned round for a moment, I could see this writing on his back – 'Infinity Specials'. Jeez, so Bailey was right. Infinity were involved in some way. Maybe they have a security division they hire out, that the Mainland's put at De Grew's disposal? Perhaps he'd got so fed up with looking for us that he'd brought in expert help? Which would explain the sudden increase in choppers.

For several minutes I was seemingly incapable of doing anything. I just sat there watching their slow but relentless progress towards us. I didn't want this to be true. Didn't want to have to go down and tell the others that it was all over. And yet, the odd thing was, when I finally did force myself, when I fronted up there all pale and serious-faced, no one seemed that surprised. There was a degree of panic, of fear, but the overriding sense, especially with the old folk, was of something closer to embarrassment, of having been such fools to have dared to dream long after dreams were known to be dead.

'Let's go up and wait for them,' Gordie said. 'Jump them as they come in.'

'There's too many,' I told him.

Gordie turned to Lena, as if he hoped she might know what to do, but one look at her expression was enough to know that she thought it was over, too.

'We gotta do something!' he cried, his voice trailing off as people started to turn away.

This eerie silence descended upon us all. I mean, what's there to say? There's no other way out. Okay, so we have our 'weapons', but this ain't kids about to find their way in. This is an army comprised of well-equipped Mainlanders plus the bloodiest, meanest survivors of the Island's natural selection process. Those who've proved more violent, more evil, than all others. Nor is there any chance of hiding in the lower tunnels. I mean, I ain't the greatest military tactician in the world, but I know what I'd do in their place: smoke us out and pick us off as we tried to make it up to the surface.

I think it was only then that I realised just how bad our situation was. Our sanctuary has become, not just a prison, but a trap. Once they get inside, the satellites can't save us. Nothing can. They can do exactly what they like, and I'll tell you something, I don't even want to imagine what that might be.

Hour after hour's gone by. Still there's very little movement or conversation. Everyone's just waiting for the sound of them coming down the tunnel. We haven't even placed a lookout up there. Not permanently. Just now and then someone's unable to resist going up to take a peep and they return a little later, ashen-faced, like they're about to be sick, with news that the Wastelords are getting closer. The whole living area, old folks, kids, are numb and pale with fear. Everyone's slumped on the ground, leaning against the tunnel wall or hanging on to each other, staring up at the roof, trying to see the surface beyond.

For a while Lena's been trying to keep busy, dishing out her remaining supplies of hooch to those who are craving it, but eventually she found her way into my arms and we're staying here the same as everyone else, awaiting our discovery.

It was one helluva mixed blessing when we realised that it was dark and they'd gone, that they weren't going to find us that day. We knew it could only be a temporary respite, that they'd be back first thing in the morning, and in some ways I think we would've preferred to get it over with.

I went up to the entrance, just to see how close they'd got, how much time we'd have in the morning. It didn't take a lot of working out. The remains of walls that stood only feet away were now part of a huge swathe of rubble that started in the distance and stopped almost at our door. In fact, they were so close, it was as if they'd known all along where we were and just been teasing.

I looked out as best I could, wondering if they'd left someone out there in case we tried to make a run for it. But why would they? Where the hell were we going to go?

I was just about to turn away, to go back down and tell the others the news, when, as my eyes skimmed across the horizon, I saw something that stopped me dead. I mean, Jesus, I hadn't even thought about it. It had been so long, none of us had. But moving in across the ocean, rearing up like some huge tidal wave, was a massive towering wall of fog.

CHAPTER NINETEEN

An hour or so later it was all around us, like some great dull vacuum sucking out our reality. Once more the rules were to be changed. Different boundaries would exist. Those things up in the sky couldn't watch over us anymore. Nor anyone else, come to that. There would be no judgements from on-high that night. It was up to us to create our own justice.

At first everything went remarkably well. Our makeshift little army rapidly assembled, got itself organised, grabbed weapons, decided who would carry the explosives. Then I realised that the kids were nowhere to be seen. I was about to ask Lena where they were when I heard Bailey give a cry of protest, followed by a lot of anxious muttering from the rest of the old folk. The moment I turned around I knew why.

It even gave me a bit of a start. Approaching along the tunnel, all dressed and made up for killing, were the kids. Gordie almost naked, his body all whited-up with huge smudges of black around his eyes; Arturo, like some dance-hall queen, long shiny red dress, blonde wig, sparkly make-up with heavy boots and a safety helmet. Luxurious was wearing an old tiger-skin rug he must've dug out of the garbage, his face striped yellow and black – he'd even tried filing his teeth and nails into points. And Hannah . . . Jesus, Hannah . . . was wearing theatrical make-up and a black – what do you call it? – tutu? Like she was about to perform a ballet.

'What the hell are you doing?' I shouted, it momentarily occurring to me that these must've been the possessions they brought with them from the Camp.

All of them gaped at me, like they didn't have a clue what I was talking about.

'Why are you dressed like that?' I demanded.

Gordie shrugged. 'Why not?'

'Don't you think we've seen enough of this?'

They all looked to one another, still not understanding what they'd done wrong.

'We always dress up,' Arturo whined.

Delilah went and stared deep into his made-up face, like she couldn't believe it was really him. 'This is the way you came to the Village,' she reminded him.

There was a long silence. No one really knew what to think or say. I mean, it's probably the most disturbing aspect of them; the way they can be so innocent and guilty at the same time.

Eventually, as if she'd been saving herself for this moment, as if the rarity of her words made them count that much more, Hannah spoke.

'We know it's different,' she reassured us.

I sighed, as ever bemused by their behaviour, their way of thinking. I mean, kids, dressed up, trick-or-treating maybe, nothing could seem more harmless. 'I want you to promise me that whatever happens, when this night's over, you'll burn these,' I told them.

There was a pause, then Gordie reluctantly nodded. I mean, I'd already forbidden them to carry machetes – only clubs or baseball bats – and I think they were still smarting over that.

'Never again!' I emphasised. 'Not for any reason.'

'Okay, okay!' he said, like I was some overreacting parent.

Bailey shook his head, as if he thought we shouldn't let them get away with it, but Delilah tried to tug Arturo into an embrace. For once he wouldn't let her, making a point of standing on his own, like a child on his first day of school not wanting to be labelled a handmaiden by his peers.

Finally, all of us were assembled and ready to go. The old soldiers unable to stop themselves forming into a couple of lines, the kids looking like they were off to a party; especially Hannah, who had gotten hold of some silver paper and wrapped it round her baseball bat so it looked like a giant wand. I looked to a couple of people, wondering why they weren't moving off, then realised everyone was waiting on me.

It was kind of embarrassing. I already told you, I take orders, not give them. However, that seemed to be what they wanted, so what else could I do? I turned, was just about to lead them away, when I noticed Jimmy wasn't with us.

'Where the hell's the little guy?' I muttered to Delilah.

'Sorry, Clancy,' she replied. 'Still in his workshop.'

I was just going to send one of the kids down to get him when he appeared from the other direction; from the garden.

'Jimmy!' I groaned.

'Okay, okay!' he said. 'I'm ready.'

Just for a moment it went through my head that maybe he'd been thinking about not going. That he'd actually prefer to take his chances down in the tunnels, in his precious workshop, than be any part of a venture I was leading.

We still hadn't made things up. In fact, what with me getting all his ready, and him presumably working on his computer, I'd barely seen him. But I still couldn't believe he'd let me down. Jimmy was a major part of things and he knew it. Tell the truth, it kind of undermined me. Not that I was about to show it, not to him or anyone else. Instead, I took a deep breath, and with one last look around me, like a general surprised at just how many troops went to make up an army, I led everyone off in the direction of the entrance.

I can't tell you how strange it felt emerging into that foggy night. Not just 'cuz of where we were going, but also 'cuz of what we were leaving behind. I made a point of closing the door behind us, but wondered why. I mean, whatever was going to happen, it wasn't likely we'd ever return. I glanced across at Lena. Even in the dull blending of darkness and fog I could see she was thinking the same thing. I moved a little closer, gave her arm a squeeze, just to let her know I understood. That place had been her home for years. It meant nothing less than life. Now she was leaving it behind forever. The garden, the living area, everything she'd worked so hard to create, abandoned down there in the darkness. For some reason it made me think of Ethel Weiss; her suitcase in the wall. Is that what was going to happen to us? Sometime in the future someone was going to stumble on the tunnels, find our things, and wonder what happened to our bid for freedom?

Slowly we picked our way through the ruins of the Old City, our collective footsteps sounding dully on the ground. I've been a part of some odd gangs in my time, but never anything like that; old folks staggering along with boxes of Molotov cocktails as if they'd just come back from doing their weekly shopping; kids looking like they'd just stepped out of some weird fairy tale. At one point Gordie whacked Arturo for giggling, which resulted in a loud cry of protest. It's moments like those you realise they are just kids, and to be honest, I could well do without them. I was about to drop back and give them a piece of my mind, but Bailey beat me to it, angrily hissing something into their faces that instantly shut them up.

Lena, of course, was in the lead. Getting along in her customary fashion, not on foot, but by something like 'all-possibility tracks'. The Wastelords might've created a hell of a mess, demolishing everything, clearing the rubble, but that meant more of a problem for us than her. She just reacted in her usual manner: last-moment changes of direction, of step and height, and no map in her head to confuse her.

As we were crossing the square, she suddenly stopped, her head cocked as if she heard something, and panic rippled back through the group 'til all of us were frozen there like a Wasteland of statues.

I strained to get my old eyes to pierce the fog, wondering if maybe the Wastelords had left someone on watch up here after all, though surely they wouldn't have stayed once the fog fell?

Eventually Lena nodded her head, touched me on the arm and moved forward. 'They're up ahead,' she whispered.

'Who?'

'Gordie's friends.'

To be honest I was a little surprised. I mean, Gordie had sworn they'd be there, waiting at the top of the hill, but I certainly hadn't been counting on it. He made this hissing noise with his teeth and soon someone called softly to us from out of the fog.

'Gordie?'

'Yeah.'

I'll tell you, to rendezvous with that bunch, to suddenly see them materialising out of the fog, just like our kids, all dressed and made up, was not a comforting experience. And the fact that there were rather more than we'd been expecting, though gratifying, also made it that much more intimidating. If they'd turned on us, if they'd attacked us then and there, I wouldn't have been the least bit surprised.

'This is Gigi,' Gordie told me, forcing himself to make introductions, maybe 'cuz he could see how ill at ease I was.

I nodded at what I quickly realised was a girl; all dirt, tangled hair and seagull feathers, but she gave me a surprisingly broad smile.

'Hi.'

There was just a moment of hesitation while everyone looked at one another, the dawning realisation of just how disparate a band we all were, but I was anxious to keep going. I mean, if anyone's going to question my leadership, now's the time for them to do it.

'Let's go,' I said, Lena following as I led them away. And you wanna know something? That almost made me burst out into a smile? Man, woman and child – damned if they didn't all tag along behind.

The plan – if you wanted to call it that – was that, when we got down into the sorting area, we'd split into three groups: Jimmy, Delilah and the kids were going to blow the drugs warehouse; Bailey and his old soldiers would toss all the Molotovs they had into the Wastelords' shacks; and, in what we hoped would be chaos, Lena and I were going to enter the main house to settle with De Grew.

I mean, I knew it was pretty flimsy, but with what we had available, it was the best I could come up with. And anyways, it's like I said, it's how the kids in the Camp reacted that'd decide the thing. If what Gordie said was true; there were others who'd join us once it got started, we had to hope the majority would get swept along with them. On the other hand, maybe they'd see their precious drugs going up in flames and chop us up and leave us for the rats.

We began to descend towards the Camp. So far we hadn't seen or heard a thing. In fact, the silence was that heavy, it made the fog seem that bit thicker. In places you couldn't even see where you were putting your feet, you had to just thrust them out in front of you, into nothing, and hope they eventually made contact with something solid. One of the old soldiers slipped and fell heavily, a real resonating thump that made you think he must've broken something, but he got up and moved on, proudly ignoring the concern of those around him.

Soon the ground began to level out and Lena turned towards the sorting area and the new garbage. This time she didn't have to tell me when we were nearing it as my senses were once again assaulted; I had that same rush of memories, mugged by nostalgia. Behind me I heard some of the Villagers getting carried away, becoming all excited, and I had to tell them to keep it down.

A few minutes later we parted company with Jimmy, Delilah and the kids. They looked so damn pathetic heading off into the fog. A little bent old man, a long twisted stick of a woman, Arturo, Gordie, a gang of children and several boxes of home-made tricks, off to destroy the most prized possessions of the Wastelords. If it wasn't for the fact that all the missions were suicidal, I would've insisted on swapping with them.

No farewells were exchanged, no wishes of good luck, but I remained where I was until the fog completely embraced them, the thought that I might never ever see any of them again having to be repeatedly evicted from my mind.

Bailey and his old soldiers accompanied us up the slope towards the Wastelords' complex, then peeled off along the path to the lower level, many of them still insisting on marching, on holding formation.

Now it was just Lena and me, all alone in that vast grey emptiness. For a moment we just stood there, feeling the ache of our place in the night, almost too daunted to go on, then she tugged at my arm.

'Come on,' she whispered.

She led me through a storage area, with lots of old oil drums and wooden crates strewn around, occasionally stopping, sniffing and listening, switching over to her different map. Which was just as well, cuz halfway up the hill we met a couple of Wastelords coming down.

She had just enough time to get us hidden before they appeared out of the fog, angrily muttering to each other, grumbling about something someone had said to them.

They were almost by us and away, when it occurred to me that they might be going over to relieve the guards on the drugs warehouse and could stumble on Jimmy and the kids. In an instant I leapt out, swung that big-bladed bar of mine and cracked the nearest one across the back of the head. The other guy turned, so shocked all he could do was to try to run. He got about half-a-dozen paces before he stumbled and fell. Lena was on him before I was. I told you she's strong, but in that moment it seemed like more. She jerked his head back, drove it into the ground; one movement and he was gone.

'Jesus!' was all I could say.

We dragged the two of them aside, threw garbage on their bodies, then continued up the hill. Below us, over to our right, a stifled cry echoed out of the fog. I don't know, it could've been anything, but it was in the region of Bailey and his group. We waited, but there was nothing more, so moved on.

It was strange. I could feel the old adrenaline starting to surge through me. I was a little more nervous than I used to be, more aware of the dangers, but I could handle it all right. In fact, I was almost beginning to enjoy myself.

A few minutes later, Lena put a hand on my arm and I realised we'd arrived. To my right there was a huge dark clot in the fog and something black and substantial looming out of the murk.

'Can you see it?' she asked.

'Yeah . . . I see it.'

Crouching low, she felt her way over to a woodpile and we squatted down behind it, not twenty yards from the house. We'd arrived. We were in place. Now all we had to do was wait for Jimmy.

Neither of us mentioned it, but I knew she had to be as worried about his part in this as I was. I mean, the little guy ain't anyone's idea of an action hero. Nor did we have a clue what he was up against over there. Course, he had all the kids with him, but, in truth, they were something of an unknown quantity. This wasn't getting all drugged up and butchering helpless old people, this was going clear-headed up against strong and mean young men they'd always regarded as their masters. Who knew how they'd react?

Five minutes went by. Then five that seemed like ten. Then five that seemed to have hitched themselves to eternity. I was making these funny little breathy noises, like I was cold and shivering, but really it was just nerves. A door slammed somewhere inside the house. A man shouted. I wondered if it was him – De Grew – but there was no reaction from Lena, so I guess not.

The only thing she hadn't been able to tell me was if he'd be alone or not. Apparently, some nights he'd have a gang up here; drinking, watching a movie, playing cards, fooling around. Other times he got all mean and spiteful, picking on people, trying to start fights, throwing them out and taking out his rage on some kid. That was one of the reasons why we had to wait for Jimmy to blow up the warehouse, to flush out whoever was in there. That is, if he ever managed it.

'Come on, Jimmy,' I urged.

'Give him time,' Lena reassured me. 'He'll do it.'

I couldn't imagine for one moment that she was that confident. It was only a hundred and fifty yards or so to the warehouse from where we'd last seen him. He should've been there ages ago. What the hell was keeping him?

'Think about the house,' Lena told me.

'What?'

'The layout! What I told you! Forget about Jimmy.'

She was right. Go over everything she'd told me; get it fixed in my head one last time. Hit the front door, kick it open, everything to my right: people, chairs, maybe a movie showing. If there were Wastelords, that's where they'd be. Maybe a few kids too, for 'entertainment' purposes. If De Grew wasn't there, it was straight ahead, through the door in the corner into his bedroom.

Course, she gave me a detailed description of him as she last knew him: thick-set, blonde hair, beard, a large face with hard and heavy cheekbones. I mean, if only one person dies tonight, it has to be him.

Suddenly the door opened, there was a momentary glow of light, a heavy masculine shape, then it closed again and footsteps approached. Lena and me crouched lower, but whoever it was passed by and took the path down the hill. I tell you, I was starting to panic. For all we knew he was also on his way over to the drugs warehouse. Jimmy must've screwed up. He was supposed to have given us ten minutes to get up the hill and get in place. It was more like half-an-hour now.

'Stay here,' I said to Lena, getting up.

'Where you going?' she asked.

'Something's gone wrong.'

'*No!*'

She shouted after me as loudly as she dared, but I was off; tripping and stumbling through the fog, making my way back down the slope. I knew I was panicking, but I had every right. We had to blow that damn warehouse, nothing was going to happen until we did.

I got about a hundred and fifty yards, maybe more, it's hard to say, when suddenly there was an explosion below me. One, then another. And then a really huge one, like something else had been ignited. An orange glow erupted across the fog like it was burning a hole in it. I immediately stopped, realising what a stupid mistake I'd made. I should be outside the house now. It was at this point I was supposed to have gone in to tackle De Grew. I turned and started to run back up the hill, cursing myself the whole way.

When I got back to the house, I couldn't find Lena. I started searching around, whispering her name into the fog, calling out for her. Where the hell was she? What had happened? Then I heard shouts coming from inside and realised she was already in there.

I rushed in after her, finding myself in the main room. One look was enough to know what had happened. The warehouse had gone up, no one had stirred in the house, so she'd assumed there were no Wastelords and entered. Trouble was, they were so stupefied by drugs, it had taken them a while to react and she'd walked in to find herself surrounded. There were eight or nine of them. Not De Grew, but they had her backed up against the wall, a couple brandishing machetes, the rest just jeering and taunting. They were relishing her blindness, her vulnerability, and she was swinging her club back and forth, daring them to come any closer.

'Come on! Come on!' she snarled, but they just continued to mock her.

Even after all this time, all these years, I still did what I always used to: just let everything go. All my emotions, my feelings, anything to do with self-control, I let them all go and released whatever it is that lies beneath. Roaring with anger, leaping in amongst them, swinging at everyone in sight. I cracked one on the side of the head, accidentally took out their video screen trying to get another, then managed to fend off a machete and received a blow to the ribs for my trouble. They were so distracted by me, Lena got in a really good shot on this guy and he went to the floor like he'd never get up again.

Only problem was, that seemed to ignite whatever it was they'd been taking. As if, up 'til then, it had only been playing with their minds, but now saw an opportunity to truly express itself. They began screaming and snarling at us, making evil threats. They were going to rip out our organs with their bare hands, stuff our still-beating hearts into our own mouths. And the things they said to Lena, just 'cuz she's a woman, a blind one at that, made you feel sick. One of them even lunged at her, laughing as he made an upward sweep with his machete, as if he was going to cut her open from vagina to mouth. She stepped back instinctively, but didn't really understand, couldn't even guess at the threat.

I tell you, I was so damn repulsed, so furious, that when he tried it again I was on him in an instant, wielding that big iron bar of mine smack into his cheek as hard as I could, with all the disgust he'd aroused in me pushing me on.

In an instant another one came at me, this look in his eyes, as if he believed nothing in the world could stop him, that the drugs had made him invulnerable. I stepped to one side, hit him so hard on the knee it must've shattered his kneecap and as he buckled over, shoved the blade into his back. I mean, you can't mess around. Not in a situation like this.

I thought that might be it, that they'd give up, but I hadn't reckoned with the one guy who always wants to prove he can succeed where others fail. He was a little older than the rest, with a heavy scar across his face that gleamed shiny and red as he advanced upon me, whirling his machete like a propeller. I just stayed where I was, as if exhausted from swinging my big metal bar, the blade-end resting on the floor. Then, once he got in range, I suddenly swung the bar up, driving the blade into that soft gap between his legs.

He squealed in agony, like I'd cut him in two, and finally I knew that, no matter what I been telling you about being a changed man, about hating violence now, I was back thirty years, through that fine wall that shores up humanity. You don't think about blood then. Nor pain. You've no regard for the flimsiness of the flesh, the scant protection offered by the body to its organs, the foolish vulnerability of the human face. You just got to destroy whatever's in front of you, irrespective of what it is and whether it screams or cuts or looks like it might damage you in return. I started swinging and slashing at everyone, and mean drugged-up sonsofbitches they may have been, but it didn't take long for that look to come into their eyes. The doubt. The fear. This old bastard was crazier than any of them. One panicked, ran for the door, and immediately the others followed.

As they sprinted out into the fog they were silhouetted against a series of explosions. Bailey and his team of old soldiers were throwing their Molotovs, trying to mop up as many as they could down on the second level. It was mayhem. Carnival time. Adrenaline was punching at the inside of my head like hot air filling a balloon. But we still hadn't achieved our prime objective.

I turned to Lena. 'Where is he?'

She didn't answer, just ran through to the bedroom and I followed on behind.

I tell you, the sight of it almost stopped me dead. Amongst all the shit of the Island, to be suddenly confronted by antique furniture, a four-poster bed, gilt and chintz, red satin draped round the walls, seemed like the biggest obscenity of all. But there was no sign of De Grew.

'He's not here,' I said, making a quick check of the wardrobes and under the bed.

'He must be!' Lena cried, furiously biting her lip.

'He's not!'

I went back out into the main room, searching through everywhere, throwing open doors, going crazy. Where the hell was he? Then she called out to me.

'Clancy!'

I rushed back into the bedroom. She was standing in exactly the same position but had the most terrible expression on her face. Pain, revulsion, I don't know, but I knew I'd seen it before.

'What is it?' I asked.

She sniffed the air a couple of times and for a moment I thought she was going to burst into tears.

'Lena?'

'He's here.'

'What?'

'He's here! In this room!'

Again I looked around. 'No!'

She started sniffing once more, slowly making her way over to the corner. I thought she'd gone crazy. There was no one there. The damn room was empty. Then she began pulling at the red satin curtains, trying to tug them down, and a concealed door swung open in front of her.

It was him, of course. Standing there wearing just a pair of striped briefs, grotesque in his near-nakedness, holding up a metal club, ready to take a swing. But it wasn't him my eyes fell upon. It was something that sickened me probably more than anything ever has in my life. He had this little garbage urchin with him. She couldn't have been any more than ten or so. Thin, naked, her body twisted in humiliation, a long trail of dried blood down her legs.

I guess he heard the commotion and hid. Probably had this secret hideaway built as a precaution against someone ever coming for him. Whatever, he sure looked relieved when he saw it was only an old man and a blind girl.

'Lena!' he sneered, like he was determined not to appear surprised. 'Welcome back.'

It was too much. After all this time, all he'd done to her, to find him like this. The little girl started to whimper and it pushed Lena over the edge. She leapt at him, screaming at the top of her voice, swinging her club with all her strength. I hesitated: this was her moment, I couldn't just wade in. She got in a couple of good shots, on the shoulder and arm, but the rest of the time she was so out of control she was just swiping and missing. He waited 'til she began to tire, 'til she swung herself off balance, then stepped forward and cracked her on the back of the head, and Lena fell to the ground, unconscious.

Never in my life have I felt such rage, such hatred, towards anyone. I swung that big metal bar at him so hard that when I missed it shattered the door frame from top to bottom. I ripped down the curtains, I put holes in the wood-panelled walls, but he was so quick I never got in one telling blow. He just kept blocking and dodging, doing all he could to survive, knowing I couldn't keep this up for long, 'til I was forced to back off to get my breath back.

We started circling one another, staring into each other's faces. Lena's description fitted him pretty well – mid- to late thirties, I guess, longish blond hair, a sculpted beard, the sort of face that looked like you'd break your fist on it, and a big muscular body reinforced with fat – but she'd left one thing out: his eyes. So pale and empty, like someone up there hadn't done their job properly and he'd come off the production line without emotions or feelings. Babies born with those eyes should be put straight to sleep. They're from another place, a world where they scream all day and eat each other at night. I remember this hit man Mr Meltoni had working for him in the early days. Boy, did he love his work. I never knew a guy who liked killing more. Someone got him one night with a car bomb. Rumour had it it was Mr Meltoni; that he just got so nervous of this guy, how unpredictable, how unstable, he was, he decided the best thing was to just get him rubbed out. What we're talking about is a madness, a raw emotion that can't even bear to live in its host body, that can't abide the restrictions of mortality. De Grew had that look about him. You could take his limbs off, one by one and he'd still keep coming for you.

He started to taunt me, sneering in my face. 'Hey. Old man. That all you got?'

I rushed him again, swinging with my bar, but I missed and he just laughed. I pivoted around, kicked him on the hip, and when he stumbled back, managed to get in a real hard blow on his shoulder before he could recover.

He glared at me, almost as if he'd been willing to make a concession or two but not anymore. 'I'm going to ram that fucking thing down your throat so far it'll come out your floppy old ass,' he snarled.

If he was trying to undermine me with all that 'old' stuff, it wasn't working. In fact, all those years of feeling bitter and alone were starting to scream out for their revenge. I leapt at him again, swinging my bar back and forth, fending off his club, and managed to put a gash in his wrist. For a moment he stopped and stared at the blood. He had this expression on his face, like he couldn't believe an old man could be doing this to him. It made me feel even stronger. I swung at him again, giving it everything I had, feeling his defences start to weaken, more and more of my blows getting through. Then I got him a beauty, right smack on the forehead, and down he went.

I mean, as far as I could see, that was it. It was all over. I raised my weapon, blade downwards, ready to drive it into his chest, and the lights went out.

I knew immediately what had happened. One of the buildings Bailey and his gang set fire to must've housed the complex's generator. We were immersed in a darkness almost as total as that of the tunnels. I stabbed repeatedly at the floor, trying to finish De Grew off, but he managed to wriggle away. I swept from side to side, thrashing around, frantically trying to find him, but became that desperate I made the mistake of silhouetting myself against the open door, and with the slight glow of the fires still seeping through, he leapt at me and knocked me over.

I was on the floor with him astride me before I even realised what was happening. He wrenched the bar out of my hands, then rammed it down across my throat. I struggled and kicked, twisting this way and that, desperately trying to breathe, to wriggle free. I mean, I could do it. Of course, I could. I was the Big Guy. There wasn't anyone stronger than me. Pushing that bar off my windpipe was going to be just like doing a bench-press: get your shoulders back, tighten your grip, then thrust with all your might. The only thing was, the bar just jerked up a little, made the slightest of movements, like a twitch, then clamped firmly back down on my throat.

I tried again. This time going right down inside myself, summoning up every bit of strength I've ever known – from the old neighbourhood, from the days of Mr Meltoni when I was the most feared big guy around – I gave that damn thing everything I had. But I still couldn't get it off me. Again I tried. Again and again, 'til finally I was forced to realise that the greatest fear of my life was coming true: this guy was too strong for me. All that training, running and lifting weights hadn't made the slightest difference – I was up against an opponent utterly unrelenting and without mercy. Or to put it another way: De Grew might've been about to beat me, but it was Time I was really falling before.

He jammed the bar down even harder onto my windpipe. I could feel it starting to collapse, the sinews of my airway cracking as they were being crushed. Pain was spreading across my chest, my vision was blurring, my head threatening to burst open. Then slowly, like the lowering of the final shroud, I felt my grip loosen, the darkness of the night going down into my soul, and I died.

CHAPTER TWENTY

I guess it was only for a few seconds, but it might've been for longer. I slowly became aware of life again, of a further unnatural dawn and this heavy dull weight being dragged off me. Not death, nor a man, just a burden. As I struggled out from beneath it, I felt a warm, wet handle sticking out of it.

Really, he hadn't stood a chance. Not in the dark. Not up against her. See, while he'd been so busy choking me, Lena had been recovering, finding one of the machetes the Wastelords dropped earlier, stalking up behind him.

Despite the pain in my throat, this feeling that it was ruptured somehow, I grabbed hold of her and hugged her for all I was worth. I mean, literally – she just saved my life.

Lena called out to the young girl, told her it was all right, that she could come out from her hiding place, but the poor kid was so frightened she bolted past us and out into the night. Lena shouted after her, even went to follow, but it was too late. I mean, you didn't have to be a genius to work out that that was the major reason why she did it. Why it was so personal. All those things he'd done to her, that she'd been festering over ever since, and now finding them being done to someone else. It wasn't only my life she saved.

I don't know how long we stayed there like that, squeezing each other as tightly as we could, binding our strength together, feeling a surge of relief coursing between us, but suddenly someone called to us from outside, begging for our help, and we realised this night still had a long way to go.

We both rushed out. It was Bailey and half-a-dozen or so of his old soldiers. Jesus, were they in a bad way. Beaten, bleeding, Bailey's arms slashed all the way up, I guess from trying to fend off blows from a machete. Four more came tottering up through the fog, two of them carrying another, her leg almost severed just above the knee.

'There were more than we thought,' Bailey gasped, desperately trying to get his breath back. 'They're right behind us!'

No sooner had he said it, the first of the Wastelords came bounding out of the murk bearing a blood-smeared machete, howling like the leader of a pack of wolves.

We didn't have a great deal of choice, there was no way out other than the way they were arriving. All we could do was stand and fight, try to exchange blow for blow. More and more of them appeared, running straight at us, the old soldier with the severed leg, left on the ground while her companions tried to make a stand, was killed with a single blow to the back of her head.

Again I started swinging that big metal bar, managing to down the first Wastelord but aware that I was tiring, that the odds against us were multiplying by the second. It was as if the fog had ruptured and blood was gushing out of it, that by killing De Grew we'd somehow made them stronger. And in that moment I realised what maybe a more intelligent man would've realised all along: things weren't going to get better, they were going to get worse. Any of these Wastelords could take over and make this place even more of a hell than it'd been up 'til now.

Bailey got cut off. Three of them chased and hemmed him in over by the woodpile. I did everything I could to get over there, to help, but there were just too many bodies in the way. Through the fog I saw him fall, gallantly struggling as they were hacking at his prone form, over and over, 'til he finally stopped.

One by one we were being overwhelmed. More by instinct than anything, Lena and me were standing back-to-back, her swinging her club, me that big-bladed bar. Looking out for each other. I mean, we knew it was all over, that she'd only given my life the most temporary of reprieves, but sure as hell this foolish old big guy and brave blind young woman were going to keep fighting 'til we felt the other fall and knew there was nothing left to do but follow. That there was nothing left to live for.

Then suddenly, above all the noise around us, the cursing and threatening, the cries of pain and distress, we heard an old familiar sound. A terrifying shrill scream that, even in that moment, made the hairs on the back of my neck stand up. For so long it had haunted our dreams, brought terror to our lives, and now it was approaching up the hill.

The moment we heard it, everyone, Wastelords and old folk, stopped fighting and turned in the direction it was coming from. As if we all knew that our efforts to settle this were as nothing compared with those who were about to arrive. Some of the Wastelords started sniggering, jeering at us, relishing what they were sure was about to happen.

They came bursting out of the night like Children of Hell, all shrieking and wild-eyed, dressed and made up in their insane fashion. And despite everything that's happened, despite getting to know some of them well, they still frightened the hell out of me. I tell you, it's something else. Something from the forbidden area of your unconsciousness, that no one ever dares enter or talk about.

For one agonising moment they paused, some bumping into the backs of others, assessing the situation, looking from Wastelords to old folk. One of the old soldiers raised his captured machete, daring them to attack, ready to make his last stand. But as one, all of the kids turned towards the Wastelords and rushed at them.

I tell you, you never seen anything like it – and you don't want to either. They fought with such ferocity, such anger, all the pain and frustration the Wastelords had channelled at us, now being turned back on them. I mean, most Wastelords are pretty big guys, and all of them were armed with machetes, but the kids outnumbered them so heavily they were like bees buzzing around lumbering bears.

I saw Gordie swinging away, making up for his lack of size with speed, winning out time and time again. Little Arturo following behind, picking up the pieces, hitting anyone who'd already been hit and looked like they might get back up. I mean, they might be kids, but this was no game. They were looking to do damage, to do as much harm as they could. I saw Hannah – I mean, shit, even amongst them, she is one helluva weird kid. She was dancing. Performing a kind of ballet. Wielding that silver bat to deadly effect, hitting anyone she could, like it was part of her routine. Grace and violence. I tell you, I didn't know what to make of it.

And it wasn't just 'our' kids either. There were hundreds of them. We weren't even fighting anymore, we got pushed aside, turned into involuntary and horrified spectators.

Jimmy and Delilah followed out of the fog, a look of relief appearing on their faces when they saw Lena and me, which must've matched ours at seeing them.

Delilah started to scan the mayhem for Arturo. Soon catching sight of him, so small amongst all that grown-up brutality, still swinging his club for all he was worth.

She turned to me, an appalled expression on her face. 'Clancy! For God's sake!' she protested. 'Do something!'

I looked at her, then back at what was going on. I saw the Oriental guy, the one who'd given me a hard time, and several of his gang, dropping their machetes, trying to surrender, but the kids wouldn't let them. They just picked the machetes up and carried on fighting, hacking at the very Wastelords who'd surrendered to them. And you want to know something? As wrong as it might seem, I thought about all those nights in the Village: the drugs, the terrible things that had been done to Lena and others, the bodies going back to the Mainland for spare parts. I thought about everything the Wastelords had ever done, and simply turned away. Tonight would be the last of it. Afterwards I'd make the kids burn their killing clothes and we'd face the problems of rehabilitation together. But for now I was going to let them do whatever they wanted. Destroy this stinking evil once and for all.

Why I didn't notice, I'll never know. I guess I was just too preoccupied. It was Lena who first realised. Maybe 'cuz she wasn't so distracted, or 'cuz she's got more of an aptitude for that kind of thing.

'Clancy!' she called to me.

I turned to her. Something about the tone in her voice, the expression on her face, froze my heart.

'What is it?' I asked.

She raised her head a little, sniffing the air, like she had the frayed edge of a smell she feared more than any other. Then she directed her face to the sky, like she was desperately trying to force her eyes to see, and I realised. *Oh, God, no!*

I screamed out to the kids, but there was so much noise going on, they couldn't hear me.

'Stop! Stop! . . . Gordie!'

I started to run towards them, hollering at the top of my voice, but I never made it. There was a sudden flash, like they opened the door of Heaven and light spilled out, and one of them fell dead. Then another. And another.

Somehow a wind had got up, out of nothing and it was rapidly sweeping the fog out of the sky. Lasers were coming back on all over, firing at us from every direction. It was wholesale slaughter. In a matter of seconds there must've been a dozen or more kids lying dead on the ground, their legs and arms twitching, as if, even in death, they were registering the shock of what happened to them. I saw Luxurious trying to force his way through to me, like he knew he was going to be next, then there was a flash that scarred right across my eyes and he was gone. Time and time again that light spat out across the night and claimed another child. It was as if this was it. This was the end. After all these years of torment and misery, they'd finally gathered us here together so they could destroy us all. I screamed out to those satellites, over and over, begging them to stop.

'No! No! . . . Not now! . . . Please! Let them be!'

And do you know something? All of a sudden, in the most abrupt of fashions, they did stop.

There was an unbearable weight of silence, almost worse than the sound of the lasers. The moon appeared so suddenly I wondered if someone had flicked a switch. Everyone was looking up, rows and rows of frightened faces waiting for it to start again. I mean, we've never seen them punish like that before. Not wholesale. We thought they must be recharging or something. Seconds went by; no one spoke, no one moved, no one even checked on the dead. Then this giggling started behind me. Not frightened, nor nervous, the other sort, kind of joyful. I turned around, wondering who the hell it was, and saw Jimmy. The crazy little bastard was sniggering like a child about to unwrap his birthday presents.

'What the hell's got into you?' I muttered.

But he just laughed even louder. 'Hey, Big Guy,' he said. 'D'you like fireworks?'

Suddenly the satellites opened up again, there was another thrust of searing light, but it didn't go to the ground, it went to another satellite. One of them actually shot another. I saw it get blown out of the sky, then start tumbling down over the ocean. Then another. And another. They all started zapping one another up there. It was like some huge version of a video game, with the whole of the sky acting as the screen. One by one, like enormous golden raindrops, the satellites came burning down from the heavens.

Jimmy was positively beside himself. 'I told you, Big Guy!' he cried. 'I told you I could change the world!'

And finally I realised what was going on. That was what he'd been doing when we left the tunnels. What he said he'd do. Setting up an antenna in the garden, trying to talk to those things, get them to do what he wanted. He must've set a program to kick in once his decoder had broken down their security.

I turned to him, too stunned to speak, shaking my head in wonder at my foolishness at ever doubting him. A satellite plummeted down on the Island, crashing onto the Head. People were starting to cheer every time one got hit. It was delirium. Over on the Mainland, far into the distance, they were raining down. Jesus, what must they be thinking? Suddenly they had no law and order. No security. The satellites were all there was. And in that moment, a thought struck me, so incredible, so awesome, I could barely hold it into my body. I just stood there, shivering and shaking, gasping for breath, unable to say what was in my mind.

And it wasn't just me neither. The same thought must've been occurring all over, 'cuz suddenly this huge roar went up. Not just from us, but from the whole damn island, from one end to the other. Even over in the Village I could hear the call, the cry, this shout of *Freedom!*

There was nothing to hold us here anymore. We could get off this filthy stinking mound of garbage. And then and there, everyone turned and started to run towards the pier. It was utter, mad chaos. People were coming from all over, scrambling over mounds of garbage, shouting and calling to each other, streaming down that moonlit hill as if peeling life off the Island. I grabbed Lena's hand and tugged her along, Jimmy and Delilah following, the kids, too. All of us joining in with this mad, irresistible surge.

By the time we got to the pier a lot of people were already in the water. You could see a line of flotsam and jetsam bobbing around as the first wave set out for the Mainland. One or two managed to commandeer boats, but anything would do: lengths of timber, plastic containers, old oil drums. Some didn't even bother to find anything, they just ran to the end of the pier and jumped in. I tell you, it was the most joyous sight I've ever seen. As if, with the restoration of freedom, we'd reawakened our humanity.

Jimmy found this inflatable under the pier, called us over, but there wasn't enough room and I sent him on with Delilah and the kids. Lena and I managed to dig out an old wooden door. It barely floated but it didn't matter. We just hung onto it, half-on, half-off, kicking away with our feet. The funny thing was, there didn't seem to be any need. Maybe it was the tide, but it felt like general momentum was carrying us over. This huge mass of people, a floating crowd, being borne across to the Mainland, a terrible wrong finally righted.

God knows how many of us there were, but in places you could barely see the moon reflected in the water, we were so thick upon it. I could see Villagers I was convinced couldn't walk, now swimming. Quietly, serenely, just a gentle sidestroke, but you knew that if they never did another thing in their lives, they were going to do this. A few were singing. Maybe Delilah started it. I don't know. Apart from paddling, all Lena and I were capable of was laughing. God knows what over. Everything, I guess. I tell you, I never knew this old body had the capacity for such happiness.

As the City got a little nearer, I noticed that new building, the huge one that Jimmy always reckoned was one of the utilities, was, in fact, the headquarters of Infinity International. Jesus, who the hell are these people? What are they up to?

Not that it matters. No way are we going to hang around here. We're going to take off into the wilderness and find ourselves somewhere to settle. I got this desire to put my arms around a tree, to feel life passing through me again; to dislodge this damn shit that's encrusted in my lungs and fill them with pure air once more.

There was an explosion behind us and I turned to see the Village aflame. I don't know whether a falling satellite started a fire, or if someone lit one as they left, but it must've ignited a chain blowout, 'cuz the whole place was now burning furiously. I turned to Lena, her wet hair trailing across a face that never looked so beautiful, and told her what was going on, automatically, the way I do now.

Garbage. Nothing but garbage. But we ain't anymore. We proved that. We also proved something else. A body can be held captive, be abused and tortured, a mind can be distorted or terrorised, but give people hope, give them something to believe in, and somehow they'll claw their way out of almost anything. I don't know what you want to call that. The survival instinct? The human spirit? No doubt you'll be able to put better words to it than me. I'm just a dumb old big guy. Simple, with simple dreams and desires. And who knows, maybe now Lena and me might be able to fulfill some of them.

I reached across to put my arm around her, the door momentarily submerging, then rising back up again. In turn, she tried to kiss me, but only managed to brush my lips before falling back into the water.

'I love you,' she told me.

'I love you,' I replied, unable to finish the sentence without bursting into laughter.

I never ever dreamed I'd see this day. Never even dreamed there was such a dream for me. I stopped paddling for a moment, holding on to Lena's hand, smiling at those around us, wanting to savour the moment. Leaning back and looking up at the moon, taking a deep breath and holding it into my body, the stench of the Island finally fading away and being replaced by something altogether sweeter.